Her Side of the Story

ANGELA SCIPIONI

CHAPTER ONE
Carolina

Knees, elbows, and fists tucked in close to her chest, that was how Carolina liked to fall asleep. When she thought about it, which wasn't often, she figured maybe that was because she'd been cheated out of a full month in her mother's womb. She could thank her parents for that, because if they hadn't been so nasty to each other while she was waiting to be born, maybe she would have stayed put instead of busting out prematurely, scrawny and screaming, her purple face pinched with rage, her frog legs kicking as fast as they could to get away from their bickering.

It was in that same curled-up position that she always awoke, precisely at four forty-five, no alarm required, thank you very much. A six-hour recharge of fitful sleep (the only kind she ever got) was all her body needed before her brain (that *never* rested) ordered her eyelids to flutter open, her thoughts racing ahead to the new day, her legs twitching to catch up. She was what people called a morning person, and always had been. As a student, she'd zipped through her homework before school, when her head was fresh with dreams, instead of after school, when it was weighed down with all the words of her teachers and classmates who never shut up. Once high school was over and done with, her parents had harnessed that early morning energy by putting Carolina to work at Caffé Cantarelli, where she rolled up the shutters before most people rolled out of bed. Six days a week, she earned her keep by serving commuters from behind the stainless-steel counter of the family-owned coffee shop in the depressing outskirts of Milan. Everyone needed something on their way to work, whether it be a shot of caffeine from a steaming espresso, a sugar buzz from a starchy brioche, or a nicotine fix from a fresh pack of smokes. While standing at the bar gobbling down their breakfasts, customers could grab tickets for the trams and buses and subways that got them to all those places they didn't want to be that day, and the occasional lottery ticket that fanned their futile hopes of never having to go there again. Carolina was really good at handling those people as they began each pitiful day of their pitiful lives. She smiled despite their grumpiness; she asked questions that made them feel interesting. She flattered them by learning their names, and those of the children and dogs and cats whose pictures they eventually showed her. She wasn't just serving those people coffee, she was serving a higher purpose: she was helping them to cope. And that was what helped *her* to cope. Until the day she met a commuter by the name of Giangiacomo Lanza and began plotting a way out for both of them.

Yep, four forty-five it had always been for Carolina, for as long as she could remember. Before jumping to action this morning, though, she rolled over to feast her eyes on Giac's muscular form in all its naked splendor. She wondered how the man could sleep with his limbs sprawled out at such improbable angles, what made him flail his arms and twist his torso so much. His restlessness was enough to drive any woman crazy, but at least he knew how to make up for it (or used to, anyway), that much she could say for him. Sighing, she swung her legs around and sat on the edge of the bed as the lone cock among her two dozen Silver Duckwing Livorno chickens crowed for the third time, reminding her that she wasn't the only early riser. She let her feet linger on the floor a moment before standing, her toes caressing the aged oak planks. Beginning and ending each day with the feel of that solid, smooth surface beneath her hard-working feet made that floor worth every argument it had caused between her and Giac (there'd been many during the blood-sucking renovations), who'd tried to pull a fast one on her by swinging a deal with a ceramics factory near Modena for a truckload of tiles sold by the pallet, with undisclosed plans to install them throughout the main building and bungalows. Sure, he'd been an accountant in his previous life, and sure, liquidity was tight (okay, more like *gone*) by the time it came to picking out floors, but those tiles had no place in the charming resort they'd dreamed of creating, and you could only downgrade dreams so much before they became a dismal reality. There was no sending the tiles back, though, so Carolina had eventually conceded that they'd be practical and easy to clean (proving she wasn't as unreasonable as Giac said), and consented to using them in the kitchen and dining room and even in the barn if he wanted to, but *not* in her bedroom, or in those of their future guests.

Carolina wasn't big on reminiscing, mostly because her brain had a knack for remembering best the things she wanted to forget most, like the Great Tile Fight. But when Giac behaved himself, it was easier for her to block out the quarrels and focus on the positive. Like how courageous they'd been to come up here, despite everyone's dire predictions of financial failure and a ruined relationship, how thrilled they'd been to leave gloomy Lombardy behind, and how empowering it had felt to take control of their own lives instead of squandering them on someone else's agenda. Up here, high above the Ligurian coast, was the place where they could create a world of their own, immersed in a fragrant beech forest of the Maritime Alps, straddling borders with France to the west and the Piedmont region to the north, yet just a few hours' drive from the French and Italian Rivieras. This was a place where they could raise their children and build their futures with their own hands by converting the crumbling relics of a peasant's property into a working farm and nature lodge. Carolina knew at once that theirs wouldn't be just any lodge, it would be an exclusive nature resort, one that would attract a certain type of clientele, people who could go anywhere they wanted, but would choose to travel up a winding mountain road specifically to come here. The kind of people who appreciated refined taste and delicious food; the kind who could engage in stimulating conversation but weren't spooked by silence; the kind who valued independence but didn't disdain pampering; the kind classy enough to soak up Carolina's attentions without treating her like a servant. And, let's face it, the kind who would pay the rates they'd need to charge in order to dig themselves out of debt. Enough reminiscing though, it was time to get cracking.

Carolina's day was marked by routines, the first of which was her morning stretch. Standing as straight as her chronic backache and uneven legs (one was shorter than the other) would allow, she breathed in through her nose, raising her arms high above her head, stretching until her fingertips tingled. Bending forward at the waist, she felt the tightness in her hamstrings as she exhaled slowly, until her lungs were as empty as they could get without her being dead. Hugging her elbows, she let her torso hang free, her long, straight hair falling to the floor, her head lolling, nodding yes and no to iron out the kinks in her neck. Where did all those millions of people find time for meditation, she asked her upside-down kneecaps (why did her skin ripple above them like that, despite her legs being so thin?) when she could barely squeeze in a quick stretch? Unrolling her spine one vertebra at a time, she began to inhale, maybe not as slowly as those yoga people had tried to teach her back in the day, but she really couldn't stand that empty-lung feeling, that oxygen-starved sense of suffocation. Truth was, she hated emptiness of all kinds: empty refrigerators and cupboards, empty plates and glasses, empty tummies, empty guest rooms, empty bank accounts, empty minds, empty hearts. Standing up straight again, she sucked in more air as she reached her arms overhead, then lowered them for a final exhale, joining her palms in front of her heart and bowing her head. This was when she was supposed to thank someone somewhere for the new day, so she thanked herself. Not to brag or anything, but if anyone deserved credit for where she was now, it was her.

At that moment, Carolina's brief journey to her inner self was aborted by a sharp snort and gurgle, something like the sound a clogged drain makes when freed by a plunger. She turned to look down on the bed where Giac lay snoring, a woe-is-me elbow bent over his brow, his dimpled chin pointing at the exposed beams she'd nearly killed herself sanding and staining. There was enough dim light filtering through the shutters for her to glimpse the little boy that still lurked within the man, with his mouth pursed in a pout, his chipmunk cheeks puffing up with each exhalation until the spent air leaked out through his sealed lips. Waking him up when he looked so innocent like that made her feel a little bad, but only until her irritation at seeing him slumber so soundly kicked in. Kneeling on the mattress, she pecked him on one cheek, while slapping him gently on the other. Well, maybe not so gently.

"Time to rise and shine, Giac!" she cooed.

Her husband swatted at Carolina the way he would have swatted at a pesky fly, then rolled away with a ragged snort, pressing his pillow over his head. The poor guy still needed a clock to tell him when to get up, like some pathetic office worker. By the time his alarm rang at six, a pot of coffee would be brewed, a batch of croissants baked, and a cake or two would be in the oven. Then Carolina would step outside to survey the morning sky, worrying about whether the weather would hold for a couple more days. They needed rain, sure, but the season was winding down, and the bungalows had been vacant since last weekend, so right now they needed the business more. It wasn't just the revenue that she needed, it was the *people*. And although they may not know it yet, *they* needed *her* even more.

CHAPTER TWO
Inge

Inge knew how he'd respond even before he opened his mouth. That was what happened when you lived with a person for such a long time. Especially if that person was a man, and especially if that man was as predictable as Severino Di Meglio.

"I *need* the window *open*," she huffed. She could already hear Rino reply that the sticky air and gritty dust and annoying noise from the road would invade the vehicle, compromising the comfort of its silent, climate-controlled interior. "And slow down! You know how I suffer from motion sickness."

"I didn't spend seventy-five thousand euros on my dream Mercedes to drive slow!" was all he *said*, but she knew he was *thinking* those other things. She lowered her window and stuck her head out, breathing in the pine-scented air. Although they weren't too far above Italy's always blossoming *Riviera dei Fiori,* with its date palms and succulents that lined the seafront promenades, the change in vegetation as they climbed was noticeable. Here it was less frivolous and decorative, more earthy and natural.

"I know that, Rino," she said. "But *we* didn't spend that kind of money so *I* could get carsick. We're not on the autostrada, we're on a steep, winding road riddled with – *woah!* Take it slow on those curves, would you?" Inge glared at her husband, recalling her initial dismay on learning the price of the car he'd been lusting after in the privacy of his bathroom, where he stashed water-spotted piles of *Automobili Oggi,* his favorite car magazine. She didn't begrudge the purchase, though, he deserved it after finally retiring officially, if not completely, from his felt business at the end of last year. Besides, every time she indulged him, it made her feel a little bit lighter, a little less guilty. Leaning out the window of the sleek sedan, Inge tried to focus on the view, but the craggy Ligurian landscape whizzed by too fast for her to enjoy the scenery, even if she weren't on the verge of vomiting.

"That's exactly why I agreed to take this road. I love the way this *bambina* performs on the curves," her husband said, downshifting as he approached another hairpin turn, then accelerating halfway through it. He could have a least bought an automatic, but no, like most men, he loved his stick.

"It's also the only decent route to get where we're going," Inge called over her shoulder.

"Call it decent!" he said. "We're lucky if we can go five kilometers without running into road work."

"Another reason to go slow!"

"I would have been happy to go so slow that we didn't go at all. We could have stayed a couple more nights in San Remo. It had everything you could ask for – restaurants, bars, boutiques, yachts, the casino – oh, *merda*!" Rino downshifted abruptly and then braked, coming to a complete stop at a temporary traffic light. Aided by a tiny bulldozer precariously perched on an incline, two sweaty, sunbaked road workers in orange vests and hardhats were clearing a section of road blocked by a rock slide. Pressing a button, Rino rolled up his wife's window, shutting them and their noise out.

"Yes, San Remo has that perfect mix that attracts the rich riffraff and tacky tourists," Inge replied, taking the deal for a closed window in exchange for sitting still. "I just can't stomach those vulgar people, Rino, and I did only agree to a stopover. What we really need to do is forget about this crazy world for a few days and focus on what's important. I was told that this place is ideal for that."

"Who told you that again?"

Inge sighed. "An ex-colleague of mine."

"Have I met him? What's his name?"

"Fabio. You only met him once, ages ago."

"Hmm. Can't say I remember him."

"No reason to. The point is, this is one of those special places, they say there's some kind of an energy vortex there."

"You mean like Machu Pichu? Or Sedona? I didn't feel much in either place, to tell the truth. Except for the overwhelming heat. And the distinct sensation of getting ripped off."

"How could anyone tune in to anything there, with all those tourists crawling all over the place like ants? This little spot is nothing like that. They don't even publicize it because they want to keep it exclusive. It seems that the people who go there feeling negative somehow leave feeling positive. Oh, and then there's the food, too. It's supposed to be excellent."

"Well, that's good news. I'm feeling more positive already."

"Delicious food. Pristine nature. Comfy accommodations. Discerning clientele. Surely *meglio* than San Remo, Signor Di Meglio?" He was proud of having "*meglio,*" the Italian word for "better," in his last name, and he liked it when she teased him about it.

"By all means, Frau Doktor Egger. You're always the expert, aren't you?" Rino said, revving his engine at the long red light.

Now he was the one making fun of her Swiss-German heritage and professional title. He tended to do that whenever he thought she was talking down to him, which honestly was sometimes hard to avoid since she knew more about most subjects than he did. It wasn't that she flaunted her cultural superiority, she simply accepted it. And so did he. After all, Rino dealt in felt, and she was a highly respected physician. She'd been listening to him talk about his business for years, and for a while, being the bright and curious person that she was, she'd even found many aspects of felt production fascinating. Rino, on the other hand, refused to engage in any conversations about her work as a gynecologist. He was proud of her, of course, and enjoyed the prestige of being married to a top member of the medical staff at a fertility clinic in Lugano, Switzerland. But it was no secret that he'd have preferred her to be a specialist in something above the belt – a cardiologist, maybe, or an ophthalmologist. Something it wouldn't embarrass him to talk about over dinner with their friends.

"Let's leave behind the doctor part of Inge Egger this weekend, please. And you put everything related to felt out of your head, too. What's the point of retiring, if your mind is always focused on the business?"

"I didn't *retire*. I slowed down."

"Well, let's both make an effort to disconnect from outside interference this weekend, and use the time to reconnect with ourselves, with each other, and with nature." Even as she spoke the words, Inge wondered whether she was capable of being just Inge Egger; whether she could tolerate forty-eight hours of uninterrupted soul searching and truth seeking and marital bonding, or whether it would only make matters worse. Nonetheless, it had sounded like a good idea when Fabio had suggested it – unlike some of the other things he suggested.

The light turned green. Rino accelerated. The burst of speed forced Inge back against the buttery leather seat. Rolling her eyes, she rolled down her window.

CHAPTER THREE
Josephine

Josephine generally enjoyed traveling by rail, a rare treat back in the U.S. But after riding from Rome to Genoa on an overcrowded interregional train with faulty air-conditioning and enough fellow passengers who believed in the evils of air currents to demand that the windows remain safely sealed shut, she'd arrived at her destination sweaty and exhausted. On the positive side, the discomfort of the train had made her doubly excited yesterday afternoon when taking possession of her rental car, a plain white Fiat Panda, which to her was a ticket to freedom. She loved the sense of independence that driving gave her, of being the one to decide whether to open or close the windows, whether to turn right or left or keep on straight, whether to cruise along in silence or listen to whatever she wanted to; in short, to have control over where she went and how she got there. It was more a state of mind than anything, though, since she'd never owned a car back in Buffalo. The truth was, she hadn't driven in months, not since coming over to Rome, so she could have used some practice with the manual gearshift before plunging straight into the spastic bowels of the Italian Autostrada. One sign had led to another, though, and she was still congratulating herself on how well she'd followed them, when she found herself on the entrance ramp of the Genoa-Ventimiglia. Her main problem at that point was to stay alive, though how she was supposed to manage that when faced with a ridiculously short merging lane wedged between a suspension bridge and a tunnel, the cars and trucks whizzing by so fast they made her compact car shake and shudder, was anyone's guess.

Her situation hadn't improved when instead of giving the engine the gas it needed to join the flow of traffic, she hesitated. Honestly, it was only a second, a fraction of a second, really, but that was long enough for the car to stall out. The Italians were kind-hearted people, mind you, and usually ready to help you out – just not while driving. And they certainly didn't make it any easier for her by honking their horns and flashing their lights while swerving around her, shouting words she luckily couldn't hear when they turned to glare at her. The gesticulating she understood, though, and it wasn't nice. Knowing the only way out of her predicament was to move forward, and fast, she restarted the engine, engaged first gear, and gunned it. The Panda obediently lurched forward into the so-called slow lane, cutting off a rapidly approaching tractor-trailer, whose massive chrome grille kept growing bigger and meaner every time her horrified eyes glanced in her rearview mirror. She absolutely had to speed things up, but first she had to get out of first gear, and what if she stalled out again with that monster glued to her tail? At that moment, almost by miracle, it was something inside her that shifted. Maybe it was the fear, or the adrenalin, or whatever, but a flash of memory took her back to a long-ago Sunday when Thomas had let her ride shotgun with him in his souped-up Mustang at the Watkins Glen race track. Driving in such a fast car had thrilled her down to the marrow of her scrawny little bones (the abundant flesh now covering them had come later), and she would have killed to get behind the wheel herself, if only Thomas would have let her. But he wouldn't. The taste of that urge was still so strong that it made her push the pedal of the Panda to the floor, clutch, and ram it into second, push it to the floor again, then into third, finally slamming it into fourth, then fifth, while crying "Eat my dust!" to the driver of the truck on her tail, and maybe to Thomas, too, and maybe to all those other people whose purpose in life seemed to be to tell her what she could and could not do.

Her confidence bolstered, she'd motored along, smiling and humming to herself, while heading southwest on the coastal A10 in the direction of Ventimiglia and the French border, but exiting after only an hour, at Savona. Though the drive was short, the day had been long, which was why she'd planned to spend the night in the port city before continuing her journey up into the mountains the next morning, rested and refreshed. This was her first time in Liguria, and she'd heard of the famous Riviera destinations like the Cinque Terre and Camogli, which she'd strained to see from the window of the train as it zipped past. Between tunnels, she'd managed to glimpse bursts of colorfully painted homes towering over rocky coves and pebbly beaches, and agreed that they did indeed look pretty spectacular. Her first impression of Savona, however, as she drove down its messy streets, was one of shabbiness, but to be fair, which she always tried to be, the hotel she'd booked online was one of the least expensive available, which was a pretty good indication that it was in one of the least desirable areas of what might well be a lovely seaside city. Since deep disappointment is only made possible by high expectations, and since she hadn't been expecting much, she couldn't really complain. Having said that, the room could have been cleaner, and the dinner included in her *mezza pensione* rate (gummy gnocchi with garlic-laden pesto, stringy roast beef with potatoes that were both half-burnt and half-raw, of which she ate every bite, being both hungry and raised in the religion of eating everything on her plate out of respect for the world's starving children), was on the difficult-to-digest side, making her toss and turn in the lumpy single bed until it was time to consume her breakfast of bitter coffee, watered-down orange juice, and a packaged croissant, also included in the rate. The upside was that, by contrast, she'd appreciate the place to which she was headed now even more. Thomas had booked her stay there, as a sort of personal time-out gift, and assured her that it would be out of this world. Which was exactly where she wanted to be these days.

Finally on the last leg of her first solo Italian road trip, she gripped the wheel of the Panda, grinning as she bounced along the steep dirt road that led to the resort, probably going faster than she should, what with all those ditches and potholes to look out for, but now that she was warmed up, the challenge of staying in control was the fun part. That was until a massive boulder appeared out of nowhere and barreled across the road right in front of her! In the time it took to blink, she could see her car crashing into it, she could hear the sound of solid stone impacting flimsy metal, of plastic breaking and glass shattering; she could feel her head banging against the steering wheel, taste the blood streaming from her face. Josephine's reflexes were quick, though, and she managed to slam on the brakes and veer sharply to the right, which avoided the crash, but sent the car into a ditch, where it landed with a dull thud, its engine dead, but its driver, luckily, alive. Her heart thumping, she took stock of her surroundings, her eyes darting here and there, scouring the thick vegetation on both sides of the deserted road, as if looking for whoever or whatever was responsible for almost killing her.

"Are you *kidding* me?" she cried, banging on the steering wheel with both hands, before sticking her head out the open window. "What was that supposed to be, huh? A *threat*? A *warning*?" she screamed to the sky. But Josephine knew what it was. It was a *test*. Well, fine, bring on the darn whole battery of tests and let's see who comes out on top! The whole point of this little expedition was to see what it felt like to go it alone, to deal with whatever came her way, in her own way. But there were not supposed to be rocks involved.

The last thing she wanted to do was call for help, especially so close to her final destination. She'd have to inspect the damage and decide how to proceed. With its front right wheel down in the ditch, exiting the lopsided car was awkward, especially with the few extra pounds she'd put on recently. Plus, there were all those snapping and rustling sounds coming from the woods, which she didn't like one bit. Luckily, she saw that the tire wasn't blown, just stuck, and also luckily, she'd landed in more than one ditch in her day, having learned to drive in Eerie, Pennsylvania, during a record-breaking winter for snowfall, and happened to know a technique that would come in handy here. First, she'd have to see if the car started, which it did, after only two tries. Next, the trick was to get a good rocking motion going by throwing it into first gear and giving it gas, then in reverse and giving it gas, first and reverse, first and reverse, making make the car pitch forward and backward, faster and faster, her rubber-soled shoes pounding the pedals, her clammy hand working the gear stick, first and reverse, first and reverse. Finally gaining enough momentum to clear the rim, the car shot onto the road, where it landed with a shocked bounce.

Josephine Fortunata threw back her head and laughed. Was it luck? A miracle? Or was she alone responsible for getting herself out of her rut? That would be something to ponder.

CHAPTER FOUR
Allegra

Allegra crouched beneath the open hatch of her twelve-year-old Citroën Saxo, taking stock of the contents one last time. Ten rolled-up yoga mats, a stack of cork blocks, some straps and bolster pillows, a pair of hiking boots, a canvas book bag decorated with a decal of the *Om* symbol, and a bulky backpack, made in Nepal. Fishing her phone from the pocket of her harem pants, she checked the time again and sighed. She didn't want to leave now, or any later than now; she wanted to leave an hour ago. And she also wanted everything to fit in her car. Staring at the trunk, then at the guitar leaning against the passenger door in hopes of a lift, then at the trunk again, she started humming her favorite mantra, *Om So Hum,* I Am That, hoping to reconnect with the Universe, and at the same time disconnect from her irritation toward one of its human components.

The neighbor's dogs at the bottom of the hill burst into a barking frenzy, making it hard for her to hear her own humming. Those poor mutts were dull, but their ears were sharp, and they could be counted on to announce every intruder approaching her little hideaway in Dolceacqua, the town tucked between the sea and the mountains in the west end of Liguria whose claims to fame, besides its wine, were its humpback stone bridge and 12th-century castle immortalized by Claude Monet. There was nothing impressionistic about the yapping of the dogs, however, now accompanied by the roaring engine and honking horn of the vehicle that shot up the steep road. Adalberto's SUV rounded the corner and flew through the gate, barely giving Allegra the time to jump out of the way, causing her to bang her head on the hatch and drop everything in her hands.

"Glad you could make it!" she cried, rubbing her scalp. She winced at the bump she could already feel forming beneath her thick head of curls, but also at her lack of self-control. She'd promised herself that she wouldn't complain if he was late, that she would simply leave. But somehow everything got reversed; she hadn't managed to leave before he got there, and she had managed to complain as soon as he did. Well, not exactly *complain*, she wasn't good at coming right out and saying things, but he'd be pretty tuned out to miss the sarcasm in her voice.

"So am I!" Adalberto said, his dazzling smile competing for brilliance with his mirrored Ray-Bans as he hopped down from the driver's seat on long, lean legs, immediately enfolding her in an embrace. Tight jeans, cowboy boots; he sure looked ready enough for a few days of country life. "Why is your car loaded up?" he asked, looking over the tousled auburn head he pressed against his chest.

"Maybe because it's time to leave?" she suggested, wishing he didn't always smell so good, wishing she didn't always crave the comfort of his arms and the heady effect of his nearness. She wriggled away enough to look him in the eye, but all she saw was her reflection in the sunglasses.

"C'mon, we must have a few spare minutes to, you know, get reacquainted?" He pulled her close again, running his hands up and down her back a few times before cupping her slender bottom. Knowing that he wanted her was reassuring as well as arousing. But his timing left much to be desired.

"We would have had lots of minutes, last night," she said.

"I know you wanted me to come yesterday, Allegra Amore. But I needed to finish a rewrite so I could free up today and tomorrow," he said, gripping her elbows. "I worked until two in the morning!"

Allegra wasn't a jealous person by nature, but she felt a familiar stab of resentment toward the time he stole from their lives together, only to squander it on those short stories it took him ages to write in the isolation of his own country hideaway. That home was also where the famous Adalberto Albertis did his best work turning commonsense advice into the pearls of wisdom published in his popular magazine column AskAda, taggable as @AskAda and #AskAda for his droves of online followers.

"I promised you I'd be here this morning by ten, didn't I?" he said, holding her at arm's length.

"Ten, *at the latest.*"

"And what time is it now?"

Allegra looked at her hand, the one that was supposed to be holding her phone but wasn't, then turned to look inside the trunk where it must have fallen together with the shawl she'd been holding but hadn't, then scanned the ground, where she spotted a piece of plastic casing sticking out from under Adalberto's front tire.

"You ran over my phone," she announced in a flat voice, crouching to examine this extension of herself lying on the ground like roadkill. She felt she would be sick, as if she really were staring at the splattered blood and guts of a hapless hedgehog.

"What?" Adalberto asked, following her gaze. "Geez, Allegra, what was your phone doing on the ground?"

"Just ... *please* ... don't ... say *anything*," she stammered, conscious of the square-toed boots coming to stand next to her, noticing that he'd taken the time to shine them. *Breathe*, she told herself. *It's just a phone.* After telling

Adalberto on more than one occasion that he was too attached to his phone, too involved in his constant self-promotion on social media, it wouldn't be right to turn this into a tragedy. Brushing off her hands, she rose to standing in one swift, supple movement. "I can't deal with this now. We have to *leave*."

"I'm sorry, Allegra Amore, but how was I supposed to see a phone on the ground? Don't worry about it, though, I'll buy you a new one, okay? Anyway, for the record, I'm actually early," he said, turning his wrist to show her his watch. "It's nine fifty-two."

"Great. So why don't you move your car, let me back out, and we can go."

"Seriously, you don't want to make the drive in your dinky sardine can of a car, do you?" Adalberto asked, jerking his thumb at the overloaded trunk. "I can tell you right now the door won't even close if you put the guitar in there. Why do you need to take the guitar, anyway?"

"Because I may want to *play* it, and because it will fit in the passenger seat."

"Did I get uninvited?" Adalberto said, taking her chin between his thumb and forefinger, the way he did when she was undecided and he wanted to make her nod her head yes or shake it no. "Or do you still want me to come?"

"Yes," she said, nodding before he could do it for her. She did want him to come, very much; she'd been surprised he'd agreed to come when she'd proposed it, and afraid that he'd change his mind at the last minute ever since. That was why the waiting had made her so tense." Of *course* I want you to come, or I wouldn't have asked you to."

"So let me run inside to pee, grab a few things, then we can move your stuff to my car. It's way better on those mountain roads. Clock me – I still have a credit of five minutes!"

Kissing the top of her head, Adalberto dashed into the house in that physically charged way he had of moving, as if every second shaved off the race of life were a second gained. Speaking of seconds, Allegra didn't want to waste even one by getting into a discussion, and he was right about his 4x4 being better to travel in. The important thing was that he was here now, and they could leave. Adalberto really was reliable, he always did what he said he would do, as long as it was something he wanted to do, and he could do it the way he wanted to. If, like he said, she was always so eager to accommodate and justify everyone else's needs and actions, she could surely do as much for him. It wouldn't be the first time.

Allegra bent over to pick up what was left of her phone and dropped the scraps into her pocket, hoping to at least save the SIM card, then began loading her yoga mats and blocks and straps and pillows and boots and backpack and guitar into the spacious and sturdy SUV. *Om so hum, om so hum, om so hum, om so hum.*

CHAPTER FIVE
Carolina

Opening the door of the gleaming stainless steel refrigerator, Carolina gazed inside, her dark eyes glistening. Blocks of sweet yellow butter, as precious to her as gold ingots, were stacked alongside two brimming bowls of the purest white yogurt, one made from cows' milk and one from their own goats' milk. Blinking with satisfaction, her eyes then roved over the assortment of fresh cheeses: the darling rounds of tasty tomino, the soft-ripened squares of delicate robiola, the spreadable slabs of creamy stracchino, all supplied by an organic farm just over the pass in Piedmont. Below those were the trinity of her own creation, three milky mounds of homemade goat milk ricotta. Smiling, she gently closed the refrigerator, as if to not disturb her slumbering treasures, and turned her attention to the counter, where a perfect dozen of freshly laid eggs huddled in a basket, the tiny white feathers of her generous hens still stuck to their shells. Next to the eggs was a container, covered by a linen towel; lifting one corner, she peeked at the chunk of waxy honeycomb that lay there oozing its golden sweetness. Cooling by the oven, a fragrant tart made with the last of the season's fresh peaches stood next to a pastry shell filled with her own apricot preserves, whose tangy taste would complement the sweetness of the chocolate pear cake. Giac would say that all this was way too much for the few guests they were expecting, (and she still had to whip up tonight's featured dessert!), that she'd overdone it again, that she must be hell-bent on throwing away their hard-earned money when she should be economizing. What the heck did he call doing all this on her own, without any hired help? If he'd learned anything at all about hospitality, he should know by now that food was a fundamental part of the guest experience and that the only thing skimping would do was ruin the reputation she'd worked so hard to build up. Her goal was to overwhelm, not underwhelm, and one disappointed customer would bring greater ruin to them than an extra cake or two.

Carolina's thoughts were interrupted by a noise she'd grown to both love and loathe: the crunching of a trolley on the gravel. She loved the feeling of anticipation that quickened her pulse now, for example, when she heard new guests arriving. And she loved the feeling of relief when the pain-in-the-butt guests finally got the hell off her property. But boy, did she hate it when the ones she really bonded with went away! Sometimes, and she wasn't ashamed to admit it, she cried after certain guests departed, though she no longer let Giac catch her in tears to avoid his sermons about keeping her distance and clinging to people in what he called an unhealthy way. The thing was, Carolina had an integral approach to hospitality that involved way more than smiling and saying *buongiorno* and *buona sera,* and feeding her clients excellent food. Sure, cooking was something she was proud of, a skill she'd acquired and perfected over the years, more like an art, really, but her talent for connecting with people was a gift she'd been born with, the way some people are musical prodigies or clairvoyants. Everyone said that about her, even back at her parents' crappy bar in Milan, though naturally the people who came to the Renovatus were on a totally different level. Of course, being wealthy enough to afford certain experiences didn't automatically qualify people to fully grasp the depth of those experiences, but those who came here with an open attitude, those who were sensitive and courageous enough to embrace change, were sure to leave this place restored and renewed, just like the name promised.

Carolina had high hopes for this weekend's guests and was anxious to greet the first arrival. Walking out of the kitchen and through the empty dining room to the entrance foyer, she spotted a plump silhouette standing on the threshold, backlit by the morning sun, making the person's face undistinguishable. "*Buongiorno!*" Carolina said. "Can I help you?"

"*Buongiorno a lei!*" the person replied, in a slightly husky voice that could belong to either a man or a woman. "I hope I'm not disturbing you?"

That settled it, it must be a woman. Men rarely asked whether they were disturbing anyone, or framed a statement as a question. Most usually just barged in to make demands or complain about something.

"Do you have a reservation with us?" Carolina asked.

"Yes, I do. At least I hope so!" the person said, in what sounded like an American accent. "The road up here was a blast, but I'd rather not turn around right away."

"Sorry about that. We've had some weather-related damage. Did you have any trouble finding us?" If Carolina had a euro for every time she'd asked Giac to fix that road, she could afford to bake *twenty* cakes a day.

"Not at all! The directions in your email were perfect."

"Good! That's what I always tell people. The only ones who get lost are the ones who insist on using their GPS." Carolina made a welcoming gesture with her arm, indicating that the woman should come in. "*Benvenuta al* Renovatus. I'm Carolina Cantarelli, the owner."

"Pleased to meet you," the woman said, shaking Carolina's outstretched hand.

"May I ask your name, please?"

"Sorry, of course, my name, yes. The reservation was made for me by a

Mr. Thomas Tomas. And I'm Josephine. Do you need the confirmation email?"

"Not necessary! I have a thing for names, especially ones with double initials. And I can tell you without checking that you're all set for two nights."

"Do you need a credit card or anything?"

"No, the room and meals have been prepaid, and I have my instructions for any extras. You'll be well taken care of. I'll just need your ID to register you."

"I know my passport's in here somewhere," the woman said, her hands shaking slightly as she rummaged around in her giant black handbag. She seemed to need some calming down.

"No worries, an ID card will do just fine," Carolina said. She actually preferred ID cards over passports, which provided less information. In the good old days before all those silly European privacy laws (and before Carolina got into this business), Italian IDs used to give a woman's maiden name, plus her marital status, married name, address of residence, and profession. Now all you got was her maiden name, address, and profession.

"Phew! I knew I had it!" Josephine said, producing a burgundy passport embossed with gold lettering. "I just used it for the first time yesterday in Savona."

"Oh, you're Italian!" Carolina noted, glancing at the cover as Josephine handed it to her.

"You wouldn't guess from my accent, right?"

"Your Italian's very good, though."

"That's kind of you. And now it's official, thanks to my Italian grandparent connection. It's good to have a backup plan these days, so it was definitely worth all the red tape. But..." The woman paused to dig around in her purse again, giving Carolina the chance to see that she was wearing a wedding ring on her right hand, before pulling out a blue passport. "This is the original and I wouldn't want to give it up!"

"United States of America!" Carolina said. "I'll swap you the Italian one for the American." Without waiting for an answer, she dropped the stiff burgundy passport into Josephine's open bag and snatched the worn blue one from her hand, as if they were baseball cards. She liked foreign passports better, especially if they were extra-European.

"Actually, I get a little nervous leaving my U.S. passport, if you don't mind."

"Oh. Sure. Of course," Carolina said. "I'll just take a photo then, and give it right back to you, okay?"

"That would be fine."

Americans were funny like that, Carolina knew, but she felt so chagrined as she snapped a quick shot of the vital information pages with her phone that she couldn't see straight. With the woman standing right there, she could hardly take her time studying details and flipping through the document to see if there were any travel visas. Imagining the places people traveled to and why they went there provided valuable pieces to the puzzle that was each person's life. Each bit of information she gleaned helped her figure out who they were, which in turn helped her figure out how to help them. She'd hoped this passport would reveal more about Josephine, especially since she had so little to go on right now, except for the name of the guy footing her bill. He was obviously her husband, maybe from a northern or eastern European country, which could fit in nicely with the wedding ring on her right hand. That was just one example of something her travel stamps might have confirmed.

"I have a couple of questions," Josephine said, holding out her hand. "but I'm a little embarrassed!"

Carolina handed back the passport begrudgingly and smiled. "By all means. Feel free to ask me whatever you want."

"Well, I already forgot your name, isn't that terrible? What was it again?"

"Carolina Cantarelli."

"Carolina Cantarelli. It has such a musical sound!"

"Thanks, I like it," Carolina said, and meant it. It did sound harmonious; plus, it had double initials. At least her stingy parents had given her that. "You can call me Carolina."

"And you can call me Josephine."

"Great! Josephine it is." She encouraged interaction on a first-name basis, which made guests feel freer; even Giac approved, as long as it came naturally. "What else did you want to ask me, Josephine?"

"*What* is that *divine* smell? It's making my mouth water!"

"I've been baking desserts. Everything you'll eat here is homemade, or locally sourced."

"Oh, good! I can't wait!" Josephine said, her clear blue eyes, definitely her best trait, widening with childlike anticipation.

"I have an idea, then. I'm afraid your room isn't quite ready yet. We pride ourselves on hygiene here at the Renovatus, and housekeeping does a very thorough job cleaning and sanitizing." No need to mention that at the moment there was only one part-time cleaner, who was still catching up with the rooms vacated last weekend, and who threatened to quit on a weekly basis. Too bad if she didn't like Carolina inspecting the rooms after she cleaned them; it was her resort, her reputation on the line.

"Oh, I know I'm early, but I'm an early riser, and I was eager to get here."

"I'm an early riser, too. So, how about a snack while you wait?"

"Well, I did already have a little something in Savona. But honestly, it wasn't much."

"I baked a couple of extra croissants this morning, and I'm told my coffee is exceptional. I make the blend myself. How does that sound?"

"To tell the truth, I don't know if it was the drive, or what, but I'm actually *starving*! I'd *love* a croissant and coffee, if it's not too much trouble."

"Not at all, it's my pleasure. Maybe you'd like to sample my cakes, too?"

"I won't say no to homemade cakes!"

"So, why don't you go sit near Ollie and fill your lungs with some fresh mountain air?"

"Ollie?"

"Oh, don't worry, Ollie's not a man! He's that magnificent old holly oak you see over there. That tree has been here way longer than us, so I thought he should have a name, out of respect. Like one of the family."

"How sweet!" Josephine said, looking relieved. "And this place, wow, it's like a garden of Eden! I just want to sit there and take it all in."

"Go right ahead and have a seat outside, then. I'll check you in as soon as your room's ready. You can leave your suitcase here," she suggested.

"Oh no, that's all right. I'm used to doing things on my own."

Carolina smiled until the shapeless but no longer nameless woman turned away, then stood watching as she wheeled her trolley over the gravel to a table, where she settled down on a hand-hewn bench, beneath the protective branches of Ollie the oak. Despite the open smile and bright blue eyes that said she was happy to be here, Carolina couldn't help thinking that Josephine Fortunata seemed tired, or worried, or tired of being worried. She looked as though she were dragging something more than a two-night trolley around with her.

But what, Carolina wondered? She shook her head and turned away, taking her musings with her to the kitchen.

CHAPTER SIX
Inge

"Benvenuti!" the woman called out, perfectly balancing two full glasses on a tray despite the limp in her step, a long black ponytail swishing behind her. Her purposeful stride and ebullient greeting combined with her compact stature gave Inge the impression she was that nervous type of woman who never gained an ounce because she burned her entire calorie intake and then some; the sort who was always on the move, but didn't waste a movement. After setting the glasses down on a table in the shade, she fluffed up her bangs and turned to face Inge, her black eyes twinkling with the joy of a child on Christmas morn. "Welcome! Welcome to the Renovatus! I'm Carolina Cantarelli, the owner!"

She was certainly very eager to greet them, Inge thought, not even giving them the time to walk in the door. Their steps on the gravel must have tipped her off to their arrival – either that or the sound of their bickering voices. An old married couple, that's probably what this woman took them for. It irked Inge that anyone should view her that way.

"Piacere. I'm Dr. Inge Egger," she said, nodding politely and smiling tightly. "And this is my husband, Severino Di Meglio." Rino followed his wife's example of not offering his hand, and that thing he was doing with his lips could hardly be called a smile. He wasn't in the friendliest of moods after banging something on the undercarriage of his car on that last stretch of unpaved road. For the sake of keeping the peace, Inge had remained calm during the ensuing tantrum, biting her tongue instead of saying I told you so, that's what you get for flying over those potholes at breakneck speed.

"It's such a *pleasure* to have you here!" their host said. "I hope you had a good drive up. I thought you might enjoy a glass of chilled white wine before settling in."

"Yes, well about the drive–" Rino began.

"A glass of wine sounds lovely, thank you!" Inge cut off her husband, her icy stare reminding him of what she'd said while getting out of the car, not five minutes ago. If he wanted to kick off their weekend complaining about the road instead of accepting responsibility for his reckless driving, he would first have to remove himself from her sight and earshot. She had no intention of standing next to him, pretending to support him, just because she was his wife.

"If you'd like to give me your documents, I'll be happy to check you in while you relax and enjoy the view. I always suggest our guests take a moment to transition when they arrive, to just sit and breathe and get a feel for this place, which I think you'll find very special."

"Actually, I'll come inside with you to take care of formalities while my wife settles down and *unwinds* out here," Rino replied. He knew when Inge meant business. "She suffers from motion sickness."

"Of course! May I bring you something else, doctor? Some herbal tea, perhaps?"

"No, thank you. I'll be fine in a minute. The fresh air will do me good." Inge eyed the two sweaty goblets as she sat down on a wooden bench carved out of a tree trunk. It wasn't one of those corny benches one often saw surrounded by statues of Snow White and her team of dwarves. This was an artistic sculpture, yet it was also surprisingly comfortable. "You go ahead and get us checked in, Rino," she added, waving him away.

"Very well then. We can step inside the main lodge, where you'll also find the indoor dining room and access to the veranda," the owner said to both of them. Turning to Rino, she added, "This way, please." Inge looked on as the woman walked away in her lopsided gait, trailed by Rino who hitched up the Bermuda shorts he could never quite decide whether to belt above or below his belly. The lodge they walked toward was built from weathered wood in the same natural tones of its neighboring trees, alternated with large panes of glass that mirrored the surrounding mountains and vegetation, making it tricky to determine at first glance exactly where the outdoors ended and the building began. Extending outward from the left wall of the lodge was a semi-circular veranda that faced the mountains on the other side of what appeared to be a steep gorge. This place was decidedly different from what she'd been expecting, even the way it had suddenly materialized in front of them, just when it seemed they would never make it out of the woods. That it made a strong initial impact on Inge was undeniable, and although it was early to say, the air did seem to be charged with a certain energy. Or maybe it was simply the absence of Rino's negativity that was having a positive effect on her.

Resting her back against the giant oak tree that stood behind the bench, Inge picked up a glass of wine, swirling it for a moment before taking a cautious sip. She should have asked what kind it was; she certainly couldn't afford to drink bad wine on top of an upset stomach. At least it was well-chilled, and crisp, the way she liked it. After another sip or two, she found herself thinking about a patient, distractedly at first, but within seconds she was mentally reviewing the delicate procedure she'd performed on the woman the day before yesterday. She was replaying the most challenging moments in her head, going over the compliments of her colleagues on the successful outcome, and just about to indulge in a round of self-congratulation, when she remembered that this weekend she'd vowed to leave thoughts of work behind to focus on her role as Inge, wife and mother. The difficulty with that was that tackling personal issues had always been harder for her than dealing with the many hurdles of her profession. But, as an intelligent and rational woman, she knew that problems, whether medical or personal in nature, didn't generally resolve themselves, and that ignoring them could lead to serious complications. Having certain matters hanging over her head was wearing her out and, above all, distracting her from her work, so she was determined to say what needed to be said this weekend, to get it over with, one way or the other. But first she'd have a little more of that white wine, which was having the startling side effect of somehow settling her stomach, as well as calming her nerves.

Inge didn't know what was taking Rino so long, but she didn't care much, as long as he didn't involve her or embarrass her. She'd take the opportunity to admire the view, get her bearings, transition her mindset. She was no stranger to the mountains, but couldn't recall ever having been in a place quite like this. Even at the end of one of the hottest, driest summers on record, the grounds were incredibly lush and blooming with flowers that usually only thrived at lower altitudes. And the mountains, while certainly not the highest or the most dramatic she'd seen, offered a sense of protection rather than a threat of danger, encircling the spot completely as if in a great embrace. If she hadn't driven up here, she might think there was no way in and no way out, except by helicopter. It was so unlike the overcrowded, overbuilt coast that it didn't seem like Liguria at all. And with all this breathing room and open space and not one ugly man-made structure in sight, it didn't even seem like Italy. Calm pervaded the air, the silence tickled by the sound of leaves rustling in the slight wind. If she strained her ears, she might hear Rino's muffled voice rambling on in the distance, but she much preferred to block it out.

Hopefully, they'd both be able to tune into that calm so she could effectively address the delicate issues on her agenda. For the most part, they revolved around their son Carl, regarding not only his future, but his past. Though she loved her son dearly, it was no secret that Inge hadn't felt any great need to become a mother by the time she'd married Rino. Already pushing forty, with her career in full swing, a baby was a complication she could have done without. But she'd said yes to his proposal, and to the child – just one – which to Rino had been a non-negotiable condition of marriage. Not being a woman who went back on her word or wasted her time, Inge had gotten the job done as quickly as possible, suffering through the pregnancy and morning sickness and insomnia and varicose veins and hemorrhoids and bloating, then enduring one of the most dreadful births she'd ever witnessed – from the wrong end of the delivery table. All that while working twice as hard at the clinic to dispel any doubts about her being able to handle it all.

Well, she had handled it all, despite her male colleagues' keenness to trip her up and then kick her while she was down. And now, as she sat under this ancient tree feeling the force of the mountains all around her, she was confident she would handle the task at hand without too much collateral damage. Whether or not there was any special energy floating around out there, being immersed in nature always gave her a boost. And so did a good white wine. Having drained her glass, she took a sip from Rino's. No sense letting it sit there and get warm.

CHAPTER SEVEN
Allegra

Allegra squealed, her white-knuckled fingers gripping the hand rests. "I hope you're having fun!" she cried.

"Way more than we would have had in your jalopy!" Adalberto laughed, taking his eyes off the road just long enough to wink at her.

"Me and my Saxo would have handled it fine! But the road is definitely worse than I remembered!" Though Allegra was loyal to her little car, she had to admit that a rugged ride in the 4x4 always excited her. Morally, she was against owning such a fuel-guzzling, environmentally incorrect vehicle, and whenever she looked out the window of her humble home and saw it hogging up space next to her outdated Citroën, its presence there seemed wrong, just like the name Defender seemed wrong, when in reality it was more of an Offender. There was no sense denying it, though, the SUV also made her feel more extravagant, more adventurous, the same way Adalberto himself made her feel. Now he was accelerating up a short, steep hill, and after a sharp bend in the road, they burst out of the woods and into a clearing, the tough tires chewing up the gravel as he made a quick turn into the parking area, braked abruptly and came to a halt.

"Whew!" Allegra said, immediately hopping down from the passenger seat, glad to feel the ground under her feet again. Placing her hands on her lumbar zone, she arched her back, staring up at the milky sky. She was looking forward to a good, long yoga practice later, hopefully with a few students.

"Wow! You were right about this place, Allegra Amore!" Adalberto said, instantly putting her at ease about inviting him along, when there were so many other things he could be doing. She admired his long, muscular arms as he stretched them high into the air, his head tilted back, his Ray-Bans glinting. The light was strong, even if the sun was behind the clouds, but Allegra wished he'd take those sunglasses off anyway. She enjoyed observing him as he observed things and often wondered whether they saw anything the same way, and if anything they saw could remind them of the same things. Because when you thought about it, just about everything you could see or smell, taste or hear, had the power to reactivate a memory connected to some other time and place where you saw or smelled or tasted or heard something similar. Even though it seemed like she and Adalberto had been together forever, they'd only been sharing experiences for seven years, and out of those seven years, they were apart half the time.

"I'm glad your first impression is so positive. Don't you just love these woods? They remind me of chestnuts!"

"Chestnuts? This high up? I don't think so."

"I'm not saying there *are* chestnuts here, but anything can spark a memory. The smell of the woods always reminds me of a certain chestnut forest where my parents used to take me when I was little." As she spoke, her mind traveled across the miles and back in time to the mild autumn days spent in the south of France, gathering chestnuts in the forests of the Massif du Maures.

"I was so young when we moved north that I don't remember much about being a kid in Naples," Adalberto said, not a trace of wistfulness in his voice.

"How about roasted chestnuts? You must remember eating them in the fall. I know I do!"

"Well, now that you mention it, yes. Sometimes my parents would buy us some off a cart on a street corner in Turin. The vendor would wrap them up in those brown paper cones."

"Right!"

"They used to be cheap, but not anymore. And forget about the marrons glacés. They're a luxury item now!"

"Marrons glacés! I used to love those! They remind me of Collobrières, this place where I'd walk around sniffing the sweetish burnt smell of chestnuts that hung over the whole town, mixed in with that autumn smell of damp leaves and mulled wine. Oh, and when my nose wasn't in the air, it was pressed against the windows of all those darling shops that sold all those fancy boxes and jars and bottles of chestnuts in every imaginable form. They had candied chestnuts and creamed chestnuts and chestnut spread and chestnut liqueur and even chestnut ice cream!"

Pushing his sunglasses up above his forehead, Adalberto stared at her, smiling. "I hope your parents bought you some," he said.

Allegra beamed back at him, happy to have his attention. "Oh yes, I was allowed to have a marron glacé, just one, probably to make me stop drooling. I used to let it sit on my tongue and savor it as it dissolved. I swear, I could feel the sugar going straight into my blood!"

"It's great that you have such good memories of your parents."

"Yeah, some," Allegra said, though being reminded of chestnuts was better than being reminded about her parents, and about the fact that Adalberto would never meet them. "I want to make lots of new memories, though. With you." She really did, that was just one of the many reasons why she wanted to spend more time with him. If she could create more memories with Adalberto, when something reminded her of something else, when that certain smell or taste or sight or sound stirred up the emotions, sensations, and experiences that made life fuller and richer and worth remembering, it would be their shared memory; not just hers, not just his.

"It's not much cooler up here, though," Adalberto said.

"What?" It took Allegra a minute to remember where exactly "here" was.

"I said, it's not much cooler up here."

"Oh, right. I know. We're at around fifteen hundred meters, but I guess that's not high enough to make much of a difference, not with this heat wave. It'll cool off at night, though, you'll see. And just having all these trees around makes it easier to breathe, doesn't it?" Even though Adalberto had already said he liked the place, Allegra felt a duty to defend it, as if she would be held responsible for everything that happened while they were here.

"Yeah," Adalberto said, taking her hand in his, turning it over to kiss the palm. "It does."

Holding hands, they inhaled a lungful of pine-scented air, holding it in as long as they could, then letting it out slowly, very slowly through their noses, the way she'd taught him. Making memories was as simple as that, and it was good.

CHAPTER EIGHT
Carolina

Carolina was steaming, and it wasn't from spending the afternoon in the hot kitchen. This kind of steamy wouldn't go away when she turned off the stove or when the sun went down. This kind of steamy she was stuck with as long as Giangiacomo Lanza thought that minding the goats and riding around on that jackass of his amounted to carrying his half of the load. Sure, she was the designated people person, they both knew that and had agreed on that from the outset. But one thing was dealing with happy people, who over an exquisite breakfast raved about how well they'd slept thanks to the magnificent mattresses she'd chosen; who over a glass of local wine praised the quality of her home-cooked meal; who by the time they left were gushing about Carolina this and Carolina that, and insisted on hugging her goodbye and maybe even leaving her their number in case she ever passed through Genoa or Milan or Turin or Nice, or wherever they came from. It was another thing altogether dealing with people who were angry from the minute they got there, for something that didn't depend on her. Turning those people around after a rotten first impression was an uphill battle, and Giac would do well to remember that Carolina was not here to fight his battles or justify his incompetence, but to bring positive change into people's lives. Any idiot knew that in order for her to do that, those people needed to be relaxed, receptive, responsive.

"Leave those muddy boots on the porch, please!" she called out to her husband, perceiving his presence by his footfall in the foyer while she bent over to retrieve a serving dish from the dining room credenza. His beloved ceramic tiles might be easy to clean, but they sure didn't clean themselves, and the housekeeper had already left for the day. Maybe even for good.

"Oooh, what got *your* goat?" Giac asked as his wife approached. He didn't disobey, but neither did he obey. He simply stopped in his tracks, grinning, his thumbs hooked in the front pockets of his jeans. He looked darn good in those jeans, she couldn't help but notice, despite her irritation. When they'd first moved up here, it had been astonishing to see how quickly he'd taken to country life, how his flabby muscles had toned up and filled out from the manual labor, how his pasty skin had taken on a ruddy bronze glow from the hours spent outdoors. Giac wasn't simply a born-and-raised Milanese man who had changed from the suit-wearing, subway-riding, laptop-toting, soft-bellied, slope-shouldered middle manager he used to be; he was a different man altogether. But sometimes he overacted the part.

"My goat was got by the road that you had all winter, *and* the winter before that to repair, when we didn't have any clients!" she said, slinging a dishtowel over her shoulder.

"Well, *you* might not have had any clients, but my animals didn't know a damn thing about tourists. They still needed to be fed and watered and herded and grazed and bred and milked and tended to. You have no idea how much work they take!"

"All I'm saying, Giac, is that last year's flooding turned the little holes into potholes and the potholes into ditches, and someone has to fix them! I myself am sick of driving around them and I'm sick of asking you to do something about them!"

"Those woods are public land, and so is the road that goes through them. With the taxes we pay, it's up to the town to fix it."

"Is it up to the town to come and talk to that guy with the Mercedes who bent his something-or-other out of whack driving up here? Is it up to the town to pay for his repairs? If so, then you can tell our guest that, because I told him to talk to you!"

"The guy with the Mercedes should learn how to drive. What's he doing coming to a place like this in a city car like that? And who needs people like him anyway?"

They needed people like him, that was who. Because those people in fancy cars attracted other people in fancy cars, and their business was essential if they wanted to survive, but she didn't have the patience or energy to explain that to Giac for the umpteenth time. Especially now that a certain someone was standing right behind him.

"Why don't you ask me?" said the bespectacled man at Giac's back. "Severino Di Meglio," he added, extending his hand when Giac swiveled around. "Owner of the Mercedes in question. I've been driving a Mercedes for decades. I've driven a Mercedes to San Moritz and Cortina and Davos and Zermatt in the deep of Alpine winters, and I assure you I have never come across such a treacherous road!"

Giac clasped the man's hand in a firm shake as Carolina looked on, hoping he wouldn't crush his fingers. "Giangiacomo Lanza, owner of this establishment," he said, though he'd stopped introducing himself with his full first name immediately after ditching Milan. "Giac" was simpler, more direct, more macho, more American-rancher-sounding, whether you pronounced it Jack or Jock. But he still liked having all those syllables to fall back on when he needed to convey a sense of authority, when he wanted to establish that he wasn't just a hired hand.

"For the record, it's clearly stated on our website and on every confirmation that the last five kilometers are on a dirt road and that the management will provide transportation from the main road for anyone who doesn't want to drive up. But that those who still choose to drive, do so at their own risk," Giac said. "And you did so at your own risk, Signor what-was-it? Milio?" Hands on his hips, Giac rocked on the heels of the mud-caked boots which he still hadn't taken off. Better that way, they made him look tougher, though he already had a physical advantage over the rotund little man whose own feet were encased in a pair of tasseled moccasins that looked as soft as kid gloves.

"The name's Di Meglio! Severino Di Meglio!" the man replied, throwing back his shoulders and thrusting out his chest. "Owner of Feltro Di Meglio, if you don't mind!"

"Hey there, wait just a minute!" Giac looked the man in the eye, poking a finger in his face.

Great, all Carolina needed now was for him to punch him in the nose! And she was the one who overstepped boundaries?

But then Giac smiled. "Did you say Feltro Di Meglio? As in Feltro di Meglio *di meglio non c'è*?"

"The one and only!" Signor Di Meglio affirmed, his eyes glinting with a mixture of pride and suspicion.

"Well, what do you know? I have a saddle liner made with your felt!"

"Is that right?"

"Yes*sir!* Made by a saddle company in Germany. They only use the best felt. Sheep felt, it is!"

"Ah yes, I know that firm well. They're in Dresden," Signor Di Meglio said, now smiling and nodding his head. "They've been clients for decades. Good people. Serious."

"Well, hey, I didn't mean to change the subject. I'm awfully sorry about your car, Signor Di Meglio. Carol here will get you our insurance information," Giac said, winking at his wife. He did that thing with her name, too, lengthening it and shortening it without her consent, according to the importance he wanted to give her.

"Nonsense," Signor Di Meglio said, with a wave of his hand. "It's just a dent, and I'm fully covered. Please, call me Rino."

"All right, then. I'm Giac." He held out his hand, and they shook a second time, throwing in pats on their backs. "Friends of felt."

Ugh! That man! She'd borne the brunt of this guest's anger because of Giac's negligence, and now the two guys were already buddies! On a first-name basis! And she was relegated to being a Carol! He'd pay for this.

Giac paused the pleasantries to jerk a thumb at Carolina. "Carol, this gentleman here is Rino. Treat him well."

"We've already met, of course. You can call me *Carolina*," she specified, smiling sweetly. "And I treat all my guests well, Rino. Trust me."

CHAPTER NINE
Josephine

When the higher-ups extended her three-month overseas transfer to six, Josephine hadn't complained. It was a godsend, really, considering she was in no rush to return to the States, let alone make any decisions about her future. Thomas was being great about it too, even though, as a man, he couldn't quite relate to her midlife crisis or existential crisis or whatever crisis she was going through as a woman. He remained his kind and patient self, listening while she talked, but offering precious little advice, a behavior which, to tell the truth, sometimes got on her nerves. He never tried to convince her one way or the other, saying that it was her life, that he only wanted what was best for her, that he would always love and respect her no matter what, that she should take all the time she needed to figure things out. Well, the only thing she'd figured out so far was that she was happier in Rome than she'd been in Buffalo in a heck of a long time. No surprise there. Buffalo was filled with the struggles of her past, piled up like the sooty snowbanks that lingered on the street corners in March, waiting for the sun to melt away their miserable existence. What a difference from springtime in the Eternal City! It was easy to fall in love with Rome at that time of year, when it was alive with people teeming in the streets, jackets slung over their shoulders, eating and drinking at sidewalk cafés, picnicking in the parks, crowding around the monumental fountains while licking their dripping ice cream cones, of which she'd sampled many. In addition to the joy of simply being in Rome, Josephine was gratified by her work there, too. Teaching in a safe environment was a welcome break, and she'd also undertaken a stimulating project, writing for a newsletter that she herself had conceived. And Rome was also where she'd met Lucia, who'd immediately become an important part of her life. It was as if this past spring had been like awakening from a lifetime of hibernation, with a revival of desires and hopes that had lain dormant for too long. But then summer had exploded, and Rome suddenly had too much of everything: too much heat and noise and pollution, too many tourists, too many distractions, too many doubts, too much pressure. Rome had been her escape from Buffalo, but by the end of August, Josephine needed an escape from Rome. Just for a few days, on her own. That was all she needed. And, once again, Thomas had come through for her.

From what it looked like, not very many people knew about this place, but, you had to hand it to him, Thomas was one of those who did. With all his jetting here and networking there, he was always in the know. All it had taken was a few emails and bingo! here she was, strolling the grounds of an exclusive Italian resort, filling her lungs with fragrant mountain air instead of carbon monoxide fumes, listening to the chirping of birds instead of the honking of cars and roaring of scooters. Always a city dweller, she'd gone off on her share of retreats to secluded places in the past, but there was something different about the silence she was experiencing here. It had depth to it, and substance; it wasn't simply the absence of irritating noises, this silence was a protagonist in its own right, presiding over the grounds with its peaceful presence. That silence was so calm-inducing, in fact, that as soon as Carolina had escorted Josephine to her essentially but exquisitely furnished wood-scented room, she'd collapsed on the most divine bed imaginable, her tummy replete with cakes and croissants, her consciousness drifting off as if carried away on a cloud. She wasn't used to napping, though, and the deep, dreamless sleep had left her feeling sticky-skinned and fuzzy-headed and puffy-faced, with a telltale pillowcase crease marking her left cheek. That was why she'd decided to take a brisk walk before showering for dinner, although the brisk part wasn't quite getting off the ground.

Yawning and blinking as she took in the scenery, she meandered along the path that led from her bungalow to the main lodge, feeling like she'd been magically transported to another dimension, smack dab in the middle of the mountains. Although their beauty was undeniable, she could swear those towering peaks were looking down on her with disapproval, their jagged features dramatized by the slanted afternoon sunlight slicing through their crown of ominous clouds. They were the kind of dense, dark clouds you saw in those religious paintings hanging in Rome's churches, the kind of clouds that parted like a rent curtain to reveal the ascension of Jesus or the assumption of the Virgin Mary or the descent of the Holy Spirit. The view was impressive, for sure, but it disturbed her, the same way those churches and their sacred paintings disturbed her lately, making her feel insignificant, unworthy, ashamed, the way she'd felt as a little Catholic girl. If only she could wash those feelings away, once and for all!

That was when she noticed the gentle gurgling. Drawn to the sound, she followed a narrow dirt path through a stand of willowy reeds leading to a shallow pond. The opposite side of the pond was edged with flowering plants arranged according to the colors of the rainbow, and the entire spectrum, from red to violet, was alive with the buzzing of plump, fuzzy bees and the flitting of butterflies with the largest, most colorful wings she'd ever seen. The pond itself was brimming with crystal clear water that trickled down from a rock garden just above. What an enchanting spot! What pure water! On an impulse, she dropped to her knees and scooped some up in her hands, splashing it on her face, letting it drip down her neck, hoping its freshness would revive her. The drops tasted so sweet on her lips that she felt the urge to drink some, first in tiny sips, then in gulps. An instant later, she was sticking her whole head in the pond, relishing the cool, tingling sensation on her scalp, imagining the water penetrating her skull, cleansing her brain, refreshing her thoughts. When she finally came up for air, it was only long enough to take a breath before dunking her head again. God, she wished she could jump right into that pond! She hadn't seen any other people around, but she couldn't very well risk stripping off her clothes out in the open. Not that she'd be bold enough anyway; she was too modest, too ashamed of her body. She remained on her knees for some time, staring blankly at the still water and at the face it reflected, until that deep sense of peace returned. The water may not have the power to wash away her problems, but it made her feel, for one astonishing moment, that she alone had the power to do so, and as far as she was concerned, that made it a miracle pond! The miracle wasn't extended to her knees, though, which had stiffened up something awful. After sitting on the bank of the pond a minute to massage them, she rose slowly to her feet and retraced her steps through the reeds, walking back down to the path and up to the freshly mown meadow below the main lodge.

"Ciao, Holly!" she said, deciding on the spot to baptize a younger relative of Ollie the oak before sitting beneath it on the cool green grass. Kicking off the rubber-soled shoes that made her feet sweat, and taking off her socks, too, she leaned against Holly's trunk, stretching her legs out in front of her. Closing her eyes, she felt grateful for the solid support behind her back, but also for the freedom of sitting barefoot, letting the blades of grass tickle her toes and feet. Solidity and freedom, reliability and whimsy. Could they co-exist in her life?

"Excuse me," a female voice said, some minutes later, or hours later, it was hard to say. Startled, Josephine looked up to see who it was, but she couldn't speak, or didn't want to speak; all she could do was stare. Clothed in flowing white garments, her sunlit auburn tresses falling to her waist, the stranger was the closest thing to an ethereal vision Josephine had ever beheld. Was she real, or was that pond water affecting her brain?

"I'm sorry, I didn't mean to disturb you," the apparition said.

"No, um, you're um, not disturbing me," Josephine stammered, thinking she should stand, but wondering if she could. Her legs felt like jelly.

"I'm Allegra," the woman said, squatting low to face Josephine, her bottom grazing the ground, her bare feet flat on the grass. How could she do that without toppling over?

"Allegra?" she repeated.

"Yes, Allegra. That's my name. And yours?"

"Mine's Fortunata – Josephine Fortunata."

"That makes us Cheerful and Lucky, I guess! How funny!" Allegra said.

"Were you waiting for me?"

"Um, no," Josephine said, confused by this woman's presence, wondering what she wanted, and why she looked disappointed by her answer. "Unless I may have been waiting for you without knowing it?"

"I *love* your attitude!" Allegra said. "And your *name*, too. First *and* last. My mother's name was Josephine. Where are you from?"

"Oh, that's a long story," Josephine said, shaking her head. She was good at evading questions, but she didn't want to be rude to someone who looked like the Madonna incarnate. She'd give her the basics. "The Fortunata part has its roots in Italy. I'm half Italian and half American."

"I'm half Italian, too, on the Scalzo side. The other half, the Verseau side, is French."

"So is it Allegra Scalzo, or Allegra Verseau?" As a seasoned teacher, Josephine had the habit of mentally registering people's names and surnames, then filing them away in alphabetical order.

"Officially it's Allegra Verseau, but that's a long story, too. Everyone just calls me Allegra, which would be great if they didn't always expect me to walk around with a big smile on my face."

"Fulfilling an expectation like that is a full-time job," Josephine said.

"Right! It's kind of like when I say I'm a yoga teacher. I've chosen this path, and I'm on this journey, but I'm only *human*. I can't *always* be yogic in *everything* I do. Hey, so, speaking of which. In case Carolina hasn't filled you in on the details, I'll be leading yoga lessons this weekend for anyone who's interested."

"Oh. Yoga. I see." Josephine forced a weak smile. She'd tried yoga once back when she was a student. Who hadn't? It hadn't seemed like a very good fit at the time.

"So, would you like to join me?" Allegra's expressive eyebrows were arched in expectation, while her fingers deftly twirled her curls into a long strand which she proceeded to knot on the top of her head in a bun, just like that, with no rubber bands or clips or anything.

"Well, I didn't really come prepared for yoga," Josephine said, running a hand over her own cropped hair.

"What you're wearing now is fine. I have the rest."

Josephine had planned to take a long, hot shower in her luxurious bathroom before dinner, which she hoped would be early, since with the help of Carolina's free pastries she'd skipped lunch to avoid running up her bill. On the other hand, it was also true that she'd been raised on quick, cold showers, and once you had a habit drilled into your head, it wasn't easy to break it. Even now, washing her hair took under a minute, and honestly, once she soaped up the critical areas and rinsed off, she was good to go and there didn't seem much point in just standing there. Sure, it felt nice, but it also felt like a waste of time and water. So, showers aside, what should she say? That her life revolved around routines? That she wasn't used to being caught off guard, to being offered options, to even consider an impromptu yoga class?

"Um, it's just that I may not be *mentally* prepared."

"All you need to be is *receptive*, Josephine. I'll do all the rest. But hey, only if you want to. No pressure whatsoever."

Josephine felt drawn to Allegra and didn't want to brush her off. Maybe she'd been sent to help her with more of that deep inner cleansing; maybe she was the follow-up to the miracle pond.

"Well, I guess I could try," Josephine said. "When's class?"

"How about right now?" Allegra suggested with an encouraging smile. "It'll just be you and me and the trees."

"I should warn you, I'm not very flexible."

"You'd be surprised, Josephine. I have a feeling you're more flexible than you think."

CHAPTER TEN
Carolina

Dinnertime was Carolina's favorite time of the day at the resort. It was the time when all her efforts came together like the ingredients in a perfectly executed recipe. She couldn't say exactly when she'd developed her passion for cooking, but she supposed she'd always had it in her, really. Back when she helped out her parents at Caffé Cantarelli, everyone used to say she had a flair for food. Most coffee bars of that type (the anonymous, depressing type, let's face it), located in the busy outskirts of a big city (also anonymous and depressing) accepted their lot and did nothing to improve things. Sure, they'd switch to energy-efficient light bulbs, or install bathrooms for the disabled if they were forced to, but far be it from them to give their customers anything to get excited about. Granted, the customers themselves, so grim-faced and dead-eyed, were also anonymous and depressing, unless you took the trouble to learn something about them, like she did, but how much of a conversation could you overhear in the time it took to someone gulp down an espresso? People rushed in and rushed out again, in too much of a hurry to even taste the croissants they dunked into their cappuccinos or the sandwiches they shoved down their throats – provided they could even spare a few seconds to eat the food there instead of taking it away in little white bags. If there was one thing Carolina hated, besides all forms of emptiness (okay, so maybe it was more than one thing), it was anything anonymous and depressing, so the only way she could cope with being stuck at her parents' bar was to give the place a creative spin. Baking croissants on the premises wasn't feasible, so she began haggling with her father until he broke down and granted her permission to add some pizzazz to their breakfast selection. Her idea was to incorporate an assortment of personalized pastries delivered fresh from the bakery each morning, with special cream fillings like Avola almond, Bronte pistachio, and Roero hazelnut, to name a few, or for those who preferred jelly fillings, there was passion fruit, quince, or fig, for example, depending on the season, on her imagination, and on what she could convince the bakery to prepare and her father to finance. The "Carolina Croissants," as they came to be known, were a far cry from the frozen croissants every other bar served, which were barely passable when warm if you were still half-asleep and starving, but after that, you might as well be eating sugary cardboard.

If the fluffy, flaky croissants with ever-changing fillings were a hit, Carolina had a harder time convincing customers to try one of the new sandwiches she prepared each morning after the first wave of caffeine guzzlers receded. At her father's insistence, she still produced teetering piles of the usual *tramezzini* with tuna and lettuce, and tomato and lettuce, and mozzarella and lettuce, and prosciutto and lettuce, glued to soft slices of crustless white bread with the mayonnaise she scooped from a giant jar. Only then could she focus on the fun part, experimenting with alternative types of bread she convinced that same bakery to provide, as long as she procured the sacks of special flour. Thus were born her famous "Super Senatore Cappelli Sandwich," a summery favorite, made with sun-dried tomatoes, grilled eggplant and fresh goat cheese, and the "Grano Arso Grand Panino," from her fall/winter collection, made with local gorgonzola, Sorrento walnuts and red radicchio from Treviso. She could always tell when someone was tempted to take a risk on one of her new sandwiches, based on how long it took them to pick the same exact one they always ordered. At first, she was disappointed that only a small percentage of their patrons took the leap and chose one of her creations over a standard *tramezzino*, either because they were too stingy to cough up the couple extra euros, or more likely because they weren't curious enough. It didn't matter much, though, because word got around, and the mere fact that the more exotic options were visible in the display case right next to the usual boring options seemed to make all of the sandwiches they sold more desirable and tastier, kind of like when dull people hang out with interesting people, hoping that some of their charm, or intelligence, or wit might rub off onto them by association.

Now that Carolina was in charge of her own kitchen here at the Renovatus, she had control over everything that went into it and came out of it. The meat she served came from a couple of sustainable farms in Piedmont which she had taken the time and trouble to personally inspect, and made it a point to visit periodically. It was ironic that she should stop eating meat when she finally had access to some she could trust, but the closer she got to the source, the less she wanted to see it on her plate, the final straw being the one (and only) time Giac had wrung the neck of a spent laying hen without her consent, somehow imagining that she would cook and eat it (in his dreams!), a crime that might have earned him the same punishment as the poor hen, were she not such a kind and forgiving person.

Carolina didn't serve meat at every meal anymore but knew that if she forced her vegetarianism on her guests, it would backfire. These rich people were used to having options, and it was only through her experience and sensitivity that she was able to strike a balance between what she *knew* they should want to eat, with what they *thought* they wanted to eat. Just the same, her meat dishes were exquisite, everyone said so, but in the end, the foods her guests raved most about were her pastas and risottos and vegetable-based dishes which featured, whenever possible, her homegrown produce. Gardening was another repressed passion of hers that had exploded once she got out of Milan and could sink her hands into some soil. Of course, she couldn't do everything herself, there were only so many hours in a day even if you got up as early as she did. After being forced to slave away at her parents' bar during her youth, Carolina would have appreciated a hand from her own kids, who instead of sticking around to help, opted to spend their summers working at some stranger's bar on the island of Ibiza (her daughter) and Mykonos (her son), just because she expected them to earn their keep. But that was another story, the theme of which was that kids were ingrates.

That was why she'd ended up engaging Florian, a deceptively skinny guy from Albania, to help with the grunt work, and his dark-haired wife Jada to give her a hand with the kitchen chores. Despite being without working papers or references, Carolina hired them (unofficially) on the spot, then dug up what she could online. They were both on Facebook, but most of their posts were in Albanian so she had to rely on the translator function. Luckily, you could also tell a lot about people by their photos, which revealed that Florian had a weird obsession with ambulances, while Jada looked a little too good for Carolina 's comfort in a bikini. Most of the pictures were with family, though – lots of family, with lots of birthdays. Carolina figured that anyone who could smile while being squashed into a photo frame with so many unattractive relatives must be fairly reliable, so she was caught off guard when first Florian, later followed by Jada, took off just because she fell behind with their pay. Good riddance to them, though, because Giac had immediately stolen Florian away from her, claiming he needed help on the farm, and Jada had gotten into this sneaky habit of sticking her paws into Carolina 's pots and pans, and if Carolina was jealous of anything, it was her kitchen, and of course, her guests; a little less of her husband, even though she'd caught him flirting with Jada more than once. Anyway, Giac paid so little attention to Carolina these days that it was hard for her to feel possessive, which was kind of sad, but that didn't mean she could stand there and watch him make a fool of himself.

Enough time wasted thinking about those two, though, when she had dinner coming up. She was looking forward to making the rounds from table to table with the excuse of checking whether everything was okay, which wasn't only an excuse, she really did want to make sure everyone was happy, and also to give them the opportunity to make her happy with their compliments. If she approached slowly enough, and took her sweet time clearing away the dishes between one course and another, she could pick up snippets of conversations that revealed all kinds of things about her guests, especially when they dined on the panoramic veranda, suspended between the mountains above them and the gorge below. The awe-inspiring nature broke barriers people weren't even aware of, priming them for an experience of total abandonment while savoring a delicious dinner as the darkness fell, the only light coming from the candles flickering on the elegantly set tables, the stars twinkling in the velvety black sky, and whatever moon rose to look down on them. The musical tinkling of cutlery accompanied by the popping of corks and gurgling of wine as it was poured (and drunk) would set the tone for intimate table talk, and provided she played her cards right, by the end of the meal she'd be nibbling on more than scraps of her guests 'conversations, she'd be feasting on them. The trick was striking the right balance between discretion and solicitude, friendliness and courtesy, chattiness and reserve.

CHAPTER ELEVEN
Inge

The evening air was snug and warm, swaddling Inge in a way she might have found comforting, if only she could relax. But with so many thoughts pressing on her mind, she could ill afford to be lulled into complacency. A brisk wind was what she needed, one that would clear both the air and her head. At least she had some dramatic scenery to contemplate as she leaned over the railing of the veranda. The rough outlines of the mountains set against the darkening sky filled her with the desire to climb, while the steep drop to the gorge directly below brought back exhilarating memories of her white-water rafting days. She wondered whether any visitors ever considered jumping to their death from here – or throwing someone else to theirs.

With an unconcerned toss of her stylish blonde head, Inge's thoughts turned to the more pleasant subject of dinner. As a person who detested being stuck indoors, particularly if it entailed the presence of people that weren't of her choosing, she was delighted that dinner would be served out here. Her craving for the open air was constant and insatiable, and the place where she loved breathing it most was high up in her beloved Swiss Alps, hiking or climbing in summer, snowshoeing or skiing in winter. Outdoors and alone, that was where she longed to be whenever she felt overwhelmed by professional responsibilities, oppressed by domestic boredom, or simply restless and dissatisfied. If she couldn't be outdoors – a luxury these days, with all the demands on her time – Inge's preferred environment was a sterile one, which was where she spent most of her waking hours. Oddly – or maybe not – she'd even elected to work with sterile couples and to practice her profession in what was probably the most sterile country in the world. When she thought of the planet's population nearing eight billion, Inge couldn't help but question the value of her vocation to help people have the babies Mother Nature denied them. But that was only when she thought about it, and she'd promised herself not to think about any of those things right now.

"No climbing on the railings, Dr. Egger!"

Startled, Inge spun around to find the owner standing directly behind her. Granted, she'd been too lost in thought to notice anyone else, but sneaking up on a guest in those soft-soled shoes the woman wore was unacceptable, and so was her silly comment. Inge was about to say as much when she was silenced by the woman's smile, so open and unguarded, almost to the point of being childish, that Inge felt compelled to smile back. In her evening attire, her host resembled a little girl in grown-up clothes, the simple black tunic hanging loosely over her slight frame, no curvy obstacles preventing it from falling straight down to the middle of her calves. Her dark hair was shiny, the bangs freshly curled against her brow, the rest pulled back in a ponytail so tight that it stretched the corners of her eyes a bit, giving her a slightly exotic look. Inge appreciated the fact that her skin was clean-scrubbed, without a trace of makeup.

"I'm sorry if I disturbed you," the woman said.

"No need to apologize," Inge said. "I was just enjoying a moment of solitude."

"I'll leave you in the excellent company of the view, then. Your table is right over there, in that far corner, when you're ready."

There were five tables on the veranda which could have easily accommodated ten, and only three of them were set for dinner, all along the railing, but spaced far apart. That was fine with Inge. She wasn't here to rub elbows with strangers.

"I thought you'd appreciate the privacy of that position," the woman added.

"Thank you," Inge said, wondering what exactly had prompted her to say that. Clearly, she couldn't see her and Rino as a couple who were here on a romantic getaway. It was more likely that she'd labeled Rino as a loud-mouthed oaf when he'd gone in to complain about his car, someone who might disrupt the relaxed ambience and the serenity of the other guests. The only thing he'd reported back to Inge after that conversation was that the woman had politely but firmly suggested that he speak to her husband about the road.

"Also, you get the best view from that angle. I suggest you sit on the right."

Inge nodded, deciding that if the woman wasn't going to leave her alone, she might as well sit down and wait for Rino. She'd still have the view, but she'd also have the advantage of checking out the other guests as they arrived, while not being forced to interact with them. She sometimes wished she didn't feel so put off by people, that she were capable of casual conversation and easy friendships. The feeling didn't usually last long, though, it was like a ping of the brain that was supposed to remind her of something, but that she'd grown used to ignoring, like all those alarms and buzzers that rang in the corridors of the clinic throughout the day, most of which didn't concern her.

"Would you like to select a bottle of wine for this evening's dinner, Doctor, or will your husband take care of that?"

"I'll choose the wine, thank you."

"Well, perhaps I can recommend an excellent bubbly to start with on this unusually balmy evening? Although we do carry some French vintages, we like to stay as local as possible. One of our favorites here is a brut Spumante from the Langa region. That's in Piedmont, just over those mountains."

"Of course. I know the Langa area well. And exactly what Spumante would that be?"

"It's called Tetillante, due to a curious story about the winemakers' father who misunderstood the French word for sparkling, *pétillant,* and turned it into a family label."

"And what grapes is it made from?"

"One hundred percent Chardonnay. But perhaps you and your husband are champagne drinkers, Doctor?"

"My husband adores champagne, but I'd like to try the Tetillante."

"Wonderful. Shall we wait for Rino, or shall I bring it now?"

"I'm sure *Signor Di Meglio* will be along shortly. You can bring it now."

"Very well, Doctor!" The woman nodded, then turned and walked away, favoring her left leg.

Champagne drinkers, indeed! What Inge really liked was a good beer, that was all she used to drink in her younger years. It wasn't until leaving her Swiss mountain valley for college that she became more familiar with wine, and she'd take Italian over French any day. Just like she'd take brown bread with butter over Beluga caviar any day. Food snobs were every bit as boorish as wine snobs, and it irritated Inge that she should be taken for either. Of course, that was a risk you ran when you went to the same places the snobs went to, and wore the same designer clothes they wore, and were more gratified when your husband draped your body with expensive jewelry instead of covering it with kisses. Looking down at her overly scrubbed hands, she spread open her long, learned fingers with their closely clipped nails. On her left hand glittered the platinum band of five flawless diamonds Rino had rewarded her with on their tenth anniversary; on her right, her fiftieth birthday gift, an emerald solitaire of five carats, one for each decade, earned by simply staying alive for half a century. The gems suddenly seemed tainted to her, like stolen property that belonged on the liver-spotted hands of some wealthy matron, not on hers. Drumming her fingers on the table, she wondered what was happening to her lately, why she often experienced such confusion about who she was as a woman; about how she came across to other people compared to how they perceived her. Maybe this brain fog that sometimes clouded not only her mind but her feelings was a long-term side effect of menopause, or possibly of the pandemic, who could say? Whatever the cause, lately she found herself recoiling from overstated luxury, the way your stomach might turn at the sight of oysters once you've tossed enough of them down your throat to make you vomit your guts out.

"There you are!" Rino called, grinning as he approached the table. His chest was puffed out like a bullfrog's, stretching the stripes of the green-and-blue polo shirt he'd changed into for dinner instead of one of the more flattering button-downs she'd packed for him. A few other people were arriving now, too, but Rino blocked her view of them.

"I hope you haven't been obsessing over your Mercedes," she blurted. "It's useless to worry about it now. When we go home, you'll get it fixed." With all the things they needed to talk about, she refused to waste another minute talking about a car. "Subject closed."

"I didn't say a word! You're the one who brought it up!" Rino replied, too loudly. All those years spent around noisy machinery had led to partial hearing loss, and the less a man heard, the more he shouted. Inge knew that, but she still hated it.

"Please. Just sit down and relax," she said, stealing a glance at the other two tables, where a youngish couple and a lone lump of a woman had taken their respective places. They were all looking their way. What was wrong with people? Didn't they have anything better to do than eavesdrop? "Now, let's not get this weekend off to a bad start," she added.

"It's too late to change the way it started," Rino grumbled, sitting down across from her. "But if you can find the time to listen, I've been wanting to tell you something incredibly interesting."

"What's been stopping you?"

"The fact that you were gone!"

"I only went out for a short walk while you were napping."

"The drive up on those roads tired me out. But I only conked out for fifteen minutes! I thought that when I woke up, after all your talk about reconnecting, we'd spend a little more time in that super soft bed together," Rino wiggled his eyebrows, giving her a moment to let his meaning sink in.

"I needed to stretch my legs after the drive. You know I can't rest unless I stretch my legs," Inge said, ignoring his allusion. She was aware that she'd stayed out longer than intended, returning just in time to shower for dinner and finding Rino missing. She simply lost track of time when she was outdoors, that was the way it always had been and always would be, and she refused to feel guilty about it. "But what did you want to tell me that's so incredibly interesting?" Inge was curious; she'd love to hear something interesting issue from his mouth for once. When he was busy running his company all he could talk about was felt, felt, felt. And after scaling down his involvement, no other new passion had stepped in to take its place, leaving yawning gaps in their conversations unless she talked about her work, but merely mentioning ovaries and uteruses, especially defective ones, was out of the question. Thank God for their son, who took advantage of the open slot and was happy to monopolize the dinner table conversation. It was precisely Carl that she needed to talk about now that they were alone. But how to begin?

Meanwhile, Rino was studying her expression, as if trying to decide whether she still deserved to hear his incredibly interesting story. "As I was saying," he began at last, "When I got up and you were gone, I went back inside to discuss the incident with my car, and there was this big fellow blocking the doorway. Before I could ask him to let me pass, I realized that the lady owner was already telling him about it and that the guy was insulting me! He had no idea I was standing right there, behind his back!"

So we *were* talking about the car again. Marvelous. Inge couldn't wait to see where this was going. She'd give him sixty seconds.

"Of course I didn't stoop to his level, badmouthing someone I didn't even know. Instead, I did the classy thing and introduced myself. Handshake and all."

"And?"

"Well," Rino allowed himself a chuckle. "This is where it gets good."

Inge supposed she should be sitting on the edge of her seat by now.

"When I said I was Severino Di Meglio and happened to drop the name Feltro Di Meglio, you'll never guess what he said!"

Inge couldn't stop her fingers from drumming. "I give up. You tell me, Rino."

"He said, and I quote: "Did you say Feltro Di Meglio? As in Feltro di Meglio *di meglio non c'è?*""

"You mean the guy recognized your name? And he even knew your company slogan?" The story did strike her as incredible, if not incredibly interesting.

"*He-he-he*," Rino laughed in that high-pitched giggly-girl laugh he reserved for particularly delightful circumstances. "He not only recognized the name, what's more important is that he recognizes the quality of our felt! He owns a top-of-the-line German saddle pad made of our very best sheep felt!"

"You don't say?" Inge said, relieved to see that the bottle was on its way to their table.

"Yes, I do say! Giangiacomo Lanza, that's the husband's name. He's actually a very nice fellow, now that we cleared the air. I stopped by again just now to give him our new catalog, and he offered me a drink. Some local craft beer Giac has a stake in. You should try it."

"Wait – in what sense did you clear the air?"

"Well, when he told Carol, that's the wife, to give me their insurance information, I told him not to worry. It's just a little dent, no big deal."

"So you let him off the hook? Just like that?"

"You're the one who kept saying it was nothing, remember? At the end of the day, he's a customer. It's because of the business of people like him, people who truly appreciate quality, who realize their lives are better because of my felt, that I could even afford the car in the first place." Beaming, Rino looked up at the woman who had come to stand beside their table and was now showing Inge the label of the bottle she cradled in her hands. "Ah, there's our Carol!"

"It's *Carolina*."

Ignoring the remark, Rino turned to his wife. "You already ordered the wine?"

"Yes, I already ordered the wine. I was curious to try this Tetillante."

"Don't you mean *pétillante*? As in bubbly?"

"Dr. Egger is right, Rino. The name is Tetillante," the woman said. "It's a sparkling wine from the Langa wine region in Piedmont, and there's a story behind that name. You see —"

"Since you've already told me, I can tell him," Inge said, cutting her short. How was it that Rino, who'd blown into this place in a rude huff, was already on a first-name basis with the woman and her husband, while she, who'd gone out of her way to be cordial, was still Dr. Egger? She appreciated the respect, of course; in fact, she usually demanded it, but right now it annoyed her. Even worse, it made her feel excluded. "May I suggest we forget about the name of the wine and move on to tasting it?"

"Certainly. Will you do the honors, Rino?" the woman asked.

"Since *I'm* the one who ordered it, *I'll* taste it," Inge said.

"Very well, Doctor," the woman said, locking eyes with Inge. Now she didn't look like a little girl at all, now there seemed to be an element of shrewdness in her stare. Then the woman glanced down, pouring a small amount of wine into the tilted glass, which she placed in front of Inge. Inge held the glass up in the evening light, her spirits already starting to lift at the sight of the bubbles streaming to the surface.

"Hmm," she said, after taking a sip, then another. "That *is* nice."

"As I said, it's a favorite of mine. It has an unmistakable character, yet it's versatile enough to accompany a meal from start to finish. Some people make a show of switching wines with every dish, but I don't believe in confusing a person's palate, or metabolism, really, any more than necessary, which can lead to headaches and all sorts of unpleasant side effects the next morning," the woman added, pouring a sample for Rino. "Having said that, you and Rino are of course free to drink whatever you like, Doctor."

"Please, call me Inge," she said, glancing at Rino long enough to register his surprise at her rare descent into the territory of familiarity. "And yes, I'd be happy to stick with the Tetillante."

"And what do you think, Rino?"

"It's fine by me too, Carol!" he said, finishing his taste and holding his glass up for a refill. When would the man learn some manners?

The owner wore a stiff smile on her face as she filled both glasses. "It's *Carolina*," she said, staring pointedly at Rino, *glaring* at him, really. Then she jammed the bottle into its ice bucket, rattling the cubes more than necessary, and retreated to her kitchen, her steps quick and tight as she walked. Inge wondered why she limped, and whether she'd ever seen an orthopedic surgeon.

CHAPTER TWELVE
Allegra

Allegra felt marvelously loose of limb and light of heart. Practicing yoga out in the open air always worked wonders for her blocked chakras. It occurred to her, not for the first time, that when she was with Adalberto she often struggled with her *vishuddha*, or throat chakra. Sometimes it presented itself as a lump in her throat, like when she swallowed a chunk of bread without chewing enough, which made it hard to get her words out. Other times, the blockage made her feel as if she were choking, and when that happened, there was no way she could speak. She figured it might be because she was so used to remaining silent while Adalberto did most of the talking. Of course, she was used to remaining silent during the long stretches of time she spent alone, too, but everyone knew that being silent on your own was different from being silent in company. Anyway, it was only natural that Adalberto had more to talk about than she did. Her work was of a more *internal* nature, while he was out in the world doing things and meeting people, between his collaboration with *Coppia Moderna* magazine, coping with fan mail and requests from his readers, being a featured guest on a live radio show, and basically being somewhat of a celebrity and all. In a way, it was gratifying that he'd chosen her out of all the women he could pick from, women who'd jump at the chance to be his sounding board, his confidante, his advisor. Allegra was more of a listener than a talker herself, anyway, so everything balanced out well. The only thing that made her feel bad was when he sometimes accused her of not paying attention. She always started out paying *total* attention, but if he kept repeating the same things, like people who talked a lot tended to do, her mind – not her – might eventually get distracted and look for something new to focus on.

Allegra was always eager to provide her feedback, but she had to be careful because although she often agreed with him, and therefore had no problem telling him what he wanted to hear, she sometimes felt compelled to challenge him, which could lead to some pretty interesting discussions. There was a fine line between encouraging Adalberto to see things from another point of view, though, and giving him the impression she was taking someone else's side, which he sometimes mistook for a lack of loyalty. Being accused of disloyalty definitely made her feel even worse than being accused of not listening, and Adalberto knew that. Not that he would intentionally say anything to make her feel bad, he just had strong gut reactions, and unlike her, no blocked chakras preventing him from voicing them out loud.

It was weird that Adalberto could sometimes read her the wrong way, because he truly did have a gift for understanding women. He understood what made them tick or trip, how to turn them on or off, why they couldn't resist the men who were the worst for them. That was why they counted on Adalberto for advice, and that was why @AskAda was such a popular column. Allegra suspected that the women who wrote to him probably had *vishuddha* issues too, or they would talk to their husbands or boyfriends instead of airing their most intimate grievances in the glossy pages of one of the few surviving ladies 'magazines, or worse, on Adalberto's social media profiles, which he used to promote his work and his image, but not to interact with his followers because what would be the point of a magazine paying him to write a column if he started offering free online advice?

She herself had met Adalberto when, through a friend of a friend, he'd called her for a consultation regarding the practice of *shatkarmas*, the series of hatha yoga techniques used to purify the body. At their very first encounter, she'd felt a deep, immediate connection with him, a premonition that she was experiencing a life-defining moment. It was the first time she'd come across anyone from outside her yoga circle who seemed sincerely interested in what she said and did, and the feeling of being listened to and respected had an even more powerful effect on her than the undeniable physical attraction. Unlike the previous men in her life, he had a way of making her feel protected, but not coddled; of challenging her while respecting her; of accepting her as she was while encouraging her to be everything else she might be. That was why she couldn't exactly blame Adalberto for her throat chakra issues; it had simply always been one of her weak points.

Anyway, she was getting off track. All that was just to say that she felt much better after practicing with Josephine, who although she wasn't there for the yoga, had proved to be a responsive novice. Since it was just the two of them, after some warm-ups and basic sun salutations, Allegra had introduced some breathing exercises followed by relaxation and meditation, and it was then that she slipped into chanting the *bija* mantra *ham*, which was exactly what her throat chakra needed to free itself up. Mantras sometimes scared people off, but Josephine was cool about it, and at the end of their hour together, Allegra felt like she'd received more than she'd given. Yoga was like that. If you were receptive and kept all your channels open, *amazing* things could happen. It was all about the flow, in and out, in and out.

"Your hair looks so pretty. It glistens like amber when it's damp," Adalberto said from across the table. "But shouldn't you have dried it? You seemed to be coming down with a sore throat when we were in the car."

"It actually feels better now, thanks. Yoga helped." One of the things she loved about Adalberto was that he noticed things, like the way she cleared her throat every time she tried broaching one of the issues she'd been hoping to talk about on the drive up. "I even had my first student."

"Great! Let me guess. Hmm, not that woman on our right, sitting with Mr. Stuffed Polo Shirt. She looks too uptight."

"No, not her. But I think she would benefit. I'll see if I can interest her tomorrow."

"So that leaves the potato-sack lady sitting in the left corner."

"That's not nice," she whispered to Adalberto. "But yes, that's her."

"She can't possibly hear me."

"Well, *I* can."

At that moment, Josephine looked up over the rim of her wineglass, and Allegra caught her eye. "*Ciao!*" she waved. Josephine smiled and waved back.

"So, is your new friend here all alone?"

"That's what it looks like."

"What's her story? Single? Divorced?" Adalberto asked, kicking off one of his favorite pastimes: speculation about other people's lives.

Allegra shrugged. "All I know is her name is Josephine Fortunata. We were practicing yoga together, not chatting." Yoga was pretty much Allegra's only way of connecting with other women. She had some acquaintances she could call casual friends, but she felt out of place doing the things they liked to do, such as shopping for clothes she wasn't interested in and couldn't afford anyway, or meeting for an *aperitivo*, those sad "happy hours" that dragged on forever, feeding on potato chip conversation and spritzy giggles.

"Come on, you must have picked up *some* detail we can use," Adalberto said, staring at her expectantly. "No wedding ring?"

"Now that you mention it, I think she was wearing a ring. Just a simple band, so I guess it could be a wedding ring. But it was on her right hand."

"*Aha!* Married to a German. Or a Scandinavian. Or someone from one of those eastern countries where people wear their wedding rings on their right hand."

"Possibly. She's half American and half Italian, so who knows?"

"You didn't tell me that part."

"I did now."

"Hmmm. Cropped hair, frumpy figure, baggy clothes," Adalberto mused. "Maybe she's married to another woman. I know lots of gay women who look like that."

Allegra also knew lots of gay women. Well, not *lots*, but a few of her yoga friends were lesbian or bisexual, or transgender or gender fluid or nonbinary, or whatever, those were only labels and didn't interest her, and to her they were all beautiful because they were receptive and strong and they cultivated not only their physical bodies, but their subtle bodies. "Anyway, it's none of our business," she said, swallowing her irritation at Adalberto's superficiality. "How was your run?"

"Great! That gravel road that goes up past the barns leads to a hiking trail. I jogged the first part up the hill to warm up for my sprints. My speed was a little slow, though."

"I don't see how you could run very fast on an uphill trail. Or enjoy it, for that matter."

"Are you kidding? Hill work is great. I pounded it for 45 seconds at a time," Adalberto pumped his arms as if he were still running, "Alternated with walking for 60. I can show you my data," he added, turning his wrist to show her his GPS watch.

Allegra nodded as Adalberto tapped through the display functions, but the readings didn't make much sense to her. Neither did sprinting.

"Wow!" she said, just to say something. To her, sprinting was the exact opposite of yoga. Yoga wasn't a sport and it wasn't about performance. It was about striving for the integral improvement of body, mind, and spirit through discipline and constancy: you had a path to follow, but it didn't matter how long it took you to get there, or whether you *ever* got there. What mattered was what you learned along the way. "You never actually mentioned what you're training for," she said, hoping he hadn't already told her.

"Well, sprints are interval work. To build up speed."

"Yeah, but why do you need to build up your speed? Are you planning to run in a race?"

"No way! No races, no marathons, no half marathons. Sprints are just quick runs. Great cardio. Great for burning calories and releasing stress. You don't need a lot of time, either. You set up your own speed-time combos. You give it all you got, then you take a break, then you give it all you got again."

"I see. I always assumed you were training to improve your *distance*."

"Nope. I like runs that are quick, but intense. It never gets boring that way. Kind of like with relationships."

"Very *funny*," Allegra said.

"Except with you, Allegra Amore," Adalberto said, taking her hand and bringing it to his lips. "Seven years is a record for me."

"I suppose I should be *honored*," she said as he kissed the back of her hand, then turned it over to kiss the palm. She loved when he did that, it was a sweet gesture, but it took more than that to stay in a relationship for seven years.

"*Mmm*, that Marseille soap smell drives me wild!" He made a purring sound deep in his throat, then bit her fingertip.

"*Ouch!*" Allegra cried, retracting her hand as Carolina approached their table. The two women had met at a yoga seminar in Pavia several years back.

They weren't what you'd call *close* friends, but they were more than acquaintances, and this was the third time Carolina had invited her back as a guest yoga instructor. Free yoga attracted clients, and free accommodations in exchange for her time attracted Allegra. Being in a position to treat Adalberto to a few days break for once, instead of the other way around, made her feel good.

"I'm sorry we haven't had time to get caught up yet," Carolina said, showing Allegra a bottle of wine, before uncorking it and pouring out a taste." I want you to try this."

"You remembered how I love rosé!"

"Of course I did."

"Adalberto can do the honors," Allegra said.

Carolina raised an eyebrow, just one, which gave her a slightly diabolic air. Allegra had forgotten how impenetrable her dark eyes could be, yet how expressive. She'd always come across as a conflicted person to Allegra, and it was a shame she'd given up on yoga so soon; it could have helped her achieve better balance, both physical and emotional.

"I'm so glad you could finally make it, Adalberto," Carolina said, sliding the glass toward him by the stem. "I've heard so much about you."

"Thanks," Adalberto mumbled. He was craning his neck, trying to read the label on the bottle. "Mimi?"

"Yes! I'm a big fan of these producers. It's a family-run vineyard in Castelnuovo Belbo."

"That's in my neck of the woods," Adalberto said. "I have an old family home not too far from there." The mention of that place made Allegra's throat tighten as she watched Adalberto swirl the wine in his glass, stick his nose in it, then finally taste it. As a rule, he wasn't fond of rosé, which he called a "sissy" wine, whatever that was supposed to mean, but he was her guest, and she was Carolina's guest, and she hoped he'd graciously accept whatever he was offered.

"That's fine, thanks," Adalberto said to Carolina, giving Allegra a conspiratorial wink. "I'm glad I could come, too. Allegra has been raving about how peaceful it is here. I could use a break right now, but I can't guarantee I won't be mulling over ideas for a short story!"

"Wonderful," Carolina said. "But keep the mulling to a minimum. And remember we turn off the wi-fi between dinnertime and breakfast."

"Oh, I didn't realize that," Adalberto said, shooting a surprised look at Allegra before picking up the phone he always set down next to his plate, a habit Allegra deplored but couldn't get him to break. He tapped on the screen, stared at it for a moment, then showed it to Carolina. "But there's really poor reception here. Look, no bars."

"At least *you* have a *phone*," Allegra said. "Anyway, you'll only be disconnected at night. And that's kind of the whole *point*." She probably should have told Adalberto about this detail in advance, but the couple of times she tried she got a lump in her throat. It would do him good to detox from his followers and media colleagues once in a while; it would do them both good. She had a few things on her mind that she'd like to talk about, if he let her. If her *vishuddha* let her. She watched Carolina pour out their wine, then raised her glass to Adalberto, and took a long sip.

CHAPTER THIRTEEN
Josephine

The grilled vegetables were quite possibly the best Josephine had ever tasted, not only in Italy but in her entire life. Carolina told her that she'd harvested the eggplants and zucchini and peppers from her garden that very morning. Hand-sliced nice and thin, but not so papery that the edges got charred and crinkly, they were grilled to perfection, drizzled with extra virgin olive oil, and sprinkled with freshly chopped herbs, resulting in a savory symphony of simple summer flavors, all the more precious because it was the tail end of the season. Despite being so busy, the owner paid special attention to Josephine, popping by her table now and then, even finding the time to explain, as if she had to justify not using their own olive oil, that their location, at an elevation of well over a thousand meters, was too high to cultivate olive trees, but that they procured their oil from a family-operated mill down near the coast by Imperia. When you put something in your mouth, Carolina said, it was important to know where it came from, and who could argue with that? Anyway, that plentiful platter of vegetables was more than enough as a second course for Josephine, especially after devouring such a generous serving of gnocchi with pesto – yes, she was perfectly aware of the fact that she'd eaten gnocchi the night before at her *pensione* in Savona, but honestly, they were so different it was more like they'd come from another dimension, rather than just another kitchen, the Savona gnocchi being from the Land of Dead Food, and Carolina's from the Land of Living Food. Josephine had a palate for pasta, her favorite thing in the world to eat, in addition to sweets made with ricotta, and she could have gnocchi every day, especially with pesto, but it must be said that Carolina's were superlative. And no wonder! She made them herself, with her own organic potatoes, and rolled them out by hand. They were incredibly light, those puffy little clouds of pure pleasure, and of course the pesto was made with the finest olive oil, blended with fragrant bunches of her own fresh basil, and her own homegrown garlic. Carolina said she'd done lots of experimentation before selecting the pink variety, *aglio rosa di Lautrec*, she called it, because it was very flavorful, but also more delicate and easier to digest. She said many cooks overdosed the cheap garlic to give their pesto a more pungent flavor, allowing them to skimp on the costlier cheese, but killing the aroma of the basil in the process. The ones

Josephine had eaten yesterday would have been immediately forgotten, had the heavy-handed pesto not repeated on her all night, while the gnocchi sat in her stomach like bubble gum balls, barely budging until her yoga session with Allegra miraculously bumped them down her digestive tract.

"How are things over here in your little corner of the world, Josephine?" Carolina asked as she approached again. Josephine had been watching with fascination as the woman moved nimbly between the kitchen and the tables, never wasting a step and never looking rushed. Sometimes Josephine treated herself to a bite out in Rome, and if there was one thing that could ruin a good *margherita*, it was seeing the sweaty waiters race around breathlessly as if they were putting out fires instead of serving pizzas.

"Everything is beyond perfect, thank you. As you can see, I ate every bite!" Josephine said, patting her tummy and glancing down at the plate she'd wiped clean with a chunk of crusty bread which was so delicious she couldn't resist eating an extra slice after the vegetables were gone, dressed with a drop of olive oil and a sprinkle of salt.

"Restaurants in Italy generally serve vegetables as a side dish, if at all, but I feel they deserve the dignity of their own space. I prefer serving them between courses, the way some of those stuffy old grand hotels serve lemon sorbet between the fish and meat courses."

"Great idea! That way the vegetables have the chance to express themselves."

"I'm glad you agree!" Carolina smiled. "I just hope you don't feel too isolated over here, all on your own."

"Not at all. Couples need their privacy, and I'm enjoying this beautiful setting. I watched those clouds keep changing color until the sky went totally dark. I feel so fortunate to be here."

"Fortunata you, and *fortunata* me. Anyone who comes here is lucky."

"And I came across the most beautiful spot earlier! I was out taking a stroll when I stumbled on this hidden pond. It gave me a deep sense of peace, as if it were some kind of miracle pond."

"That's exactly what my husband and I call it! I don't tell anyone about it, because I believe our guests should wander to wherever they're drawn, and discover what they're meant to discover. Sometimes I do have to intervene, though, because not everyone always knows what's best for them, do they?"

Josephine shrugged. "Not always."

"By the way, have you met the others?" Carolina said, leaning in closer.

Josephine glanced at the older couple sitting at the far end of the veranda. The wife was a strong-looking, stately woman, probably a head taller than her husband, who looked like the softie of the couple. They both had that well-groomed aspect of the wealthy, with their styled hair and pampered skin, and jewels that glinted in the candlelight. At the middle table sat Allegra with a startlingly handsome man, who kept taking her hand in his, and kissing it in the most romantic way.

"Well, I've met Allegra, the yoga teacher. I even took a lesson."

"Good for you! Allegra's wonderful. In her unique way, of course."

Josephine waited for Carolina to say more, but she didn't, and Josephine didn't know either one of them well enough to ask her to elaborate.

"Do take advantage of the opportunity, though. People say she's a good teacher."

"I hope it's not too expensive?" Josephine said, feeling her cheeks turn warm, if not pink, given her olive complexion. It embarrassed her to bring up the subject, especially at dinner, and especially because whatever it cost, Allegra was worth it.

"Not to worry! It's a complimentary service we're offering all our guests this weekend."

"Oh, well, then!" Although Josephine had benefited from her time with Allegra, she wasn't sure how much time she wanted to dedicate to yoga right now, so she'd almost been hoping it *would* be too expensive. But then if it was, she would have felt uncomfortable backing out for that reason, because Allegra was clearly the generous type, and she was pretty sure that she'd insist she come anyway and offer her special treatment.

"Have you met her boyfriend?" Carolina asked, lowering her voice a notch, even though her back was to Allegra, who was seated several meters away. As she bent toward Josephine, a tantalizing whiff of something delicious on the tray she was holding reached Josephine's nostrils, making her wonder what it was. "He's way out of her league, though, not exactly marriage material for a girl like Allegra, if you get my drift."

Josephine shook her head, not quite sure what she was supposed to think, and not inclined to say anything.

"He's famous, you know? Adalberto Albertis?" Carolina waited for a reaction, but Josephine drew a blank. "He has that column in *Coppia Moderna* magazine? He 's also on a radio show? You must have heard of him! He has tens of thousands of followers!"

"I'm not really into those things. Sorry," Josephine said. She didn't want to come off as someone who snubbed magazines and talk shows out of a sense of superiority, but neither did she want to encourage more talk about the personal life of a woman she'd just met.

"Oh, me neither! Who has the time for that stuff? Anyway, keep it to yourself, but he just told me he'll be working on a story while he's here," Carolina said. "So next time you hear his name, and you will hear it, mark my word, you can say you met him here."

"I'll be happy to make his acquaintance if Allegra wants to introduce me."

"We'll all be great friends before the weekend is over, you'll see. Some people due to arrive tomorrow canceled – as if a few possible drops of rain could spoil a weekend here! So it will just be the five of you guests, and the two of us. Me and Giac that is, I don't know if you've met my husband yet? Anyway, it'll be more intimate like this, so don't worry, you'll never feel alone!"

Josephine smiled, but not the usual toothy smile that Thomas affectionately teased her about, saying it reminded him of a toothpaste ad. "I don't mind being alone, really," she said. "That's what I'm here for."

"Mr. Tomas said as much when he made your arrangements. He must be a very sensitive man to know that this was where you needed to be." Carolina looked at her expectantly.

"Yes, he is," was all Josephine said.

"Listen to me chewing your ear off, while your food is getting cold! But no harm done, it came straight out of the oven and I didn't want you to burn your tongue!" Carolina said, setting down an individual terracotta baking dish. "I thought you'd enjoy this Ligurian specialty. Wild porcini mushrooms baked with potatoes. I picked them yesterday, in my secret spot in the woods."

"Oh my! I don't think I can!" Josephine said, her blue eyes wide. How could she find room for more food? But how could she resist wild porcini mushrooms?

"Nonsense! Mushroom season is very short, so you can't pass up the opportunity! Besides, they have very few calories, if that's a concern."

"I know it should be, but it's not. At least not this weekend. And I've never had wild porcini mushrooms before. In Buffalo, it's mostly champignons and portobellos." Josephine stared down at the cute little casserole, the potatoes still bubbling a little around their crisped edges. The aroma wafting up to her was so irresistible that she nosedived in for a good sniff, closed her eyes, and sighed. "The smell alone is a feast!"

"Go ahead, taste it! I love cooking for people who appreciate good food."

Josephine really was full, but she didn't have the heart to disappoint such a dedicated chef, who wasn't going to move on until she expressed an opinion. Fork in hand, she plunged it into the dish, fishing out a slice of mushroom and a chunk of potato. Glancing up at Carolina, she took a moment to blow on the still steaming food, a bit uneasy in her role as a food critic, when she was just a regular woman with a healthy appetite. Finally placing the morsel in her mouth, she savored its taste and delivered her verdict. "*Mmmm!*" she groaned. "How can a little chunk of mushroom contain all the earthy flavors of the forest? How can a simple potato become a perfect accomplice? And your final touch of chopped parsley isn't just pretty to look at, but a perfect accent!" She hoped that sounded good, not too over the top. It was all true, too.

"*Bravissima*, Josephine!" Carolina said, with a little clap of the hands. "I'm delighted! Now I'll leave you alone to enjoy the rest of your meal."

"Mm-hmm," Josephine said, nodding as she swallowed another bite.

"Now eat it all, if you want dessert!" Carolina said, wagging her finger and speaking in a high-pitched voice, as if she were talking to a child. It was a little weird the way she could do that, how in a single conversation she could sound so professional, then so chummy, then just plain, well, *odd*. But no matter the tone, she was definitely talking Josephine's language when she talked dessert.

"Oh, my! Dessert! You wouldn't have any more of that pear and cocoa cake I tried earlier?"

"I have something better. Trust me."

And God help *me*, Josephine thought, digging her fork into the mushroom casserole. But God helps those who help themselves, right?

CHAPTER FOURTEEN
Inge

Rino's face flushed a deeper shade of pink each time he slid his spoon into the *Nuvola al limone* then raised it to his mouth, his eyelids fluttering as he swallowed. After scraping the bottom of the bowl, he licked the spoon one last time, wiped his lips with his napkin, and sat back in his chair, a satisfied man. It disturbed her to see that look on his face, that same expression of total abandon he had during sex, which she used to find so off-putting. Not that the dessert didn't deserve the undivided attention of whoever had the pleasure to savor it; somewhere between a meringue and a custard, it was as fluffy and light as a lemony cloud, exactly as its name suggested. Inge was no glutton for desserts, which were invariably too rich and sweet for her taste, but she must admit that this creation was the perfect ending to a delicious dinner. And strange as it may seem, whether it was the effect of the so-called special energy of this place, or of enjoying the magnificent meal beneath tonight's starless, moonless sky, Inge admitted to feeling strangely relaxed, more so than she'd felt in a long time. She almost hated to spoil it by talking, but talk she must.

Her husband looked nothing short of blissful sitting there across from her, an excellent meal settling down for the night in his tummy and several glasses of bubbly buoying his spirits. The first bottle had gone down so well that he'd ordered a second, which they were in the process of draining now. Rino took a sip and sighed. "It's at times like this that I miss a good cigar."

"Oh, please!" Inge said. "I don't miss that stink one bit. Thank God you listen to the advice of what you call your 'real' doctor better than you listen to me!"

"When you're used to doing what you want when you want, it's hard to adjust, Cara. Stop working, stop smoking, stop eating, stop drinking. That cardiologist might as well have said to stop living! But the meal was healthy, wasn't it? And a little extra bubbly is better than my usual *digestivo*, right?"

"Absolutely. You're doing great." Inge rolled her eyes, but with her eyelids closed. Now was not the time for discouragement or contradiction; now was the time for encouragement and cohesion. Toying with the stem of her wineglass, she could feel Rino staring at her, admiring her. He still did that sometimes, looking at her as if she were important to him, *really* important. She felt a pang of regret that most of the time she ignored those loving gazes, either because she was too preoccupied with other concerns, or simply not in the mood to return them. She'd married Rino because he made her feel secure, protected, and comfortable, not because she couldn't live without him. That didn't mean she wasn't fond of Rino; she did love him, in her own way. Besides, they were a family, Rino, Carl, and her. And where she came from, families stuck together, not because any laws or religion told them they must, but because they formed a common front against the outside world. Together they could fend off the enemy, the intruder, the adversities of life. That's what mountain folk did, and at heart, she was still one of them.

"What are you thinking about, Cara?" Rino asked.

Inge sighed, trying to decide how to answer one of the most loaded – and dangerous – questions anyone could be stupid enough to ask their spouse. He'd given her the opening she wanted, now she needed to nail the approach. "Actually, I was thinking about Carl."

"Ah, well, he happens to be one of my favorite subjects, too!"

"I know. It's hard to believe he'll soon be eighteen, isn't it? This will be his last year of *liceo*. He'll have to decide something about university soon."

"Well, now, who's to say that going off to some fancy school would be the best thing for him? I had no time for college, I stepped up to the plate and worked by my father's side at Feltro Di Meglio, so that when my turn came to run the business, I would be ready. And that worked out pretty well for all of us, I'd say!"

"Carl already has a clear idea of what goes on in the factory, I think. You've been letting him tag along since he was a toddler."

"Darn right! He's known what excellent felt feels like since the day he was born! Remember how I used to bring home those swatches to line his crib?"

"Of course I do. Every color of the rainbow was in that crib. And no matter what toys we bought him to play with, he loved that little felt lamb your secretary made for him better than all of them." Chatting about the past was a good way to lead into the future, as long she kept the sugary sentimentality to a minimum. "He couldn't wait for those Saturday mornings when you took him on your morning rounds."

"And how about when he was on school vacation? He was always begging to come with me and following me around like a shadow. *La piccola ombra*, the guys used to call him! Yes, my boy has felt in his blood, I tell you! Why, even as a tiny tyke he could tell the difference between sheep and goat and camel fibers! And when he got a little older, you should have seen how his smooth little brow used to wrinkle with concentration when he learned about moistening and rolling and compressing. Those processes are fundamental for the perfect matting that makes our felt stand out. That's why we can truthfully say, '*di meglio non c'è!*' There really is nothing better in the whole world!"

Inge smiled as he spoke, sipping her wine. They were getting deeper into felt territory than she liked. But it really had been heartwarming over the years to witness the tenderness with which Rino treated Carl, and the pride that oozed from his pores at every step of their son's development to puberty, then adolescence. And now he was on the brink of manhood! Part of her did wish she could instill in him the same all-consuming passion for felt as Rino, but when she looked at Carl, so tall and trim and smart, always glowing with a healthy tan from skiing the Alps in the winter, and sailing Lake Como and the Mediterranean in the summer; when she casually conversed with him in Italian or German or French or English, languages in which he was fluent thanks to the international schools and study programs abroad he'd attended; when they discussed his prospects at the London School of Economics, or Stanford University, or the Swiss Institute of Technology, all of which he had the grades to get into and they had the money to afford, how was she supposed to coax him to stay home and work with his father?

"Speaking of the whole world, you do know that times have changed, don't you?" she said. "We live in a global economy, and businesses are run differently than they were in your father's day. Don't you think it would be a good idea for Carl to pursue his education away from us, and away from the little world of Faloppio, so he can return with the proper tools to bring Feltro di Meglio into the twenty-first century?"

"There is nothing backward about the way I run my business! And what's wrong with Faloppio? We have everything we need there!"

To start with, the name of the place was wrong. No sense reminding Rino how embarrassing it was for a gynecologist to live in a place called Faloppio. Even if the spelling was different from the name of a woman's egg-conveying tubes, the fact never failed to raise a giggle, which was why she usually just said she lived in nearby Como.

"We have a custom-made home with a heated swimming pool!" Rino continued. "And central air conditioning! And even a basement cinema, complete with reclining armchairs! It may not be right on the lake, and it might not be right around the corner from your clinic, but it's home!"

Before Rino could list all the other advantages, she did it for him. "Yes, and I'm quite aware that a similar home in Lugano would cost a fortune, and that it's a reasonable commute unless I get stuck in traffic going back and forth over the border. But that doesn't mean it's necessarily the place a young man would choose to live his life. Doesn't our son deserve to make his own choices? The only way for him to be truly happy is if he's passionate about what he does. But first, he needs the chance to find out what that is."

"Felt makes people happy! It's been making the world a softer, safer, warmer place for humankind since ancient times!"

Inge couldn't allow this discussion to be about felt. Felt was fine. She had nothing against felt. Who was she to judge, maybe Rino's mission of giving people access to good felt was more vital than her mission of giving people access to parenthood.

"I'm not disagreeing with you, Rino. All I'm saying is that I want Carl to be happy, and I know you do, too. But he deserves to make his choice freely. Parents have no more right to match a child to a profession than they do to match them to a mate."

"And what about me? What about everything I've worked for? Am I supposed to stand by and let that incompetent oaf of an accountant run my business from his computer?"

"He's only managing things temporarily. Everyone knows he could wear twenty pairs of thick felt socks and never fill your shoes. If Carl wants to step in, all the better; if he doesn't, you'll find someone else. Or sell."

Rino tossed his napkin on the table and rose to his feet. "Giac invited me to stop inside for a grappa nightcap. I'll meet you back in the room."

Inge knew better than to tell him that he needed a shot of grappa like he needed a hole in his head. You couldn't convince a man like him to do anything he didn't want to do, and whether he knew it or not, Carl was very much like him in that regard. All Inge wanted was for the two most important men in her life to reach an agreement that would satisfy both, or at least leave neither disappointed, resentful, and bitter for the rest of his days, with her stuck in the middle, constantly explaining, negotiating, moderating, reconciling. Inge intended to remain loyal to both, as long as they didn't make it impossible for her.

The discussion hadn't gone as well as she'd hoped, but precisely as she'd imagined it going. She'd need to work on making Rino more pliable, more understanding. Because that wasn't even what she'd brought him here to talk to him about.

CHAPTER FIFTEEN
Carolina

Dinner went well, don't you think?" Carolina said, pouring herbal tea into two oddly shaped mugs, the sole survivors of her failed foray into the elusive craft of pottery a few years back. Her plan had been to organize residential workshops for their guests, to help pick up some business in the slack shoulder season. However, the only thing she'd picked up was the bill for the kiln that stood stone-cold in one of the barns. That, and a couple of nasty burns on her hands and forearms.

"It always does, doesn't it?" Giac said, wrapping his calloused fingers around a steaming mug. He did rugged work, okay, but would it kill him to put a little more effort into at least cleaning his nails?

"It always does, because I always work my butt off to make damn sure it does!" she said. "I saw you having a drink with Rino while I cleared the tables. You could have offered to help me."

"You could have had your kids here helping you if you didn't make life so miserable for them. Besides, I was helping with guest relations, calming Rino down, getting him to mellow out."

"Why? Didn't he like the dinner? What was wrong? What did he say?"

"Now don't go getting all paranoid. He loved the dinner. My guess is that his wife put him in a bad mood."

"Why can't people just leave their problems at home when they come here? *Why?* I can't have that negative energy in the air. It affects everyone, and I won't allow it. I *won't!*"

"Easy does it. He just wanted some male companionship, then he went to bed."

"Open this, please," Carolina said, passing Giac a jar of *millefiori* honey, a gift of their resident bees. Giac opened the jar and handed it back to her.

"Wouldn't you like some?" she asked, scooping up the pure golden honey with a wooden dipper and drizzling it into her tea. The brew was made from the herbs she'd taken the time to select, gather, and dry, a blend of malva, sage, and melissa leaves.

"I'm good, thanks. I'll add some of this instead," Giac grunted, rising just enough to reach the bottle of grappa on the shelf.

"Utkatāsana."

"What?"

"Nothing. Your position just reminded me of a yoga pose. Chair pose. I always hated it," Carolina said, finally sitting down across from him. "That stuff will rot your gut out sooner or later."

"What, yoga?" Giac said, pulling the cork and pouring a shot of clear liquid into the tea.

"No, grappa," she sighed. "Didn't you already have some of that with Rino?"

"Yeah. Piergiorgio gave me a couple of bottles. It's naturally distilled."

"Not everything natural is good for you, you know."

"Amen to that," Giac said. "This place will be the death of me yet."

"Please don't ruin my evening by complaining now. We've been building our business back nicely. It's a good sign."

"Well, enjoy it while it lasts. Who knows when the next catastrophe will strike?"

"Thanks for the optimism. Anyway, if and when it does, we'll cross that bridge when we come to it," Carolina said, taking a tiny sip of the scalding tea. "As my mother always used to say."

"And as I always still say, you're gonna burn your mouth like you always do. Can't you wait five minutes?" Giac said, sloshing a dose of grappa into her tea. "There, that'll cool it off for your tongue. And warm your cold, cold heart."

"*Gia-ac!*" she whined. She'd been looking forward to having a chat over tea, then going into the office to register her guests, which she hadn't had time to do all day. She certainly didn't have the energy to make a fresh pot, and fat chance Giac would do it for her. Lifting the mug to her lips, she took another cautious sip. Temperature-wise, it was more drinkable, but the harsh grappa killed that herbal honey combo she liked so much. Not that she was a teetotaler, not at all, she enjoyed a glass or two of good wine and she dabbled in producing some pretty powerful cordials herself. The most popular was the *limoncello,* made with lemon zest, but she also concocted liquors with *erba luisa,* or lemon verbena, and *mirto,* that one was with myrtle berries, or *sambuco* (not to be confused with sambuca) made with elderflowers. Grappa was so senselessly strong. It had no point, no flavor. It was just overbearing and hard to swallow, like some men. Giac was right about it warming up your insides, though. Not exactly what you needed on a balmy night, but it did take the edge off. After taking another sip, she opened and closed her mouth a few times to unclench her jaw. She wondered if she was grinding her teeth at night again, but her husband hadn't remarked on it. How could he notice anyway, with the way he slept?

"See you upstairs?" Giac asked, pulling himself all the way up this time, moaning as he pressed a hand against his lower back. Shuffling to the sink, he poured the remainder of his tea down the drain, then served himself another shot from the bottle on the table, tossing it down his throat straight.

"Sure, I'll be up in five, ten minutes. Fifteen tops," Carolina said, extending her arm so that Giac could help her to her feet. "Ow!" she cried at his rough yank.

"Remember what you promised," Giac said. "Do what you need to do, then get off that damn computer." Turning away, he plodded up the stairs that led to their living quarters above.

Carolina stood there rubbing her shoulder for a minute while looking around her kitchen, her domain. It gave her a sense of peace and pride to see everything in order and spotless at the end of the day when the guests had eaten and retired to their rooms. In order and spotless except for Giac's mug, which God forbid he should rinse out and put away. And also except for the open bottle of grappa on the table. She picked the bottle up, sniffed it, then poured another drop into her tea, before hammering the cork back in place with the heel of her hand and returning the bottle to its shelf. She had just one more job to do, then she could go to bed. It was a job she couldn't (and wouldn't) skip.

Carolina walked to the door where a sign reading "*Direzione - Privato*" informed people that the office behind it was where the management conducted its business. So what if Giac called it her cubbyhole, and so what if it was right next to the pantry? It was her private space, off limits to everyone including her husband, which was probably why he didn't like her spending so much time there. Call it what you want, it was big enough to accommodate a small desk and a single swivel chair, her computer, printer, a few storage shelves, and the three-drawer filing cabinet she'd managed to squeeze into the space beneath the tiny window. Carolina flipped on the light, took another sip of spiked brew, then set her mug down on her desk. Now, then. Her first order of business was to turn off the Wi-Fi router. She always felt a certain satisfaction when she pressed that little black button, knowing she was performing a service for the good of her guests regardless of how much (or little) they appreciated it at first. Sometimes at the beginning of a weekend (like tonight), she left the connection active until after dinner, to let people settle in a bit, give them a little weaning time, so to speak. That way, instead of feeling deprived, they felt like they were getting something extra (call it a bonus, or a grace period) when they checked their phones after dinner like they always did (even though she always reminded them of the rule), and found they were still connected to the internet. You should see how they grinned! It also gave Carolina a sense of something else (she might call it power, for lack of a better word) to change the cutoff time every day, according to her personal discretion. The guests knew they had until dinnertime, and she always respected that, rules were rules, but it could be fun (if it wasn't so pathetic) to see how they kept sneaking a peek at their phones during the evening meal to see if they could squeeze in one last pointless text, one more pitiful post, one more useless email, one more fake news feed, then watch their faces fall when they waved their phones in the air, searching for a signal that wasn't there, for some sign of life beyond the infinite forms of life that surrounded them, if they would only take the trouble to notice.

It was of course indispensable for Carolina to have access to internet 24/7, so her computer was hard-wired via an ethernet cable to the landline, but she wasn't about to tell them that. Try living and working way up here where the reception was spotty on good days, and on the bad ones, you might as well forget about it. Anyway, now her computer was booted up and online and it was high time to get down to the business of registering today's arrivals. Since she couldn't be expected to just drop everything and go do the office work every time a new guest turned up, and since some of them got all hot and bothered (especially the foreigners) if she asked them to leave their documents with her, Carolina used her phone to snap a picture of each person's photo ID so she could take care of things when she was good and ready, without anyone breathing down her neck. There were plenty of family-run hotels and B&Bs out there that would skip the whole registration baloney and try to get paid in cash. Not her and Giac, though, they'd made a pact from the get-go that they would run their business by the book, and that's what they did (except for maybe when unreliable kids and seasonal workers left them in the lurch and they needed emergency help they couldn't afford to hire). Besides, the prices at the Renovatus were on the high side, and honest people didn't travel with wads of cash in their pockets anymore, only crooks and tax evaders, and those scum could take their business elsewhere, thank you very much.

"Very well, then," Carolina said, her eyes bright as she swiped her phone screen. "Let's see who we have here this evening, shall we?" She had the habit of commenting out loud when performing certain tasks, and it was only natural that she should assume a proper tone while recording personal data to report to the authorities, as if they were present in the room. Accessing the photo gallery, she couldn't resist a quick scroll through the hundreds of stored documents (she kept meaning to delete them, but you know how it is when you never have time for anything, and when you do, you couldn't possibly remember all the things that need doing, besides she did enjoy looking at her favorites now and again). "Ah yes, here we are," she said, locating the most recently added photographs, beginning with the day's first arrival. "Thank you for your patience." Pinching out the image, she peered at the passport photograph, a little blurry on account of her hands shaking when she'd taken it. "Ah yes, that's our American guest. Blue eyes, short hair." With a quick bit of mental math, she discovered that the woman had recently turned forty-seven, though she looked a good five years older with that silver hair (good for her, though, for refusing to dye it). Carolina was holding the phone in her left hand, her right poised over the keyboard, when she froze. "Oh. Well. Now this is unusual. Highly unusual!" Taking a sip from her mug, she smacked her lips. "Why, that anonymous-looking woman has two identities! An *alias*! It says right here her name is Marisa Tomas *known as* Josephine Fortunata!" That was highly suspicious! And why would a normal person need to carry around two passports anyway? Now she wished she'd looked inside the Italian one, too. Who could say what name was on that? Carolina hated that it was too late now to investigate the matter further without pissing Giac off, but investigate she would. Gulping down what was left in her mug, she proceeded with the business of wrapping up her work. Yet she couldn't stop speculating about Josephine, even after moving on to those stiffs who could only be from the Lombard hinterland, as she'd guessed, though the wife was Swiss. Despite the broomstick up her butt, Carolina was already getting the lady doctor to loosen up, and if she was reserved it was because she had way more class than the husband, Giac 's new pal Severino Di Meglio. She decided then and there that she'd baptize him Rino the Rhino, but only in her head, of course. Coming up with pet names for her guests always amused her, and it was harmless fun, really. Lastly, there was Allegra, who'd finally granted her an introduction to Adalberto Albertis (an AA, by the way!) in the flesh, and what a hunk he was! No wonder she 'd kept him to herself all this time. How someone like Allegra managed to nail down a guy as handsome and fascinating and self-assured as him, who still didn't strut around like he was God's gift to women, was a mystery to her. Hopefully, he treated Allegra better than her last two boyfriends. She just didn't know how to pick them, poor girl. She was too distracted, too trusting, too, well, flaky.

Carolina leaned back in her chair, swiveling slowly from side to side a few times (the motion helped her think) before shutting down her computer and finally rising to switch off the light and lock her door. Stopping off in the kitchen, she washed the mugs then wiped down all the surfaces for the second or third or fourth time, it didn't matter, she liked to see everything gleaming when she came down in the morning. She hoped Giac would be sound asleep so he wouldn't bug her about the hour, but not snoring so loud that he'd prevent her from sorting through all the new information to be filed away in her head. Tomorrow couldn't come soon enough.

CHAPTER SIXTEEN
Josephine

So much for seeing what it felt like to sleep in. Old habits were hard to break, and Josephine had been getting up too early for too long. Once a body got six or seven hours' rest, it seemed a sin to let the day waste away. As her Italian grandmother, whom she'd never met except through her mother's reminiscences, used to say, "*Sette ore per un corpo, otto ore per un porco.*" Seven hours for a body, eight hours for a pig. That was a little harsh maybe, but it seemed about right, especially if you slept alone.

Speaking of which, she would have appreciated having someone to cling to last night when all those animal sounds kept waking her up. It had started with the blood-curdling screeching noises, probably some owls or ravens or whatever giant birds cruised around at night, stealing innocent little bunnies and kitties from their mommies. Oh, and then there were all the squealing and grunting noises literally just outside her window that were probably the reason behind that weird dream she had where she was being held prisoner on an industrial farm, and a man in black was forcing her to herd panicky pigs onto a truck. Bad as that was, and it was bad, it was the howling that really gave her goosebumps. She'd bet any money there were wolves out there, even though she'd never actually heard a real live wolf or even a coyote howl, except in movies. Anyway, between all the noises of nature and the eerie silence that they broke, she'd spent chunks of the night with her eyes wide open, staring at the dark ceiling. And talk about dark! With no other buildings around, no street lights, and not even a moon to illuminate the night, the dark here was *really* dark.

But the bed! Oh, the bed was divine, she'd already discovered that during her nap, which may have been to blame for her fitful sleep. Then at one point a rooster started crowing, and a bunch of different birds started chirping, but in a more genteel way than those on the night shift, so she lay there lazily listening on that incredibly comfortable mattress, also because she didn't know what to do with herself. She didn't want to go wandering around and risk waking people up, especially if she could barely see where she was going, and there were all those wild animals out there. When at last the faintest sliver of gray light slipped through the slats in the shutters, she decided she'd had enough of bed.

Upon entering the bathroom she was pleasantly surprised to find the tube of toothpaste still capped and rolled up from the bottom, not squeezed from the top. Even seeing her few toiletries all lined up and facing the front, just the way she'd left them, was a treat, reminding her of what a rare luxury it was to have a bathroom all to herself. After using the toilet, whose lid was still properly lowered, she washed her face and brushed her teeth. Slipping out of her cotton nightie, she folded it neatly and placed it under her pillow, then pulled on a pair of sweatpants and her faded blue Buffalo Bills hoodie. She did her best to ignore the unmade bed, but only made it halfway to the door before turning around. Again, habits were habits, and she simply wasn't used to having people tidy up after her, so why fight it? After straightening the sheets but leaving the bed to air, she grabbed her favorite shawl, the old red one the mother of a favorite former student had crocheted for her as a Christmas gift, then stepped into her shoes and walked out to see what the new day looked like to a woman of leisure. Standing on the porch of her bungalow, she filled her lungs with the cool morning air, feeling pretty darn lucky to have all those idle hours stretching ahead of her in this strangely luxurious, strangely wild hideaway. Once her eyes adjusted to the dim light, she headed down the path, stepping gingerly over the gravel so as not to disturb anyone, then crossed over to the grass, which turned out to be her first mistake of the day because it was thick with dew and her feet got soaked. Climbing up to the clearing where she and Allegra had practiced yoga the previous day, she spotted a slab of rock near the oak tree and decided to sit there and think for a spell.

Though the stone wasn't as wet as the grass, it was damp and cold, which made her thankful for the sweats she'd been undecided about packing until Lucia told her not to, as if people would think less of her for wanting to be comfortable, and if they did, as if it mattered! Drawing her knees to her chest, she pulled up her hood and draped her shawl over her head and face, then tucked it in all around her, creating a cocoon for herself. Ah, that was better already, she thought, hugging her knees. Maybe if she could sit still enough for long enough, she'd tune into some of that inspiration she'd come looking for. Better yet, maybe a massive bolt of illumination would strike her, Damascus style, revealing what she should do with the rest of her life, now that she'd almost survived the first half-century. After all she'd been through, she considered that a pretty miraculous achievement and she wasn't about to blow it now.

Before a nasty detour had thrown that well-planned life off course, she'd been fairly good at praying. As a child, she'd learned all her Catholic prayers by rote, including all the mysteries of the rosary: the five joyous, the five sorrowful, the five glorious. Out of habit, she still carried a rosary with her, transferring it from pocket to pocket of the clothes she changed into and out of, as you would your house keys, your hanky, or your lucky charm. And again, out of habit, whenever she needed a little help she dipped her hand into whatever pocket she was wearing to finger the smooth mother-of-pearl beads, which was precisely what she did now. Finding the cross, she closed her eyes, while her lips began moving of their own accord, ready to recite decade after decade of Hail Marys punctuated by an Our Father and a Glory Be, her fingers tracking her progress along the smooth little beads until they circled back to the cross. And then it was over. As far as she could tell, no inspirations or revelations or guiding spirits had descended upon her in the quarter of an hour it had taken to make the rounds. Then, precisely when she was wondering whether it was faith or superstition that prompted her to pray, the darkness of her cocoon was pervaded by an incredible sensation of warmth and light. Was her Nonna looking down on her? Or the Madonna sending her a sign? Shaking off her shawl, she was nothing less than astonished to find herself spotlighted by a ray of the rising sun! But how could that single sunbeam burst through all those dark clouds at this exact moment? And how could it find her here, in this exact spot where she was sitting?

"How's that for a start?" said a voice.

"What … who?" Josephine stammered, falling off her rock as she turned to see a figure draped in white sitting on the ground behind her.

"Is that you?" Josephine whispered, not even sure who she meant by "you."

"Namaste," Allegra said, bowing at the waist, palms joined in front of her heart.

"What are you *doing* here?" Josephine didn't know whether to feel spied on or flattered.

"Isn't this just the perfect spot to meditate? You can face east in the morning and west in the evening. Pity the sun won't last, otherwise we could practice *surya trataka* together."

"Sir what?"

"*Surya trataka.* It's the practice of staring at the rising sun while maintaining gestures of awakening called mudras. The sun reflects on the inner you, which is reflected back on the sun. You become the seer, the seen, and the seeing."

The seer, the seen, and the seeing. She wondered how she would see herself, if she were the sun. She wasn't sure she'd want to know. But she would like to bask in that beam again, if it hadn't already been gobbled up by the greedy gray clouds.

"It's one of those things it's better to experience than talk about. Maybe we can try tomorrow," Allegra said. "Anyway, I was surprised to see you out here meditating. And so early! Good for you!"

"I always get up early," Josephine said. "I need my quiet time."

"Same here. It's so important to start the day with a clear mind and an open heart."

Josephine wondered what kinds of things could clutter the mind and heart of this fairy-like creature. She looked so light and innocent, with her freckled face and her wild red curls, still tousled from their night on the pillow.

"Is there something special weighing on your mind this morning, Josephine?"

Josephine wasn't big on confessions, but she surprised herself by nodding her head. "Yeah, but it's a little personal. And very complicated."

"Oh hey, I'm sorry. I just thought, well, that maybe you came to this particular spot for a reason. Like maybe you could use someone to talk to."

There you go, that was the big drawback of traveling alone for a woman like herself. No one would ever think Josephine *wanted* to be alone. No one would ever think she was an artist in search of inspiration, or an intellectual working on some new theory, or an outdoorswoman here to explore nature. People would always view her as pathetic and lonely. Pathetic, lonely Josephine. Forget the Fortunata part. But at the same time, she knew it was wrong to resent Allegra for what other people might think. She was just trying to be nice; in fact, she *was* being nice.

"No need to apologize, Allegra," Josephine said, turning to face her fully. "I appreciate your concern."

Allegra smiled, and it was such a warm, caring smile that it was a little like being in that sun ray again. Maybe she was right; maybe it would be a good idea to share her thoughts with someone, to outline the pros and cons of her dilemma to an impartial party, to confess her fears to someone who had no vested interest in her decision, to hear some thoughts from outside the box she'd been shut inside for so long. But where to begin?

"This is a tough time for me," she heard herself saying, before she could think too much about it. "I've devoted over twenty years to a life I'm not sure I want to keep living."

"I see," Allegra nodded, waiting, but not pushing, for more information.

"I ... um ... maybe I should give you some background first." Josephine stared at the sky, pausing for a full minute before looking into Allegra's kind green eyes, flecked with the same copper color as her hair. "Sorry, I always get a lump in my throat when I say this out loud. I had a tumor. More than one, actually. Breast cancer."

"Oh, gosh! I tend to get those, too!" Allegra said, giving Josephine's shoulder a sympathetic squeeze.

Josephine gasped. The thought of this poor girl going through what she had gone through was too much!

"Lumps in my throat, I mean!" Allegra blurted, her pale cheeks flushing crimson. "Not in my breasts! Not cancer!"

Josephine remained speechless as she stared at her, not quite sure how to react to such a ludicrous misunderstanding. She didn't want to dredge up the details of her disease, and she certainly didn't want Allegra's pity. Whatever it was that she wanted, the only thing that came out of her mouth was a giggle. Allegra's response was a twitter so awkward that it made Josephine chuckle, which gave Allegra the go-ahead to join in, and then they were both laughing so hard they were soon doubled over, then rolling onto their backs, kicking their legs, waving their arms, holding their tummies. Josephine wasn't a lonely, pathetic woman at all. She was a woman with a new friend, and they were giggling like schoolgirls in the grass still damp with dew, beneath a night too reluctant to surrender to morning, and a morning too weak to chase away the night, and caught between the two, all they could do was laugh.

When her belly finally stopped jiggling, Josephine lay flat on her back to catch her breath, dabbing her eyes with a corner of her shawl. Turning her head to look at Allegra, she spotted a silhouette standing in the window of the main lodge. "I think someone's up," she said.

"Must be Carolina," Allegra said. "Want to go see if we can get some coffee?"

"Do I ever!" Josephine said.

Sometimes you didn't know what you needed until you found it. Sometimes it could just be someone to laugh with, even when there was nothing to laugh about.

CHAPTER SEVENTEEN
Inge

"Where are you off to already? It's barely light out," Inge said, stretching her body to its full, well-proportioned length on the bed, her hands over her head, her long legs straight, her toes pointed.

"My morning jog! Some rooster has been crowing for the past hour so I thought I might as well get up." Rino replied, sitting on a chair to put on a pair of turquoise running shoes she'd never seen before. "Especially since I skipped yesterday in San Remo. That place inspires vices, not virtues."

"Yes, good habits can be hard to keep when you can choose from so many bad ones," Inge said. "Unless you have a strong will, of course."

"Meaning I don't?"

"I didn't say that." Inge scooted up in the bed as Rino bent down to lace up his shoes. She was touched by a mixture of tenderness and sadness at the sight of his pate, viewed at its worst angle, with his thinning gray hair losing ground to the quickly spreading patches of pink scalp. She continued to observe her husband as he pushed on his knees with both hands to help himself back up to a sitting position. His face was flushed, and his glasses had slid down the bridge of his nose, until coming to a stop against its blunt tip and wide nostrils.

"Wouldn't you rather take a walk in the woods, Rino? The terrain looks a little rough for running. You could twist an ankle." Inge wasn't the anxious type, but having assisted her husband after surgery to repair a torn meniscus, she wanted to make sure nothing like that happened again – for both their sakes. "If you give me a few minutes, I'll join you."

"We can walk later if you want. But I can't skip running two days in a row, or my average will go down."

"Your average?"

"Yes, you know. My average. The number of kilometers I run per week divided by the number of days in the week, which no matter what distance I log in, is always seven. I don't need to explain the math to you, do I?" He double-checked that his Apple watch, which he kept on at night to track his sleep patterns, was securely fastened to his wrist, then swapped his spectacles for his prescription sports glasses.

Inge sighed; she hoped he wasn't going to let yesterday's discussion about

Carl poison the new day. "No, you don't need to explain the math to me. I know what an average is. Are those new running shoes?"

"Yes!" he answered, immediately brightening. "Meet my new Merino runners. Spiffy, huh?"

"That's one word to describe them." Inge leaned forward to get a better view of the shoes being modeled by her husband. She smiled indulgently as he strutted to the door, hands on his hips, performed a little pivot, pointing one toe in, one toe out, then returned. Regrettably, admiring his shoes also involved looking at his legs, and although she admitted that over the past few months his exercise regime seemed to have improved his overall muscle tone and stamina, she never could bear the sight of an older man in shorts. And now, here she was, married to an older man in shorts. One with hairy legs and knobby knees and a paunch to top it all off. Better to focus on the shoes.

"But woolen running shoes, Rino? Won't your feet melt down to the bone in those?"

"No! That's the beauty of felt. It keeps you warm in winter and cool in summer!"

"Yes, I've heard that somewhere before," Inge said, her voice flat. It was hard, very hard, to talk felt before coffee. "Don't they look a little like slippers?"

"Slippers? Ha! Just look at this lightweight sole! And the foam footbed and wool insole! Designed specifically to wick the sweat!" Rino said, sitting next to her on the bed, grunting as he hoisted his right ankle over his left knee to pull off the shoe he'd just put on. "This insole is one hundred percent virgin wool, mind you! Plus, it's interchangeable!"

"Imagine that," Inge said, her head sinking into her neck, her neck sinking into her chest, like a turtle retreating into her shell, as Rino thrust the shoe in her face.

"Feel how soft the upper is! How light! How it stretches!" He took Inge's hand in his and guided it over the top and sides of the supple shoe.

"All right, you win!" Inge said, waving him away with a laugh. "It's a marvelous piece of footwear. I can't wait to see how it performs for you."

"Me neither!" Rino wiggled his foot back into the shoe and laced it up again.

"Well, if you're set on going I think you should stop wasting time talking to me, and get out there while it's still cool."

"And that's exactly what I plan to do. *Auf Wiedersehen, Frau Doktor Egger!*"

"*Arrivederci, Signor Di Meglio,*" Inge replied. "Do your best, but *don't* overdo it!"

"A Di Meglio does nothing *but* the best!" Rino called over his shoulder, slamming the door as he left.

Inge flinched at the banging. Why couldn't he be gentler with doors? Sinking back into the luxuriously fluffy yet surprisingly supportive pillows, she placed her hands on her abdomen. Let's face it, she wasn't as taut and firm as she used to be, either. Doughy, that's what her tummy was. Not that anyone would notice, because no one ever saw her naked anymore. Did she regret that? Sometimes. Did she know what to do about it? No. Sex with Rino had been passable enough at the beginning, thanks largely to him, that much she had to admit. Inge was more physical than emotional by nature, and her body, trained to perform to its fullest capabilities in any discipline, knew how to respond to the right stimulation in bed. And Rino, eager to please her, had taken the trouble to learn what that was. Until at one point, she'd started brushing off her husband's advances; it hadn't been a conscious decision, but rather a gradual slide into indifference, and she'd done nothing to arrest the process. One night she had clinical reports to catch up on in bed, another night she needed to research something on her laptop, and almost every night she was too exhausted. On those increasingly rare occasions when she did give in to Rino's insistence, achieving any sort of climax was more work than it was worth. Before she knew it, the weeks of abstinence had turned into months, the months into years, and now here Inge was, already on the wrong side of menopause, and still barely on the right side of sixty. It saddened her to realize that her existence as a sexually active woman could, in effect, be over, unless she did something about it. But what? The thought of trying to rekindle the sputtering flame they'd started out with was totally unappealing. What she needed from Rino — what she'd always needed from him, really — was comfort; a warm body next to hers as they nodded off while reading; a solid back to press hers against when they rolled over onto their opposite sides; a pair of toasty, felt-warmed feet to thaw her icy toes.

Was it because theirs had been a steady, practical kind of love from the start? A love that took the backseat to their true passions? They were mature adults when they'd met, and even then, it was clear that Rino's first love would always be his felt, just as hers was her profession. Well, after Hans, that was. Hans had been passion and recklessness personified, and a love like the one they'd shared could burn forever without fizzling out. It was the kind of love that was hard to live with, but harder to live without. Yet she had no choice but to live without. Was that what it meant to grow old? To have life's most powerful emotions relegated to the archives of memory?

Lying in her bed alone, Inge gently rubbed her tummy, then let her hands wander over her expensive silk nightie up to her breasts, still firm and full for a woman of her age. She briefly considered taking out the vibrator she used occasionally as much to stave off the risk of vaginal atrophy as to resuscitate what lingered of her libido, but not even that inspired her. Instead, she crossed her arms over her chest in a hug, her hands squeezing her shoulders, running up and down her strong upper arms to chase away a sudden chill. More than sex, what Inge missed most — what she *craved*, if she were honest with herself – was the type of intimacy that followed sex. Swinging her feet to the floor, she headed for the shower before the ache became unbearable.

CHAPTER EIGHTEEN
Allegra

"Don't just stand there like a couple of lost souls! Come on in!" Carolina cried, throwing open the door. Allegra jumped back, surprised. She hadn't even touched the handle, so Carolina must have spotted them from the window. "What can I do for you? Can I get you some coffee?" Flapping her arms like a mother hen, she ushered the two women to a table in the dining room before they had the chance to answer.

"Sure, that would be great," Allegra said.

"We'd hate to disturb you though!" Josephine said, biting her lip. "You look very busy already."

"Oh, I'm *always* busy! But the day taking care of my guests *disturbs* me is the day I'll hang up my apron!"

"Really, though, Carolina," Allegra said. "I used to know my way around the kitchen, I can go make the coffee myself."

"Don't be silly! Besides, you know how I am about my kitchen. Especially now, after what happened with Jada." Carolina shook her head and rolled her eyes. "But that's the *last* thing I want to talk about. Though I know I could trust *you*."

Allegra couldn't remember if she'd ever heard anything about a Jada, but it was clear that Carolina was itching to remedy her deficiency. The woman always wanted to tell you something in confidence, especially if you were willing to drag the details out of her the way she dragged them out of other people. Allegra, on the other hand, felt that if something wasn't offered to you, you shouldn't try to take it, even if it was only information. That was one reason why their conversations never really got off the ground.

"Unless of course you really *want* to know." Carolina winked.

"Maybe later. Right now, we sure could use that cup of coffee."

"At your service!" Carolina said, rushing off. Now she seemed offended. Allegra sighed, remembering how she used to confuse her with her sudden mood swings during the few retreats they'd attended together. Even the way she'd thrown herself into yoga obsessively and then suddenly vanished from the scene completely was weird. And when out of the blue she called Allegra a few years later to gush about the Renovatus, she'd acted as if they'd never been out of touch!

"I'm going to use the ladies' room," Josephine whispered, though there was no one else around to hear. Allegra nodded absently, strolling around the dining area to see why it looked so different from the last time she'd visited. She was noticing how much bigger the room seemed with the addition of the adjacent veranda, and how out of place that stuffed boar's head hanging on the wall seemed, when she got the funny feeling that she was being watched. Glancing at the kitchen door, she thought she saw a blur of movement behind the porthole window. Was Carolina keeping an eye on her? Or was it just that appalling trophy staring down at her with its glass eyes?

"Do you think she's annoyed that we turned up so early?" Josephine whispered, returning to her seat.

"It's hard to tell," Allegra said, keeping her voice low, too. "She does seem a little on edge this morning."

"I'd hate to impose on her hospitality. After all, breakfast doesn't start until eight. But whatever's baking in the oven sure does smell good."

"We always used to have coffee together around this time in the past."

"Well, then, since the two of you are friends, maybe it's *me* she doesn't like."

"Who wouldn't like *you*?"

Josephine sighed, as if she could name a few names.

"*Eccoci!* Here we are!" Carolina announced, bursting through the swinging doors with such unexpected enthusiasm that the women both started. "A full pot of hot, strong *caffè* for you early birds! With plenty of foamed *latte*!" Balancing the tray on the edge of the table, Carolina set down a thermal carafe and a jug of steamed milk, whisking away the empty tray and turning on her heels before they had the chance to thank her.

"But Carolina!" Allegra called after her. "What's the big rush? Can't you join us?"

"Me?" Carolina said, her ponytail whipping her on the cheek as she pivoted back around to face Allegra. "I have things to do, you know? Giac will be down any minute now, and before you know it people will be wanting their breakfast. Busy, busy, busy, from sunup to sundown. That's me!"

"But it's still really early. And there are only a few of us here this morning. Come on."

"Well, if you insist, I suppose I have a few minutes."

Insisting was another thing Carolina was fond of, but Allegra wasn't; she was happy to encourage anyone who needed a little push but beyond that, she believed each individual should do what felt right, when it felt right, without being cajoled, because you never knew the reasons holding them back. She also knew Carolina well enough to know that she often hid behind her busyness and although she certainly had things to do, right now she did want to sit with them. Allegra wanted her to sit with them, too, and so did Josephine, so it seemed simple enough to her. But right after making the suggestion, Allegra began wondering whether it was such a good idea. The way Carolina just stood there balancing the empty tray on her palm while openly scrutinizing Josephine's appearance made Allegra notice for the first time her friend's bedhead of punky spikes, and the ratty red shawl draped over her sloped shoulders, and the faded football hoodie and baggy sweatpants that hid whatever figure might be lurking within.

"You Americans love your sweatshirts, don't you?" Carolina finally said.

"Oh, this old thing? Just about everyone in Buffalo has one of these, it's like a passport to the city. The Bills are our football team, you know?"

"I don't follow sports," Carolina shrugged. "But it looks very comfortable."

"It is! But listen, I'm sorry I'm not dressed for breakfast," Josephine replied, blushing. "I didn't plan to barge in like this. I only left my room to go –"

"Nonsense!" Carolina said, waving away the comment with her hand.

"We're very informal here. Like family. Better yet, like a bunch of friends. Friends are way more fun than family, don't you think?"

"Well, I, um, that's not an easy question for someone like me to answer," Josephine stammered.

"Someone like you?" Carolina asked, cocking her head. "What do you mean by that?"

"Well, between us women, my background wasn't –"

"Yes, you're one hundred percent right about friends being more fun than family, Carolina!" Allegra interjected. It was best to prevent Josephine from revealing too many personal details in Carolina's presence, at least until she got to know her better, at which time she could decide for herself. "All the more reason to make time for a coffee with two friends, one old and one new."

"Okay, okay!" Carolina said. "I wouldn't want to *offend* anyone!" After retrieving a third cup and saucer from the credenza, Carolina pulled out a chair and sat down. Despite her alert eyes, her face looked drawn, as if she hadn't slept well.

"Now, you sit back and relax for once, and let *me* serve *you*," Allegra said. Maybe she just needed coffee, she thought as she poured; maybe they all just needed coffee.

"How nice that the two of you have already become such *amiche per la pelle*," Carolina absently stirred her black beverage, despite not having added any sugar or milk. "That's how we call best friends in Italian, Josephine."

"Yes, 'skin friends,' that's an interesting way to put it," Josephine said.

"Like how we say 'bosom buddies.'"

"In our case, we're more like tree friends," Allegra said. "We're both drawn to that oak out front."

"I decided to call it Holly!" Josephine said, smiling.

"You named *my* tree?" Carolina asked.

"Well, since you mentioned the other one is called Ollie, I thought Holly would —"

"As I was saying, we happened to meet by that tree twice, but aside from that, we hardly know each other, do we, Josephine?" Allegra said. She already felt closer to Josephine than she wanted to let on, but Carolina was giving off seriously bad vibes this morning. Not only was she jealous of Josephine, she was also jealous of the tree. But you couldn't *own* a *tree*, even if some deed said you owned the land it was on. And you certainly couldn't own anyone's *friendship*.

"It's a perfect spot," Josephine said. "You must have created it with yoga and meditation in mind."

"Well, I didn't see much of either going on out there this morning! All I saw was the two of you rolling around in the grass!" Carolina said, her lips screwed into a tight smile. "Is that one of those new techniques you yoga people are always coming up with, Allegra? Laughing yoga? Like goat yoga? Or beer yoga? I don't have time to keep up with those silly fads."

"Beer yoga? Oh gosh!" Josephine laughed. "I wouldn't know about those things either, Carolina. To tell the truth, this whole yoga business is pretty foreign to me. We were just having a good old-fashioned giggle. Gosh, it's been ages since I laughed that hard. My stomach still hurts!"

"And what could you have possibly found so funny, at this hour of the day?" Carolina asked, staring at the space between her two guests over the rim of her cup.

"Well," Josephine paused to sip the coffee she'd topped off with a pile of frothy milk. "Oh, that's *so* good! Anyway, it didn't start out funny. You see, when I confided to Allegra that —"

"You have some foam on your nose, Josephine," Allegra butted in, tapping on the bridge of her own nose.

"You were saying?" Carolina urged Josephine to continue.

"Let's let it go for now, Carolina," Allegra answered before Josephine could speak for herself. "It's a delicate subject."

"I see," Carolina said, her saucer rattling as she set down her cup. "So you're already sharing secrets, then. My, my, you still move fast, Allegra."

"What?" Allegra said.

"Don't play dumb. You know what I mean. You've always been better than me at making friends."

"What are you *talking* about?"

"When we were at those seminars together, you were the one people wanted to bunk with, not me. You were the authentic yogini. You had the right look, with your guru pants and ankle bracelets. You already knew the names of the *āsanas* and you could recite the mantras for the twenty-four sun salutations in Sanskrit. You even knew how to play a bunch of those Indian tunes on your guitar. You always outshone the rest of us."

"It wasn't a *competition*, Carolina. It's just that my parents lived and breathed yoga, and got me started when I was a little kid. Getting back to it after so long felt a little like speaking a language I grew up with. I thought maybe it could be a way to reconnect with them."

"Did it help?" Josephine asked. She looked a little lost, as if she'd walked into a party she'd been invited to for unknown reasons, and couldn't spot anyone she knew. "I mean, did you reconnect?"

Carolina glared at Josephine, but Josephine was staring at Allegra, as if she'd finally found a conversation she could latch onto.

"In a way," Allegra said, feeling the urge to open up to her, despite her wariness of Carolina. Or maybe to counteract it. "But not physically. When my mother died, my father went off to India. That was his big dream."

"I'm so sorry about your mother! Have you been to visit your father?"

"Only once. That was enough. He lives in one of those communities where no one owns any personal property because they take it all away from you when you move in. Not that he ever had much, just my mother and me, and a very small roof over our heads."

"I know what those communities can be like," Josephine said. "And you don't even have to go to India to find them. Everyone is supposed to share and care and look after one another, right? It sounds like the perfect life, but unfortunately, people aren't perfect. So it doesn't always work out that way, does it?"

"All this time I've known you and you never told me about your mother, Allegra," Carolina said before Allegra could answer Josephine. "Or your father."

"It's a complicated story. I don't talk about it much. I don't even know how it came out now."

"Well, for what it's worth," Carolina said, "I'm sorry, too."

"That makes three of us," Allegra said, her hands wrapped around her coffee cup.

The women sipped their coffee together in silence, a silence that was more respectful than companionable, a silence in which they seemed to accept all their broken and missing parts. A silence that was interrupted by Giac's footsteps thundering down the stairs, stopping briefly in the kitchen, then bursting through the doors.

"The croissants were burning!" he said. "Lucky for you I took them out."

CHAPTER NINETEEN
Carolina

So much for establishing some semblance of order in this place! Just because people paid good money to stay here didn't mean the whole world revolved around them. Sure, they were the sort who were used to barking orders, like Rino the Rhino, who ran his own company. Probably inherited everything he had from his father, without so much as lifting his pudgy little pinky. Young men who reaped all the advantages of a family business without sowing any of the sacrifices required to build it up treated their employees like crap and paid them peanuts; she knew that from all those years watching Giac squeeze his paycheck out of the entitled clutches of a born-rich boss. At least that had made him keen to get out of the rat race and move up here, where he didn't have to answer to anyone, where his sweat and toil weren't wasted on making a rich person richer. The wife, Inge the Hun (Carolina was liking that nickname; the things you conjured up when you couldn't sleep!), was just as bad as the Rhino, if not worse. Doctors floated through life on a cloud of privilege, as if they belonged to some superior species, more like demigods than humans. Combine that with being Swiss, *and* being spoiled by a wealthy husband (who could miss those rocks flashing on her fingers?), *and* being an attractive lady (past her prime, okay, but Carolina knew classy beauty when she saw it), and *voilà!* that was the recipe for one arrogant bitch. Well, there wasn't any sick patient lying in bed at her mercy or hanging on her fancy medical words here, no crisp white jacket flapping to the beat of her hurried steps telling the world that she was a big shot, no stethoscope hanging from her neck like Olympic gold. If you were curious enough and clever enough (which Carolina was), you could learn all kinds of things about doctors, especially now that people were posting reviews about them online as if they were flunkies flipping burgers at some roadside diner. Not that you could take a reviewer's word as gospel, she knew all too well that people could be snarky and use the internet to dump their hostility onto you like a load of steaming cow manure whenever and however they felt like it. She herself had never received any bad reviews at all until this year, and the thing that killed her was that it wasn't even her fault. She was working harder than ever, and was better than ever at what she was doing; it was the other people who'd gone crazy, maybe they were still suffering from all those restrictions on their freedom during those lockdowns and their judgment was still impaired, who could say, all she knew was that if they didn't get what she was trying to do here, she was better off without them. A couple of times she'd shared the comments with Giac, expecting at least a show of solidarity, but no, he had the nerve to side with the complainers! But that was another story, she was getting off track thinking about her two-faced husband instead of focusing on Rino and Inge. She was so tired last night that she barely scratched the surface with them, but then when she got to bed, she was so keyed up she could hardly sleep.

And of course, the one morning when she takes time out to indulge her two friends who insist on chatting with her over coffee (after all, they were guests too, and deserved her attention, she couldn't be rude), everyone else decides to get up early, too, just to throw her off schedule, and as a person who prided herself on efficiency, Carolina *loathed* being thrown off schedule. She'd still managed to set up a gorgeous buffet of sweet and savory breakfast delights in the dining room on time, though, with a good fifteen minutes to spare, and with fresh bouquets of wildflowers and herbs artistically arranged on the tables. Allegra had gone to give a good morning kiss to her *bello*, while at Carolina's insistence, Josephine had stayed put, transitioning seamlessly from an early coffee and an almost-burnt croissant (or two) to the full-blown breakfast spread before retreating to her room. And now of course Inge insisted on sitting outside. So what if it looked like it was going to start pouring any minute? So what if she made her walk all those extra steps to serve her? But that's what Carolina would do, because catering to her guests, even the most capricious ones, was what Carolina did best.

"Are you sure you wouldn't be more comfortable indoors, Inge?" she asked, smiling as she set down a pot of strong coffee with hot water on the side (some people really knew how to ruin a good thing).

"Absolutely! I'd much rather be outdoors, in the fresh air," Inge replied.

"Fine." Of course it was fine, of course Carolina would make sure it was fine, like she always did. "Can I bring you anything else at the moment?"

"No, I'll just have the coffee while I wait for my husband," Inge said. "Oh, there he is now. *Rino! Here!*" she called, raising her index finger in the air. None of that undignified waving and *yoo-hoo, honey!* business for her. She was a woman used to issuing orders and having them obeyed immediately.

Following her gaze, Carolina spotted two men in shorts approaching from the gravel path. Rino the Rhino was dragging his flamboyant feet as if each step might be his last, but his buddy looked like he'd just jumped out of a sportswear ad. Skimpy black running shorts that showed off his muscular thighs, a sleeveless T-shirt that clung to his lean torso, and red running shoes that didn't even seem to graze the ground when he walked: this was Adalberto Alberti first thing in the morning? Not only was he fit, he probably didn't snore, either, or suffer from nighttime halitosis. Allegra had all the luck.

"This young fellow ... gave me ... a run ... for my money!" Rino sputtered.

"It worked both ways!" Adalberto said, slapping Rino on the back. "Your time wasn't that much worse than mine!"

"You two perspiring men keep your distance please," Inge said, holding her arm out, though they were still several meters away from her. "And you be careful not to catch a chill, Rino."

Rino said nothing, but untied the warmup jacket knotted around his waist, put it on, and zipped it up.

"If you aren't going to introduce me to your lovely wife, I'll do the honors myself," Allegra's hunk said. "I'm Adalberto. But my friends call me Ada."

Carolina wondered why he or Allegra hadn't told *her* to call him Ada yesterday when they'd met. They were closer in age, and closer to being friends than these two stiffs would ever be.

"It's a pleasure to meet you, Adalberto," Inge said. "I'm *Doktor* Inge Egger and I'm not fond of nicknames."

"Are you ready for this, Inge?" Rino said excitedly. "It's not only his sprinting speed that this guy's modest about! My friend Ada here is none other than Adalberto Albertis! *The* Adalberto Albertis! The writer!"

"Of course," Inge said, her polite smile a pretty good indication that no bells were going off in her doctorly head. It was probably too crammed with medical information, and the remaining space was too full of herself.

"My ex-secretary reads all those little books you write, Ada. She loves that '*Cento Pagine d'Amore*' series," Rino continued. "You always know what you're getting: a hundred pages of a love story, and some are pretty steamy, I hear! And the print font is nice and large, easy on the eyes. At least that's what I'm told!" He shot his wife the glance of one who does not wish to be interrupted for once. "Very clever of you to put out two new stories every year, one just in time for Christmas, and another one just before the August holidays. They make great gifts!"

Inge said nothing, but glared at her husband, and oh, the priceless expression Carolina caught on her face now! Maybe books weren't the only thing Rino gave that secretary of his. At Christmas, or Ferragosto, or the rest of the year. How pathetically banal. But worth remembering.

"My wife isn't a big reader of fiction, I hate to say, or I'd give them to her, too, of course," Rino said. "All she reads is medical journals and clinical charts. In bed, of all places. Not nearly as romantic as your stuff. According to my secretary, anyway. I don't read love stories. Sorry."

"Most men don't," Adalberto said. "Though it sure wouldn't hurt them!"

"One thing I'd like to ask since you're right here and all. My secretary always said the stories ended too soon, just when everything was starting to work out. She said that falling in love was the easy part, that she always wanted to know where the couple went from there, how they'd handle their future together. You ever consider writing more than a hundred pages?"

"Well, since that particular series is called 'A Hundred Pages of Love,' I sort of have to stick to that length. It works better for the podcasts, too, because every hundred-page story breaks down to ten bite-size episodes, you see? And because of their busy schedules, today most women prefer a quick listen to lugging a book around. But you make a good point, Rino. I've considered it, but to be honest – and I'm telling you this in confidence – after a while, I get fed up with my characters and their lives. They're so limited, you know? And if I get bored, my readers are bound to get bored, too. I think modern women want a fast-paced, emotional rollercoaster ride to compensate for their stale relationships and tedious lives. Monogamy and monotony tend to go hand in hand!"

"Sure, sure. Good thinking," Rino nodded in agreement. "You're a genius." Turning back to Inge he added, "Ada also writes a column for one of those ladies' magazines. He's an expert on relationships. You know, couples, families, friendships, whatever. He gives women emotional support and advice, that kind of thing, right Ada?"

"Oh, a therapist! So, on top of all that, you're a doctor as well?" Inge said.

"God, no!" Adalberto chuckled. "I started out studying pol sci in Turin, but after two years I realized I needed to do something more creative with my life. Something that would not only make me feel better, but that would help others feel better about themselves."

Inge raised her eyebrows; Rino jumped in again. "I'll bet lots of your clients read his column, Inge."

"Patients, Rino," Inge sighed.

"What do you mean, patience?"

"I mean *patients*. They're not clients, they're patients."

"I know, I know. What's the name of it again, Ada? Sorry, but I only read car magazines."

"Yeah, well I'm fond of those, too, Rino!" Adalberto chuckled, turning to Inge. The magazine is *Coppie Moderne*, and the column is called @AskAda, you know, with the little 'at' symbol front of it. That's for social media."

The Rhino kept looking at the Hun and nodding, as if he were expecting her to ask @AskAda for an autograph or something, which was obviously something she would never do, even if she did get who he was, which she didn't.

"But Cara, with all your commuting, you must have at least heard him on the radio? He 's one of the regulars on RadioNord!"

"RadioNord? That's the station I listen to on my drive to work, for the news at 7."

"Keep listening then! Audience share is of vital importance these days when people have so many entertainment options to choose from!" Adalberto said. "The show airs right after the news. It's called —"

"Oh, now I know! *Parlami di te*, right? That program where listeners call in and tell you things they can't tell anyone else? I catch that occasionally if I'm stuck in traffic. I find it fascinating to hear what people are willing to share about themselves on live radio, first thing in the morning." Inge said, shaking her head.

"What can I say?" Adalberto flashed a fake sheepish smile. "Women open up to me."

Rino grinned, looking relieved that he'd finally made a dent in his wife's thick Swiss skull. He gave Adalberto a chummy clap on the back, and Adalberto smiled an even bigger smile, shaking his head as if to say *you guys!* Carolina had to admit that his was one of the most dazzling smiles she'd seen on a real live off-screen man – and he knew it. Oh yes, he was good at flaunting those perfect white teeth, and he timed the smile just long enough for you to notice those cute dimples (yes, he even had dimples – in both cheeks!). But Carolina was also getting one of her vibes right now, and it was telling her that this super handsome, super popular guy was a little too slick for the likes of the socially challenged Allegra to hang on to. In fact, she had plenty of questions for Allegra about this boyfriend of hers, and she could kick herself for letting her foul mood blow her shot at what could have been a revealing conversation earlier. Never mind, she'd find another chance. Luckily, it was hard to make Allegra really mad. She was one of those rare (and let's face it, annoying) women who never held a grudge, was always ready to forgive and forget, let bygones be bygones, and all that crap. If Carolina didn't know her and like her as well as she did (because she *did* like her), she'd think she was a poor sap. Better leave Allegra for later, though, and focus on who she had in front of her now.

"Getting people to open up is quite a talent, Adalberto," Inge smiled. Well, well, not even the doctor seemed immune to his charm.

"As I said, feel free to call me Ada." Back came the dimples.

"Yes, and I'll also feel free to *not* call you Ada."

"Fair enough! You know, it was my editor who insisted on shortening Adalberto to Ada, and then it kind of stuck. Since it's an advice column for women, the idea was that they would be more likely to confide in an Ada – their favorite aunt Ada, their best friend Ada – than to an Adalberto, which can sound a little, you know, *pompous*, with its noble origins and all. My identity isn't a secret, not by any means, there's even a profile pic of me in plain view. Women who want to see me as a man and ask the advice of a man are free to do that, but the funny thing is, most write to me as if I were one of them. I suppose there's a bit of role-playing involved."

"My job also requires some of that," Inge said.

Adalberto scratched the fashionable stubble on his chin as he considered her comment. "Really?"

"Yes. I often need to change my approach according to whether I feel my patients are more comfortable seeing me as an empathic woman or as a neutral professional. It takes a particular set of skills to make people speak openly about their most intimate concerns. Whether they be of the heart or the body."

"You know, you're *so* right about that, Doctor," Adalberto said. "Both of our jobs involve getting inside people's heads. In my case, to relate to them, and in yours, to cure them."

"Yes, I suppose you could say we're both in the business of improving people's lives, couldn't you?" Inge said. "And please, do call me Inge."

"Will do! Thank you, Inge."

"If I may make a suggestion," Carolina said, taking a step toward Ada the Adonis (that just came to her, another good one!) and his groupies. They all turned to look at her, as surprised to see her walk and hear her talk as if she were a tree that had suddenly assumed a human form, like in one of those fairytale forests. "Why don't you all come on inside and indulge in the breakfast buffet that awaits you?"

"I'd prefer to stay outdoors," Inge sniffed. "If you put these two tables together, we'll have plenty of room to continue our chat over breakfast."

"Great idea, Inge! But only if it's not an imposition." Adalberto said. "We do seem to have a lot to talk about."

"No problem whatsoever," Carolina said. No problem lifting the heavy wooden table, or running back and forth to serve them yogurt and cheese and eggs and pastries and cakes and bread and coffee and milk and tea and honey dripping off its gooey goddamn comb, no problem at all! Josephine had been quite happy eating inside and had already gone back to her room. But she could tell that once these people sat their privileged butts down, they weren't too likely to get off them anytime soon. She could already hear how it would be for the next couple of hours with their "I'd *love* a little more of this!" and "*Do* bring me a little more of that!" with no regard for the fact that she needed to start lunch preparations.

"But I'll move the table, not you," Adalberto said to Carolina, throwing in a double-dimpled smile and wink as he waved her aside. "Then it's a quick shower for us, right Rino? Five minutes, tops, and we'll be back."

He really *was* a nice guy, Carolina thought, letting her eyes rove from his full head of wavy hair, down to the little tattoo at the nape of his neck, across his well-proportioned shoulders and muscular back, taking in every detail of his remarkable physique as he rearranged the tables. Carolina never totally trusted the nice guys, though.

CHAPTER TWENTY
Josephine

Still in her sweats, Josephine leaned in and turned the water on full blast. She wanted to make sure it was the perfect temperature before stepping into the gorgeous shower stall tiled with natural stone, positioned directly beneath a round window in the ceiling. She'd never seen a skylight in a bathroom before, and the idea of showering in the shaft of light it cast exactly where she would stand was what had helped her to choose the shower over the Jacuzzi tub, a separate luxury that took up an entire corner of the bathroom. That, and the fact that filling the tub would be a selfish waste of a community resource. Of course, so was running the water in the shower with no one standing under it, so what was she waiting for? Taking off her clothes, she took the time to fold them and place them on a stool, wondering if she would ever learn to accept pleasure without some form of guilt nagging at her. For this one weekend at least, she was determined to enjoy whatever came her way, to follow her instincts, go with the flow, free her mind free from the weight of regrets and remorse and schedules to follow; she'd promised herself that, and she'd promised Thomas that. So far, she was doing a pretty good job of keeping her word. She'd stayed in bed as long as possible, then walked out without worrying about what to wear or who she'd see. She hadn't planned to confide in Allegra or share a laugh with her, but she had. She hadn't planned to hang out with Carolina on her own, but she had. And now, with nothing on her agenda, she was going to indulge in the longest, hottest shower of her life, then pamper herself with all those courtesy toiletries in the "Created exclusively for Renovatus Resort" lineup, instead of saving them and taking them home, where they would gather dust on a bathroom shelf, too precious to use and too precious to toss.

Josephine couldn't remember ever feeling this excited about taking a shower, but simply standing there in the light of day, letting liters and liters of hot water rain down on her, was pure bliss. This type of shower, so gentle, so soft, did not encourage rushing; in fact, it didn't even allow it. Opening one of the bath gels, she sniffed the fresh, herbal scent, then began soaping up her skin, slowly, generously, while she revisited the morning's events. After Allegra excused herself, Carolina had practically begged Josephine to stay put right there in the dining room, while she scuttled back and forth to set up the buffet. Josephine, used to playing the peacekeeper both at home and at work, felt uncomfortable that her instant connection with Allegra had aroused jealousy in Carolina, so she agreed to linger for a bit to even things out. She had to eat breakfast anyway, and it was fun at first, because every time Carolina burst through the kitchen doors to present another enticing cake or tray of pastries or platter of cheeses, she insisted that Josephine taste some of this or that and tell her what she thought, and of course Josephine didn't even try to resist the temptation. Quite frankly, overindulgence in food wasn't at the top of her list of things to feel guilty about these days. So she ate the goodies, and drank the coffee, and showered the beaming chef with compliments.

At the same time, once she felt its chilling effect Josephine couldn't ignore the undercurrent of negativity that now and then broke through the shimmering surface of Carolina's hospitality. Having spent years working in a predominantly female environment, she'd often witnessed, and most likely been the object of, criticism by those women who felt compelled to comment on another woman as soon as she exited the scene. And that was precisely what Carolina started doing after Allegra left. Dropping snippets of unsolicited opinions as she ferried food from the kitchen, she managed to insinuate that Allegra's life was hopelessly rootless; that her relationship with Adalberto, like all of her previous relationships, was doomed to fail; that she'd never hold a steady job, live in a decent house, or raise a family of her own. When Josephine's jaw kept chewing instead of dropping, Carolina finally switched course and began asking her casual questions about herself, about how different Buffalo must be from Rome, about how much she must miss Thomas and her family. Not being fond of talking about herself in the best of circumstances, she took her cue from Allegra's caution, and instead of answering questions she started asking them. Nothing too personal, just things like where did Carolina come from, how did she end up at the Renovatus, did she have any children, that kind of thing. But instead of sticking to the kinds of things you'd tell a stranger, Carolina provided Josephine with an unwanted glimpse of a miserable past at the hands of parents who'd made her life hell, of an exemplary mother whose children despised her, of a devoted wife whose husband didn't appreciate her. That final point was no secret, after seeing with her own eyes the way the guy treated her, accusing her of burning the croissants right in front of her and Allegra (Josephine had eaten two, just to prove they weren't so bad), then stomping off without even wishing his wife a good day. Giac was gruff, that's what he was. Some men thought that behavior made them more virile, but Josephine had never felt comfortable around those types and couldn't understand why a woman would ever be attracted to one, let alone marry one.

What had saved the conversation, in the end, were her questions about what Carolina planned to prepare for lunch, a subject Carolina was eager to expound upon. Josephine was still so full she couldn't even think about those mouth-watering descriptions now, but she already knew that within a couple of hours, they would be all she could think about. Right now, in fact, she didn't want to think about anything or anyone. Closing her eyes, she soaped up her head with way too much shampoo for the few inches of hair that graced her head, then just stood there in the beam of steamy light, letting the water rinse the suds from her head, over her shoulders and arms, down her legs to her toes. Her olive skin had a rosy glow to it by the time she finally stepped onto the bath mat and wrapped herself in the plushest towel she'd ever had the pleasure to encounter, while briefly entertaining the idea of snuggling up in that fluffy bathrobe, then going to sit in that designer armchair, just to see how it felt to do absolutely nothing for a while. But since she only had two mornings here, she couldn't justify wasting the first one like that. No, the smart thing to do was to get dressed right away and continue making the most of it. The problem with that was that she couldn't get dressed until she decided what to wear, and she couldn't decide what to wear until she decided what to do. Now would be a good time to try out the set of watercolors and sketchbook Lucia had given to her for her birthday, for example. The landscape was certainly inspiring, and she could go sit on her private porch to try her hand at painting something, but she already knew that her utter lack of artistic talent would end up frustrating her within the first fifteen minutes. She could always dig into one of the five novels (two Agatha Christies, a Patricia Highsmith, an Anne Tyler, and a Jane Austen) she'd brought along for the pure pleasure of reading fiction instead of studying texts, but maybe she should save those for later, just in case it rained. So why not opt for the healthy choice and take a vigorous hike on one of those trails to work off her breakfast? Of course, all that physical activity would make her eat more at lunch, in addition to exhausting her and making her feel out of shape.

Free time with no claims on it was something Josephine was unequipped to handle. Maybe it was because her strict upbringing had offered her so few options that she'd chosen an adult life that didn't allow them. It was easier to keep her ambitions in check when she had no hopes of a brilliant career, easier to keep her passions in check by never having cultivated them, easier to feel virtuous when she kept a safe distance from temptation. She didn't have enough fingers to count the times she'd been called a masochist for the choices she made. She didn't have enough breath to explain how little phrases like "you deserve" and "you're entitled to" meant to her. But what if her critics were right? What if she had it all wrong? How could she find out? Certainly not by standing here all alone, too undecided to make any move at all, in any direction whatsoever.

Sighing, she shuffled her slippered feet over to the closet. Getting dressed was never much fun when you didn't like the way you looked in anything, which was why she always wore one of the same three boring outfits to school every day. Today, however, was not a school day, and she did have that brand new pair of jeans dangling right in front of her, just waiting to be broken in. Still tucked in her towel, she reached for the pants, but the cuffs got stuck in the hanger and during the battle to free them, her towel slipped to the floor. With her jeans in one hand, she snatched up the towel with the other, clutching it to her chest. When had the habit of covering herself become such an ingrained reflex? There was no one around to hide her body from here, no one to criticize her lack of modesty, or worse, pity her unappealing appearance. No one but herself. She didn't expect to find solutions for all of her problems in one weekend, but maybe she could work on resolving this one little hangup right now, right here.

Letting the towel drop to the floor again, she stepped in front of the full-length mirror, an amenity she didn't have or want in her own bedroom, and looked herself in the eye. She'd been told many times that her eyes were an incredibly bright and beautiful shade of blue, and even she had to admit they were her best feature. For that, she could thank the genes she'd been blessed with, because those eyes received no preferential treatment: no lash-lengthening mascaras, no shape-defining pencils, no bag-reducing serums were used to enhance them. The thing that she liked most (and sometimes least) about her eyes was that they were honest. If she was happy, they shone with joy; if she was insecure, they clouded over with embarrassment; if she was sad, they reflected her inner darkness. Enough about the eyes, though, what about the rest of her face? Her cheeks were a little too chubby, but the upside was that her skin was smooth and still pretty much free from wrinkles. She also thought that her plumpish plainness offset her Roman nose and full mouth, which otherwise might have been overbearing. Whatever the case, it was her face, and she was used to it. What she couldn't get used to, even after all this time, was her chest. Looking in the mirror as if she were observing another person, she touched the gnarled tissue crisscrossing the area where her breasts used to be. Those beauties had developed sooner than she would have liked, grown larger than she would have liked, and drawn more attention from the other kids than she would have liked. Why hadn't she let more of those horny boys squeeze them back then? Why hadn't she let more men looking for love and comfort close enough to bury their faces in them? Had it been fear? Confusion? Guilt? Lack of interest? She couldn't even remember, and now it was too late. As her fingers traced the scars across to her armpits, her chest quivered and her throat tightened with all the emotions she'd silently swallowed over the past few years. Right after her diagnosis she'd wanted those breasts cut off of her body and kicked out of her life as soon as possible. She'd been too scared of dying to mourn their loss, too relieved at having survived to be concerned about her appearance, then too worried about the cost to consider cosmetic reconstruction, though Thomas had urged her not to worry about the money. This wasn't the first time she stopped to think about these things, but it was the first time she did so while looking at her body in the light of day, instead of shrinking away from it.

Fanning the fingers of her right hand over her chest, Josephine watched her left hand, the so-called devil's hand, slide over her soft, round tummy, and down to the area between her fleshy thighs. She dipped her fingers into the dampness, searching her inner warmth for the fulfillment she'd become so adept at avoiding. But before she could find it, she stole a glance at her eyes and, seeing them clouded with shame, she cast them to the floor. Grabbing the towel that lay there, Josephine hurried to the bathroom for a second shower. This one would be quick, and cold.

CHAPTER TWENTY-ONE
Allegra

"Can I interrupt a sec?" Allegra whispered, leaning in close to Adalberto. They were still seated at the table where that man Rino had been dominating the conversation for what, an hour now? Allegra had hoped to enjoy a leisurely breakfast alone with Adalberto to talk over a few things now that her throat had loosened up, but he was so enthusiastic after his morning run with this guest who turned out to be a fan of his that she had no choice but to accept that breakfast would be a foursome.

Allegra loved many things about Adalberto, and the way he treated his fans was one of them. He accepted their flattery graciously, signed their books tirelessly, and posed for selfies smilingly. That was a huge part of his job, and his job was a huge part of who he was. Sometimes he acted like all that attention made him uncomfortable, but in reality, he thrived on it. One thing he did not talk about openly was his private life, and he was an expert at turning questions around and cutting interviews short if he felt his personal territory was being invaded. Allegra still didn't know whether it was because he believed an aura of mystery made him more appealing, or he simply didn't want people to know where he went, what he did in his free time, or who he was attached to. It made sense that as a columnist and commentator and creator of fiction, he was more interested in mining *other* people's lives than shedding light on *his*, so when Rino started directing questions at him and Allegra as a couple – where they lived, whether they had kids, even corralling him into a group photo which included Allegra – Adalberto deflected him by asking about Rino's line of business. Ask men about their feelings, and they writhed and wriggled and replied with one-liners; ask them about their jobs and they could talk for hours. As a result, the impromptu breakfast club was treated to an in-depth disquisition on felt, ranging from its ancient origins, to its astonishing versatility, to Rino's merits in transforming Feltro Di Meglio *di meglio non c'è!* into the thriving business it was today. Rino was thrilled to have the ear of a famous narrator to tell his own tale to, and now he was all Ada this and Ada that, which was getting on Allegra's nerves, especially since his wife, Inge, instead of reining him in, just went on eating her breakfast as if she couldn't hear him, and didn't even try to make conversation with Allegra, which made her feel like some kind of alien, especially because of the way she kept staring at her when she thought she wasn't looking. Allegra was relieved when the doctor finally excused herself to call her clinic, giving Allegra an opening to make her getaway, too. She was pretty sure no one would have noticed if she just walked away, but first, she needed something from Adalberto.

"Sorry, can I interrupt you?" she repeated, squeezing his elbow.

"Please excuse me, Rino," Adalberto said, turning from him and winking at her. "What's up, Allegra Amore?" Maybe he'd had enough, too, but knowing him, it was more likely that he was amusing himself with this character and imagining his warm, padded existence in the muffled world of felt. Maybe he was already carving out a role for him in a future story, the boring husband and his frustrated wife, resigned to living their boring life, until one day the wife...

"I wanted to ask if I could borrow your phone," Allegra said.

"My phone?"

"Yeah, you know, that little rectangular device people use to communicate with people in other places. I used to have one of my own, but someone ran it over with his car," Allegra smiled. "A *big* car."

"Oh, right. Ouch." Adalberto grimaced, as if he could feel the pain of the crushed phone. I'll buy you a new one when we get back home. If you can wait that long. Otherwise, we can pop down to Ventimiglia and pick one up now. No problem."

"Driving down to Ventimiglia is *incredibly* low on the list of things I 'd like to do today. And so is buying a new phone. You're the only person I really need to keep in touch with, anyway. Luckily, you're right here with me."

"Luckily is right. You know how I worry when I can't reach you," Adalberto said, kissing the palm of her hand. "So who could you possibly need to call now?"

Allegra knew he wasn't just saying that. Although he had no qualms about leaving her alone for several days on end while he retreated to his family's old farmhouse near Alba to think or write or record his podcasts or whatever he needed to be alone to do, he freaked out when he couldn't get through to her. He hardly ever asked what she was doing or who she was with, so it wasn't a *jealousy* thing, he was hands down the most *un*jealous man she'd ever been with, and she was grateful for that, not being a possessive person herself. No, when he called it was more like he needed to make sure that she was safe and sound, just the way he'd left her. The problem was that if *she* needed to talk to *him* for some reason, she had to wait for *him* to call *her*, because to avoid being distracted from his various urgent deadlines, he kept his ringer off. He always had all those themes to ponder, plots to plan, characters to develop, words to weigh, and each part of this complicated creative process needed to be nurtured in a very private mental space he called his "brain bubble," which could burst at the slightest intrusion. Allegra could understand that, she too needed to be free from distractions when she meditated, or taught yoga, or composed music, but to be honest, Adalberto's short stories didn't seem all that *complex*; they just seemed, well, *short*. Sure, they were decently written, and his readers gobbled up the tidbits of romance like buttered popcorn, but Allegra knew that he could write more meaningful literature if he tapped into all of his resources, even if it meant giving up the radio slot and magazine column, and stopped spending so much time feeding his ravenous followers on social media. More than once she'd suggested he try adding more *layers* to his characters, dig a little *deeper* into the complexities of modern relationships since he knew so much about them, thanks to all the information people willingly provided to him for free, but those conversations never went too well. Adalberto tended to take a defensive stance, as if she were *attacking* him instead of *encouraging* him. He said that real relationships were already too complicated, that if his readers wanted a steamy love story with a happy ending, who was he to deny them?

Anyway, getting back to the phone, she really didn't like the way he used his, not answering her calls when sometimes all she needed was to hear his voice, and instead all she heard was the ringing. Oh, he always called her back, sooner or later, but by then it didn't matter; by then she felt lumped in with all the other "distractions" he wanted to shut out. So now, to avoid subjecting herself to that awful sense of rejection, she left the calling to him.

"Earth to Allegra!" Adalberto said, giving her shoulder a shake.

"Huh?"

"I said, who could you possibly need to call?"

That's right, she was asking about the phone. Adalberto was right about her mind sometimes wandering off on its own, but she hoped he wouldn't get into that now.

"I thought you wanted to forget about everything but us and yoga," he continued.

"I do. But then I started thinking about Papa while I was meditating this morning. I got this strange feeling that something might be *wrong*, and since today is Saturday, the only day I'm allowed to call, I want to check on him."

"I don't think you should worry about him, Allegra. He's right where he wanted to be, surrounded by an entire community of people who look after each other, right? Besides, even if he did have a problem, how could talking to you help him, when he's all the way over in India?"

"The same way talking to you could help me when I have a problem and you're all the way over in Alba." Allegra felt her fair cheeks flush, betraying her feelings on this sore subject. "A flat tire. A bad dream. A tummy ache. An existential doubt. Hearing the voice of someone who cares can help a *lot*."

"That's different."

"If you say so. Anyway, I *am* his daughter, you know. His only living relative."

"Who he didn't think twice about leaving behind," Adalberto said in a soft voice, gently tucking a stray spiral of hair behind her ear.

"If you met him you'd know it was more complicated than that. He's always followed his own path, regardless of what other people wanted or needed from him. You can probably relate to that, right?"

"What do you mean by that?"

"Never mind." Allegra swallowed, trying to clear a scratchy tickle in her throat. "So, may I *please* use your phone? The internet's back on and this is a good time of day for me to reach him. I'll use my Skype account to call his landline. I always keep a credit on balance so I can make toll calls to people who don't have internet."

"Landline? Toll calls? People who don't have internet?" Adalberto rubbed his chin, grinning. "Do those things still exist?"

"Actually, yes. So, can I use it?"

"Sure you can. Just give me a second." Cupping the phone in his hands, he unlocked it, sighed, and started tapping away with his thumbs. That still looked weird to Allegra, who never did get past typing with her index finger. "These people never give me a break," he said, shaking his head.

"It's Saturday, Adalberto. Try not looking at your phone for the rest of the day. Like you do when you 're in Alba."

"Good idea," he said, finally handing the phone over.

"Thanks!" Allegra said, hopping to her feet.

"Hey!" he called as she turned to leave. "Where are you going?"

"Inside. The wi-fi signal is stronger near the router, and that's in Carolina's office," she called over her shoulder. "I won't be long."

"Women, right?" Allegra heard Rino chortle, as she skipped away. "As I was saying …"

"Hey, Carolina!" Allegra called out, figuring Carolina must be in the kitchen. "It's only me, Allegra! I don't need anything, I'm just making a call!"

The slamming of cupboards and banging of pots confirmed that Carolina was definitely in the kitchen, and probably wrestling with a case of nerves. Allegra would have to make some time to sit down with her to see if anything else was going on besides her usual obsession with perfection and frustration with Giac. But first, she had her father to check on. Walking into the deserted dining room, she pulled out a chair and sat down, anxious to make her call so she could shake off her apprehension. Signing into Skype and dialing her father 's number, she tried to remember when they 'd last spoken; her log showed an outgoing call back in May, and she sure didn't need an app to remind her that he never called her. How could it be that they spoke so infrequently? How could they have so little to talk about when they did? Even when she managed to get through to the number, getting through to him as a *person*, as her *father*, was another story. He was the only one she could reminisce with about her mother, but he never wanted to. If she asked him a specific question about his life or the people in his community he would answer in a vague way, but never shared anything spontaneously or asked her anything about herself. In fact, she couldn't remember having *any* personal conversations with him, *ever*. He had pushed her to seek her highest levels of consciousness through the practice of *āsanas* and *prānāyāmas*, yet he wouldn't take her to see his birth family, or even tell her whether they were alive or where in Italy they were located. He taught her how to tune a guitar by ear and change a broken string, but not how to find harmony in a relationship or mend a broken heart. He and her mother never talked much to each other, either, at least not within her earshot. They communicated plenty through their *bodies*, though, you could tell, and through their music. They had a special intimate space to escape to together, a bubble of their own, just like Adalberto – only *theirs* had room for *two*.

"Anything I can help you with?" Carolina asked, the kitchen door swinging behind her as she entered the room.

"No, thanks," Allegra said. "I'm trying to reach my father on Adalberto's stupid iPhone. I *hate* iPhones."

"Oh, well, don't mind me then," Carolina said, a tray of loose silverware rattling in her hands. "I have to put these things away, though."

"Of course," Allegra nodded, pressing one ear against the phone, and plugging the other with her index finger.

"Where exactly was it in India that he ran off to?" Carolina called from across the room, loud enough to be heard over the racket she was making.

No answer. The call got dropped. Allegra redialed.

"He didn't run off," Allegra said. "It was more like he was transported there by some force he couldn't resist, after dreaming about it for so long."

"At least he had a dream," Carolina said, opening a drawer of the credenza and dropping in a fistful of forks. "My parents are still working themselves to death by boredom in the Milanese suburbs. Some people are born to be wild, right?"

Every time the flatware rattled, and it rattled plenty, Allegra winced. And now the connection wasn't even going through. She was redialing one more time when a notification flashed across the top of the screen like breaking news, then vanished. Pressing the phone even harder against her ear, she recalled how as a child she'd slept for months holding her ear to a seashell she'd dug up in Brittany, imagining she could hear the ocean. What she imagined now was an old-style telephone jangling off the hook in a simple room where the air smelled of sandalwood incense and masala chai, and a thin old man with a long white beard sat cross-legged on the floor, refusing her intrusion. That jangling in her head was as real as Carolina's cutlery concert, and Allegra was just about to tell her to *please* stop when the phone fell silent, the line dropped, and Carolina slammed the drawer shut.

"You stubborn old man!" Allegra muttered, staring at the phone. At the same instant, another notification flashed across the screen, and right after that another. This time she couldn't help seeing the name of the person bombarding Adalberto with messages. And once she saw that name, she couldn't un-see it.

"Gisella Giostra?" she said. "*Gisella Giostra!*"

"What or who is that?" Carolina asked.

Allegra stared at her. "What?"

"Who's Gisella Giostra?" Carolina repeated.

"No one," Allegra's voice came out in a pathetic squeak. She could hardly swallow, let alone talk. "She's *no one.*"

Allegra rushed away before Carolina could ask again, before she was tempted to call her father again, before she gave the phone the chance to *ring* and *ring* and *ring* and make her feel *rejected* again.

CHAPTER TWENTY-TWO
Carolina

Finally, everyone was done asking her for things, at least until lunchtime. For a minute it made Carolina sad to think such a thought, when being right here, tending to the needs of her own special guests at her own exclusive resort, was exactly what she wanted to be doing. When she got caught up in one of those fleeting (or not so fleeting) dark moments, when it could seem a struggle to make everything run precisely the way she wanted, she reminded herself that what she was doing went far beyond some self-serving ambition to make her mark in the world of hospitality. If she was such a perfectionist it was because she was motivated by a burning desire to offer a unique, customized experience to people who'd done it all, seen it all, had it all. She wasn't devoting her life to just a job; hers was a vocation, a mission, really, to teach a lesson or two to the ones who thought they knew it all, to open their eyes to things they didn't want to see, to make them realize that inner wealth was far more valuable than worldly riches. She hadn't fully grasped the importance of that at the beginning, and if she had, she wouldn't have been stupid enough to announce it to the folks back in Grislengo Lombardo, who were all so envious that she and Giac were getting out that all they could do was criticize them. Everyone said that it was a ridiculous scheme, that they'd be sorry, that it would ruin their marriage. Her parents were dead set against Carolina moving away, which was ironic, considering how much they'd always complained about how she did her job, accusing her of wasting too much time gabbing with customers who didn't want or need her advice, instead of just serving them. Yet they'd done everything in their power to make sure she never left.

It was their fault if she was born with a short leg, and their fault they never sought medical attention to fix it. To them, it was a perfectly good leg to stand on all day behind the counter of their crappy bar. Even worse, they almost seemed pleased about her disability, and were quick to use it against her any time she dared to share her latest adolescent dream about doing something exciting with her life, something that would give her the power to make the world beyond Grislengo Lombardo a safer place, like joining the police force or, better yet, enlisting in the carabinieri (now that they let women in), or maybe even become a helicopter pilot, which would allow her to save people's lives while sitting down.

Anyway, that was just to say that her parents had done absolutely nothing to support any dream of hers that went beyond introducing a new line of sandwiches. She'd stopped counting how many times they'd told her, after she broke the news about their plans, that she was crazy, idiotic, delusional; that they had no intention of investing in her wild scheme; that she could forget about coming back to work for them when she and Giac ran back down to Lombardy, up to their eyeballs in debt, before most people even had the time to notice they were gone (which wasn't exactly a kind thing to say to your own daughter). Luckily, Giac had always been a headstrong man, the quiet but defiant type, and the more her parents undermined her confidence, the more he bolstered it. He'd been a ready and willing accomplice, eager to take a chance, looking for a dream to latch onto, and had made her dream his, theirs.

So it also made her a little sad to feel relieved that Giac, who was acting super grumpy lately, wouldn't be back to eat any of the fantastic food she was making her guests for lunch. She hardly saw him at all these days because of that project he was working on, way up in the most remote corner of their land where he pastured the goats in summer. He didn't share the details of what the project was all about, just that he couldn't afford to waste time running back and forth just to eat. Carolina, who still made an effort to at least *act* interested in what he was doing (unlike him) had suggested tagging along one day to see what he'd accomplished, but Giac said to leave it to him, that she had enough to do as is.

Boy, things had changed a lot since their early days at the Renovatus when they couldn't stand to be apart for more than a couple of hours, and Giac couldn't keep his hands off her! The children would be at school all day, and if the weather was decent she and Giac would take their break by the little pond they'd come across after chopping down a swath of reeds, knowing a water source had to be there somewhere. Discovering that it was spring-fed had excited them beyond belief, and just sitting there was enough to replenish their sometimes flagging energy and optimism, which was why they'd called it the miracle pond. There was an old fallen trunk to sit on, and Giac would slice up some salami with his pocketknife while she broke open a crusty loaf of bread with her bare hands, and they'd lop off chunks of cheese and sometimes sip on a glass of wine, while their conversation flowed like a rushing river after a rainstorm. In those days, they couldn't talk fast enough to squeeze in everything they had to say about the projects they were working on, individually or together. They always cheered each other on, complimenting one another on their progress, and congratulating themselves on making the best decision of their lives. Sometimes they even snuck in a quick nap with the benefits they couldn't enjoy at night, because by evening they were always dead tired and more likely to get into a fight about one thing or another, sometimes it was the kids, but mostly it was about the money, because Giac did the bookkeeping after dinner. Everything seemed more beautiful and doable during the day, and sometimes they even made love right there, out in the open, by the miracle pond. If it was warm enough they might take their clothes off and splash each other with that nice fresh water first, but even when they were dirty and sweaty, they were so into each other back then that neither one of them cared.

Whether or not Giac missed those days she couldn't say, because he never said much about anything anymore, but what she could say for sure was that he'd be missing a fabulous lunch today, unless of course the rain drove him home early. She'd been hoping the weather would hold at least until dinnertime and had said as much to her guests when they finally got up from the breakfast table, but those clouds ganging up in the sky and that pain throbbing in her hip said otherwise. It sucked that the heat wave would finally break today instead of waiting until Monday, but the weather was something she couldn't do anything about; what she could do was get cooking. She planned to make her guests forget about the bad weather with a lunch so special that they'd be seeing rainbows and hearing birdsong, even if they'd have to eat in the dining room. She'd add some extra touches to make sure it was super cozy, maybe even put out candles if the day got dark, so they could eat and drink to their hearts' content and get in the mood for one of those naps with benefits. Except of course for Plain Jane Josephine (these nicknames just kept coming to her!), who had no one to get romantic over, but who'd be happy to take a plain nap after all she'd be sure to eat.

Carolina was dying to spend some time doing research in her office, and her new priority was to figure out what the hell had caused Allegra to run out like that earlier, repeating that silly name over and over like a mantra. Could she have received some bad news from India, so horrible that it made her go all pale and shaky? That couldn't be, because Carolina had been standing right there while she was trying to place the call, so she knew for a fact that she didn't even get through to her father or anyone else. Before she could start investigating, though, she still had to dislodge Rino and Adalberto from their table so she could clear the area, then focus on preparing the amazing lunch she'd already described to her guests, who all said they were looking forward to it.

Grabbing an empty tray, she walked out the door in time to see Josephine crossing the lawn with stiff-legged determination, heading straight for the trailhead. When Carolina had asked her earlier how she planned to spend her morning, she'd mentioned possibly taking a hike in the woods, and Carolina had told her that if she did go, to be sure to stop by for a map and some tips. Honestly, she seemed like an obedient kind of lady, so why wouldn't she take the advice of a person who had her well-being at heart? A person who, by the way, had given her word to that same lady's husband that she'd take especially good care of her! At least she could see that she was wearing sensible sneakers, long pants, and that hooded sweatshirt she'd had on earlier, which as awful as it looked, would protect her arms and keep her warm in case it was chilly in the woods.

"Hey, Josephine!" she called, waving her tray in the air.

Josephine glanced in her direction and waved back, but didn't stop.

"Let me get that map for you!"

Josephine waved again but kept on marching.

"Listen, be sure to stick to the trails, okay? Follow the easy one, it's marked with two red balls. Got that?"

Josephine paused to shout back, "What?"

"The trail marker, it's two red balls! And look out for poison ivy! Oh, and the rocks might be slippery! They get mossy in the shade!"

"Got it!" Josephine called.

"And if you come across any snakes, don't worry! Poisonous ones are rare!" There, that should make sure she didn't stray too far.

"Snakes?!"

"And it might actually rain soon, so don't be gone long, okay?" she added.

Josephine stopped for a moment as if rethinking her plan, then resumed her walk. "Okay!"

"Don't forget, lunch is at one o'clock!"

Josephine replied with a thumbs-up. "I can't wait!" she shouted.

Carolina watched the woman as she slowly soldiered up the hill, figuring she'd probably be back within the half-hour, forty-five minutes, tops. Carolina never found the time to hike anymore, but if her memory served her well, the so-called easy trail would start to get pretty steep after the first ten minutes. Easy, in these Ligurian mountains, didn't mean flat.

CHAPTER TWENTY-THREE
Inge

"Isn't there somewhere you'd like to go, Signora?" the skinny woman with the stringy hair suggested from behind the surgical mask Inge had asked her to put on.

"It's *Dottoressa*," Inge said, sitting down in the cute little bamboo armchair by the window. Carolina had pointed out that the piece was part of a sustainable furniture project by some Milanese designer whose name Inge had already forgotten, and it did fit in nicely with the other artistic furnishings Carolina had commissioned, made from reeds that grew right there on the property – if you liked that kind of thing. Inge didn't have time to waste on decorating, and her taste was more classic, so for her own home she preferred solid, serviceable furniture, the kind you could count on for comfort at the end of the day, and that could be relied upon to last a lifetime.

"They say it's going to rain, Signora," the woman said, plugging in the vacuum cleaner.

"I *know* that!" Inge snapped. She wanted to stay put and supervise the cleaning of her room, but she also wanted to get in a hike before lunch. Jumping to her feet, she walked over to the cleaning cart and inspected the supplies. "Ugh! All these so-called natural disinfectants only make a room *smell* clean. Find some bleach and use it wherever you can. Especially in the bathroom."

The woman nodded, then switched on the vacuum. Probably to drown out her voice, Inge thought, only partly annoyed with the woman who didn't even know the proper way to address a guest. The rest of her annoyance was with herself. Here she was, tucked away in this haven of natural beauty, yet she still couldn't relinquish her need to be the boss. The problem was that she'd learned the hard way that if you wanted things done when you wanted them done and how you wanted them done, you had to assert yourself, especially if you were a woman. So what if some of the staff called her a bossy bitch behind her back? What mattered was how they acted in front of her. With respect and obedience. That was what mattered.

"And leave the windows open!" Inge called to the maid over the noise of the vacuum cleaner, gesturing to make sure she understood. After lacing up her hiking boots, she grabbed the backpack branded with the logo of the pharmaceutical company that had sponsored last year's conference on endometriosis, then marched out the door of her bungalow, across the lawn, and past the table where Rino was still talking the ear off the resort's most famous guest. Inge wouldn't have minded getting to know this Adalberto Albertis a little better over breakfast, if only out of curiosity; she didn't have the opportunity to meet popular radio-star speaker-authors every day, especially such attractive ones, but no, the guy had to ruin things by asking Rino about his business, and of course Rino had latched onto him like Velcro to felt. From what she gathered about his stories or novellas or whatever he sold them as, Inge was quite certain they were appalling, and that their author was basically a fraud. But she had to give him credit, he was slick enough to be successful at what he did, and charming enough, between his good looks and trained speaking voice, to make even Inge warm up to him. That kind of appeal was superficial though, and only lasted as long as you were in his presence, or naive enough to fall for it, like the man's girlfriend or muse or guru, or whatever she was.

Even if Allegra hadn't introduced herself as a yoga teacher at breakfast, hinting that Inge might join her for a lesson later, she'd already guessed her so-called profession by the fluidity in her barefoot step, calm demeanor, and unstructured clothes. Inge had tried yoga – who hadn't, at some point? – but quite frankly, taking classes on posture and breathing and meditating was pointless for a woman like herself, who could spend the day climbing a mountain and still have oxygen to spare before relaxing at the summit, where she was perfectly capable of meditating on the marvels of nature without any outside guidance. Inge didn't disapprove of yoga per se, but so many of those so-called yogis were big fakes who wouldn't know spirituality if it clobbered them over the heads they stood on, when they weren't sipping smoothies or shopping at Whole Foods or color-coordinating their fashionable little outfits, a single one of which cost more than it would to feed an entire family in Calcutta for a month. At the other end of the spectrum were the misfits, those unbalanced women with their unkempt hair and fading tattoos, who suffered from anxiety, depression, failed relationships, and so forth, who used yoga as a crutch instead of falling back on a real religion or the old standbys of alcohol or drugs.

Inge judged Allegra to be a member of the misfit category, yet with some qualities that could conceivably attract a guy like the Albertis man. Maybe because he saw her as a project to fix that complemented his pseudo-therapist role, maybe because he saw her as an artistic type that suited his literary persona. In addition, Allegra did project a mix of childlike vulnerability and unaffected femininity which some men found irresistible. Thin as a wisp, she had fine bones that looked like they could snap as easily as twigs, and an oddly angular face, with chiseled cheekbones and a pointed chin. Inge had noticed how her innocent, round eyes observed the others feasting on croissants and cakes and eggs and cheese, as she breakfasted on goat milk yogurt with honey, and not a word came from her heart-shaped mouth during Adalberto and Rino's animated conversation. Her features certainly weren't practiced in the art of deceit; the poor thing looked, well, honest, was the word that came to mind. If it wasn't for her flaming head of curls, she was the type of woman that other women wouldn't even notice, let alone perceive as competition.

Inge waved at the men, indicating she was headed for the woods, but she didn't see any point in stopping to ask her husband again if he wanted to join her, since he'd already declined her perfunctory invitation, and since he'd never enjoyed hiking to start with. Rino's playground of choice had always been the water, whether it be sailing with Carl or cruising in his speedboat. Inge smiled to herself, recalling how silly they'd been at the beginning of their relationship, pretending to share one another's interests. Inge had subjected Rino to some rather demanding Alpine hikes, outings which he declared to be, between all his huffing and puffing, *fantastic!, amazing!, spectacular!,* then limping off at the end of the day to the bathroom, where he could pop his blisters in private. Inge had done her part, too, faking a love for the water long enough to participate in a few dreadful lake cruises, during which she pretended to look for fish over the side of the boat whenever she needed to vomit. Once they were married, the faking – at least over the little things – quickly faded.

CHAPTER TWENTY-FOUR
Carolina

By now Carolina knew that there was always a personal price to pay when you took other people's problems to heart the way she did, and it was her nagging worry about Allegra (Giac would call it *obsessing*, he was always accusing her of that), that pushed her to chop the vegetables faster and faster until the blade was moving up and down in a blur of shiny steel that sent bits of onions and carrots flying, but it wasn't until she was halfway through the celery stalks that the tip of her left thumb ended up in the wrong place at the wrong time. Mind you, Carolina was no amateur when it came to handling sharp knives (if anything, she was more prone to burns than cuts), but all it took was a moment's distraction and there you were, bleeding like a stuck pig all over your cutting board. The nick was nasty, dammit, and the bandage kept getting soaked, which meant she had to keep dropping everything to put on a fresh one. As anyone who spent any amount of time in the kitchen would understand (if anyone ever tried to understand *her*), an injured thumb is a massive pain in the you-know-what when you're trying to cook, especially if you were already under as much pressure as she was! But Carolina was a pro, and she managed to get the diced vegetables into the pot to sauté together with some garlic and red wine before adding the tomato paste and a bouquet of handpicked herbs, then the boar meat which she'd minced after marinating it overnight (to tame the wild flavor), and, finally, the hot vegetable broth, and now the sauce was simmering on the stove (freshly ground pepper and a grating of bitter chocolate, her secret ingredient, would be added later), already filling the kitchen with an incredibly enticing aroma that would make her guests' mouths water the minute they set foot in the restaurant. Anyone who wasn't into meat, like Allegra, could have the homemade ravioli (Carolina still had to prepare the pasta dough!) dressed with olive oil, fresh sage, toasted pine nuts, and parmesan, but honestly, this smell could make even hardcore vegetarians see things from another point of view, especially if they were hidden away up here, far from prying eyes, with no one to impress with their virtue. In the meantime, Carolina finally found a finger rubber to slip on over her injured thumb so she could proceed with the *crema pasticcera*, without running the risk of polluting its creamy white pureness with so much as a drop of crimson.

What it boiled down to was that thinking about Allegra made her heart race and her hands shake, and those symptoms, that intuition that she could feel in the very marrow of her bones, were clearly calling her to fulfill another duty, above and beyond that of chef (call it a Divine Duty, if you must!), to find out what was upsetting her, then force Allegra to face it and resolve it. Normally, she would focus her talents on the problems of her paying guests only, but she and Allegra went back a long way. Sure, they hardly ever saw each other, which, not to point any fingers, was totally Allegra's fault, seeing how she was free as a bird and had a standing invitation to come visit (no yoga strings attached!), but no, she was too busy boosting the ego of her Adonis Ada to worry about nurturing a longstanding friendship. It went without saying that with all Carolina's responsibilities, if Allegra ever insisted that she go visit her in Dolceacqua (like she'd insisted earlier about having her sit down for a cup of coffee), Carolina would have to refuse, but at least she'd have the satisfaction of saying no. Of course, in order for that to happen, Allegra would first have to invite her, which she never did. That was okay, too, Carolina was used to being on the giving end of relationships and expecting nothing in return, but could somebody please tell her why people were always so disappointing? And why no one ever gave *her* feelings a second thought? Or even a first one? Take for instance all those things that were suddenly coming out, all those "details" that Allegra had "forgotten" to disclose, like the not-so-minor fact of her mother *dying* and her father moving to freaking *India*. You'd think a *friend* might tell you those things, but no, she had to learn about them at the same time as a woman they hardly knew! Well, Carolina would find more out about Plain Jane Josephine soon, but in the meantime, if that was the way it was, so be it, Carolina couldn't hold grudges against everyone who let her down or she'd be the Queen of Grudges instead of the Goddess of Goodness. She'd chalk up this latest "oversight" to Allegra's general weirdness, and rise above her petty behavior. And to prove just how superior she was, she'd do everything in her power to help her friend.

Meanwhile, the name Gisella Giostra was spinning around in Carolina's head like the pastry cream she stirred constantly over a low flame to avoid lumping as it came to a slow boil. Once the cooked cream cooled, she'd use it to fill the individual hazelnut tortes (at least she'd baked those before taking a slice out of her thumb!), which she would garnish, just before serving, with a dollop of unsweetened hand-whipped cream and one perfect *marron glacé* (not those broken bits of sugared chestnuts you could buy in bulk). This sumptuous dessert was her way of rendering homage to the approaching autumn, and although it may be on the rich side, some days simply called for a little sinful indulgence, did they not?

Promising herself it would be her last cup (her shakes were getting worse, and no wonder, with all the stress of having so much to do and no one to help her!), Carolina pressed a sheet of plastic wrap over the hot custard, then brewed herself a pot of coffee in the old Bialetti she kept for her personal use. The coffee was still bubbling up when she grabbed the pot, splashed a dose into a little cup, and downed it in a few scalding sips before ducking into her tiny office, where that indispensable tool of investigation, her computer, was up and running. Shaking out her hands to limber up her fingers, she took a deep breath, then began with a classic Google search, typing the name Gisella Giostra (an easy name to remember because of its silly sound *and* double initials), in the search bar. As expected, there were only a couple of matches that combined both names, then lots of women named Gisella something-or-other, followed by a bunch of results relating to merry-go-rounds and carousels and all kinds of spinning objects, which fit in with the definition of the word *giostra* in Italian.

It only took a minute or two for Carolina to hone in on the only viable candidate, a young woman who'd published some articles on tattoo removal, who turned out to be a dermatologist with a practice in Savona, which was slightly disappointing, not to mention a little boring. There was a LinkedIn profile on her too, but reading about a person 's education and professional background was even more tedious, so she 'd save that as a last resort and head over to Facebook. She found only one Gisella Giostra there, but one was all she needed, especially since this was undoubtedly the same dermatologist. Her feed was loaded with public posts and photos, but those were pretty boring, too, with all those links to articles on psoriasis and acne, eczema and herpes (complete with yukky images), and a series of disastrous tattoo stories, none of which were very helpful in connecting the doctor with Allegra. Gisella clearly wanted to keep this page professional, fair enough, but with 3,253 friends to her name, she couldn't be *that* selective and must have posted some more useful stuff just for them. After shooting off a friend request, Carolina giggled to herself, thinking that there was more than one way to skin a skin doctor, especially a young one that was so attractive and socially active. Grabbing her phone, she logged into Instagram with one of the fake usernames she'd created for investigative purposes.

As it turned out, our Gisella was way more into Instagram, where she had 50,999 followers – make that an even 51k with Carolina. The dermatologist, her newest follower noted, was quite photogenic and had such a striking Instagram presence that she could well be on her way to becoming some sort of skin care influencer. In addition to flattering photos of her stunning self in stunning settings, there were images of many other attractive people sporting tattoos, not the botched jobs Gisella cautioned against on Facebook, but some very classy stuff – if you liked tattoos, which Carolina didn't. She was several rows of images down the feed when she spotted the two necks, side by side, and instantly got that telltale feeling on the sole of her right foot, a tingling sensation bordering on numbness, like when your foot fell asleep and started to wake up. The doctors called it neuropathy, but she knew it was a sign of telepathy, tipping her off that she was close to making a discovery. Holding her breath, she clicked on the thumbnail to enlarge the neck image. Yes! Dr. Giostra was seen from the back, looking over her bare shoulder, her long hair brushed to the side to reveal a butterfly tattoo at the nape of her swanlike neck, and inside the butterfly's wings, there were some symbols – no wait! they were letters. Yes, two pairs of letters, which appeared to be two Gs coiled around two As. The other neck, clearly a man's, had an identical tattoo at the nape – same butterfly, same letters! Which might have been unremarkable, except for the fact that Carolina had seen that tattoo before. That very morning. On the neck of her celebrity guest with the double initials AA!

Breaking her promise to herself, Carolina hopped to her feet and went to grab another cup of coffee. This assignment might take a while, and she needed to be alert for it.

CHAPTER TWENTY-FIVE
Josephine

It made Josephine feel like a thief to slink off like that, but the last thing she needed right now was to get ensnared in another chat trap with Carolina. She was sorry about Carolina's problems, and Allegra's problems, the same way she was always sorry about Thomas's problems, and Lucia's problems, and her students' problems, and everyone else's problems. But she was here to focus on her own, for God's sake!

It was no use pretending to be a carefree lady of leisure when her whole life risked blowing up in her face, and she was the one holding the grenade. Being alone in her room had led her to a dark place, and when that happened she knew it would take physical activity – meaning something more vigorous than eating – to restore her mental state to a condition in which she could reason clearly and think positive. A solitary walk in the woods would be good for making her take stock of where she was, step by step, and figuring out where to go from there. As long as there weren't any snakes involved. She despised snakes, poisonous or not. She hated worms, too, and grubs and caterpillars and everything else that slithered or crept or crawled. The thought of coming across any of those creatures, or worse, running into any of the wild animals she'd heard during the night, made her regret she hadn't invited Allegra to come along. Having a companion would have made her feel safer, and she was pretty sure the idea would have appealed to Allegra, who could have turned it into some kind of guided walking meditation. But Allegra already had a companion of her own to hike with, and from what Carolina had insisted on confiding to her, Allegra should devote every free minute this weekend to strengthening her bond with the man in her life, not listening to the woes of a complex-riddled, middle-aged frump in the throes of an existential crisis.

She wondered how it was for Allegra, trying to keep up with such a lively, fascinating man like Adalberto, who so obviously thrived on attention, but might possibly come up short in the reliability department. The only experience Josephine really had with men was with Thomas, her personal champion of solidity, selflessness, and sense of duty. Thomas had known her for so long that he could read her thoughts and anticipate her needs before

Josephine herself had the chance to realize them. But what did he think of her as a woman today, provided he even saw her as a woman anymore? Could he really understand where she was coming from, and grasp what she needed at this juncture? Which brought her to Lucia, headstrong, impulsive Lucia, who'd only come into her life a few months ago, instantly turning her world topsy-turvy, making her question the foundations she'd always taken for granted, and desire the rewards she'd always believed were beyond her reach. And now here Josephine was, caught between two continents and two very different kinds of love. The love wasn't a problem for her, she had enough of that for everyone. The problem was the loyalty; that did not fall under the category of things you could divide and multiply. Sooner or later a choice would have to be made, and she would have to be the one to make it before someone else did that for her. Choose it or lose it, that was the deal.

Meanwhile, it was a good thing she had all that caffeine stoking her step because this trail was way steeper than she'd expected. And she was already in a sweat, between all those calories burning away inside her, and the hoodie she'd put on at the last minute out of some need for privacy, or protection, or both. She could understand why her teenage students back home hid under those hoods, it was like living in your own little cocoon. What she didn't understand was why the heck she'd put on these new jeans instead of her sweatpants, or why she'd bought the stupid jeans in the first place, when she already owned a perfectly good pair. The denim was so stiff she could hardly bend her knees, and the waistband was cutting into her stomach. That was what she got for scavenging the men's department of an unfashionable clothing store in Rome for the sturdy kind of jeans that cost half as much as the kind that were already half worn out and sometimes even had holes in the knees. Once she broke these in, though, they'd last her a good ten years. As long as she kept her weight down, which she would. She was sure of it, and she was starting right now, with this hike. In the meantime, she'd unbutton the top button. Or maybe the top two. And maybe she'd take off that sweatshirt now, before she passed out.

Stopping for a minute was actually a good idea because she hadn't really taken the time to notice the changes around her as she left the open meadow behind and entered the thick of the woods. The air was different here, a little cooler but more humid and musty smelling, probably on account of the dead leaves that had already fallen to the ground, exhausted by the hot, dry summer. Looking up, she could hardly see the sky because of the canopy of tall trees. Some of them were oaks, even she knew that because their leaves were easy to recognize, and also because there were acorns on the ground, but she didn't know what the other ones were. Looking behind her and around her, she realized that, like the sky, the resort had disappeared from view, too. She knew that her parked Panda, and the bungalow where she'd slept, and the veranda where she'd eaten, and the main lodge and barns and outbuildings were somewhere down there, but suddenly not seeing them made her feel a little disoriented, which she knew was silly, because she was still on the trail with the two red balls, and all she had to do to get back to home base was retrace her steps. Retracing her steps wasn't what she'd come here for, though, was it? What she'd come here for was to find a way forward. Was she or was she not up to the challenge?

Spurred on by her desire to prove something to someone, she pushed ahead, hoping the trail would level out, but it just kept climbing. She probably should have brought some water with her, she thought, but she'd only planned to be gone about an hour, and she didn't like to see herself as one of those American women who sucked on water bottles all day long. They went to the grocery store, they sucked. They went to the gym, they sucked. They went for a walk, they sucked. They sat at their desks, they sucked. Anyway, in a few minutes she was bound to get to the top of something, and then she could at least say she'd made it there, wherever "there" was. It was then that she spotted another trail, off to the left, and at the same time noticed the tree ahead of her, whose trunk was marked with two balls and a triangle. That must indicate a different path that went who knew where, while Carolina had specifically told her to stay on the two-ball path, that she remembered distinctly. She didn't see any markers on the path to her left, but maybe that was because of all the moss covering the rocks, and the vines clinging to the trees. It looked like it went deeper into the woods, but the first part was definitely flatter, then quickly sloped down, probably circling back to the lodge.

Downhill could be good, right, even if it seemed less challenging? What was that aphorism she'd learned in Philosophy 101? Something Kafka had said, about a man being amazed at how easy the road to eternity was, before realizing that the one he was on was going downhill.

CHAPTER TWENTY-SIX
Allegra

Allegra was sitting on a patch of soft grass wrapped in her mother's white shawl, her legs crossed in the lotus position, her purple flip-flops abandoned at the edge of the pond. She loved water: being immersed in it, listening to it, staring at it. When she was restless or in need of direction, she sought out a river or a stream, where the water passed without stopping on its way from one place to another. When she needed to find acceptance, she looked for it at the sea, where the water was pulled toward and then away from the land with implacable repetition, with no say in the matter. This little pond, so still, so limpid, was perfect for introspection. The entire universe seemed to be contained in its quiet body shimmering with the reflections of the sky and the mountains, the trees and the flowers. It was like a mini-world, one that was easier to face, one that saw who she was and mirrored that person back to her. That was why this secret pond was one of her favorite places to come and think in solitude. Hidden by the reeds, she could see no one and be seen by no one, only the bees buzzing and butterflies flitting among the colorful array of blooms, and the birds that swooped in and out for a bath or a drink. Hearing a rustling sound behind her she turned, hoping she'd see a pretty one.

"Ah, there's my beautiful friend!" Carolina called, emerging from the reeds. "By my beautiful miracle pond. I figured you might be here."

"And here I am," Allegra answered, her heart sinking.

"Good choice. I hardly ever have time to sit anywhere, let alone here. This spot sure brings back lots of memories, though. But I don't have time for those, either."

Allegra said nothing.

"Where did Ada go?" Carolina asked, plopping down next to her like a marionette whose strings had suddenly been severed. "I saw him take off with Mr. Felt."

"Yeah," Allegra sighed. "They went for a drive."

"Why are people so restless these days? I thought he was here to chill out, to connect with the Renovatus energy. And with *you*."

"Me too. He said he needed to buy something. And that Rino was itching to take him for a spin in his car. You know how guys are."

"How come you didn't go?"

"Why would I want to go on a drive when I can stay here? Besides, I wanted to be available for yoga."

"You can forget about Josephine. I saw her heading out for a walk. How come you didn't go with her?"

"She didn't ask." Allegra shrugged, trying to keep the disappointment out of her voice.

"Maybe Inge the H – I mean, Inge the doctor will be interested."

"No, I saw her leave a while ago, too."

"Where did *she* go?"

"She was dressed for a serious hike, backpack, walking stick, the whole works."

"Well, they'd better all be back here by one. I've been cooking up a storm! Speaking of which, there's definitely one brewing," Carolina said, glancing up at the sky, before turning to Allegra. "You know, I'm actually glad everyone else is gone. I was hoping to get in a little alone time with you. Between your hot boyfriend and your new girlfriend, you're making me jealous!"

Not knowing quite how to respond, or even wanting to, Allegra didn't.

"Come on now, don't go making that face. I was only joking," Carolina said, giving her a shoulder bump.

"Of course you were."

"But look at me, barging in on you when you were probably in the middle of another meditation session. But really, how many times a day does a person need to meditate, anyway?"

"I wasn't meditating, just thinking. There's a difference."

"I've been thinking too, Allegra. And worrying."

Carolina placed her hand on Allegra's back and began rubbing her spine, but instead of making Allegra relax, it made her shiver. She squirmed out of reach, wondering what the heck was going on with the woman. She'd always been a little too clingy, a little too curious for Allegra's taste, but now she was acting like the old Carolina on steroids. "Is everything okay with you, Carolina?"

"With me? Of course it is, can't you see that? It's you I'm concerned about."

"Me?"

"Yes, you. I'm not blind, and I'm not deaf. I saw how upset you were when you were trying to call your father."

"It's so hard to get through to him at that place. It's frustrating!"

"I can imagine. But I'm not so sure that's what upset you."

Allegra stared at the glassy water, and at their reflections in it. She saw herself with Carolina, and saw herself seeing herself with Carolina.

"Correct me if I'm wrong," Carolina continued, twisting around to make Allegra look at her directly. "But my guess is that it had something to do with a certain *Gisella*."

That *name*! It was lodged in the folds of her brain like a tapeworm, and no amount of meditation had been able to rid her of it.

"I don't know what you're talking about," she said, bending forward to pluck a daisy before she could stop herself. She didn't mean to pick it, she was sorry she had, but there it was, already transitioning from alive to dying to dead, as she twirled it between her thumb and index finger.

"I'm talking about *Gisella Giostra*." Carolina tried to take Allegra's hand, but Allegra was quicker, hiding her own hand with its murdered daisy under her shawl. "The name you kept repeating while you were looking at Ada's phone."

"That name doesn't mean anything, Carolina. Just let it *go*."

"No, I will *not* let it go. I will not sit here and watch one of my very best friends be made a fool of!"

"I appreciate your concern, I really do," Allegra said. She did not appreciate being called a best friend, though, because it wasn't true, and she did not appreciate being called a fool, because she feared it *was* true. "But I think your imagination is getting the better of you."

"I didn't imagine that name, Allegra. And I certainly didn't imagine the effect it had on you," Carolina said. *"Gi-sella Gio-stra! Gi-sella Gio-stra! Gi-sella Gio-stra!"* she taunted in a singsong voice, like a school bully at the playground.

"Stop it! Just *stop* it!" Allegra said, clapping her hands over her ears.

"See what I mean!"

"It's only a name from the past. I just want to *forget* it."

"Only yesterday, today's past was the present."

"I'm not talking about *yesterday* past. I'm talking about the *past* past. As in many *months* ago."

"Look, it's me you're talking to," Carolina cooed. "We used to confide in each other, remember? Why don't you just tell me about this name from the past? Getting it off your chest will help. I promise."

All Allegra wanted was to end this conversation and be left alone. But it was true that hearing the name repeated out loud like that seemed to divest it of its power, even make it sound *ridiculous*. Honestly, what kind of name was Gisella Giostra, anyway? And maybe she *had* let her thoughts run wild and blow things up out of proportion; maybe talking about it would put the situation into perspective, the way hearing the name did. She just had to be cautious, giving Carolina only enough to get her off her back, but no more than that.

"All right, then," she said, hoping she wouldn't regret it. "If it will make you feel better."

"No, it will make *you* feel better. Believe me."

"If you say so. Let's see. Where should I start? Well, you know I've had some experience in music production, right?"

"Yeah, you've had more careers than I have fingers. God knows why you ended up picking the least lucrative."

"I do gain things from what I do, just not much *money*. But that's another story. Anyway, after the big boom in online courses, I decided to launch a series of yoga seminars. People got used to the convenience of working and studying remotely so I thought, why not me? I love being with people, but I also love it when I can stay put in the country without driving all over the place to teach."

"I totally get that! Look at us, living up here. Sure, it's isolated, but we wouldn't trade this place for anything."

"So, about the remote teaching. The only thing that was holding me back was that I had to wait for the phone company to bring high-speed internet to my area. When I finally had access to a decent connection, I hooked up to it right away. In the end, I created a pretty nice set-up, with high-quality audio and video. Who wants to sit through a yoga seminar with garbled voices and frozen images, right?"

"Who wants to sit through a yoga seminar, period? I mean, I liked the exercise part, but talking about that stuff is torture, with all those terms in Sanskrit. I suppose people even had to pay for it?"

"Well, yes. As you know, teaching yoga happens to be my *job*."

"Whatever."

"So, I was all ready to go, but then I had the problem of getting the word out. Adalberto insisted I open a Facebook account in order to advertise, so I did. He even took some nice pictures of me and helped me write some great marketing copy. He lives and breathes that stuff, while I hate it."

"I'm with you on that!" Carolina shook her head. "I only use Facebook when I really *have* to."

"Anyway, Adalberto has always stood behind me and encouraged me, but was never really interested in practicing yoga himself. When I told him about my upcoming session on breathing techniques and he asked me if he could sit in, I was all for it. He'd already written an article years ago, but he was interested in following up with a more in-depth piece about the benefits of controlled breathing. He said he'd even quote me, to give my credentials a boost."

"Speaking of breathing, didn't it bother you to have him breathing down your neck while you worked? I hate it when Giac hangs around in the kitchen while I'm cooking, sticking his fingers into sauces and batters, telling me there's not enough sugar or too much salt."

"No. It made me feel good that he was so interested. His plan was to interview any students who were willing to share their experiences, so I thought that would be stimulating for everyone."

Carolina sighed. "That sounds fantastic, Allegra. But would you get to the *point*, please? You're supposed to be telling me who the hell *Gisella Giostra* is!"

"Would you stop saying that *name*, please? And don't interrupt me again or I won't say another word!" Allegra closed her eyes and took a deep breath, exhaling completely before continuing. "As I was saying, my students began logging into the session and one by one their faces started popping up on my computer screen. First came another teacher I already knew from Pavia, then a guy from Vercelli, then a woman from Asti, and a teacher in training from Novara, and we all said hi and I checked to make sure no one had any technical issues. Adalberto was sitting right next to me so he could introduce himself, too, and everybody seemed eager to be interviewed by him. We were waiting for the one late person to finally log in, and when she did we stopped to greet her too because she was a new student from Savo —"

"From Savona? Don't tell me she was from Savona?"

"Well, yes, how did you —"

"Never mind, go on."

"As I was saying, this last woman, from Savona, she was a doc —"

"She was a doctor, right? What kind of doctor?"

"I told you to stop interrupting me!"

"Just tell me! She was a dermatologist, right?"

"If you already know everything, why do you need *me* to tell *you*?"

"Okay! Okay! Not another word!" Carolina made a pantomime of zipping up her mouth.

"Dermatologist or whatever, it doesn't matter! What matters was that before I could even finish welcoming her, that woman blurted, '*Ada?* What are *you* doing there?' And Adalberto, who's *never* at a loss for words, got all tongue-tied and turned white as a sheet. Then the woman left, just like that. She signed out and disappeared from the screen, never to be seen or heard from since. Meanwhile, Adalberto was on his feet and running up the stairs, mumbling something about a sudden deadline. It was so embarrassing, the way he left me hanging there in front of my students. I wanted to run after him and ask him what the heck it was all about, but all those little faces on my computer screen were staring at me, waiting for me to get the session back on track."

"So Ada and this Gisella already knew each other," Carolina said, chewing on her lower lip. "But how?"

"Adalberto explained it to me later. He said he met her while he was researching something for his column, and they became friends. He doesn't give out advice without consulting professionals, you know. He's not some hack, making up answers as he goes along. That's why people like him so much. That's why they trust him."

"Especially the *women*."

"Well, yes, it *does* happen to be a women's magazine, and women *do* happen to talk more openly about their problems than men, don't they?

Anyway, the subjects that come up in his help column give him insight into the kinds of issues women are dealing with, and that's all material that inspires his feature articles, and what he writes in his feature articles comes in handy for his short stories, and without his short stories he wouldn't have his podcasts."

"Right, so between the column and the articles and the stories and podcasts, he's basically recycling used words and churning them out in a different form."

"Well, they *are* his words. He's free to use them however he wants to," Allegra said. The fact that she agreed with Carolina made her feel a greater duty to defend Adalberto. "He's good at what he does, or he wouldn't be so popular."

"You're trying to sidetrack me, Allegra. Don't do that."

"What do you *want* from me?"

"I want you to *unburden* yourself to a *friend*. I want you to tell me why Ada ran away when he saw Gisella Giostra, and why she deserted your session. I want you to tell me why she's sending him texts now, and why that fact makes you so upset! And I want you to tell me what she wrote!"

"How would *I* know what she wrote? I don't *read* his messages."

"You *don't?* You must be joking." Carolina cackled, as if it really was the funniest thing she'd heard in ages.

"No!" Allegra said. "That would be *awful!* Have you ever heard of such a thing as a right to *privacy?*"

"Yet you already knew that Gisella lived in Savona and that she's a dermatologist. How'd you find that out without doing some snooping of your own, little Miss Marple?"

"Because she provided that information by email when she signed up."

"So *she* was the one stalking *you!*"

"No! She was totally caught off guard when she saw Adalberto next to me."

"So Ada was hiding who *you* were or maybe even the fact that you *existed* from her, then!"

"No! Why would he do that? He just probably never mentioned me to a woman he met through work. There's nothing *strange* about that, is there?"

"Oh, he mentioned you to her all right, you can bet your bloomers. With all the yoga teachers out there, she honed in on *you?* Sorry, but I don't buy that she didn't know who you were. She wanted to check out the competition, see what she was up against!"

"I told you, they were just *friends.*"

"Then why did she disappear when she saw Ada? And why hasn't he introduced you to her yet? Couples share friends, don't they?"

"Not *always.* Not *all* of their friends. And we don't exactly live nearby, so we wouldn't really have had the chance to meet yet. If it happens, it happens."

"So she's just *his* friend. And she keeps texting him. And that bothers you, doesn't it? I saw your face."

Allegra didn't *want* it to bother her, but it did. A *lot*. "Well, a little," she admitted. She hadn't yet had the chance to talk to Adalberto about today's barrage of texts and didn't know if she should, or how she could, without him accusing her of spying. "But I can't tell him not to communicate with his friends, can I? I don't *own* him, do I?"

"Ha! Your words or his?"

Allegra cleared her throat, cringing at how scripted this conversation, and her relationship, sounded. It was time to end this halfhearted heart-to-heart.

"And what if they aren't just friends?"

"Let it drop, Carolina. *Please*."

"What if Ada were to stop off and see his friend Gisella in Savona on his way to your house in Dolceacqua? Would that still be okay with you?"

"Why would he do that?"

"Because they're friends, right? For someone highly motivated to see someone in Savona, it could sort of be considered on the way from Piedmont."

"Adalberto said that they only talk on the phone. And only occasionally."

"And what if Gisella were to stop off to see Ada at that house of his, wherever the heck it is, in Piedmont?"

"Oh, he'd never let her do that. That's his private space, and he doesn't allow *any* outsiders there."

"I see. So what do you think about that tattoo on the back of his neck?"

"The butterfly?" Allegra shot a glance at Carolina, afraid she was finally onto something. "What about it?"

"Take a closer look at it, next time you have the chance. It's not just a butterfly. It's a *code*."

"What are you talking about? What *code*?"

"Two *A*s in one wing and two *G*s in the other, joined by the body of the butterfly. Do you happen to know anyone with those initials?"

"What? No! Now you're *really* imagining things!" Allegra said, clutching her stomach. She shouldn't have drunk so much coffee, it tended to give her spasms lately. And now her heart was racing, too. *AA* and *GG*. Adalberto Albertis and Gisella Giostra. "That tattoo is too tiny for all that. I've been sleeping with it staring me in the face, and I never noticed any initials, so I don't see how you possibly could have!"

"Unlike you, I *notice* things. The tattoo may be small, but that didn't stop me from noticing it when I walked behind him to clear his plate at dinner. Then I got a better look at it again at breakfast when he was moving the table. Then I saw it in a picture. I had to search her feed to find it, but there's a closeup of it on Gisella Giostra's Instagram profile. And she has one just like it. I enlarged the image, and I'm telling you those two have *identical* butterfly tattoos, with *identical* initials, in the *same* place on their necks! If you don't believe me, go on Instagram and see for yourself!"

"I don't do Instagram. And if I did, I wouldn't go snooping around like that."

"Oh, come on! I suppose you never looked at GG's Facebook page, either?"

"No! I only opened that account because of yoga, but I already shut it down."

"But Facebook is an *invaluable* source of *vital* information!"

"I'm not interested in digging around in other people's lives like some *voyeur!*"

"Well, that's your first big mistake if you want to keep your relationships in check! You're lucky to have a friend who cares about you so much. Someone who lives in the *real world* and knows what *real men* are like."

"And that *friend* would be *you*, I suppose?"

"Yes, it would! Friends should be honest and open! I gave up my precious time to learn some very interesting information I feel compelled to share with you right now."

"I don't want any more information, *thank you very much!*"

"Fine! Suit yourself! Just remember, friends like me are hard to find!"

"Thank *God!*" Allegra cried, grabbing her flip-flops as she scrambled to her feet and darted off.

"Be back for lunch!" Carolina shouted. "Don't forget, it's at one!"

But Allegra was already clear of the reeds and running off as fast as her legs could carry her up the hill, past the lodge, across the meadow and into the woods, her purple sandals dangling from one hand, her white shawl trailing from the other.

CHAPTER TWENTY-SEVEN
Inge

Exactly one hour and thirty-five minutes was all it took, meaning she'd shaved a neat twenty minutes off the time indicated at the trailhead. Not bad, but back in her prime Inge would have halved it. The fact that she was in far better shape than most women her age was of meager consolation; she detested the qualifier, and she detested admitting that she was no longer at the top of her physical form. That didn't mean she would admit it to anyone else, of course. She'd endure the stiff legs tomorrow, even look forward to the sore muscles that would prove she'd made them work during the steep uphill push, the same way she was enjoying the sweat beading on her brow, and the T-shirt sticking to her torso right now. If only she were oxygenating her blood with some of that pure, Swiss Alpine air her lungs had grown up on instead of this muggy Mediterranean mush! On the upside, it beat hospital air, and city air, and indoor air of any kind. Apart from catching her breath – not that she was exactly winded – Inge needed to rehydrate, so she allowed herself a pause to grab her water bottle; like her backpack, it too was a pharma freebie. Between sips, she checked her phone for messages but to no great surprise discovered there was no service, which was just fine with her. She'd advised the staff at the clinic that she would be unreachable over the weekend, and had left the number of the Renovatus in case of an emergency. She wasn't worried about Carl, who was spending the weekend at the villa of his best friend's family, in the hills above Bellagio; she and Rino had known the parents, both financial advisors, since their boys had attended the same pricy preschool and become playmates. As for Rino, he was in the good hands of *his* new best friend, Adalberto Albertis. She couldn't understand why her husband had insisted on going for a spin in the Mercedes, though, when Adalberto's SUV was so much more suited to these roads. No, that wasn't quite accurate, she actually *could* understand because, in addition to wanting to impress a man who so thoroughly impressed him, Rino hated not being in control. That made him an unbearable passenger, a fact of which he was well aware, which was why he'd rather risk damaging his precious car again than risk annoying his new idol. As long as her husband came back in good spirits and relaxed enough to hear what she had to say without overreacting, she didn't care who drove which car, or where they went with it.

Returning her water bottle to her backpack and tucking her phone into the pocket of her fluorescent safety vest, Inge shook out her legs, then took a moment to stretch her hamstrings, harboring more than a little resentment that not even here her time was her own, that not even here she was free to keep on hiking until she was adequately exhausted. It was no use pretending that she'd come up here to hike, though, when the real reason was to talk things over with Rino. Thoughts of that unavoidable discussion made her even more reluctant to turn around, but that wouldn't change the fact that she'd have to do just that, and very soon, because Carolina had made it clear to all of them that the midday meal would be served at one o'clock sharp. In a world where luxury was often synonymous with laziness, the woman deserved credit for running a tight ship, and Inge had to respect that. She herself took punctuality seriously, having zero tolerance for open-ended programs or vague commitments, whether it be in one's work or private life. So if her host said lunch was at one, Inge would be showered and seated by one, not one-thirty, or even one-fifteen. Regardless of lunch or marital obligations, she'd need to head back soon anyway, due to the weather. As a serious outdoorswoman, she checked the forecast religiously before setting off on any excursion, and this morning's latest update predicted rain before two. She'd welcome a downpour to clear the heavy air once she was back at the resort with Rino, savoring what Carolina had promised would be a delicious lunch, accompanied by enough wine to loosen her tongue and kick off her dreaded conversation. And even if the rain came a little early, she was, as always, equipped with a waterproof jacket, of the same bright orange as her safety vest.

Glancing at her Swiss Military Chrono watch, a quick calculation told her that if she jogged back down the trail instead of walking, not only would it make her return trek more challenging, but the time saved could be spent on a quick dash up to that clearing she spotted ahead of her to check out the view. There was no way the panorama could compete with the majestic mountain vistas she was used to, but this rugged side of Liguria, hidden from the masses of tourists that clogged its chaotic coast from savvy San Remo to posh Portofino to the cramped Cinque Terre, held a certain appeal for her. She'd always felt a degree of contempt for people who had it too easy, living in mild climates where ripe fruits fell into their laps and abundant crops sprung up from fertile soil. Up here it was different; up here she could perceive the hardship its inhabitants must have endured, trying to eke out a living by shepherding and farming among the rocky mountain valleys, hunting and gathering whatever could be found in the dense forests. Thoughts of that bygone life brought to mind the sacrifices made by her long-dead father, and her father's father, and even further back in time, not only to survive but to provide their children with the opportunity for a better life, generation after generation. As if squeezing her father's hand in a gesture of silent gratitude – the only kind he could ever tolerate – she tightened her grip on the walking stick she'd brought along, a time-worn piece of wood he'd hewn from a branch. Inge had saved his collection of sticks, some with intricately carved handles, and used them on all but her most serious climbs; like her father, they were sturdy and reliable but unbending, and with each shared step they reminded her of the man who had encouraged her to be strong and adventurous, and instilled in her an enduring bond with nature. Was she passing on to Carl any of those precious values she'd grown up with, she wondered? And how about Rino? What would be his legacy to their son, besides his felt business, which he didn't even want? What had the two of them been doing all this time, while Carl was growing up? They'd been good providers, but had they been good parents while they were still in time to make a difference? It was hard to fathom that her little boy was already seventeen years old, soon to be eighteen. She could feel the promise she'd made to his father all those years ago tightening around her neck like a noose, as that day, for so long in the distant future, now approached. Without answering her own questions, she dug her stick into the ground and pushed off, staring down at her hiking boots as they marched briskly ahead until they were forced to a sudden stop, nearly tripping over themselves when they ran into a horse blocking the trail, placidly munching on leaves from a low-hanging bough. The animal was unsaddled, but wore a lead and a brightly striped blanket, the kind you'd see in an exotic location like Nepal, or Mongolia. Both equally surprised, they locked eyes, then the beast snorted and tossed its mane. Parting its hairy lips, it bared its yellow teeth and emitted a whinny that crescendoed into a shrill wail, telling her she wasn't looking at a horse at all, but a mule.

"Jack!" she heard a man shout from a distance. "What the hell's the matter with you?"

Inge froze, uncertain whether to present herself or hide, while instinctively ducking back into the trees for cover.

"What's going on, Jack?" another voice called, this one female. Seconds later, Inge spotted a young woman through the leaves, her shapely hips, crammed into a pair of very tight jeans, swinging as she walked. Inge was relieved that she'd come across a couple rather than a lone man, but caution strongly suggested she remain out of sight. From what she could see, the woman was rather attractive, in a vulgar sort of way, with lots of dark, curly hair that fell past her shoulders. Her skimpy cropped T-shirt, covering her bust while leaving her tummy bare, looked like something she'd outgrown in elementary school.

"*Cattivo*, Jack! *Djale i keq!* You naughty boy, eating leaves! They could be poisonous, you know!" she said, patting the mule on its flank to make it turn around, as Inge crouched low to the ground. "Come back here where we can see you. C'mon, let's go! *Andiamo! Shkojme!*' Inge couldn't tell what language she spoke besides Italian, but Jack the mule understood and obeyed her, backing up a few steps before doing an about-face and exposing its sturdy hindquarters to Inge, as a shirtless guy in jeans also came into view for a second before turning around to walk away with the woman and the mule. Inge could only see the man from behind, which wasn't a bad point of view at all, with those broad shoulders and muscular back, tanned to a deep brown. Inge was craning her neck, hoping to get a better look at both of them as they walked away, when the man suddenly stopped to look around, one hand shielding his eyes like a visor. Inge ducked again, wishing she'd taken the time to shed her bright orange vest.

"The wolves are back, you know," she could hear him saying. "They got at Giovanni 's sheep up in the high pasture yesterday. Killed fifteen of 'em So don't let the dog wander off, and bring him at night, too, when you round up the goats."

"Oh no! You be careful when you're out riding. We don't want any wolves getting at our Jack. Or at our *Jack*!" the girl said, giggling as the mule nudged her bottom with its muzzle. "You two boys follow me, and I'll give you both something sweet."

At our Jack or at our Jack? What did that mean? Inge could have made her getaway at that moment, but instead she found herself transfixed with curiosity as the guy bent over a stone trough and began scooping up water, splashing it onto his chest and face and under his arms, while the woman tied up the mule, then sneaked up on the man from behind. In one swift movement, she pounced on him, dunking his entire head under water, giggling crazily as he yelped then screaming as he filled his cupped hands with water and doused her repeatedly, causing the mule to whinny wildly and a hound on a chain to yelp and howl at them. Inge was fascinated by their playfulness, something that had been missing from her life for a very long time, together with the only man who'd ever inspired it in her. Now was certainly the time to leave, she knew, but found it impossible to budge.

"Jack, no! *Ju lutem*, Jack!" the girl cried, jumping out of range, while the man dashed to the other side of the trough. Now the two of them stood still, eyeing one another to study their next move. At that moment, Inge caught a better view of the man's face, and it was then that it hit her: the second Jack was actually *Giac*! None other than Carolina's Giangiacomo! But who was this foreign girl, where had she come from, and what was this bastard doing up here, screwing around with her like a teenager while his wife singlehandedly ran the resort? Now, even if Inge wanted to walk away, even if her scrupulous respect for privacy demanded it of her, she simply couldn't. After silently slipping off her backpack and vest, she rose slowly to her feet, standing behind a tree she wished was a fat, full fir instead of a tall, skinny beech. From this position, she could spot a small stone hut in the clearing, the sort of shelter once used by shepherds. It was certainly old, but looked freshly plastered, and there were even some potted plants on the windowsill. Then the girl, making her move, caught her attention again as she grabbed a bucket, dipped it into the trough, and managed to throw half of its contents at Giac before he could snatch it away from her and dump the rest on her head. The girl shrieked, the mule screeched, and the dog wailed, which made the girl laugh so hard she finally had to take a break, doubled over and clutching her tummy, to catch her breath. With water dripping from her hair and face and arms, she cried, "You won!" then scampered away into the hut, her braless breasts bouncing under her soaked T-shirt. Giac stood there looking after her for a moment, rubbing his jaw and running his fingers through his soaked hair, then followed. He was about to cross the threshold when Inge's phone blared its ringtone of trumpets playing the "*Sweizerpalm*" – her beloved Swiss anthem!

Inge froze. Giac's head swiveled in her direction while Inge held her breath. But no, maybe he hadn't heard, maybe there was only one thing on his mind, because a second later he disappeared inside the hut. The damn phone wasn't done ringing, though, and it was only because she had nerves of steel that Inge managed to grab the vest she'd dropped on the ground, rip open the Velcro flap, and silence it in a matter of seconds. But by then, Giac was outside again, shotgun in hand.

"Who's out there, Gringo?" he shouted at the hound, howling and lunging as far as his chain would allow, while the girl came running out, pulling on her T-shirt. Now it was too late for Inge to come forward, now the only thing she could do was get the hell out of there before Giac could see her, or worse, take a blind shot at her! In the time it took him to free the dog, she grabbed her vest and backpack from the ground and started running as fast as her legs could carry her. Headlong through the trees she fled, through the thorny underbrush attacking her ankles, through the low branches lashing her face. In her frenzy to escape, she wasn't sure whether she was heading back to the same trail she'd come up on, she just knew she was careening down the hill, skating over twigs and leaves, tripping over rocks and roots, her arms flailing as the vines reached down to grab her and rip her belongings from her hands, while her feet flew so fast it was impossible for the rest of her to keep up with them, impossible to stop them from stumbling over a fallen trunk while her mind raced ahead, trying to remember something about the best way to fall, when she was already somersaulting to the edge of a drop, digging her nails into the dirt, tumbling and rolling and flying until, at last, her body came to a stop and everything went dark.

CHAPTER TWENTY-EIGHT
Carolina

Carolina could never understand why women got all touchy and defensive when you tried to help them. She took no joy in causing Allegra (or anyone else) any pain, but the plain and simple truth was and always would be (and it wasn't just one of those expressions) that the truth sometimes hurt. Wasn't it better for women to know it regardless, rather than to continue living in ignorance, telling themselves the same old stories, repeatedly justifying the very same people who deceived them? The liars and misleaders, the cheats and the cowards who didn't take responsibility for their actions, those were the people who hurt the women they pretended to care about, certainly not her. Her mission was to expose the lies to the light of day, not bury them just to spare someone's fragile feelings. And her greatest satisfaction was seeing guests leave the Renovatus at the end of their stay with a clearer picture of the world they lived in and an honest insight into the people they shared it with. Time was a precious commodity, and we had so little of it, less than we realized until it was too late, which was why it was so important that it not be wasted on dead-end relationships or squandered on those who don't deserve us. People might not always thank her right away, but sooner or later most of them came around, and realized she was the true friend they'd always needed but never had, the one person they could count on to confront them with what must be said. And even if they didn't, well, too bad for them. Carolina wasn't in this for glory or for profit. Knowing she'd done the right thing by opening their unseeing eyes and prodding their power to reason was reward enough for her. She'd be their best friend, whether they liked it or not.

As for Absent Allegra, she was sorry she'd reacted so badly, turning against her like that, instead of thanking her for shedding light on a shady situation. She'd recover after a walk in the woods, where she could whimper and wail, or gnash her teeth, or pull out her kinky red hair or whatever she did when she lowered herself to the level of real human beings with real emotions, instead of acting all spiritual and detached and in control. Not that there were any excuses for Ada's disgusting behavior, but Carolina could see how maybe an exuberant man like him would find her a little too, well, what was the word she was looking for here? Calm? Dispassionate? Maybe even, let's admit it, annoying? Maybe their relationship had worked so far because her virtues balanced out his faults (and vice versa), but in cases where two people were so different, sooner or later what seemed like complementary traits revealed themselves to be incompatible traits. People (read: MEN) want what they want, and they want to be with people who want the same things, and above all, who want to give them what they want. And, not to speak ill of a good friend like Allegra, but sometimes those overly vegetarian types like her (not to mention the vegans), seemed bloodless themselves, especially the pale, skinny ones, with no extra meat on their brittle bones, no spare padding to soften their falls, no womanly flesh for a man to sink his hands into. Crunchy, outdoorsy women clad in eco-friendly garb, from their sustainable woolen shawls down to their organic cotton undies and clunky ergonomic shoes, might attract a certain type of man going through a vulnerable stage of life, but let's face it, most guys would rather be pinned down by a pair of stilettos than clobbered by clogs.

One thing at a time, though. For now, it was best to let Allegra digest the tattoo story before spoon-feeding her any other disturbing facts. Thanks to Gisella's generous sharing of information and Carolina's skill in finding and interpreting it, Allegra now had solid proof of certain peculiar goings-on to back her up when she confronted Ada about today's text messages. If she was too wimpy to lean on him and make him admit that he and that woman were more than pen pals, Carolina would. Unpleasant and thankless a task as that may be, she'd gladly undertake it for a person as dear to her as Allegra.

One brief weekend wasn't much time to straighten out the lives people spent years messing up, so Carolina had her work cut out for her. Now that she had prepared Allegra's consciousness for the next level of awakening, she could put her friend's situation on hold and dedicate her efforts to someone else. Her curiosity had been instantly piqued by her first guest ever to present herself under an alias, the so-called Josephine Fortunata, or, as she turned out to be, Mrs. Marisa Tomas. But since she'd left her husband Thomas Tomas behind (why this convergence of so many people with double initials? was it a sign? of what?), and since he'd been so concerned about reserving her accommodations and prepaying her stay so she would have nothing to worry about during her "time-out," Josephine had probably already discovered that the kind and generous two-timing-Tommy had been a naughty boy, which would explain things like that pensive look that kept clouding her clear blue eyes, and that unwise impulse to run off into the woods alone, not to mention relegating her wedding band to purgatory status by transferring it to her other hand. Again, like with Ada vis à vis Allegra, Carolina tried to be fair in her assessments and avoid passing excessively harsh judgment on men (even though they usually deserved it), but she could maybe see this man's point if he was momentarily distracted by someone with a little more, let's say, feminine flair than Josephine, who, God love her, came across as a little butchy. Not the manly, aggressive type of butch, but the more passive, sack-of-potatoes type. Personal impressions aside, Mr. Tomas could very well be repentant for having mistreated such an innocuous, plain woman who would cause him no grief in the wandering wife department, and may be patiently waiting with open arms for her to come around again, so he could slide that wedding band back onto the finger where it belonged.

Of course, it was never as simple as that, a woman didn't get over profound disappointment in her partner or bounce back from a betrayal with a snap of the fingers, especially when she's invested the best years (isn't every year a best year?) of her life in a relationship. But all things considered, Carolina had a hunch that that was what Josephine was bent on doing, and in that case, she'd leave her to her internal struggles and private debates and pseudo-meditations with Allegra or whatever soothed her suffering soul. When Carolina felt the call to intervene, she would, but she'd keep an eye on her in the meantime, well aware that when a woman was pushed to a critical crossroads by the man she loved, reconciliation was not always the road back to happiness. Sometimes the hurt was so deep that the pain kept festering, oozing bitterness. She'd seen many a ruined couple who treated each other with such rancor that witnessing their destructive dynamic made her physically ill. If Carolina's work wasn't characterized by such a subtle, behind-the-scenes type of guidance, she'd be tempted to take the direct approach of one of those brutally blunt (and ridiculously expensive) therapists, and come right out and ask those couples why they insisted on staying together, why they hadn't already left each other last year, or five or ten or fifteen years before. Why they continued throwing their lives away when they could still call it quits before they destroyed what little good remained. So, although she wished Josephine well, it should be remembered that sometimes it was necessary to excise the source of infection before the wound could truly heal. Sometimes more drastic measures were called for, measures like punishment, like revenge, like *get the hell out of my life*. Only then could a person move on, even if it meant doing so alone, and only then could the pain finally subside. And although Carolina 's mission wasn't to assist the men, but to defend the women against the men who said they loved them, men often benefited from her efforts too. That was what happened, and you know why that happened? Because men were rarely the ones to speak from the heart, or to make life-altering decisions. Because for women the letter "c" stood for *courage* and *change*, while for men it stood for *cowardice and convenience* That's why.

Carolina was still sitting by the pond where she'd found Allegra when a plump drop of rain plonked down on her head, derailing her train of thought. She 'd been so engrossed in her reflections, practically in a trance, really, that she hadn't even noticed the sky getting darker. This spot still had the power to make her lose track of time and place, which was why she'd stopped coming here with Giac some time ago, then altogether. Now she did her thinking on the fly, while she was cooking or cleaning or gardening, whenever she could squeeze it in. She wasn't a woman who could afford to just sit there and think or meditate or whatever you called doing nothing, it was all the same to her. Jumping to her feet, she brushed off her bottom, waved goodbye to her dimmed reflection, then retraced her path through the reeds and hurried back to the lodge.

As soon as she entered the dining room, she was hit by the aroma of the boar meat sauce she'd prepared earlier, which triggered a series of boings and grumbles in her stomach. That was a good sign, but also a reminder that she hadn't eaten anything in hours (how could she eat with her stomach all in knots?). For a minute, she just stood there, breathing in the smell as if she could taste it and swallow it and be nourished by it, while at the same time looking over the three tables she'd set up to perfection. She'd never liked tiny tables for two (there was no room to put anything), and since there were so few guests, each of the tables she prepared could have accommodated six. That would also allow people to pull up a chair and converse with the guests at another table if they were so inclined. With her scrupulous attention to detail, it had taken almost an hour of adjusting and tweaking to get it just right, in a way that would ensure privacy but encourage conviviality. The tables were neither too close together, nor too far apart, so people could have private conversations without having to whisper, but still exchange comments with the other guests (to praise the food, for example) without shouting. Her finest Irish linen tablecloths and napkins (natural white) dressed the tables, and she'd chosen handmade stoneware dishes of a different color for each one (green for Inge and Rino, blue for Allegra and Ada, and robin-egg speckle for Josephine). Carolina, meanwhile, would never be far from their sides, the discreet and impartial observer who would not only to serve them, but listen to them, in order to better guide them.

Obviously, Carolina wasn't thrilled about the crappy weather approaching, but she was a pro, and as such she knew how to adapt to what some people might consider adverse circumstances, and how to make them work in her favor. She'd go all out with the stormy Saturday kind of mood, which could either shake things up or tone them down, depending on how people reacted; they could get all romantic and cozy, or go the claustrophobic and grouchy route, that part was up to them. She might even light a little fire in the hearth, but only if the storm cooled things off considerably, because right now just thinking about it made her sweat. For now, the thick, low clouds that had rolled in made the room nice and dark, almost gloomy, but she could work with that. She'd definitely go for candles instead of turning on the lights, which would cast annoying reflections on the veranda doors and spoil the effect of all those dramatic gray tones. You didn't need much light to eat (if you could trust your chef), and if she didn't believe the saying "*l'occhio vuole la sua parte*" (the eye wants its part), she might be tempted to go all the way and try blindfolding her guests during the meal. That would really make them focus on each piece of food they put into their mouths, savor every flavor, make them appreciate, bite by bite, all the work she put into each dish. But her instincts told her that they weren't ready for that yet; they were still too unsettled, too all over the place. Who could say, maybe at dinner?

The thought of dinner jarred her back into action. She'd lost way too much time on creating the perfect ambiance, and now she had to finish up in the kitchen or she'd fall behind schedule for lunch. Luckily, she'd been quick enough to roll out the ravioli dough and fill it before getting involved with Allegra, and now she opened the refrigerator to admire the puffy pasta squares lined up on their trays under a dusting of flour, ready for their scant two minutes in boiling water, but not before everyone finished enjoying their antipasto. With all the time it took to prepare a meal of this quality, Carolina wasn't about to let people just shove it down their throats. She was in charge here, and she'd make sure this was a leisurely lunch, with absolutely no rushing. Still inspecting the contents of the refrigerator, with all the other goodies in the wings waiting for their moment to shine, she paused to take a closer look at her custard cream, jiggling it to test its consistency (was it too firm? she hated it when it was too firm, but not as much as when it fell apart at the touch of a teaspoon, kind of like Allegra at the mention of Gisella).

Finally shutting the refrigerator door, she filled a large aluminum pot with water and heaved it to the stove, but didn't turn it on yet (or should she? sometimes it took forever for the water to boil). Despite not being a meat-eater, she couldn't *not* taste the wild boar sauce. Smacking her lips and rolling her eyes with pleasure, she tasted it again, just to be sure. God, was that good! Divine, really! Perfectly suited to her vocation as an ambassador of authentic, locally sourced cuisine! Then, as both chef and critic, she tasted it one last time. Maybe it was too salty? Not salty enough? Had she made a mistake by throwing in a few extra grains of juniper? Fighting the urge to keep tasting, she slammed the cover on the saucepan, then stomped up the stairs to freshen up before people started arriving. Where the hell were those vagabonds, anyway?

CHAPTER TWENTY-NINE
Allegra

Allegra couldn't stop running, not until she'd left the lodge behind her, her bare feet flying over soft grass and crunchy gravel and rocky dirt until she was well into the woods, but she'd have run over a bed of nails to escape Carolina's persecution. Unlike her spirit, still tender despite all the beatings it had taken, the soles of Allegra's feet were toughened from her lifelong habit of going shoeless. That was why she didn't feel the pain right away, why she didn't even notice her feet were bleeding until she stopped to catch her breath. Spotting a boulder at the side of the trail, she sat down, brushed away the worst of the debris stuck to her cuts, then slipped on the flip-flops she'd been clutching in her hand as she fled.

Why couldn't Carolina just leave her alone? Why did she have to go sticking her nose into things that didn't concern her? Because she'd always been *jealous* of Allegra, that was why. But again, *why*, when Allegra had accomplished so little, possessed so little, and mattered so little to so few people? All she'd ever wanted was a simple life, a conflict-free, positive-minded, honest existence, possibly with a little love thrown in. Was that too much to ask? Couldn't Carolina imagine the tremendous suffering she would cause by revealing that Allegra's partner, the one person she cared for and counted on like no other, was involved in a secret relationship with another woman? If only she knew how much *work* it took for Allegra to accept his friendship with that woman, how much *self-control* it required of her, if not to convince herself it didn't matter, to at least pretend. Because the truth was that Adalberto had indeed "slipped up," as he put it, with that Gisella. Allegra had picked up on that right away, the very moment she saw his reaction to the woman's appearance on her computer screen. But at least he'd respected Allegra enough to admit it when she pressed him for an explanation. He also *swore* it hadn't meant anything to him – but who could know how much it meant to that woman? And *hello!* in case anyone was interested, it sure meant an *awful* lot to *Allegra*.

She'd been wise to feed Carolina only part of the story, but now she regretted talking to her at all and could kick herself for running away like a bullied child instead of standing her ground like a grown woman. But who was she trying to kid? She sucked at standing her ground, especially with someone like Carolina, who acted like she genuinely cared, and maybe even did care, but took it too far with that way she got in your face and didn't know when to get out of it. Allegra let out a heavy sigh, trying to figure out how to make what she'd been told by Carolina fit in with what she'd been told by Adalberto, and knowing she couldn't go back until she did. Standing up, she tied her shawl around her waist and began climbing the trail marked with two red balls and a triangle, not because she remembered where it went, but because when you needed direction, any symbol was better than no symbol.

Speaking of symbols, Carolina's theory was absurd, far-fetched, ridiculous! Butterflies were probably one of the most common tattoos out there, and that whole thing about the initials was as crazy as Carolina was for dreaming it up. Besides, now that she stopped to think about it, Adalberto 's fling was definitely already a thing of the past by the time that little butterfly turned up on the nape of his neck. At least that was what he said, and Allegra either believed him or didn't believe him, and she'd decided long ago that if she wanted to stay with him, which she did, she had no choice but to believe him, because what was a relationship without trust? Oh, it wavered, and it shook, but so far she'd been able to prop it up with the sheer power of her will. Then along came Carolina, who didn't think twice about taking a sledgehammer to that trust, and now until Adalberto explained what was really behind that tattoo he'd suddenly decided to get in one of the most painful spots on the human body, she'd be plagued with doubts, and what Allegra did *not* need in her life was more doubts.

Just thinking about that stupid tattoo made her charge up the hill faster, her heart pounding, her legs pumping, her toes clutching her flip-flops. Carolina couldn't possibly know it, but Allegra's reaction to Adalberto's tattoo went way deeper than jealousy. It had its roots in her childhood, in her vivid memories of her father and the creepy old tattoo artist he loved to visit in Marseille. She could still see the skinny man hunched over Diego, cigarette dangling from the corner of his cracked lips, the ashes falling wherever they would, as he inked one of the few remaining patches of skin with yet another Sanskrit symbol while Allegra looked on, her red eyes stinging and her crinkled nose itching from the smoke. To make matters worse, every few visits her father convinced her mother to get another tattoo or two. It was another one of those things that made Allegra feel excluded, as if they belonged to some secret society of which she would never be a member. Her parents didn't bother to ask her if she minded those tattoos, which she did, though they did say she could get one too, if she wanted, which she didn't. It seemed an exaggeration to even refer to them as parents when they were simply two people who happened to have a third little person following them around, who didn't even call them *papa* and *maman* but Diego and Josephine.

They adopted the attitude that kids had the right to decide things for themselves, so they never made her do anything, like eat, or wash up, or sleep, or go to school. Though they never came out and said it, Allegra could tell by the look on their faces that her wanting to do all those things with regularity disappointed them. But at least they never forced her to get a tattoo.

Allegra suddenly felt tired, too tired to continue climbing a trail to who knew where, one that seemed steeper with every step. She was out of breath, out of energy, out of answers, but she needed to get a grip on herself before she could even consider going back. To do that, she needed to focus on Adalberto and the present, not on her parents and the past. Okay, so it was true that Adalberto had gotten that tattoo without mentioning it to her first, but it was also true that he didn't know the background story, so she couldn't exactly blame him for not imagining how she would react. These days (according to him), everyone had tattoos, and she was probably the only yoga person (whatever that meant), who *didn't* have one. Besides (he said), it wasn't anything obscene or gaudy, just a cute butterfly, in a spot at the nape of his neck where it wouldn't bother anyone, wouldn't even be visible if he let his hair grow a little longer again. His radio audience wouldn't see it, and his readers wouldn't see it, not even he would see it, but to Allegra, that was exactly what made the whole thing pointless, and even more offensive. *She*, the *one* person who was disturbed by it, *saw it*. Every time she massaged the kinks out of his neck with arnica oil, *she saw it*. Every time she curled up against his back in bed, *she saw it*. How could she ever stomach the sight of it now, knowing that if there was any truth to Carolina's absurd allegations, that this Gisella had a twin tattoo? And even worse, *way* worse, was the thought that both *her* initials and *his* initials were permanently etched on each other's necks. Why would a man who clung so fiercely to his freedom, who sometimes accused Allegra of wanting to *own* him just because she wanted to be *with* him more, agree to be *branded* like that? Maybe Allegra had it all wrong when it came to relationships, maybe it was an illusion that she'd learned enough through her past failures to get it right this time. Maybe with Adalberto she should have been more possessive, more present, instead of meditating herself into independence. Maybe she should have spent more time standing up for her needs as a woman and companion, and less time standing on her head. Maybe she should have let her emotions flow as freely as her *prana*, instead of hiding her heart's deepest desires, leaving Adalberto wide open to establish the terms of their relationship.

It was then that Allegra realized she hadn't taken another step, that she was paralyzed in place, her chest straining to contain her sadness, her throat tight with frustration. It struck her that it was suddenly darker in the woods and that there was a faint tapping sound she hadn't heard before. Tilting her head back, she looked up at the small patch of sky visible through the treetops towering over her. It made her dizzy to stand there like that, watching the rain begin to fall, slowly but steadily, its drops landing on her face like pinpricks, teasing out her tears.

"Aaaarrrggh!" she cried to the sky, as her bubble of pain burst. The sky answered with a rumble of thunder, warning her to head back. But she heard something else, a split second later, that told her the opposite. It was the high-pitched scream of a woman, and it came from somewhere deep in the woods.

CHAPTER THIRTY
Josephine

Why the heck couldn't Josephine have stayed in Rome to do her thinking? Why in God's name flee the very place to which people from all over the world flocked for inspiration? Weren't there enough magnificent churches in the Eternal City standing there with open doors, eager to be entered? Didn't each one of them offer endless rows of polished pews dying to be sat in? And armies of saintly statues begging to be prayed to? And batteries of votive candles yearning to be lit? And in between churches to pray for guidance at, weren't there all those cheerful streets pulsing with all those chatty people, and all those bustling cafés with their frothy cappuccinos and flaky *cornetti* and cream-filled *maritozzi*? And all those enticing *rosticcerie* where you could grab freshly fried *mozzarella in carrozza* and *supplì di riso* to munch on? And all those lively *trattorie* where a quick lunch of *spaghetti alla carbonara* or *bucatini all'amatriciana* or a simple plate of *tonnarelli cacio e pepe* could lift your spirits to the heavens and fill your tummy with joy? Surely, all of that God-given goodness could have consoled her as she wrestled with her state of limbo, instead of risking her life in the freaking woods!

"*Oh, sweet Lord!*" she screamed, as a slimy snake slithered across her path. It was the second one she'd seen in the past fifteen minutes, which was two more than she'd seen in the past fifteen years. She knew nothing about snakes, had absolutely no idea how to distinguish the poisonous from the innocuous, and had no desire to further her knowledge out here, all alone, with no way to call for help if she got bit. Of course she'd brought her phone with her, she wasn't that ill-prepared, but a machete would have been more useful, considering the only coverage available was from the vegetation, which was frighteningly dense at this point, with all those thorny creepers sticking to her sleeves and pawing at her pants. She hadn't seen any of those red balls or triangles in a while, but since she hadn't veered off her chosen course, well, except for back at that fork, they must be buried by the undergrowth, together with who knew how many more snakes and other creepy crawly creatures. She just hoped she wouldn't run into anything bigger, none of those animals on the prowl she'd heard grunting and howling in the middle of the night. When she thought of those, which was more often than she wanted to, in fact practically constantly, she told herself she should turn around, but then she scolded herself for thinking that, because that was exactly what she *shouldn't* do, because this hike in the woods was turning out to be a trial, a test, a perfect example of what it meant to make a choice and stick with it, whatever the consequences.

Besides, the farther down into the woods she went, the less the idea of clawing her way back up to the main trail appealed to her. She'd figured that the downhill path would be easier, but this seemed more like the path to hell. Which, at this point, wasn't even a path at all. It was steep as heck, treacherous, really, and slippery too, and it was all she could do to just stay on her feet. That was why she had to keep calm and remember that she'd be out of the woods and sitting down to a delicious lunch before she knew it. She'd probably feel so stupid for even thinking she could have been lost, while in reality she was so close to the lodge, that everyone would get a good laugh out of it, she could see herself telling the story now, leaving out the part where she started to panic. Let's face it, she was a city person, and to be even more specific, she was an *indoor* city person, and that person swore that this hike would be her last of the weekend, maybe even her last *ever*, period. The trick was to stay motivated, and to do that she needed to focus on her most immediate goal, which meant thinking about something she'd already been thinking about pretty much since breakfast, which was the lunch menu. She did have a couple of snacks with her, but what if the smell of peanuts attracted the boars? Besides, she wanted to save her appetite for those handmade ravioli Carolina had described in great detail that morning, before reminding her to show up nice and hungry at one o'clock sharp. *Pfft*, no problem there! Josephine was already starving. Carolina evidently took great pride in her ravioli and liked everyone to know how much work went into them, starting with the selection of sixteen secret herbs for the filling, without revealing what they were of course, or they wouldn't be secret. Anyway, she either grew those herbs herself or picked them in the wild, and then she did whatever you were supposed to do with sixteen wild and/or domestic herbs, then blended in the rest of the ingredients, including her own eggs and ricotta, those weren't secret. You could either have the ravioli with meat sauce or drizzled with olive oil and seasoned with chopped fresh sage, toasted pine nuts, and topped off with grated parmesan. The meat sauce must be very tasty, seeing as it was made with wild boar, but Carolina said you could better appreciate the subtlety of the herb stuffing with the simpler dressing, and Josephine tended to agree. Which was why she thought maybe she'd ask for two tastes, not full portions of course, that would be overdoing it, just one little plate of ravioli with the sage and olive oil dressing, and one little plate with the meat sauce, in order to compare the two. If for once she was offered an opportunity to *not* decide, why not grab it?

Thinking about food calmed her down a bit, except for the fact that it was making her stomach growl, and of course it couldn't distract her forever, so before long the image of her sitting at the table and digging into a plate or two of pasta was replaced by the image of her hopelessly lost in the woods and becoming herself the meal for some hungry animals. That was silly though, right? There weren't any deadly predators in these parts of Liguria, no wildcats or bears that would jump out and attack her, right? There were boars, though, which might not eat her, unless of course they were as starving as she was, and what's worse, she'd read that wolves were repopulating the Maritime Alps and Apennines, now that there was such an abundance of free pork, which brought her back to the noises she'd heard last night. Distinct, wild animal noises, she was sure of it, even though Carolina had tried to dismiss them. On the positive side, it was broad daylight now, well maybe not so light, but it was definitely daytime, and didn't wild animals do their prowling and preying at night? So even if she heard some strange sounds now, she couldn't allow her imagination to get the better of her, she couldn't let every swooshing branch or snapping twig send her into a panic, could she? The only thing to do was to push on with determination before it really started raining because those few drops she felt promised there was more on the way.

Still, she might as well admit that she was more than a little worried, she could tell by the way her thoughts rambled on and her eyes darted around and her skin crawled and her spine tingled and her heart thumped at every sound. Like now, for example, what was that? She was making so much noise herself that she had to stop in order to listen. No, the rustling definitely wasn't coming from her, because she wasn't moving at all now. In fact, she was as immobile as one of those saint statues she would go light a whole row of candles under if she ever got out of here alive. And that heavy breathing wasn't hers, either, because now she was so scared she couldn't breathe at all. And there was some grunting and snorting going on too, off to her left, and what was worse, the breathing and snorting and rustling were getting closer. Not knowing if it was the *right* thing to do, but knowing it was the *only* thing she *could* do if she didn't want to find herself face to face with a wild boar, which she definitely, absolutely, one hundred percent *did not want to do*, Josephine charged into the brush, her chubby legs churning as fast as her stiff jeans would let them, her bare hands wrestling with the prickles that raked her face and jabbed at her eyes. She was panting and boy, oh boy, was she sweating, but she wouldn't stop, no sir, no stopping allowed, but those damn brambles were grabbing at her viciously, wrapping themselves around her, sticking their nasty thorns into the thick cotton weave of her sweatshirt to pin her down. Not being able to move *really* made her panic, so she did the only thing she could do, which was to wriggle out of the ensnared sweatshirt, even if it broke her heart to leave it behind, and get the heck out of there. Breaking free, she trudged on as fast as possible, shielding her face from the thorns with her bare arms, until another, even more terrifying sound made her stop dead in her tracks.

"*Aaawwwww!*" The desperate cry sounded like a human in horrible agony, the kind that accompanies the throes of birth – or death. Josephine's nerves were buzzing with panic, every hair on her body stood on end. Frozen in place, she looked up, telling herself she'd see a hawk or a buzzard, well maybe Italy didn't have buzzards, she was no expert, but at least a crow or some big bird to pin the screech on. "*Aaawwwww!*" came another scream. And no, it wasn't coming from the sky, but from somewhere behind her, and she could swear it came from a woman. Was she being attacked by some beast? Should she turn around and see? Josephine had no desire to die a martyr, but neither could she let a woman get mauled to death while she ran away to save her own hide. She hadn't done that in Buffalo when she nabbed that armed man trying to rob an old lady, so why should she be so scared now? If only she could stop shaking and think straight. If only God, or someone, anyone, would tell her what to do! Just this once, for *Chrissake!*

"*Eeehhh!*" Another shrill scream made her blood run cold, and she had no doubt that this one came from a human, a female human, except that it came from the opposite direction, from ahead of her, and sounded much closer. Had she stumbled upon an entire herd of killer hogs, lying in wait for hapless hikers? Was she being sniffed out and stalked even as she stood there, as frightened as a doe caught in a car's headlights? Had she chosen *this* path because it was her destiny to *die* here?

"*Aaayyyy!*" the closer voice cried.

Josephine opened her mouth to respond, but her throat was in a vice, and all that came out was a gurgling sound, as if she were being strangled. It was then that she heard Allegra's voice in her head, calmly instructing her to just breathe in and out of her nose, in and out, in and out, then to fill her lungs completely with one long breath and hold the air in until she couldn't hold it a second longer. With her chest fully expanded, she imagined grabbing her lurching heart with both hands and pushing it back into its proper place. She imagined the vital force of her breath burning in her lungs, she imagined channeling the compressed air into her voice and letting it fly into the woods.

"*WHO'S THERE?!*" she screamed, her body shaking with fear, a surge of adrenalin forcing her to charge ahead, ready to do what she must do to save a fellow human, and herself, from danger, even death!

"*Aiutoooo!*" the voice called. "*Heeeelp!*"

"*Hang on!*" Josephine cried. "*I'm coming!*" Storming through the bush like a commando in the jungle, she tore through the vegetation, bare-armed and bare-handed.

"*Down here!*" the woman cried, already sounding closer. "*Hurryyyy!*"

That urgent plea for help made Josephine push through another snarly mass of creepers at turbo speed until she suddenly found herself in a clearing, which would have been a huge relief, except for the fact that this clearing was *too* clear. Luckily, her hands were quicker than her head and instinctively latched onto a bough a split second before her mind could process what her eyes saw – and didn't see. Her arms stretched above her, her legs dangling below her, Josephine was hanging over the edge of a precipice. Pedaling her feet frantically, the tips of her sneakers miraculously made contact with a rock just behind her, so that now her not-so-supple body was stretched, from fingers to toes, into an arc. Josephine the Arc, she had time to think, in that weirdly detached way she had of thinking when confronted with the inevitability of something bad that was about to happen, because something *very* bad was *definitely* about to happen since there was no way she could stay in this position and there was no way she could get out of it, except for a way she didn't want to think about.

'I'm down here!' the woman cried.

The last thing Josephine wanted to do was look down there, no, actually that was the *second* last, after not wanting to *fall* down there. She tilted her head toward the voice to see who it belonged to, which was enough to make her body sway, which was enough to make her feet push against the rock, which was enough to dislodge a clod of dirt next to the rock. Horrified, she watched the clod crumble and tumble to the rocky debris at the bottom, which not too long ago must have been part of the hillside. "*Sweet Jesus!*" she cried, shifting her eyes desperately to the sky. So this really *was* it, this was where she was meant to die. Dying while trying to save someone else would be more heroic than the other slow and painful death she'd imagined for herself for so long. But Josephine didn't feel heroic. Nor did she feel ready.

"Call for help!" the woman cried.

"Help! We need help!" Josephine yelled to the sky, before mustering the courage to look down at the woman whose life she wouldn't be able to save. She couldn't see much, except for a blonde head of hair and a body splayed across a pile of rubble. But the hair was all Josephine needed. "Hey! You're the lady from the lodge!"

"Egger is my name! *Doktor* Inge Egger! I'm injured and in pain and lost my phone! You have to call for help!" the woman shouted.

'HELP!!!' Josephine cried.

"Not with your voice! With your phone! Use your damn *phone!*"

"It's in my pocket!" Josephine shouted. Her hands were killing her, her arms were shaking, and her spine was about to snap, but she knew she mustn't move. Every muscle burned with effort, sweat streamed down her face and neck, but even worse, her hands were slipping, losing their grip on her branch, which was the only thing keeping her on this side of dead. It almost made Josephine laugh to picture herself in this situation, and it almost made her cry to think that it could really end this way. And so what if it did? No more decisions to make, no more people to disappoint…

"Scheisse! Merda! Shit! What is it that you don't understand?" the woman hollered. "You need to call a rescue team! *Now!"*

"I can't hang on and call at the same time!"

"Use one arm to hang on and one arm to call!"

"Do I look like Tarzan to you?" Josephine screamed. "Or even Jane?"

"I'm in pain down here!"

Josephine's arms were being wrenched from their sockets, her hands massacred by the branch as they slid, excruciatingly, inexorably, over its rough bark toward its willowy tip, while her legs seemed to be getting shorter with each passing second, putting her foothold on the rock at risk. She was still trying to estimate not how many minutes but how many seconds longer she could resist when she heard the first sickening snap. Funny, she was convinced the bough would be stronger than she was, yet it was breaking first.

"Here I come!" she wailed.

"No! Stay up there! I need help!"

"Heeeelp!" Josephine called, plunging feet first into the pit, wondering how loud a crack her bones would make on impact.

CHAPTER THIRTY-ONE
Inge

"Mein Gott!" Inge exclaimed, staring slack-jawed at the woman who'd crashed to the ground a short distance ahead of her, where she lay flat on her back. After her stint as an ambulance volunteer during medical school – and especially after what had happened to Hans – Inge had come to loathe medical emergencies and kept her involvement in urgent care to a minimum. And now here she was, herself a medical emergency, with at least a fractured tibia and a dislocated shoulder, forced to face another medical emergency! Gritting her teeth to avoid crying out in pain – even if such weakness would be witnessed by no one – Inge dragged herself over the dirt and debris toward the immobile body.

But while the ski-jumping, mountain-climbing veteran Inge had tumbled down a less devastated section of the hill before landing in the pit with an aerial somersault for her grand finale, that hapless woman had taken a direct plunge down from approximately ten meters. She could be dead, or paralyzed, or have suffered brain damage, or internal injuries, in which case there was precious little Inge could do to help. And in any case, there was even less that woman could do to help *her*. Infuriating, that was what it was, to come *this* close to getting rescued, and now instead of being saved she had another person to save!

It mortified her to feel so helpless, wriggling through the muck like a mutilated crayfish, but she'd rise to the occasion and take control, as she was always expected to do, and always did. She was close enough now to verify the slow rising and falling of the woman's chest, so at least she was still breathing. There didn't seem to be any blood pooling around her head, either, which was another positive sign, but it was hard to be sure, when the victim was lying on a mound of dirt. She'd have to check the back of her skull, of course, but first, she'd take her pulse. Placing two fingers on her wrist, Inge glanced down at the sweeping second hand of her Swiss military watch, with a mixture of pride and irritation that the object had survived her disastrous fall unscathed. Reliable, that's what we Swiss are, she thought. Whether we like it or not.

The woman's heart rate was accelerated, if a little weak, which was only to be expected after such a trauma, so Inge decided that the first order of business was to find that phone and call for help, then continue her examination. She'd said it was in her pocket, but which one? The most logical place would be the back pocket of her pants, but fearing a spinal injury, she didn't dare roll her over unless she had to. Patting her front pockets first, she felt promising bulges in both of them. Honestly, though, she couldn't help thinking, what was this woman doing out in the woods, dressed like this? Her bare arms were horribly scratched, and those jeans were way too tight to hike in. So tight, in fact, that it took some effort for Inge to slip her fingers inside the right pocket to pull out what she found there. Great, a packet of salted peanuts. After worming her fingers into the left pocket, she extracted another little box.

"He-he!" the woman giggled, her eyelids fluttering.

"Scheisse!" Inge cried, dropping a package of crushed cookies onto the woman's stomach.

"Yummmm!" she moaned.

"Where's your phone?"

"Hmmm?" The woman's head lolled to one side.

"Your phone. Tell me where it is," Inge ordered. "But don't move."

"Oh, I won't. I *like* it here." The woman looked up at Inge, batting the lashes of her big blue eyes. She must be concussed, but at least she was conscious.

"Can you tell me your name?"

"Am I alive?" the woman whispered. "Or are you an angel?"

"I can confirm that you are alive. But you need to remain perfectly still until I examine you further."

"Are you a doctor-angel?"

"I am a doctor. Period." Despite not having her pocket flashlight which had ended up who knew where, she used her thumb and forefinger to spread open the woman's right eye, noting that the pupil seemed reactive, if somewhat dilated. She repeated the procedure on the left eye, which responded in a similar manner. "Now, can you tell me *your* name?"

"Um. Gimme a second," the woman said, her speech slow, and slightly slurred. "Oh, now I know. It's Josephine."

"And then what? Josephine what?"

"That's easy. Fortunata. Like me."

"Do you consider falling off a cliff *fortunate?*"

"Yeah, cuz I landed in an angel's arms."

Inge didn't answer but began gently palpating Josephine's abdomen. Tell me if you feel any pain."

Josephine whimpered softly as Inge proceeded with caution, slowly walking her fingers from the abdomen toward the sternum. "No, not there."

"And how about here?"

"I said, *no!* Not *there!*" Josephine cried, sitting bolt upright and slapping

Inge's hands away.

"*Ayyy!*" Inge howled, clutching the bump of bone protruding from her shoulder. "What the hell's the matter with you?"

"Don't touch my chest!"

"I'm a *doctor.* I have no interest in pawing your breasts."

"I don't have breasts."

"What?"

"They're gone. For good."

"I'm sorry."

"That's okay. I'm alive, right?"

"Yes, you're alive. Your spine seems fine, but you need to stay calm. And keep your hands to yourself! For your information, I'm injured too." She felt a little bad, for about a second, about not showing more compassion, but this was no time to rehash the woman's sad story. This was the time to find a way out of the present, potentially tragic one. "Listen, I need your phone. Now!"

Josephine rolled onto her left hip to expose her muddied backside, smiling over her shoulder. "Come and get it."

Wondering whether this bizarre behavior was normal for her, Inge reached over and wriggled the phone out of Josephine's back pocket. She stared at it, shaking her head. "Damn! The screen's cracked."

"I bought it that way."

"You bought a cracked phone?"

"Yeah. Used. Things can look bad and still be useful, right?" She was still reclined on one hip, her head propped on her bent arm, as if she were lounging languidly on a *dormeuse* rather than on a pile of dirt.

"Well, now it's totally *useless!*" Inge said, tapping the screen furiously with a finger, then with all of her fingers, then knocking on it with her knuckles, and finally punching it with her fist. "Now it's *destroyed!*"

"If that's how you're gonna treat it, give it back!"

"Here!" Inge said, thrusting the phone at her. Take the damn thing. It's beyond repair."

"Nothing is ... nothing is ..." Josephine muttered, jamming the phone into her front pocket. "But boy ... oh boy ... kinda woozy ... think I'm gonna ..." Leaning over, she retched into the mud a couple of times, then pulled herself back up to a sitting position. She burped once, loudly, then wiped her mouth on her bloody forearm. "Pardon me."

Inge grimaced, pulling a handkerchief from her pocket. "Here, take this."

"Thank you, my angel!" Josephine said, her eyes filling with tears.

"Enough with angels, okay? I don't believe in them. Don't you feel any pain at all? Anywhere?"

"Everything everywhere hurts. But like I said, I'm alive." Josephine dried her eyes and blew her nose. "It's a miracle."

"I don't believe in those, either," Inge said. "Can you tell me where you feel the most pain?"

"My left leg," she said. "Ankle."

"Can I roll up your pant leg to take a look?"

"Be my guest. Hairy leg alert."

"I've seen worse, in my line of work," Inge said, struggling with the thick denim. She wished she could just cut right through it, but her damn Swiss knife was in her damn backpack that was lost in the damn woods, together with her damn flashlight and everything else she'd brought along on her damn hike.

"*Owww!*" Josephine yelped.

Instead of apologizing for causing her pain, Inge scolded her. "What on earth were you thinking, wearing these jeans on a hike? Thick, stiff fabric impedes your range of motion! And if it gets wet, it stays wet. And if you wear wet pants, you get chilled! Haven't you ever heard of hypothermia?"

"It's still summer, for God's sake!"

"God has nothing to do with it! When you venture outdoors you have to be aware of the hazards, every day of the year!"

"It was just a walk in the woods!"

"Yeah, well, look at you now! Let me tell you this. When I was in medical school, I worked summers for the local ambulance service in my valley, and I saw more than my share of imbeciles head up into the mountains for a so-called walk. No physical training, no proper equipment. If they only risked killing themselves, that would be fine, but no! Those *criminals* constantly endanger the lives of the squads that have to go rescue their stupid asses!"

"Okay! Got it! Geez!"

Inge paused, clasping her shaking hands to still them. Between the shock and the pain and her overall state of mind, she was feeling excessively vulnerable, and vulnerability was one thing Inge did not do well; what she did well was control. That was why she had to defuse the mounting avalanche of latent grief before it came crashing down on her; before she was crushed again by the pain of losing her adored Hans, the man she'd never stopped loving, the man she would have married, but who instead had died a horrific death, slammed against a mountainside by a gust of wind while hanging from a helicopter. All to rescue a Dutchman who thought nothing of undertaking a four-hour trek in sandals, despite an approaching storm! People like that had no business climbing the Swiss Alps! People like that should stay home to grow tulips, on land that was as flat as their brainwaves!

"Hey, Angel?" Josephine said, touching Inge's leg. "Are you okay?"

"What?"

"How do *you* feel? You suddenly went pale, and your eyes are all glassy."

"Yeah, well, what do you want me to say?" Inge shook her head, took a deep breath, and stared down at Josephine's leg to avoid looking into the big blue eyes full of concern. "As for you, I think that ankle might be fractured or at the very least sprained. How badly does it hurt?"

"It's throbbing like the devil on speed." Josephine winced as Inge untied and then loosened her sneaker.

"And you should wear hiking boots when you go for a hike!" Inge snapped, engulfed by a fresh surge of fury for that world-class fool of a sandal-wearing Dutchman who'd killed her Hans, and gotten away with no more than a broken leg! "That's why they call them that, that's what they're made for! Feet need grip and ankles need support! Something you don't get from that flimsy footwear you people wear on your holiday frolics!"

"Wait just a minute now, Doc," Josephine said. "I don't know what got into you, but in case you're suffering from amnesia, I'm not down here on account of my jeans *or* my Nikes. I'm down here because I heard *you* screaming for help. *You're* the one who had the accident! *You're* the one who tripped over your tough lady boots and landed down here with your tactical trousers split at the crotch and your fancy panties all in a twist. *You're* the one who needed rescuing!"

Inge's cheeks burned in outrage. "I did *not* trip over my own feet! I was being chased!"

"So was I! This place is swarming with wild boars!"

"Boars wouldn't chase you without a reason!" Inge shot back.

"Well, they sure chased me!"

"If they did, they must have felt threatened." Inge was beginning to feel threatened herself, imprisoned, impotent, as she surveyed their surroundings. There was no way they could find a way out of that pit, not in their condition. But boars could find plenty of ways in. And so could wolves. With both of them incapacitated, they would be easy prey.

"All I know is they were snorting and grunting and practically charging me when I heard the screaming," Josephine continued. "They were on some kind of a *rampage!*"

"The last thing you should do is run!"

"That's what *you* did!"

"But I wasn't being chased by a boar! I was being chased by a *man!* With a *gun!*"

"Yeah, right!"

"I'm serious!"

"Well, a man with a gun I can handle! I'm from Buffalo!"

"Oh, is that so? Well how about *wolves*, then?" Inge asked, watching Josephine's panicky eyes dart from side to side. Good, she was suitably scared, but for some reason Inge wanted to scare her more, to punish her, to make her pay for something that wasn't her fault. "Could you handle a pack of wolves, now that you can't run?"

"Well neither can you!" Josephine cried, her eyes turning a darker shade of blue. "Do you really think they're out there?"

"Oh, they're out there, all right. The guy with the gun was talking about them."

"But they won't come before dark, right? And they wouldn't have any reason to attack us, right? They can eat the boars, right?"

"Who would you rather attack if you were a wolf? A wild boar with razor-sharp teeth and tusks, or two lame ladies?" Inge couldn't resist saying, although that was a scenario she'd rather not think about. Watching Josephine's fear turn to terror, she decided she'd said enough. "We need to get out of here before dark. And to do that, we need help."

Josephine looked up at the sky, cupped her hands around her mouth, filled her lungs, and focused on bringing out that voice she'd found in the woods. "*HELP!!*"

Inge let her scream a few times on her own, before joining in.

"*HELP!!*" they cried out, together, faces to the sky, as the rain began to fall.

CHAPTER THIRTY-TWO
Carolina

Carolina slathered a leftover breakfast croissant with organic hazelnut chocolate spread (over her dead body would any of that industrial crap cross the threshold of the Renovatus!) and shoved half of it into her mouth. She wasn't big on sweets, except when she was on edge. And who wouldn't be on edge, in her place? Who wouldn't be so freaking on edge that they were tempted to jump right off that edge? After working like a dog to make sure every detail of today's lunch would be perfect, it all just sat there, simmering on the stove, chilling in the fridge, while she paced the floors. How could those women still be romping around in the woods, with no regard for the time, no concern for the weather, and no respect for her, their host? And how about those men? Rino and Ada were probably guzzling an *aperitivo* in some seedy bar, ruining their appetites and indulging in the mutual stroking of their male egos. No sight of Giac, either (not that she was expecting him), who could have ditched his rancher role today and come home for lunch, seeing as it was bound to rain all afternoon, and seeing as his wife just might appreciate some help here, for once. Cramming the rest of the pastry into her mouth, she swallowed it so fast she started gagging and had to wash the gooey lump down her throat with the first thing she could lay her shaking hands on, some cold coffee she'd left by the sink. No worries about ruining *her* appetite for lunch, she thought, waiting for the tightness in her chest to pass; *her* mealtimes were spent working, and *her* meals were everybody else's leftovers.

She glanced around the kitchen again, one of the few places where she felt totally in control. Here, she knew how to measure and dose and regulate and time things to achieve the outcomes she wanted. But what control could she have over people who wandered way out of her range? Or over the weather, which after cooperating for most of the morning, seemed as fed up as she was with cutting those people a break? Instead of wishing the rain away, now she hoped it would start to seriously come down. Oh yes, she'd be pleased as punch if it *poured* rain, if it *pissed* rain! That would send the women running back here where they belonged, where she could see them and feed them and listen to them and talk to them, all in order to help them. She'd give them another fifteen minutes, then she'd start making some calls.

Meanwhile, she'd stop treading the tiles and put her time to better use in that other place where she felt totally in control. Tossing back the remainder of the cold coffee (she hated cold coffee, but needed the kick, and who had time to make a fresh pot?), she ducked into her little office, leaving the door open a crack and perching on the edge of her chair so as soon as she heard people come in she could jump up and greet them. She began by swiping through the photos on her cell phone, stopping when she came to Inge the Hun's ID card. She was a pretty good-looking lady, even if she was, let's see now, pushing sixty. Of course, you had to like that sturdy, athletic type, the kind who had that masculine way of walking without swaying her hips, the kind who knew how to put together the right hair and jewelry and accessories to achieve the female version of the professional power look. You could tell she was a natural blonde, too, just starting to gently go gray, not that ash blonde or whatever they called that neutral shade-of-nothing older women liked to dye their hair. You wouldn't catch Carolina dying her hair, no way, because she didn't care what the labels said about no ammonia and no parabens and no nickel-testing or whatever, those toxic substances seeped straight through your scalp and into your brain. One of these days it would come out that those "safe" dyes were connected to dementia and Alzheimer's and tumors, and that they'd known it all along but no one cared because the problem only affected women, particularly older women, who were doing what they were expected to do, which was to keep looking good for their men.

But Carolina had already met Inge in person, already knew what she looked like before seeing her photo, already knew she was a doctor before reading *medico* listed as her profession. What she did learn now was something funny, really, because this doctor named Egger was not only a gynecologist, but a resident of a place called Faloppio! It struck Carolina as so comical that she had to google it between giggles to make sure it was an actual place – and there it was, located just outside of Como! *Close* to the lake, but not *on* the lake. Come on, the Di Meglio family could do *di meglio*! With all their money, why didn't they own a nice waterfront property? Sure, not everyone could drop double-digit millions like George Clooney when he bought Villa Oleandra (any villa worth its salt had a name as its address), not to mention the bundle he spent fixing it up for Amal (so now it was worth ten times what he paid for it!), but between that and living in some bourgeois *villetta* in the outskirts (she pictured it spacious, but not sprawling, with a two-car garage, surrounded by a manicured lawn and sculpted shrubs, and a brick barbecue and pizza oven out back, but no dogs because they pooped and barked and tore up the grass, all enclosed by wrought iron fencing and secured with an alarm system); *anyway*, as she was saying to herself before interrupting herself, there was a whole spectrum of options between a Villa with a capital V and a *villetta*. When she was still living in Lombardy, Carolina had driven up to Como once, specifically to check out the Clooney mansion. There was no getting near the place, between the security surveillance and the massive gates and all, but what she really hoped was to catch a glimpse of George tooling along the lakeshore on his Harley, back when he still drove a motorcycle, before nearly getting himself killed in that awful accident she'd read about. If someone asked her who she'd pick if she could have any guy she wanted, she'd say Clooney, hands down. Not everyone saw it right away, but there was something about Giac that reminded her of George, she'd told him that as soon as she laid eyes on him. It wasn't one specific trait, just that strong, symmetrical look, that chiseled sort of jaw that prevented a man from looking like a sap, which was especially important if the guy had kind eyes and a sweet smile. As for height, Giac was actually taller, he had a good few inches on Gorgeous George. All in all, she was pretty lucky to have him warming her bed (even if that was all he did there these days, besides snore), and now he was even more handsome in his rough and tough rancher incarnation, way sexier than the soft-bellied Milanese middle manager she'd married. Like George, he was also rocking the going-gray stage. Men had all the luck when it came to aging. All they had to do was not get fat. Or boring. And keep their flies zipped. With those three things, a wife could tolerate the rest till death did they part.

So anyway, this Inge Marie (she had a middle name) Egger lived in Faloppio and worked in Lugano and was married to Severino Di Meglio (though she'd opted not to indicate that on her ID card). Talk about men getting boring. And fat. The part about zippers remained to be seen, but Carolina had a hunch she could dig up something on him, if need be. Most men slipped up at least once, especially ones who owned successful businesses and the bank accounts that went along with them. Money made men feel powerful, and power made men feel as randy as a tomcat in spring. The scent of money was an aphrodisiac for plenty of women, too, and it wouldn't matter to a mistress (were they even called that anymore?) if the guy dealt in felt, as long as he didn't talk about it to her all the time, that's what a wife was for. Anyway, she'd get to Rino the Rhino soon enough, but first she still had to check out Inge's social media presence. Logging into one of her fake Facebook profiles, she searched for Inge Marie Egger. There were plenty of Inges, and plenty of Eggers, but no combination of Inges and Eggers that matched her, and no Inge Marie Eggers at all. How could that be? She'd have to check out Instagram. Still no luck! It was time to broaden her range and hit Google. Oh boy, here she found several pages referencing the esteemed doctor, but Carolina was skilled in the art of skimming and could see at a glance that most of it was pretty technical medical stuff. Oh, there would be some interesting details buried in there, no doubt, if one had time to go through it all with a fine-tooth comb, but today her time was too tight.

Speaking of time, when Carolina got all engrossed in her investigations like that, with one clue leading her to another, and pleasant thoughts like

George worming their way into her brain along the way, she got distracted enough to totally lose track of it. Hopping up from her chair, she hurried through the dining room and out to the main door to take a look outside. There was still no one in sight. The sky had turned to lead, and the intermittent drizzle had turned to rain, a detail she'd been too busy to notice through the tiny window in her tiny office, what with her eyes constantly glued to her phone and computer screens. Good. Now they'd all make a mad dash back to shelter, but of course they'd be soaked to the skin, which would serve them right, but which also meant that they'd need time to dry off and change before coming to lunch. Heading to the kitchen, with a quick flick of her wrist she switched off whatever flames were still burning. So what if people had to wait a few minutes for the water to boil again? Maybe that would teach them to turn up on time. Or maybe not. But at least she'd make a point. And believe you me, she'd drive that point in until it hurt, but always with a smile on her lips and a spring in her step, you could count on that. Meanwhile, she couldn't just stand there watching the pot not boil, letting her nerves get the better of her, not when half her mind was still speeding down a different track in pursuit of intel on Inge. If there was no direct route to her personal life, she'd get there through her husband.

Severino Di Meglio, she typed in the Facebook search field, using the legal name on his ID card, but not surprisingly there was no exact match, because let's face it, who would want to be known as Severino? When she tried *Rino Di Meglio*, Meta worked its magic and showed her what she wanted to see. With only 147 friends, Rino clearly couldn't be what she'd call a friend fanatic (unlike Gisella Giostra, who'd already friended her back) meaning that if she sent him a request (which she did) he probably wouldn't even see it for days. No biggie, she'd start with what he'd put out there for the whole world to see, which was plenty. Scrolling down his timeline, Carolina was treated to images of Rino in swimming trunks, his rhino rolls of belly blub blatantly displayed as he stood at the helm of a boat, most likely on Lake Como, judging from the mountains in the background; of Rino slurping up a slimy oyster from a platter of two dozen chilling on a bed of ice, at the Café de Paris in Monte Carlo; of Rino basking in glory as he was awarded a plaque from the Chamber of Commerce (while the lady standing beside him was bursting with proprietary pride: she wasn't Inge, so who *was* she?); of Rino smiling ear-to-ear in an official photo taken in front of the Feltro Di Meglio facility, where he stood between a smartly-dressed woman who *was* Inge and a handsome young man, a head taller than Rino, who was tagged as *ta-da!* Carl Di Meglio. That must be the son, the heir apparent. She might as well get the goods on him, too.

Carl Di Meglio's cover photo showed a crew, probably during some regatta, getting doused by sea spray in a sleek sailboat listing so severely that just looking at it made Carolina want to puke up her croissant and coffee. His profile picture was a close-up of Carl in a white polo shirt, his twinkling blue eyes set off by a deep tan and a thick shock of wavy, dark hair the girls must adore running their fingers through. So, it looked like the striking young Di Meglio had inherited his mother's eyes as well as her height, but it was hard to tell what he'd inherited from his father (definitely not that hair!), besides a foreseeable future in felt. Carolina was getting dizzy with all the clicking back and forth between father and son, and Facebook and Instagram (where Carl posted more), and getting all confused at the way some traits of Carl's struck her as familiar but didn't seem to have been passed down from either of his parents. She tried to remember what she'd learned about dominant and recessive genes in high school biology, like whether some characteristics could be the result of a blend, a sort of hybrid, rather than coming from one parent or the other, which made her think about the creepy biology teacher who had the hots for her, and who'd even tried kissing her once at an after-school study session, which made her hate attending the course so much that she nearly failed it, and in fact probably would have if she hadn't slipped him that note telling him what she'd do to him if she didn't pass.

A sharp clap of thunder made her jump in her chair, then run through the deserted dining room to the door, her heart pounding, where she saw no one, absolutely *no one*, running toward her in the rain.

CHAPTER THIRTY-THREE
Allegra

Knowing that it was the wrong thing to do but doing it anyway, Allegra dashed under a tree for cover. Maybe this rain was just a passing shower, maybe that sound wasn't thunder, maybe there was no chance of lightning. The problem was, when other people only heard the pitter-patter, Allegra heard her mother's voice telling her that anytime there was rain, there could be lightning. And anytime there was lightning, Allegra's rule-free upbringing was suddenly riddled with do-nots. *Do not* walk out in the open, *do not* take shelter under a tree, *do not* go in the water, *do not* touch metal. Since her mother cautioned her about so few things, Allegra took those warnings seriously, as if death by lightning were a very real danger. As, in fact, it was, and living proof of that (well, no longer living) was her mother's *Cher Oncle* Léon of Lyon, the only relative she ever mentioned, who every December helped set up *La fête des lumières,* the city's traditional Festival of Lights. An electrician by trade, poor Léon had been struck by lightning *three times* in his career, twice escaping with severe burns, while his third jolt, delivered during preparations for the famous *fête,* had *killed him on the spot*!

Allegra didn't doubt her mother's word, but because of her natural curiosity about the bigger picture, she was always on the lookout for lightning-related stories. That was how she'd recently learned that France, Italy, and Switzerland attracted more lightning than any other European country, with ten to twenty lightning-related deaths per year *in Italy alone.* Around the world, an estimated one thousand people a year were struck dead by lightning. *One thousand* human lives lost in a flash! Every *year*! But it was better not to think about that now, because although Allegra would have eagerly heeded her mother's warnings and run to safety as fast as her legs could carry her, she firmly believed that her actions should follow her conscience, not that her conscience should accommodate her actions. And in good conscience, there was no way she could turn around if someone out in the woods needed help.

What she wished now, apart from the storm to change its course, was that she hadn't allowed Carolina to make such emotional mush out of her. It was such an *infantile* thing to do, and now here she was, in the woods, in the rain, with a possible emergency on her hands and nothing more than flip-flops on her feet, while a perfectly good pair of hiking boots sat idle in her bungalow. Well, just because she'd run away from Carolina didn't mean she was a coward, just because she was afraid of lightning didn't mean she couldn't handle an emergency. Who do you think saved the van from burning that time her parents fell asleep without snuffing out the candles and the curtains caught fire? Who do you think drove that same van to higher ground that time in Normandy, despite being only eleven years old, with legs barely long enough to reach the pedals, that time her parents had wandered off, leaving her to read on a beach in the rising tide? When your whole childhood felt like an emergency, you learned to be alert, you learned self-reliance. Better like this, because when push came to shove, who could you rely on in this world but yourself? And if you couldn't rely on yourself, how could other people rely on you? And Allegra wanted to be someone people could rely on.

"*HEEEY!*" she shouted, leaving the questionable shelter of the tree. Squishing along in her flip-flops, she continued uphill, stopping every few steps to call out again. She knew from previous visits that there were numerous points of access to these trails, and not all of them started at the Renovatus, so there was no telling who could be out there. Anyone driving up from the Ligurian coast or across the pass from Piedmont could have come out on a Saturday excursion and gotten lost, or tripped, or twisted an ankle. Or it could be Inge, she'd seen her set off earlier, but it was hard to imagine such a well-equipped, mountain-born woman getting into trouble on such a simple walk. It was that gut feeling that Allegra sometimes got, that intuition she couldn't help listening to even when she didn't want to, that told her the person in trouble may very well be Josephine. There was something childlike, almost innocent, about her new friend that had made Allegra feel protective toward her from the moment they met, and she would never forgive herself if any harm came to her. No, she would never forgive *Carolina*, who had seen her leave, and never should have let her go off on her own like that! It was *her* job to look after her guests, it was her *duty*!

"*HEY YOU!*" she cried out again, bending over to retrieve one of her useless flip-flops after it slipped off her foot for the third time. The on-and-off rain wasn't making her search any easier, either, between turning the terrain muddy and confusing her hearing with its drumming on the leaves. Standing still, she took advantage of a lull and tried again. "*HEEY! ANYBODY THERE?*"

"*AIUTO!*" she heard, then "*HELP!*"

A reply! What was even more reassuring was that there seemed to be two separate replies, from two different voices, which fit in perfectly with her theory of the day trippers. No doubt Josephine had cut her walk short and was already back at Carolina's, eager to devour a plate of ravioli. And Inge, with her long, sturdy legs and too much experience to get caught in the rain, must have made quick work of this hike and was back at the lodge, too. Yes, she was pretty sure of that, and she was also pretty sure that the voices she'd just heard weren't coming from the trail above her, but from somewhere down below her, off to her left.

"*I'M COMING!*" she hollered in that general direction, debating her next move. For a second, she thought about running down to the lodge to call for help, but that would be a waste of time when she couldn't provide an exact location or any details about the emergency. Allegra knew her way around here a little, she'd find a shortcut through the woods, see exactly what the situation was, *then* she'd go for help, if necessary. Leaving the trail behind, she set off down the steep decline through the trees, quickly realizing as she slid over the mud and sticks and stones that her flip-flops posed a greater danger than lightning.

"Enough of this Cinderella business!" she muttered, after finding herself semi-barefoot again. Reaching down, she grabbed the flip-flop on her foot and flung it towards its mate sticking out of the mud several meters behind her. And yes, she told her conscience before it could reprimand her, she knew she shouldn't leave two pieces of purple rubber behind in the woods, and yes, she had every intention of coming back to get them. First, she had to find a way down this treacherous slope, but not seeing any easy way, it looked like the only way was to just go, and let momentum do the rest. Her cautious steps quickly accelerated to a run as her bare feet flew over the rocks and mud and twigs, her arms grabbing onto branches or hugging a tree trunk whenever she risked careening out of control.

"*HEY!!*" she screamed like some crazy kamikaze as she raced down the hill, until the descent leveled out slightly, ending in front of a narrow but steep gully. The only way around was to zigzag through some rough terrain, but luckily a path had been plowed by some animals, most likely boars who'd been digging for roots. Soon finding her way blocked by a boulder, she climbed on top of it, thinking it would be a good place to get her bearings and catch her breath, though the voice in her head strongly disagreed, because standing on a rock was right up there with standing under a tree, on the list of *do-nots* in case of lightning.

"*HEY!*" she screamed.

"*HEY!*" came the immediate reply. "*DOWN HERE!*" She was getting close!

"*I'M COMING!*" she yelled, scrambling down from the boulder and charging into a section of wildly overgrown vegetation. The brambles kept getting caught in her curls and snagging her clothes, but she pushed forward as best she could, her arms shielding her face from the thorns that left trails of blood on her bare skin. She could have sworn those voices were just minutes away, but all she could hear now was her own panting and rustling, and all she could see was the low ceiling of dense brush pressing down on her, making her feel like she would suffocate, disorienting her so she couldn't tell which way she was going anymore, or if she was even going anywhere at all. The thought struck her, suddenly, violently, like the lightning she feared would find her, that she could very well *die* here, that she might *never* find that pair of hapless hikers, just like no one would ever find her. By now she was crouched so low she was practically crawling, her legs shaking with exhaustion, her feet on fire with pain, her chest gripped in panic. If she counted on getting the hell out of there, which she did, she must take a minute to calm down, to breathe, to regain control. Dropping to her knees, she balled up into child's pose and focused on breathing, in and out, in and out, trying to hear the *om so hum* mantra in her head instead of the *do-nots. I am the universe*, she repeated to herself, *I am breath, I am present.* Then she heard something else, and it wasn't coming from inside her head. It was the sound of twigs snapping, not far behind her, off to the right. Taking a deep breath, she raised her head and slowly turned it toward the noise. She'd seen plenty of boars roaming wild where she lived, digging up gardens and rummaging through garbage, but she'd never seen one up so close that she could look into its beady eyes! She'd never smelled a boar's fetid breath or gamey hide. She'd never seen the nostrils of a boar's mud-smeared snout quiver as it snorted. All she could do was stare in silence, willing her heart to stop thumping and her body to stop shaking, as the animal stared right back at her. She knew how to talk to cats and dogs and even horses, but she did not know how to talk to a boar. All she could think of was using her eyes to tell the beast that she meant no harm and feared no harm, though the second part was far from true. The instant their eyes locked, she concentrated on channeling those thoughts into her gaze and conveying them to the animal. They were both still frozen in place, neither one advancing nor retreating, when something else caught Allegra's eye. It was something blue, ensnarled in the vegetation behind the boar. It was a blue sweatshirt with red letters. Josephine's Buffalo Bills sweatshirt!

"NOOO!" Allegra cried.

The startled boar squealed, baring its long, curved fangs. Then it turned and fled, grunting as it plunged into the cover of the woods.

CHAPTER THIRTY-FOUR
Josephine

"It's her! I know it is!" Josephine said, pulling herself onto her knees. What she wanted to do was jump up and down and run around, scream and shout and wave her arms. But this was the most she could manage.

"Whoever it is, or rather *was*, seems to have gone," Inge said, glaring up at the dark sky. Josephine wondered whether she always looked so indignant when she didn't have control over things. Which probably wasn't often. "No one with any brains would risk getting caught in this weather."

"Allegra would *never* abandon us. And it's not even raining right now," Josephine said. She, on the other hand, never had the illusion that she could control anything, which made it easier to trust that someone, somehow, somewhere, would intervene at the right time.

"It's just a brief break. Make no mistake, the storm is coming."

Josephine ignored her. "*HEY YOUU! YOO-HOO!!*" she howled.

"Are you trying to attract the wolves? Because there's no one else out there."

"Why are you giving up right now, when someone's coming?" Josephine said. "It's not like you."

"What do you even know about me?" Inge snapped.

"Enough to know you're not a giver-upper."

"Look, I don't know who was there, but hopefully they went for help. If not, you can forget about anyone finding us anytime soon."

Josephine didn't believe that, not for one second. She thrust her good leg forward, not an easy feat in those damn jeans. Planting her foot firmly on the ground, she pulled herself up to a half-stand while attempting to put weight on her other foot. "*Owww!*" she cried, falling back down to one knee.

"Sit still, I told you!" Inge ordered.

Instead of answering, Josephine figured she might as well pray, as long as she was genuflecting. "Please God, let her hear me!" she whispered, then took a deep breath, sucking in as much air as her lungs could hold. "*ALLEGRAAAA!*" she screamed with such force that it felt like her eyes and ears would pop right out of her head. One thing that did pop was the third button of her pants.

"You can scream all you want, but let's face it, the only one we can count

154

on to get us out of here is *me!*"

"*ALLEGRAAAA!*"

"How am I supposed to think straight with all your screaming?" Inge said, rubbing her temples.

"You know, if you hadn't screamed, I wouldn't have found you!"

"I screamed after I heard you scream," Inge replied.

"And I screamed because I heard someone else scream before I heard you scream."

"How can you be so sure you heard another scream?" Inge's doubt made the skin between her eyebrows pucker, and a series of tiny vertical lines to form above her pursed lips. She looked a lot younger when she was sure of things.

"I'm telling you, I know what I heard!" Josephine insisted. "It was a different kind of scream, though, the *emotional* kind, not the SOS kind. And it was coming from another direction."

"I don't how you can be so sure of that."

"But I am. And I'm positive that it was Allegra." If Josephine had any doubt whatsoever, it vanished. Zero doubt. If there was one thing that made her surer of something she was convinced of, it was someone else questioning it. "But you were the one screaming for help, so I came to you first. And now Allegra will come for us, you'll see."

Inge stared at her, shaking her head.

"Besides, if it wasn't her, who was it?" Josephine asked. "Other than you, I didn't come across one single person out here."

"Well, I did. Don't forget about that guy with the gun. And he had a woman with him."

"You didn't tell me about any woman!"

"There was nothing to tell. I was more worried about the armed man! And the dog he tried to sic on me!"

"Do you think that guy was holding the woman against her will?" Josephine asked, her voice rising in alarm.

"That wasn't the impression I got," Inge said, staring at the ground. "Whatever she was doing there, she seemed to like it just fine."

"So she wouldn't have been the one I heard screaming, right?" Although Inge was the last person she'd suspect of telling tall tales, she wasn't quite sure she believed her bizarre story. "Are you sure that man had a gun?"

"Of *course* I'm sure," Inge said, grimacing as she shifted her weight, trying to find a more comfortable position. She was stoic, Josephine had to hand her that, sitting with her butt in the mud, not complaining about the atrocious pain she must feel in her leg and shoulder. "I know a gun when I see one, and I *don't* make things up!"

"Well, neither do I!" Josephine said, then cupped her hands around her mouth and began shouting again, "*ALLEGRA! AL-LEE-GRAAA!*"

"JOSEPHINE? IS THAT YOU, JOSEPHINE?" An answer!

"YES! IT'S ME! DOWN HERE!" Josephine cried, up on both knees, waving her hands over her head, her eyes searching for a glimpse of Allegra.

"I'M COMING!"

"Did you hear that? She's coming!" Josephine cried.

"Yes, of course I heard that," Inge muttered, pulling herself up on her sit bones. *"IT'S DOKTOR INGE EGGER HERE!"* she shouted. *"WE'RE BOTH INJURED! SEND FOR HELP!"*

"HANG ON!" Allegra cried. *"I'M COMING AS FAST AS I CAN!"*

"NO! GO SLOW! AND WATCH YOUR STEP!" Josephine yelled back.

"DON'T COME! JUST CALL FOR HELP!" Inge called.

Then Allegra appeared, in a spot not far from where Josephine had fallen. Twigs and leaves stuck out from her tangled mop of hair, her yoga pants and gauzy tunic were streaked with blood and in tatters.

"You found us!" Josephine clapped. "I knew you would!"

"What happened to you two?" Allegra called to them. "How did you end up down there?"

"The same way you're going to, if you don't watch out!" Inge shouted up at her. "There must have been a rock slide no one knew about! Or if they did, they didn't bother to tell us!"

"You're too close to the edge, Allegra! Stay back!" Josephine cried. "And hang onto a branch, like I did! Just in case!"

"Forget the branch!" Inge ordered. "What you need to do is call for help! Immediately! Neither one of us can walk, and I have a dislocated shoulder!"

"Hold on! I'll figure it out!" Allegra cried, hopping back a few steps as a large chunk of dirt fell from the exposed roots of a tree that tottered at the edge of the pit.

"There's nothing to figure out, dammit!" Inge shouted, barely flinching as the clump crashed to the ground and disintegrated right in front of her. *"JUST CALL!"*

"I don't have a phone!" Allegra replied.

"You went out on a hike all alone, with no phone?"

"I didn't go out on a hike! I only went for a walk! I was about to turn around when I heard the screaming!" Allegra said.

"You went for a walk in the woods in your pajamas? With no shoes?" Inge called. "You're worse than this other one I'm stuck down here with!"

"Stop that, Inge!" Josephine said, slapping her on the shoulder, a little harder than she should have. You're not being kind!"

"Ouch! How dare you!" Inge cried. "Get your filthy paws off of me!"

"I'm sorry! But you don't know what you're saying! How could you stay so calm before, and start losing it now that help is here?"

"I'm losing it because *two* people – not one but *two*! – both manage to find me, and neither one can call for help! It's women like you who give us all a bad name! You're clueless! Helpless!"

"Hey! Calm down! And listen up!" Allegra cried, as the tree she was standing next to creaked and groaned and shivered. All three women stared at it, wondering what it would do next. "And get away from there! *MOVE! NOW!*"

CHAPTER THIRTY-FIVE
Carolina

Screw lunch, now she was really starting to worry. Carolina hated worrying, and she hated people who made her worry. Thanks to them, an entire repertoire of worst-case scenarios was playing out in her head instead of just the original reel where a bunch of muddy-shoed people waltzed in horribly late (already over an hour, and counting!), chatting and giggling and expecting to be waited on. Thanks to them, she was forced to bite the bullet and try calling Giac, even though she knew he'd tell her what he always told her when she couldn't keep that sharp edge of agitation from creeping into her voice, that she was freaking out and blowing everything out of proportion. So to prove that she wasn't, she got herself all psyched up to calmly ask him to please take a ride through the woods on that hag of his and herd those women back home before the weather got any worse. That wasn't too much to ask, right? It would even make him look good, right? But no, the man couldn't even be bothered to pick up!

There was no way Carolina could just stay here while everyone drove her crazy with worry, but there was no way she could leave, either, because this was home base, this was where people would return, sooner or later. If she couldn't count on Giac to man up and help, her next-best option was Allegra, especially since she already had her number stored on her phone. And even though she'd run off like the drama queen that she was, Allegra wouldn't refuse to answer her call out of spite, she wasn't that type. No, Allegra was the type who worshipped honesty as if it were something sacred, so once she got a good cry out of her system, she'd be grateful to her, and she'd assume (wrongly) that Carolina was calling to apologize for upsetting her. She was still deciding exactly what to say when that awful automated voice kicked in to inform her that the number she had reached was currently unavailable. It wasn't until she tried getting through two more times that she remembered that Allegra (it was a miracle she could remember anything at this point!) had used Ada's phone that morning to call her father in India because something had happened to hers, and that was what had unearthed the whole Gisella Giostra story in the first place. Talk about useless!

Pacing back and forth between the front door and the dining room, she debated who else she could try calling. The person she was most worried about was Josephine. She was a city girl, she wasn't in great shape, and she'd been gone way too long. And after seeing the way her lips twitched in anticipation when she'd described her famous ravioli to her, she was absolutely sure, as in one hundred percent *positive*, that Josephine wouldn't have skipped lunch if her life depended on it. Not that her life was in danger out there, it wasn't the Amazon jungle for God's sake, it was just a beech forest with well-marked trails even a foreigner could follow and where no one, absolutely *no one*, had ever gotten lost! So even though she promised all her guests that she would never, ever disturb them when they wanted to be left alone, the time had come to break that rule. Josephine wouldn't mind. Josephine would be *glad* someone was looking out for her. She would be *grateful*. Rushing to her desk, Carolina shuffled through some papers until she found Josephine's registration form, hoping she'd filled in the optional field for her phone number. Yes! Good girl, Plain Jane Josephine!

After tapping in the number she returned to her spot by the door, chewing her thumbnail while hoping the call would go through, because let's face it, reception was shitty out there. When after a few tries the phone finally rang, she got so jumpy that she had to start pacing, four steps one way, four steps back, back and forth, back and forth. But Josephine didn't pick up, then finally the line went dead. She tried the number again, pacing faster now, eight steps one way, eight steps back, back and forth, back and forth. There were lots of reasons why a person didn't answer the phone, she told herself. Maybe Josephine was lost in thought, after all she'd come here to think, right? Or maybe she didn't feel like talking, or didn't hear the phone ringing, or had purposely left it behind in her room. But Carolina got certain vibes about phones, she was sensitive that way. She could tell by the sound of the ring if someone wasn't picking up because they *wouldn't* (like Giac, 95% of the time), or if they didn't pick up because they *couldn't*. And she didn't like the sound of that ring one bit. It sounded weak. It sounded lonely. It sounded scared. Then it stopped. Trying again, she stepped up her pacing, again walking back and forth, then in circles, then in figure eights, but this time she got another one of those chilling voices telling her that the number she had reached was unavailable. "That's ridiculous!" she screamed back. "I just called!" This was way too much for her, it must be all that coffee she'd drunk that was making her so nervous, because let's be honest, what could have happened? Unless … yes! She'd bet her bottom dollar that Josephine and Allegra had found each other out there, that they were off hugging trees or chanting mantras together and simply lost track of time. Or, maybe if Allegra was still crying when she caught up with Josephine, Josephine would have been all concerned and asked why she was crying and Allegra would have told her that it was on account of Carolina, and then Josephine would of course take Allegra's side, and they'd *both* be mad at her! Maybe they'd even run into Inge, and started badmouthing her to her, too! Maybe they'd even called the guys and convinced them they should *all* leave! Sure, that was it, they were all ganging up on her! Boycotting her! Plotting to *ruin* her!

"Now you *are* freaking out!" she screamed out loud, cupping her hands over her ears. "Stop it! Stop it right *now!*" Her heart pounding, she leaned forward, hands on her knees, and tried a few of those breathing tricks to calm down, which worked wonders because right after that she realized her theory didn't hold water because Inge was too frigid to get all worked up over another woman's messed-up relationship and probably wouldn't even lose any sleep over her own. She was too self-centered, right? Too cynical, right? Which made her precisely the perfect person to check in with for a status update, right? She didn't care if she risked annoying her, she'd just say she was terribly sorry for disturbing her precious alone time, but as a precautionary measure, in view of the impending storm, she was calling to inquire as to her whereabouts, and while she had her on the phone, could she confirm by any chance whether she'd seen the other women out there? Yes, Inge the Hun would be the one to call! But in order to do that, she'd need her number, and Rino the Rhino, not she, had checked them in, and she couldn't very well call Rino (where was *he*, anyway? and Ada?) to ask for his wife's number without tipping him off that something was wrong, and that was the *last* thing she wanted to do! Maybe she could try that old client of hers, that Dr. Fustello, who'd called last night to check whether his colleague Dr. Egger had arrived, and while he was at it, *again* put the pressure on Carolina to treat her and her husband especially well (as if she needed to be *told* that!). The man *must* have her number. Carolina was frantically scrolling through her call log, trying to figure out which unsaved number could belong to him, when the phone on her desk started ringing. Whoever it was at the other end of the line, she absolutely had to talk to them! She was in such a rush to make it to her office that she knocked over a freaking chair, which made her trip and fall, but she wasn't about to let that slow her down. Crawling on her hands and knees until she regained enough balance to stand, she sprinted the last few steps and grabbed the receiver, but her hands were sweaty and it slipped through her fingers and crashed to the floor. She snatched it up but fumbled it again before finally grasping it with both hands and pressing it to her ear.

"Renovatus Resort!" she said, breathless. "Carolina speaking!"

"Di Meglio here!"

"Oh! I was just thinking of calling you!" She tried to sound calm, though her heart was racing and her knee was throbbing from her fall.

"And I've *been* calling you! And you know what I've been calling you? Every name in the book, that's what!"

"Why? Is there a problem?" she asked, bristling. How dare he talk to her like that! But there was no way she'd swallow his bait and stoop to his level. Angry men were tricky, you had to be quick, stay one step ahead of them or they could throw you off, making you say the things you shouldn't say when the thing to do was to make them say the things you needed them to say.

"How can you be so *irresponsible?*" Rino yelled.

"Irresponsible?" Had word somehow gotten back to him that his wife and two other women were lost in the woods with a storm brewing? No, don't talk about anyone being lost, she had no proof that they were lost, just that they weren't where they should be right now, which was here.

"It borders on criminal *negligence!*" Rino sputtered.

What did he know that she didn't know? "I'm sorry, I'm not following you, Rino." Asking him to explain was a good idea, it would reinforce his stupid male conviction that women needed to have things spelled out for them.

"Well, I don't see how you *could* follow me, because I'm not going anywhere!" Rino bellowed in a voice so loud that Carolina had a good mind to slam the phone down.

"Where *are* you, anyway?" she managed to say, reasonably politely. "And why are you and Adalberto not here for lunch?"

"Where do you *think* I am? Sitting on your goddam dirt road, that's where!"

"What are you doing *there?*" The attitude on that man! She'd had just about enough of his shit! "You should have been back here *ages* ago! I've been holding lunch for you!"

"Hey, yeah, Ada here! You're on speaker, by the way. Sorry about lunch! *Totally* my fault. I was organizing a surprise for Allegra and then when we stopped in the village for a drink we ran into a lady who was a huge fan of mine and she called some friends over and they refused to let us go until I signed some books, and the time just got away from us!"

"Too bad no one had the common courtesy to tell *me* that!" She knew she was getting snappy, dammit, and she didn't want to get snappy. But *really?*

"For your information, I texted my wife!" Rino said. "I told her to inform both you and Allegra so that no one would worry! What *you* need to worry *now* about is getting us out of here. We blew a tire because of you!"

"Well if –" She bit her tongue – literally bit it so hard she could taste the blood! – before telling him it was his fault if he didn't know how to drive! "I mean, don't you have a spare? Between the two of you, I'm sure you could change it, right? You're both smart, strong men."

"There *is* no spare! Just a useless repair kit. This is *not* a little puncture! It's a huge *gash!*"

"Hey, Carolina? Ada here again. Yeah, the tire is *totally* blown. As in exploded. I made a few calls since Rino here was a little, um, *flustered*. The insurance call center kept putting him on hold and when –"

"There aren't any *people* there! I refuse to talk to a damn *robot!*" Rino cried.

"Yeah, as I was saying, I figured it would be faster to call a tire shop directly, but the nearest one is an hour away and they were closing for the weekend. Besides, they'd have to special order a replacement."

"Which will *certainly* be deducted from my bill!" Rino gasped. Good Lord! She could actually *feel* his blood pressure going through the roof, she could practically *see* the veins in his neck bulging.

"You really must calm down now, Rino!" she urged. "Why don't the two of you come back here, have some lunch, and wait for the weather to improve? We can deal with the car later."

"I don't have much of a choice, do I? You can send someone right away."

Who was she supposed to send, for God's sake? One of her liveried valets, perhaps? Besides, the last thing she wanted was for them to be hanging around here stressing her out about why the women were out in a storm! As if she knew! As if they weren't adults! As if she were everyone's freaking *babysitter*!

"It would probably be faster if you walked," she said. "I don't know where exactly you are, but the entire access road is only five kilometers long."

"You expect us to *walk*?" Rino asked.

"You seem to be athletic types, you were out running earlier. From the looks of it, you're both in fantastic shape." A little flattery couldn't hurt.

"Yes, but earlier we *wanted* to run. We were *dressed* for it. Now, we want to be picked up before it starts pouring again!"

"Ada here again! You know, well, Rino might be a little worn out from all the, um, excitement, so we really could use a lift. Sooner rather than later."

"I'll call Giac right away, but I'm not sure how soon he can get there."

"You know, just tell Allegra to come in my SUV. The keys are in our room."

"Ah, sure. Okay." No sense telling him that after her intervention, Allegra would probably prefer to see him face-down in a mud puddle than be his chauffeur. "I'll go look for her right now."

"And while you're at it, tell Inge what's going on," Rino said. "She's not answering her phone."

"Yes*sir*," she said, hanging up before anyone could get another word in. How long would they wait before pestering her again? Or deciding to walk?

Grabbing the binoculars she stored in the credenza, she stationed herself just outside the main door, scouring the edges of the woods, from the trailhead all the way across the field to the barns and beyond. Still no sign of anyone approaching. It was then that she got the idea, one she must put into action right away, while there was still some visibility. But first, she had to go rinse that metallic taste of blood from her mouth.

CHAPTER THIRTY-SIX
Inge

Inge was quick to react. Digging the heel of her boot into the mud, she pushed back with every iota of strength in her good leg, at the same time reaching out for Josephine with her good arm. The tuft of hair she caught in her hand wasn't long enough to drag her by, but more than enough to make Josephine scream.

"*Oowww!*" she wailed, but Inge lunged at her again, grabbed a fistful of T-shirt, and tugged her along with force, causing Josephine to fall flat on her face.

"Move that ass!" Inge yelled. Finally snapping to action, Josephine scrambled away on all fours, while Inge frantically retreated in reverse. The women had barely cleared the tree trunk's trajectory when it crashed to the ground, groaning and cracking and knocking the two women down with its crown of branches.

"*Ayyyy!*" Inge cried, flat on her back, through a blanket of leaves.

"*Owwww!*" Josephine moaned, belly-down in the dirt.

Grimacing, but not groaning, from the pain shooting through her injured leg and shoulder, Inge grabbed a branch and pulled herself up to sit. Wiping a hand across her face, she was relieved to find there wasn't much blood mixed in with the dirt, and that her eyes hadn't been poked out by the branches. Sticking her head through the leaves, she spotted Allegra monkeying her way down the toppled tree towards them.

"Josephine! Inge! I'm coming down!" she cried, swinging from branch to branch with her arms, shimmying down the truck with her legs. "Say something! *Pleease!*"

"Great!" Inge muttered. "This party just keeps getting better!" But at least Allegra had the full use of her limbs – impressively strong and limber limbs, she had to admit – *if* she didn't kill or maim herself on the way down.

"Be careful!" Josephine called. Although she wasn't in a position to admire Allegra's acrobatics, she could certainly feel the shaking caused by every jump.

"Thank you, tree!" Allegra cried, leaping to the ground as soon as she was low enough. "Now we have a bridge!"

"Not that it's going to do *us* any good. No one down here can follow that act," Inge said from under her leafy blanket. "Impressive, by the way."

"Life's funny, isn't it? You never know when you'll use what you learn along the way. I spent a year in a French circus school. *L'école de Cirque de Lyon.*"

"Well, save the clowns for later. What we need is a rescue team, and we need it stat! Neither one of us can walk, so as much as I hate the idea, we'll probably need to be airlifted out."

"One thing at a time, okay?" Allegra said.

"*Hello?* I'm being crushed to death down here!" Josephine cried from under the branches.

Allegra was already standing near the top of the tree, her bare feet planted firmly in the mud, her hands around the trunk. "*Uuggh!*" She grunted, hoisting it high enough to free the trapped women. "Wiggle out, you guys! Fast!"

Inge made a quick job of scooting back on her butt, while Josephine clawed her way toward Allegra on her stomach, boot camp style. "I'm so … happy … to see … you!" she moaned before flopping down flat on her face again.

"Hey, I hear ringing!" Inge said, flashing her eyes at Allegra. "What game are you playing, anyway? You said you didn't have a phone!"

"I don't!" Allegra replied, squatting to drag an inert Josephine completely clear of the tree.

"It's mine!" Josephine cried. "I can feel it vibrating by my stomach! I told you it wasn't kaput!"

Inge wiggled closer. "Well answer it, dammit!"

"I will! If you help me get it out of my pocket!"

Inge pushed while Allegra pulled, flipping Josephine over onto her back. Sucking in her stomach, Josephine shoved two fingers into her front pocket and tweezed out the phone, still ringing and vibrating. Her hands were shaking as she swiped the screen to answer, then swiped it again, and again, but the phone kept on ringing.

"Your passcode! Punch in your passcode!" Inge cried.

"I don't have one!"

"Give it here!" Inge snatched the phone from Josephine's hand. She tapped and swiped, tapped and swiped, but the phone kept ringing and vibrating. Then it stopped. "I can't believe it!" she cried. "I literally *cannot* believe it! We're lucky enough to have reception, and you're lucky enough that someone's looking for you, and there's no way to answer because of that goddamn broken *screen!*" Inge shook the phone in the air as if to knock some sense into it, then slammed it onto a rock.

"You really need to calm down, Inge," Allegra said, speaking in the annoying tone and smiling the silly smile of a fool who thought that positive attitudes could save the world. "Things happen for a reason."

"Is that all the yogic wisdom you can come up with? Can you at least back that up with some examples? Because I'm having a hard time finding a good reason for being trapped down here with broken bones and defunct phones!"

All three women stared at the smashed device lying on its altar of stone, as if its death demanded a moment of silence. Allegra was the first to step away – not surprisingly, since she was the only one who could stand. The moment she moved, a rapid rustling sound came from beneath the fallen tree, a branch or two twitched, some leaves quivered, and Josephine, sitting at Allegra's feet, screamed.

"Yikes!"

Allegra jumped up and down, yelping, her lithe legs high-stepping in place. "*Ohmygod!*" she cried. "*Ohmygod!*"

"What's wrong?" Inge asked. "What happened?"

"A snake!" Josephine cried. "Allegra got bit by a snake! I saw it!"

"Stop jumping around this minute!" Inge ordered. "What kind of snake, Josephine?"

"A *long* one!" Josephine whined, shaking out her hands as if warming up her fingers for a piano recital. "A slithery, *disgusting* one!"

"Big help that is!" Inge said. "Sit down next to me right now, Allegra, and let me see that bite. And you get a hold of yourself, Josephine. You have to describe that snake to me!"

"I'm sure it's nothing," Allegra said, her face suddenly drained of color.

"What did its head look like, Josephine?" Inge asked. "Was it triangular?"

"It was *ugly!*" Josephine said. "With beady black eyes!"

"What shape were the eyes? Round or oval?"

"They were, um, I don't know! But they were *evil!* It happened so fast! Aren't you supposed to cut into her and suck out the poison or something?"

"Don't be ridiculous!" Inge said, examining Allegra's ankle. "You've been watching too many westerns. If it were poisonous, the best thing to do would be to immobilize the leg and stay as still as possible. And the only poisonous snake in Italy is the viper."

"It wasn't a viper," Allegra said.

"Yes, from what I can see, it must have been a common smooth snake. The bite left a series of small marks, while a viper's fangs would have left two deep marks."

"Yeah, I know. I've been bit before."

"Yet you still romp around in the woods barefoot?"

"Yes, and I'm still alive," Allegra said, already back on her feet and smiling down at Inge. "And well."

"It's a *miracle* it wasn't a viper!" Josephine said.

"It's nothing, Josephine. Really. I'm fine," Allegra said, sighing deeply. "Phew! We're all a little jumpy, aren't we? But let's focus on you two. Are you in a lot of pain?"

"Well, if you don't think a dislocated shoulder and fractured tibia are painful, I've never been better," Inge said.

"And how about you, Josephine?"

"I had a lucky fall. Ask Inge, she saw it all. She said I could have been killed or paralyzed! But somehow, I only injured my left ankle. It was a *miracle*, really!"

"And that makes how many, Josephine?" Inge glared at her, half in envy, half in pity, then glanced at Allegra. Sometimes she wished she were ignorant enough to believe in all those mini-miracles and trite aphorisms that provided such consolation to simpler folk.

"Okay, so, one thing at a time," Allegra said, back on her feet, hands on her hips, as if she were used to being in charge, though it was hard to imagine of what. "Inge, I may be able to help with your shoulder. If it's just dislocated, I know how to pop it back into place."

"*Nein*. Not an option," Inge said, shaking her head. "Reducing a dislocated shoulder may look like a simple procedure on those medical shows you people love to watch on TV, but an untrained person can cause serious damage."

"I *never* watch those shows," Josephine said. "I can't stand the sight of blood."

"It's up to you, of course, but as I said, I can help," Allegra said. "And for the record, I don't own a TV."

Inge couldn't bear being talked down to like that by a yoga-speak circus freak while she sat there with her tush in the mud. "Obviously, a layperson like yourself wouldn't know this, but there's a very real risk of tearing a muscle or a tendon, or even damaging nerves and blood vessels!" she continued.

Allegra stared down at her, nodding. "Uh-huh. You must be in terrible pain, though."

"It's *excruciating*," Inge admitted. She hated that tears were springing to her eyes, and she hated that the pain made it hard to think straight. And unless she could think straight, she'd never find a way out of there.

"Can I at least take a look?" Allegra asked.

Inge sighed. "I suppose so."

"Tell me if I hurt you." Crouching down next to her, Allegra pushed up the sleeve of Inge's T-shirt, gently sliding a hand up to her shoulder and collarbone. "Oh yes, I'd definitely say it's dislocated. The bone is protruding, and there's considerable swelling already. Do you feel any numbness? Any tingling?"

Inge eyeballed her. "*I'm* the doctor here, remember?"

"Of course. But there's a good chance that I've treated more dislocated shoulders as a yoga instructor than you have as a fertility specialist."

"That could very well be. You people are good at torturing your bodies, twisting them into the most unnatural positions. There's a limit to what the human anatomy is meant to do."

Allegra took a deep breath but said nothing.

"There is some numbness," Inge admitted, satisfied that she'd made her point. "But my circulation doesn't seem to be affected."

Next, Allegra examined Inge's lower arm, then her hand, placing it between both of hers. "I agree. There's no blueness, and your hand feels warm to the touch. So what do you say?"

"You do know you could seriously injure me, don't you?"

"Yes, you mentioned that. I also know I can alleviate your pain in a matter of seconds. But it's up to you."

"I don't care how many times you've done this before, you have to follow my instructions. Agreed?"

"Agreed. Do you want to remain seated or lie down?"

"Let's do it lying down," Inge said, relying on her reasonably strong abs to slowly recline to a supine position.

"Now try to relax," Allegra said. "Do you want to calm down with some breathing exercises first?"

"No, I do *not* want to calm down with some breathing exercises first! Let's get this over with!" Inge snapped.

Steadying herself with another deep breath, Allegra took Inge's right arm by the wrist and slowly eased it out to the side and up to shoulder level.

"Make sure the arm's at a ninety-degree angle! That will allow the head of the humerus to slide back under the shoulder blade."

"Right. Ninety degrees. You've got it."

"I can't watch this!" Josephine said, screening her face with a hand while peeking through her fingers.

"Can I anchor my feet against your body for better leverage?" Allegra asked, tightening her grip on Inge's wrist.

"If you must." Although Inge was already wallowing in the mud, the thought of having those filthy blood-caked feet pressed against her torso was highly unappealing, to say the least. "Just remember, when you start pulling –"

But Allegra was already pulling – slowly, steadily, firmly, then *clunk!* The pop was audible.

"*Ayyy!*" Inge screamed.

"Oh, my *God!*" Josephine cried, wide-eyed. "I've never seen *anything* like that!"

"Done!" Allegra proclaimed. "Is that better?"

"Yes! Oh, yes!" Inge moaned, already starting to sit up. "What a relief!"

"Take it slow, now," Allegra said, propping Inge's back as she rose. "Let me just bind that arm up in a sling until you can get it looked at. I have something that will work perfectly." She patted her hips a few times, but her hands didn't seem to find what they were looking for. "Oh, no!" she cried, her face falling. "My shawl! I lost my mother's shawl! It was tied around my waist!"

"No problem. We can use my scarf," Inge said, freeing a large silk scarf from around her neck. All her scarves, even for hiking, were made from top-of-the-line Como silk.

"Didn't you hear what she just said?" Josephine asked. "She lost her mother's shawl! It meant a lot to her. And she was willing to use it for your sling. Do you even appreciate what a generous gesture that was?"

"Of course I do. Thank you, Allegra. Really. But there's not much we can do about finding that old shawl right now, is there?" Inge said. "Like you said, things happen for a reason."

"What reason could there be for losing a precious memento, except to make her miss her mother more?" Josephine blurted, then sucked in her breath. "Oh no!" she cried.

"Now what?" Inge said.

"I just realized I lost something too!"

"I know, Josephine, I saw your sweatshirt, that's how I knew you were in trouble," Allegra said.

"It's not so much the sweatshirt," Josephine said. "But I had my Nonna's rosary in the pocket. I always carry it with me."

"Well, I hope this will be a lesson for you both if we ever get out of here and you ever go on another hike," Inge said. "Dress sensibly, equip yourself properly, and don't bring along anything you can't live without!"

Instead of admitting that she was right, Allegra and Josephine simply stared at her.

"Well? What *is* it?" Inge asked. "Look, not all of us can afford to let sentimentality rule our lives! I'm a rational professional and I deal with patients so besotted with the romantic notions of becoming parents that they lose their ability to reason. I need to keep a clear head at all times, and I can't just switch the clinical Inge on and off at will. It doesn't work that way."

The other two women kept staring at her as if expecting her to go on. Well, they could rot on the spot if they were waiting for her to admit to shortcomings she didn't have.

"Look, I'm sorry about your shawl, Allegra. And about your rosary, Josephine," she finally conceded. "If it's any consolation, in addition to my backpack and my phone, I also lost my father's hand-carved walking stick. It was one of his favorites."

"I'm awfully sorry about that," Allegra said, looking even more glum. "I guess it would be better to let go of things, rather than have them taken away from us. That goes for people, too. *Especially* for people."

"Meaning what, exactly?" Inge couldn't stop her eyes from rolling but did manage to speak in a slightly kinder tone of voice. After all, Allegra had dealt with her shoulder effectively. Plus, she was their only ticket out of there. "Is there something you need to say? Have you lost someone?"

"I may have. Or at the very least, an idea I had of someone." Allegra shook her head slowly, her eyes on the ground.

It was no use; Inge's patience was wearing thin. Some women simply weren't able to come right out and say what they had to say. "And? What's your point? Is there something else you want to share? Because this isn't exactly the time or place for idle girl talk."

"It's just that sometimes you go on for years thinking you know a person, then they say or do something that makes you realize that you never really knew them at all. It's as if they were an imposter all along."

Inge stiffened. "Oh, come on. We're all imposters. At work. At home. We even fake it with ourselves."

"Anyway, you're right, Inge. This is no time for chitchat. We have more important things to worry about now." Taking the silk scarf from Inge's hand, Allegra quickly fashioned the makeshift sling under the silent scrutiny of the doctor, who tucked her arm in close, like an injured wing. Inge did not like that feeling. Not one bit.

CHAPTER THIRTY-SEVEN
Carolina

Deep down, emergencies thrilled Carolina. They tested your reflexes, your intelligence, your bravery. They turned ordinary people (she *despised* the very idea of ordinary!) into heroes. That was why ever since she was a young girl she'd dreamed of becoming a helicopter pilot, of suiting up and rushing out on rescue missions to save wounded animals and stranded people, to airlift food and water to disaster victims, to fight raging wildfires, to transport the seriously injured and deliver transplant organs to life-saving hospitals. When she revealed her intentions to her parents, they laughed in her face and said that was a ridiculous idea because in the first place, what kind of work was that for a woman who had a family to raise (she was just twelve at the time, with only two menstrual cycles to her credit), and in the second, third, and fourth places, where would she go to helicopter school anyway, and who would pay for it, and who would help them at the café if she left? So she didn't. Between brewing espressos and frothing milk and serving snacks and, yes, falling in love, she was reassured by the voice in her head that told her there was still plenty of time to do whatever she wanted with her life. It wasn't until she somehow found herself in her thirties, saddled with a husband and two toddlers, that she realized it wasn't exactly true. Not anymore. One minute you were a kid, holding onto your dreams like a bunch of brightly colored helium balloons, convinced they could make you fly. Then along came the attachments (*pop!*) and the responsibilities (*pop! pop!*), and with every year that passed a little more gas leaked out of the remaining balloons, until they were so saggy and deflated there was no chance in hell they'd ever get you off the ground. People said being grounded was a positive thing. And sure, even grounded people had choices, you had choices right up until the day you died if you wanted to see them and dared to make them. But astronauts and brain surgeons and Olympic medalists needed young bodies with quick reflexes and alert minds. And so did top gun chopper pilots. Let's face it, that possibility was no longer on her table of life's choices, but it was no use being bitter about it. She'd followed another path, pursued something she was damn good at, successful at, and proud of. So what if she dropped a couple thousand euros on a drone if it allowed her to hang onto a tiny scrap of that little girl's dream?

Brushing a stray tear from her cheeks (what was *that* all about?), she watched her shiny red drone lift off and take to the sky. It was airborne! Again, she congratulated herself on not being one of those cheapskates who skimped on quality just to save a few euros. She didn't care how much Giac ragged on her, her hard-earned money would not be squandered on a drone that was little more than a glorified child's toy. No ma'am, she'd done her homework, researched her options, watched YouTube videos late into the night, and then gone straight for a heavy-duty waterproof chopper equipped with a 4k HD camera and GPS. Operating in this environment, with the mountains and forests and constantly shifting air currents, she needed a robust craft, one that could be relied upon to function seamlessly, even in adverse conditions, while consistently delivering high-quality images. With its extended range and long battery life, her SkyHiPro would allow her not only to keep an eye on their property without leaving home base, but to create spectacular images and videos she could use for marketing purposes. She was still in the process of obtaining her official pilot's license from the Italian civil aviation board (she was studying for the online exam, but who could find the time?), which was compulsory for all but the tiniest toys. So what if she sneaked in a few test flights in the meantime? Who was going to catch her way up here? Plus, now she had a *real live emergency* to justify it.

It amazed her to see how fast and far the drone could soar away in a matter of minutes! It also scared her a little, not because she lacked guts, no, the only thing she lacked was a little experience. She was still a rookie, after all, still a bit wobbly at the controls, plus the weather kept deteriorating, and now she was having trouble keeping an eye on the spunky little rascal! Grabbing her binoculars with her left hand, she scoured the dark sky, her mind racing. Didn't out of sight mean out of range? And didn't out of range mean out of control? Juggling the binoculars and the joystick frantically, unable to see anything at all on her phone, she sat down on the wet ground before she could drop everything, terrified that the wind would pick up and dash the drone into the trees! Or slam it against the rocks! Or that the rain would damage its electronic circuits! Even the best pilots with nerves of steel knew when it was time to abort a mission, and *she* was the one in command here. It was up to *her* to make the call. She didn't *want* to do it, but she *had* to do it. With shaking hands and a heavy heart, she engaged the return-home switch (a costly optional, but *so* worth it!), which was more than a little humiliating, but giving Giac a crash to rub her nose in would be downright mortifying.

Peering up at the sky for what seemed like forever, she kept raising and lowering the binoculars expectantly, holding her breath one minute and hyperventilating the next, until she finally caught sight of that precious red dot in the sky approaching home base! When at last her beloved craft touched down in front of her, she scooped it into her arms and kissed it, then wrapped it in a fluffy towel and deposited it in her private storeroom, where it would be out of harm's way. Dying to find out what she'd recorded, she removed the camera and rushed to her office, popping out the memory card on the way. So what if she'd cut the mission short, she was thrilled to have her baby back in one piece, having possibly recorded footage that could lead her to the missing women!

"What the hell, Carolina!" Giac boomed, charging into the foyer and slamming the door behind him. "I told you that if I catch you spying on me again, I'll run that damn drone of yours over with my tractor!"

Carolina spun around to face him. "Spying?" she asked. Why did he think it was always all about him? "Surveillance is only called spying by people who have something to hide."

"And how many times do I have to remind you that you *cannot* fly that drone until you get your license!"

"You don't have to remind me at all! I already know that! I'm working on it!"

"It's a goddamn multiple-choice exam, Carolina! Just take it if you're serious about flying that thing!"

"I know, I *know!*"

"And you need insurance! If you get caught flying without insurance you can get up to six months! And a fine!"

"Okay! Message received! Now, if you can lay off the Mr. Law Enforcement act long enough to listen, I'll tell you why I was forced to bend the rules! While you were off doing who knows what, which included not answering my calls, I've been dealing with one emergency after another!"

"What emergencies could you possibly be dealing with, all cozy and safe here? Your dough didn't rise? Your cake fell? What?"

"First of all, all three of our female guests – Inge, Josephine, and Allegra – took off on separate hikes without consulting with me or telling me where they were going, and still aren't back. I can't reach any of them by phone."

"Since when can you ever reach anyone by phone around here?"

"Well, that's why I sent out my drone, to search for them!"

"Why don't the men go looking for them?"

"Because the men are the other emergency! They're stuck in a ditch with a flat tire! Rino called, and he was beyond furious! He insists on being picked up, even though they're already on the access road. The man does *not* know how to drive! You'd better go get them."

"Oh, for God's sake! How can five people cause so much trouble? We should just shut this place down and stick to farming!"

"These are our *paying guests*, Giac! We're responsible for their safety, which, by the way, is precisely why I'm always on your case, as you put it, to make sure the trails are well-marked and well-cleared! You have to go rescue Rino and Ada, while I examine my video to see if I can locate the ladies."

"No way! You're not going to waste time watching a video when we *both* know you're not good enough to record anything!" Giac said, snatching the SD card from her hand. "I'll go get the guys, and if you're that worried about the women, suit up in your rain gear and go look for them. And grab a walkie-talkie!" At that, he marched his muddy work boots back out the door, leaving Carolina to scowl at his tracks.

To think he was such a gentleman when they got married! He sometimes forgot that this was not the Far West, that just because she was as strong as an ox and worked like a dog didn't mean that she wasn't a lady and shouldn't be treated like one. That was the problem with men, as soon as you showed them how unnecessary they were for your survival, you were screwed. It was always the helpless looking types like Absent Allegra and Plain Jane Josephine (to cite a couple of handy examples), that brought out the protective side of men. And hers too, she had to admit. The thought of those women roaming the woods during a storm made her don her slicker and boots in haste, throw a few utensils into her backpack, and head up the trail into the woods. At least she had Giac's permission to use the walkie-talkie. He was so possessive of his tools and toys, like a spoiled little boy, really.

CHAPTER THIRTY-EIGHT
Josephine

"Hey, you two! Look! Over there!" Josephine shouted, waving her arm at the livid sky.

"Damn! It's going to start pouring again any minute," Inge said. "And it's not going to be nice."

"Did you see lightning?" Allegra asked, staring at the ground.

"No, over *there*! Look!" Josephine repeated, jabbing her finger at a specific spot in the sky.

"That red thing, you mean?" Inge said.

"Yes! It's a helicopter! They're coming to get us!" Josephine clapped. She wanted to be rescued, just not by helicopter, but she tried to sound excited. "Yay!"

"I think I see it too," Allegra said, finally glancing up at the sky. "But a helicopter? It looks too small to me. Plus, I don't hear any chopper noise."

"It just looks small because it's still far away," Josephine reasoned, making giant waving gestures over her head. "And we must be upwind, that's why we can't hear the noise."

"How would they even know where to look?" Allegra said, rising to her feet.

"It's another miracle!" Josephine cried. She had to trust that everything happened for a reason, just like Allegra said.

"What miracle? They used your phone!" Inge said. "Even if we couldn't answer that call, the authorities tracked the location. Someone must have reported that we were all missing!"

"*Yoo-hoo!*" Josephine cried, cupping her hands around her mouth. "*Over here!*"

"Hey, Josephine. Don't waste your breath," Inge said, shaking her head. "That is *definitely* not a helicopter. It's a drone."

"No, it's a helicopter! A red helicopter, like the ones from the fire department!" Josephine insisted. "Can't you see that?"

"I'm telling you, I've seen plenty of helicopters in my day, and that thing is a drone!" Inge said.

"Allegra, *you* tell her! And help me get *up*! We need something to signal with!'"

"Come on, Josephine," Allegra said, hooking her under the armpits to hoist her up on her right foot, then slipping an arm around her waist to support her left side. Josephine hated being a burden, but Allegra didn't make it seem that way at all, she was so strong and gentle at the same time. "I'm afraid Inge's right. But a drone is good, too! That means they're out looking for us."

"*HEY!*" Josephine called to the sky, as if she hadn't heard.

"Just keep waving! The camera could pick us up!" Allegra said, making big circles in the air with her free arm.

"And in any case, they could spot the landslide," Inge said.

"Right, that should be pretty visible from the air, shouldn't it?" Allegra said.

"I would think so," Inge said. "And if the person reconnoitering is any good at their job, they would know this is the spot to search."

"Hold on a sec," Allegra said, squinting at the sky. "Is it me, or is that red speck getting smaller?"

"No, no, it's getting bigger! It's coming for us! I think it really is a helicopter!" Josephine cried, waving more vigorously. "*HEY! OVER HERE!*"

"It's *not* getting bigger, and it's *not* a helicopter!" Inge said. "And stop screaming!"

"It turned around!" Allegra said. "Can you believe that?"

"Actually, yes," Inge said.

"But they saw us, right?" Josephine asked.

"Who knows?" Inge frowned. "But I wouldn't hold my breath waiting for some superhero to save us. The storm is about to break, and before you know it, night will be falling. You're the only one who can walk, so you'll have to go for help, Allegra. We'll wait here. We have no choice."

"No! I don't want to be left behind!" Josephine figured her voice must be worn out from all the shouting, because the one she heard coming from her mouth was thin and whiny, like a child's. "Can't I come with you, Allegra? There's not even any place to shelter from the rain here! And there's –"

"Shhh – what's that?" Allegra said, cocking her head. "Does anyone else hear howling?"

Josephine's eyes widened. "Oh, my God! It's a wolf! They must have sniffed us out! They can smell fear, you know!"

"That is *not* a wolf," Inge said. "It's a dog. A hound."

"What hound? Whose hound?" Allegra asked.

"The hound of a man I saw earlier."

"What man?"

"The man with the *gun!*" Josephine said. "But I still think it's a wolf!"

"What are you talking about?" Allegra turned to Josephine, then back to

Inge. "What's she talking about?"

"It's a long story. But yes, there was a man who had a gun, and a dog, and a – never mind. I was running from him when I took a tumble, otherwise I wouldn't have ended up here in the first place!"

"And you're just mentioning that now? So casually?"

"Like I said, it's a long story!"

"Allegra, you can't leave us here with men with guns and boars and snakes and wolves closing in on us!" Josephine cried. "You *can't!*"

"Stop acting like a baby, Josephine!" Inge said. "Allegra needs to go, and she doesn't need anyone holding her up!"

"But I'm not –"

"Hey!" Allegra cut in. "Have you seen those incredible ferns over there?" She pointed across the pit to the section of hill opposite the landslide.

"Look, no one loves nature more than I do, but this is *not* the time for a lecture on botany!" Inge said. "You need to get moving. *Now!*"

"Stop ordering her around!" Josephine said. "Those ferns are really pretty, Allegra. And *giant!* I've never seen anything like them."

"I spotted them before we got distracted by the drone, and I got this funny feeling of *déjà vu*," Allegra continued. "And now I know why. I've been here before!"

"You're not going to start in with that reincarnation nonsense now, are you?" Inge said.

At that moment, a flash of lightning illuminated Allegra's pale face. She squeezed her eyes shut, as if she were on a plane that was about to crash. Tightening her arm around Allegra's waist, Josephine could feel her trembling. Then came the rumble of thunder, low but menacing. When it was over and Allegra opened her eyes again, she sure looked strange. Spooked, that was the word for it. That look was enough to make Josephine's spine tingle.

"This is important, Inge!" With a quick shake of her head, Allegra picked up where she'd left off. "I really *have* been here before. In *this* life. I *know* this spot! It's called *La Valle delle Felci*. The Valley of Ferns. I discovered it during another stay here when I took a hike coming up the other way. This whole area was carpeted with ferns. *Giant* ferns! They were amazing! And now they're all buried."

"Buried is what we'll all be if we don't get out of here!" Inge said. "You see all these piles of rocks and dirt around us? You see that tree that could have killed us? Well, more of the same is going to slide off that hill and come crashing down here as soon as the real storm hits. And believe me, it's coming."

Josephine didn't know what to say. She wanted Allegra to be safe from the storm which obviously terrified her, but she was just as terrified to stay behind with Inge. All she could do was trust her friend and accept whatever she decided.

"Give me your hand," Allegra said, reaching down to Inge, who simply stared back at her. "Come on! Your hand!"

Inge finally obeyed, for once without protesting. Extending her left arm, she let Allegra clasp her hand, then lock wrists with her. Allegra was firm on her feet, pulling hard, while Inge held on tight, rising first to a squat, then to her full, frightening height, balancing on her left foot. Josephine didn't know what the plan was, but she put every effort into doing her part anyway, which was to not topple over.

"Good work!" Allegra said, supporting Inge's right side, while still holding up Josephine's left side. "Both of you. We can do this. I know we can."

"Do what?" Josephine asked.

"Walk together. If you each put your best foot forward." Allegra looked at Josephine, then at Inge. "And we take it slow, one step at a time."

"Look, there's no way in hell we can climb up the tree you came down on, with or without your help!" Inge said.

"We can't go back the way we came, but we can still get where we need to go. Through the Valley of Ferns," Allegra said. "It won't be easy and it won't be fast, but together we can make it over that mound. From there, we can continue down the lower route through the pasture which should lead us home. That way no one stays behind, and no one goes it alone."

No one said anything, but Inge, leaning on the shorter Allegra to her right, took the first step forward with her left foot; Josephine, leaning on the taller Allegra to her left, took a step forward with her right foot. Wobbling a little under their weight, Allegra took two steps forward.

CHAPTER THIRTY-NINE
Carolina

Marching up the hill at a good clip, despite the permanent limp in one leg and the newly bruised knee of the other, Carolina tried to remember the last time she'd ventured into the woods, but couldn't. She used to know these trails like the back of her hand, not because she was a passionate hiker, but because she was a champion picnicker. In their early days, Giac and the kids used to call her *La Regina del Picnic*, The Queen of Picnics, because of the surprise gourmet treats she packed whenever they could get away for a family hike. Their favorite spot was that secret waterfall, especially in summer, when they had such a blast splashing around and shrieking under the cascade of icy water. She probably wouldn't remember how to get there now, and maybe wouldn't want to, because she didn't think she could stand it if it had dried up in the meantime. Kind of like her family.

Why she ever bothered to reminisce was beyond her grasp, but it was also beyond her control. It just happened, when she least expected, desired, or was equipped to deal with it. Besides being a futile mental exercise, nothing ever came from it except for that churning, hollow feeling in her gut, a cross between a bad bout of nausea and starvation. And right now, she had absolutely no time or energy to waste on sentimentality. No ma'am, she was a woman on a mission, and this was the time for action. Shoving nostalgic memories back into the black hole they'd crawled out of, she stepped up her pace, moving along so quickly that if she didn't have such a keen eye, she would have sped right past the purple flip-flop sticking out of the sloping terrain to the side of the path. And if she hadn't been sitting on the ground next to a pair of purple flip-flops exactly like this one that very morning, and if she hadn't seen Allegra snatch them up in her hand as she fled, she might wonder who it could possibly belong to.

"*ALLEGRA!*" she shouted, abandoning the path to recover the flip-flop. Hands cupped around her mouth, she pivoted in a circle, calling out her name repeatedly. No answer. Grabbing the two-tone emergency whistle that hung from her neck, she filled her lungs and blew it as loud as she could. What was that rule again? A series of six whistles, one every ten seconds, then wait a minute. But that was when you were *calling* for help, not when you *were* the help, right? She began shouting and whistling, shouting and whistling, not stopping until all that blowing made her dizzy: still nothing. Then, just as she was turning around again, she spotted something purple several meters below her: the second flip-flop! Allegra had been here, no doubt about it. The question was, where had she gone from here, in bare feet, and why? She thought about radioing Giac with the news of her discovery but if he was with the men, Ada was bound to hear too, and until she knew what she was dealing with, the last thing she needed was for them to get all alarmed and start barking orders, demanding answers, and accusing her of imaginary crimes. No, what she needed was to round up all three women and return home a hero. Meanwhile, the rumbles of thunder were getting closer, warning her to turn back, daring her to continue, threatening her ability to think clearly. But there was nothing to think about, really. She had no choice, and no time to waste. Tying a red banner onto a branch to mark the spot where she'd recovered the evidence, she shoved the flip-flops into her backpack and set off again.

The downhill trek through the trees was tough, but Carolina was tougher. Soon she was in a sweat and panting, blowing her whistle and crying out Allegra's name as she ran. When the undergrowth became too dense, she slashed through it with her sickle, clawing, crouching, and crawling her way out of the thorny vines that wrapped themselves around her like recurring doubts. How could she be sure that this was the right direction? How could the half-naked, shoeless Allegra have made it through here, if she herself, fully dressed and equipped, was struggling so hard? Had she given up? Changed her course? Was she even out there, or was she already back in her bungalow? And what about the others? Maybe all three had made it safely back to the lodge by returning down the main trail she'd left behind, and were at this very moment wondering where *she* was. There were too many questions, too many unknowns, too many variables banging at her brain, forcing her to stop and hold her throbbing head in her hands before it exploded. And now there was that pain gripping her chest, too, that made it hard to breathe, and she was racked by shivers but soaked in sweat, her ears ringing and her eyes darting around in a panic. It was then that she spotted something blue ensnared in the brambles and now on top of everything else, she was overwhelmed by a sickening, roller-coaster feeling that started deep in her gut, then rose like fire in her throat. On all fours like a dog, she began retching, over and over until there was nothing left, until she felt like her lurching stomach would writhe its way up her gullet and plop down on the ground in front of her. But then the spasms stopped as quickly as they'd started and she rocked back on her heels, uncomfortably aware that her undies were soaked. Using her bandana, she wiped her mouth, closed her eyes, and told herself that if she didn't get a grip, she would not only not be a hero, she'd be dead. After steadying herself with a few deep breaths, she reached her arm through the vines and nabbed the blue garment with the tip of her sickle. She'd known what it was as soon as she'd seen it: the same old sweatshirt Josephine had been wearing that morning while explaining that the Buffalo Bills were her hometown's football team. But why the hell would a woman as unfit as Josephine venture into such a rugged part of the woods? More importantly, what had happened to her?

"*JOSEPHINE!*" she screamed. "*WHERE ARE YOU, JOSEPHINE?*" Again, she tried blowing her whistle, but there was no reply, not even a snort from the boars, who'd certainly been rooting around here but seemed to have moved on. Exactly what an ear-shattering clap of thunder was warning her to do now. Quickly tying another red banner to a branch to mark this second spot, she stuffed the sweatshirt into her backpack on top of Allegra's flip-flops and took a drink of water from her flask. All she needed was one measly minute, sixty seconds of mental silence, to regain her bearings. She had an exceptional sense of orientation (even Giac used to tell her that) and an excellent (if rusty) knowledge of these woods. That combination could and would get her out of here. But only if she stayed calm. In fact, she was already feeling pretty sure that she was heading towards *La Valle delle Felci*, possibly already following the path that was buried under all these brambles because someone by the name of Giac hadn't cleared the trails like he was supposed to! That made sense; Allegra had gone all gaga over that spot when she'd first discovered it, raving on and on about the giant ferns and what they symbolized to different cultures, everything from eternal life to fertility to hope to sincerity and anything else you wanted to throw in. Yes, that was it! After running away like a lunatic that morning, that was just the place she would go to seek her inner peace and realign her kooky chakras or whatever. She must have caught up with the snail-paced Josephine, who was probably fed up with hiking and ravenous for ravioli, so Allegra convinced her to tag along down to the amazing ferns, taking what should have been a shortcut through the woods but turned out to be a tangled, overgrown trap. That didn't explain where Inge was, but she doubted she was with them. With her long legs and no-nonsense stride, she'd probably already planted a Swiss flag at the top of the mountain by that time, and was already back at the lodge, bitching about no one being there to serve her lunch.

Armed with her theory and her sickle, Carolina chopped and hacked her way forward with renewed zeal, silently thanking the boars (she didn't mind the beasts, as long as they kept their snouts out of her vegetable garden) for trampling paths through parts of it. With each rumble of thunder and flash of lightning, her arm swung faster, but there was no way she could outrun the storm. And with the downpour came clarity as to who was to blame for this situation: *Allegra.* This was all *her* fault! If anything happened to Josephine, she'd hold *her* accountable! With every straining muscle in her body, with every inch of territory gained, Carolina grew more furious with the woman. Angry thoughts drenched in rain blinded her to the point that if she hadn't been inspecting her surroundings like a hawk, she might have missed the tattered piece of fabric caught in a branch. But not only did she see it, she recognized it right away. It was that ratty shawl Allegra always dragged around with her like a security blanket! She'd come this way, meaning her hunch was right! Ripping the rag from the branch, she stuffed it into her backpack and tied a third red banner to a branch. Again, she paused to blow her whistle and call out the women's names a few times, but hearing nothing, she pushed ahead.

Or rather, she would have if she could have freed herself of all the creepy crawly brambly vines that were really starting to freak her out again! Gripping the sickle, she began hacking away crazily, determined to not be demoted from hero status to that of a woman who couldn't find her way out of a bush! She was pushing and hacking away so furiously that when she finally broke free she slipped in the mud, but was quick enough to plant her sickle into a tree trunk to break her fall, just as her legs flew out from under her. Flat on her butt, she was stunned to find her feet hanging over the edge of a steep pit that didn't used to be there. Because that was where *La Valle delle Felci* was supposed to be! Scuttling back to safer ground as quickly as she could, she watched gape-mouthed as a clod of earth she dislodged with her boot disappeared over the edge. Why hadn't Giac told her about this landslide? Surely he would have, if he'd known about it. So why didn't he know about it? Was it because it had just happened? Had her drone captured the catastrophic event on video? More importantly, had the catastrophic event captured Allegra and Josephine? And maybe even Inge? If so, someone would find a way to blame her, make it her fault, ruin her. And that was something she could not, would not, allow to happen.

Scrambling to her feet, Carolina surveyed the disastrous scene in front of her. She could see no way to cross the valley of buried ferns and circle back to the lodge from the other side, unless she was stupid enough (which she wasn't!) to risk breaking her neck climbing down one of those fallen tree trunks with the remote possibility of finding a passable connection to the other trail. No, the only sure way back was the way she'd come. Storm or no storm, she'd retrace her steps, at twice the speed. First, she tried raising Giac on the walkie-talkie, but unsurprisingly, he was out of range. And as expected, phone reception was a no-go, too. Today was not her day for being heard. But she'd get her chance, soon enough.

CHAPTER FORTY
Allegra

Allegra wasn't exactly rocking her role of heroic martyr. She was only doing what she felt she had to do, but no matter how deep she dipped into her well of masochism, she couldn't dredge up any enthusiasm for being crucified by the two lame women wrenching her arms from their sockets with every excruciating step. After hobbling through what was left of the fern forest together, she'd lugged them up a slope that was longer and slipperier than it had looked, her flagging energy boosted only by her dogged optimism. An alternate route back to the lodge was out there, she was sure of it. The question now was, could they limp on long enough to find it?

She had no one to blame but herself for creating such a cumbersome threesome. The idea had been hers, but like so many of the *creative* ideas that popped into her head, it translated poorly into practice. If only she'd followed Inge's more *logical* idea of going for help on her own! It made her feel selfish even to think it, but by now she might already be safe from the storm and tending to her wounds, while someone who was *trained* to be a hero conducted the rescue. But how could she leave Josephine behind after seeing the sheer terror in her big blue eyes? And if she let Josephine tag along, how could she abandon the half-crippled Inge in the pit alone? So here they were, and Allegra would keep putting one bloody foot in front of the other until she secured a safe shelter for all three of them, somehow, somewhere, even if it was just a barn. *No one gets left behind, and no one goes it alone.* Those were her words, right?

"Come on, Josephine! Step it up!" Inge snapped, hopping ahead like a hare.

"I'm going as fast as I can!" Josephine cried. "I can't help it if your legs are twice as long as mine!"

"That's enough, you two!" Allegra said, not much enjoying the role of leader, either, when all she wanted to do was curl up in a ball and cry. "That field can't be far now, but we have to take things at a pace that *everyone* can manage! Either that or we *all* fall flat on our faces."

"Right!" Josephine said. "Besides, don't you have *any* consideration for Allegra? Look at her feet! It's a miracle she can even *walk*!"

It was true, her feet were on fire, but it didn't do any good to think about it, much less talk about it. Better to think positive thoughts and talk positive talk. "Let's try to think of ourselves as one entity instead of three separate ones, then focus on putting all our energy into the whole," she said. That sounded kind of smart, actually. "Imagine us as a three-headed, four-legged, woman-creature. We are *strong*, and we can *do* this!"

"Last I looked, we still had *six* legs," Inge muttered.

"But only *four* of them are doing the walking," Allegra said.

Josephine stopped in her tracks, nearly causing a crash. "This is so *wrong!*" she cried. "Allegra's part of the woman-creature has *two* feet to walk on but *no* shoes, while our parts each have only *one* foot to walk on and *two* shoes!" Hanging on tight to Allegra, she bent over with a grunt, wobbling on her right foot. Pulling off her left sneaker, she handed it to Allegra. "Here, put this on. Now Inge, you take off your right boot and give it to her."

"But we're not even the same size!" Inge said. "I'm a 42 and she can't be more than a 38."

"Give her your boot!" Josephine ordered. "*Now!*"

Inge must have been so shocked by Josephine's burst of bossiness that she obeyed. Meanwhile Allegra, despite the women pulling and tugging on her for support, relied on her remarkable balance to stand on her right foot and lift her left leg, wriggling her swollen foot into the sneaker. It was too small, so she laced it loosely, her heel sticking out over the back. Then she took the boot that Inge was holding, shifted her weight to her left leg, and put the boot on her right foot. It was, in fact, huge, so she laced it up tight. Her poor feet weren't happy with the arrangement, but at least they'd be protected from further devastation. And she did appreciate the gesture. "All set!" she said, trying to sound perky. "Thanks!"

"Can we *please* get moving now?" Inge said. "Or do you want to swap T-shirts, too?"

"*Andiamo!*" Allegra said, taking the first step.

The trio forged ahead, not any faster, but more smoothly and silently, as if someone had oiled their cogs. The rain was falling, steady and cold, when the field finally came into view, illuminated by a flash of lightning. Her heart pounding, Allegra sped up their pace a notch. Wouldn't you know it? The worst of the storm was heading straight for them, just when they were approaching the open field! Was that what fate had in store for her? To finally set her up for the lightning which had been stalking her since childhood, patient waiting for the right chance to zap her?

"Hey! What's that?" Josephine asked, again coming to such a sudden stop that everyone stumbled, but Allegra managed to keep them on their feet. She heard the noise, too, a high-pitched squabbling, screeching sound that would have given her goosebumps even if she hadn't already been shivering.

"What do you *think* it is?" Inge said. "Chickens."

"Then we must not be far from the henhouse!" Allegra cried. "That's fantastic!"

"Not for the chickens!" Inge said.

"What do you mean?" Allegra asked.

"They're making *way* too much noise," Inge said.

"Maybe they're afraid of storms?" Josephine said.

"At least they're inside," Allegra said.

The women stood still for a moment, listening.

"Oh, good. They're quiet again. They must have calmed down," Josephine sighed, as if the emotional state of hens topped today's list of things to worry about.

Allegra felt a little calmer too, now that shelter was just minutes away. But even without all the squawking and screaming there was still an eerie feeling in the air, probably because it was charged with electricity. It made the women huddle close together, immobile, alert.

"They're quiet because they're dead," Inge declared.

"What do you mean, *dead*?" Josephine said.

"Chickens don't screech like that, then suddenly decide to shut up. Money has it they had a visitor."

"Who would be visiting the henhouse in this weather?" Allegra asked. "Giac? Carolina?"

"Wolves."

"*Wolves*?" Josephine cried.

"Can't you smell the *blood*?" Inge smirked, her eyes wide, as if she were reading a scary story to a child.

"You're not funny!" Josephine said.

As if taking its cue from Inge, an animal released a long, loud, blood-curdling howl. Allegra's skin prickled, every hair on her body stood on end.

"I'm getting the hell out of here!" Josephine cried, hopping on her good foot, this time so impatiently that she finally fell over. "I'll crawl if I have to! I'll crawl!"

"Calm down and get up!" Inge said. "They won't attack us unless we try to take their food. Let's get moving and leave them to their chicken dinner."

"She's right, Josephine. Come on!" Allegra said, grabbing her arm and pulling her up.

And then they were moving as fast as their four shod feet and throbbing limbs would allow. *Hop-step-step-hop-step-step-hop.* Despite her exhaustion and pain and fear, Allegra couldn't help thinking about those poor birds being gobbled up alive, their feathers flying as the wolves' bloody fangs tore them apart. Then she couldn't help thinking about Carolina, who despite not being an animal lover was crazy about her Livorno hens and their exceptional eggs. She'd be devastated at the loss. Though why Allegra should worry about Carolina's feelings now, or ever, was beyond her.

A terrifying bolt of lightning shot across the dark sky in a jagged horizontal streak, crackling with electricity. Again, a wolf howled. Then another one. Then the hair-raising howling was drowned out by the deafening thunder. And then the rain turned to hail, hard little balls of ice that hammered their heads and pelted their skin. Josephine leaned in closer, trembling like a tub of jelly. Allegra wanted to tell her not to cry, but she couldn't. Her throat was closed so tight she couldn't even scream, which was what she really wanted to do. Keeping her head down so she wouldn't see the lightning dancing around as it tried to strike her, she plowed through the field as fast as she could, hauling along her hobbling companions, with no intention of stopping for one second until she reached the lodge.

CHAPTER FORTY-ONE
Josephine

Unbelievably, mercifully, and yes, please just let her say it, *miraculously*, the precise instant Josephine was on the verge of collapsing into a sobbing, soggy heap, Allegra gave her arm an extra-strong squeeze. The gesture made Josephine raise her drooping, dripping head to a shocking sight. She blinked a few times to be sure, but yes, straight ahead, emerging from the gloom, was the lodge! The women's relief could be heard in their heaving sighs, but no one uttered a word, because no one had a surplus smidgen of strength to spend on speaking. After the chicken incident, they'd hit an awkward kind of stride, their syncopated movements so well distributed that it was hard to tell who was channeling how much energy into that collective burst that pushed them through to the home stretch. Josephine couldn't say whether that force was fueled more by the fear of not making it, the determination to make it, or the faith that they would make it, but somehow, at last, they had made it. As they finally approached the rustic building made of stone and wood, drenched to the bone and chilled to the core, Josephine was overcome with emotions more powerful than the jaw-dropping awe she'd felt on that glorious spring day in Rome the first time she'd stood in front of Saint Peter's Basilica. Tears of relief sprang to her eyes, washing away those of despair. She would survive! She would be cared for! And now that she was sure of making it, the hunger pangs hit her empty stomach like a boxer's barrage of punches.

"We're here! I can't believe it!" she cried over the drumming rain, impatient to get inside and off her feet, or rather, her foot. But instead of heading straight for the door, Allegra led them under the shelter of the eaves, disengaged herself from Josephine, propped her against the wall like a broken bicycle, then parked Inge next to her. Though she'd been glued to Allegra's side every step of the way, it wasn't until she faced her that Josephine could see how utterly spent she looked, with not even a flicker of light left in her sunken eyes. She could see right through those flimsy clothes that stuck to her skin, and even her body itself seemed transparent, like the empty shell of a person whose vitality had been sucked out by two leeches named Josephine and Inge. Allegra, more than anyone, deserved to be taken care of. "Adalberto must be worried sick about you!" she said.

"Who?" Allegra said, wincing as she shook out her arms, rolled her neck and shoulders. "Oh … right. He does worry when he can't get in touch with me."

"Tough luck for him," Inge said. "Rino never worries about me. He knows I can look after myself."

"Yeah, well, the only one I saw looking after anyone was Allegra," Josephine said.

"Look, Rino's car isn't even down there," Inge added. "The guys must still be out."

"Wherever anyone else is doesn't matter right now, what matters is that we're here together," Allegra said. "You two hang one more minute. I'll go find Carolina and we'll come right back for you." Pushing open the heavy wooden door, she disappeared inside.

Josephine didn't want to wait there, and she didn't want to let Allegra out of her sight. She was her angel, she'd saved her from that hellish deathtrap. And she'd saved Inge, too, though it killed the woman to admit it.

"I can't find her," Allegra declared, reappearing a moment later and immediately sliding her arm around Josephine's waist. "Let's get you inside."

"I can't believe we made it!" Josephine repeated as Allegra ushered her through the shadowy entrance and into the dismal dining room, where she seated her on a chair. This wasn't the scene Josephine's head had conjured up to keep her body going. There was no hero's welcome to celebrate their safe return, no crackling fire to warm up next to. No sizzling sounds were coming from the kitchen, either, but Josephine's well-trained nose did detect the smell of something so delicious that her gastric juices started flowing, begging for something to attack. Some elegantly set tables stood to one side, waiting to be of service, but the only light came from a sliver below the door connecting the dining room to the kitchen. "Why is it so dark? I hate the dark."

"Carolina!" Allegra cried in the direction of the kitchen. "We need help!" Without waiting for a response, she hurried off to get Inge, still calling out when she returned. "Carolina! We need you! *Now!*"

She led Inge to a chair next to Josephine, but Inge balked. "For God's sake, give me some breathing room! We've all been attached at the hip long enough!"

"Don't you *ever* stop complaining?" Josephine asked.

"I need some space. And my leg needs to be elevated," Inge said.

"I know. So does Josephine's," Allegra said, plopping down on a third chair. "Just give me a second to take off these shoes."

Looking on, Josephine cringed at the sight of her friend's filthy feet, covered with gashes and scratches. If only she could walk as far as the kitchen on her own, she'd run her a basin of warm water with baking soda and after her feet had a good soak, she'd rub them gently with some of Carolina's best extra virgin olive oil. Josephine's ankle was throbbing with pain, though, and Allegra was already back on her feet, grabbing two more chairs by their backs and dragging them across the tiles, positioning one in front of Inge, the other in front of Josephine.

"Be *extremely* careful!" Inge said with a clenched jaw, as Allegra propped her leg up on the chair. Allegra didn't answer.

Josephine handled emotional pain better than physical pain, and although she did manage to elevate her foot without any assistance, she wasn't able to do so noiselessly. "*Ayy, ooh! Sooo*, where the *devil* is Carolina anyway?" she cried, partly to mask her whimpering.

"Your guess is as good as mine!" Allegra said, hobbling to the kitchen. A few moments later, after more calling for Carolina and rustling around, she returned with some plastic bags filled with ice and a stack of kitchen towels, stopping by the door to flip a switch with her elbow. Two wall sconces with light bulbs in place of candles illuminated half of the dining room.

"Blessed be the light!" Josephine said.

"Any sign of our hostess?" Inge asked.

"Nope. But here, take these," Allegra said, handing a couple of towels to each of the women, and stopping to tie a bag of ice to their injured limbs with another one. She gave an extra one to Inge for her shoulder. When she was done, she used another towel to pat herself dry and wring out her dripping hair. "I'm making some hot tea."

"Forget the damn tea!" Inge snapped. "Find a phone."

"It may surprise you to know that I can do both. I already put the water on, and now I'm going to the office. That's where the phone is." Seconds after she disappeared around the corner, a bolt of lightning struck so close that it made a loud crack. The mighty rumble of thunder that followed rattled the credenza, making the silverware jingle and the stemware tinkle.

"No luck!" Allegra gasped, rushing back to the dining room, her face ashen, her eyes bright.

"What do you mean?" Inge asked.

"The office is locked. Carolina never lets anyone in there."

Inge groaned. "So kick the damn door down!"

"I'm not a door-kicker-downer!" Allegra cried, but she wasn't looking at Inge, she was staring wide-eyed at the lightning show visible through the veranda. She'd seemed like one of the strongest, most courageous women Josephine had ever met the whole time they were actually in danger, and now that they were safe she looked like a scared little girl.

"Well, then go out and look for Carolina and Giac! They have to be around somewhere! They wouldn't just *leave* us here!" A crackling bolt of lightning pierced the sky, a boom of thunder on its heels.

"I am *not* going back outside!" Allegra said, headed in the opposite direction, toward the kitchen.

"Look, we're safe here, right?" Josephine said to Inge.

"We need medical assistance!"

"We *need* lots of things. Like food," Josephine replied. "Allegra will make sure we get them."

A few minutes later Allegra returned to hand out mugs of steaming tea. "Here, let's drink this and warm up while we wait. I added some honey for energy."

"Honey?" Inge asked, wincing as she shifted her weight on the chair. "Couldn't you find anything stronger?"

Without saying another word, Allegra shuffled off to the kitchen again.

"Stop ordering her around, would you?" Josephine whispered to Inge. "She's not your servant."

"Oh, get over your crush!" Inge said. "She likes it. It gives her a sense of fulfillment. Besides, I can't exactly do anything for myself at the moment. Which, by the way, I *abhor*."

This time when Allegra returned, she was carrying a bottle of grappa. "Good girl, that's more like it! And don't be stingy!" Inge said, holding up her mug, which Allegra filled to the brim, forcing Inge to slurp it up in order not to spill it.

"Josephine?" Allegra asked, offering the bottle.

"What the heck," Josephine shrugged. "If it's for medicinal purposes."

"It is," Allegra said, a sudden shiver making her hands shake as she poured. "I guess I'd better have some myself."

"To us!" Josephine said, raising her drink. "To the three-headed, four-legged woman-creature who survived deathly falls, escaped wild animals, defied the elements, and made it back alive!"

"To us," Allegra said, smiling a tiny, tired smile at Josephine, who smiled back. Then the two women turned to Inge.

"What? Why are you staring at me?" she said, gulping her tea. After a roll of her eyes, she finally lifted her mug and mumbled, "Oh, all right. To us."

They were sitting there in their little circle, dazed and anxious, shivering and aching, sipping on their comforting beverage, the weight of exhaustion pressing their bodies into their straight-backed chairs, when another lightning bolt struck, so violently that all three women screamed. Allegra's mug crashed to the floor, followed by Allegra herself, who curled up into a ball, her arms hugging her head. The lights flickered once, then twice, then went out altogether, leaving them in the dwindling dusk. Seconds later, an ear-splitting clap of thunder shook the building to its foundations.

CHAPTER FORTY-TWO
Inge

"Get a hold of yourself, girl!" Inge cried to the trembling figure on the floor. "It's lightning, not an earthquake!"

"Don't be so mean!" Josephine said, leaning forward on her chair and reaching her arm out. "Allegra, honey, it's okay. Give me your hand."

Without raising her head, Allegra stuck her hand in the air, waving it in the direction of Josephine's voice.

"You're safe here," Josephine said in that annoyingly empathic voice of hers as she grabbed Allegra by the wrist and pulled. The two of them really did suit each other.

"I feel so *stupid*," Allegra said, sitting back on her heels. Letting go of Josephine's hand, she wrapped her arms around herself.

"Well, yes, being terrified of a summer storm when you're inside a sturdy stone building definitely qualifies as stupid," Inge said. She could have said more on the subject of irrational fears, but seeing how pale and drawn Allegra looked, how frail and vulnerable her birdlike body appeared inside her soaked tunic, she refrained. "You're overreacting because you're cold and exhausted. You need to get out of those wet clothes. We all do."

"We need light, too, before it gets so dark we can't see a thing!" Josephine said. "There are some candles on those tables over there. Could you go get them, Allegra?"

Allegra nodded, rising from the floor to her feet in that effortless way of yoga practitioners. Inge had never managed to do that, maybe she was too tall and muscular, or maybe she never saw the point of trying, not being fond of floors in the first place. Keeping an eye on Allegra in case she keeled over again, she watched her gather the candles from the tables, bring them over, and set them down on an empty table by their chairs. As if on automatic pilot, she then went to the credenza, found some matches in a drawer, and returned to light the candles.

"Phew, that's better!" Josephine sighed. "Any chance you could start a fire, too?"

Allegra gave her a blank stare, as if she didn't understand how that could happen. "With what?" she finally asked.

"You're holding a whole box of matches in your hand, aren't you?" Inge said.

"Yeah, but the wood's outside."

"Oh, right! And so is the storm," Josephine said. "Never mind!"

"*Mein Gott*," Inge sighed, closing her eyes and pinching the bridge of her nose. When people were paralyzed by fear, it was better to give them precise orders, assign them a task they could handle. "Listen Allegra, how about if you go back over to those tables, grab the tablecloths of those three tables, and bring them over here?"

Allegra didn't hesitate to follow the request, in fact, she seemed rather reassured by it as she walked purposefully toward the tables, swept aside the dishes and cutlery and glasses, barely reacting when some of the items fell to the floor with a crash. She systematically – and noisily – slid off the first tablecloth, then the second one, then the third one. "Well done!" Inge called to her. "Now bring them over here."

Allegra hobbled back over to Inge and delivered the tablecloths, as instructed.

"Now take off those drenched rags of yours, and wrap one of these around you," she said to her. "Here, you take one, too," she said, bunching up a tablecloth and tossing it to Josephine with her good arm.

"Hey, I caught it!" Josephine said, smiling proudly. "But I'm *not* taking off my clothes."

"Do as you like," Inge said, spreading a tablecloth over her own shoulders as best she could. "It's as big as a blanket, so pretend it's one. Linen isn't warm like wool, but this is darn good quality. Believe me, I know my fabrics."

Allegra stood there in her panties, which Inge was a little surprised – and relieved – to see she was wearing, already wrapping the tablecloth around her torso like a toga. Seeing her in the candlelight like that, with her pallid face and green eyes offset by her damp auburn curls, she managed to look rather striking, in that slightly spooked, malnourished way of cocaine-addicted top models and anorexic actresses.

"Here, drink my tea, Allegra," Josephine said. "It'll do you good."

Allegra accepted the mug, drank down the spiked tea in great gulps, then looked around and blinked, as if waking from a dream. "I'm starving," she said. "How about you guys?"

"You know, now that you mention it, I could eat something!" Josephine said.

"How can you even *think* about food at a time like this?" Inge asked. What she thought about was the cache of painkillers in the medical bag she'd left in the car, which would certainly be back, along with Rino, any minute. Take some drugs and get the hell out of there, that was what she thought about. Until then, she'd settle for some more grappa. She held up her mug. "Allegra?"

Still obligingly obedient, Allegra sloshed another generous dose of liquor into Inge's mug, then topped off Josephine's as well.

"You can leave the bottle with me," Inge said. "I'll take good care of it."

Allegra shrugged, setting it on the floor next to her. "There were some pots on the stove," she said. "I'll go see what's in them." Then she hobbled back to the kitchen, taking a candle with her.

"Wow, that's strong stuff!" Josephine said to Inge, as if they were old drinking buddies. "I didn't notice it so much before, with the tea and honey."

"That's the whole point."

"Do you drink much?"

"Do you eat much?" Inge said, her eyes roving pointedly over Josephine's abundant curves.

"Yes. And you are rude," Josephine said, draining her mug. "I'd like some more grappa."

"Serve yourself," Inge said, holding out the bottle. "And leave the cap off. I can't manage all that screwing and unscrewing with my arm in this sling."

The women sat without speaking, listening to the rain beating against the panes and the thunder rumbling through the valley, backed up by Allegra's banging in the kitchen. Inge wondered whether she was always that clumsy around housewares.

"I hardly touch alcohol these days," she said. "But we of Alpine heritage learn how to hold it at a young age."

"So do we Americans. Especially those from messed-up families. Which is basically all of us," Josephine tried to laugh, but her lips twisted into a wry smile. "I don't drink much either, though. Just wine, now that I'm in Italy."

"Same here. I used to adore a tankard of ale after a day of hiking. And when you come in from a good ski, nothing warms your insides better than a nip of something strong. Now I have too many responsibilities to drink. Or hike. Or ski." Grabbing the grappa bottle, she started to pour herself another shot, but instead took a swig straight from the bottle.

"What the hell?" she cried, bottle still in hand, on hearing a bang that didn't come from the storm, but from the kitchen. A cart burst through the door, pushed by Allegra, wearing a fancy apron over her tablecloth toga. Josephine's face broke into a giant grin of joy as the candlelit cart laden with all kinds of food was wheeled over to them. Parking the cart in between the two women, Allegra went over to ransack the dining tables again, picking up some plates, cutlery, and wine goblets, which tottered and tinkled as she carried them back and handed them out.

"Oh, I had some of that Parma prosciutto at breakfast!" Josephine exclaimed. "It's so tender it practically melts in your mouth! Had I known it may have been my last meal, I would have eaten more!" Stabbing a slice with her fork, she tilted her head back and lowered it to her tongue. "*Mmm!*"

"Care for some homemade bread?" Allegra said, holding out a basket.

"Is the pope Catholic?" Josephine chuckled as she chewed. "This is my favorite kind, dense on the inside, crusty on the outside. Who wants to eat bread that doesn't put up a fight? No *grazie*, I'll save the fluffy stuff for the day – God forbid – I lose my teeth."

Watching a woman go so wild over food would have normally disgusted Inge, but now it was stimulating her appetite. Especially since the grappa seemed to be dulling the sharpest edges of her pain. She spooned some little black olives from a bowl onto her plate, popped one into her mouth, nibbled on the savory pulp, and spit out the pit.

"Aren't those *divine*?" Josephine said, piling more prosciutto onto a thick slice of bread. "They're *taggiasca* olives, meaning they come from the Taggia area of Liguria. Carolina told me that."

"There's cheese here, too," Allegra said, pointing to the tray. "Carolina's goat milk ricotta. And look at all this fresh fruit I found in the pantry."

"I *adore* ricotta!" Josephine said, chomping on a chunk of crust. "But I prefer it in sweets, you know, like cannoli and such." She took a break to wash down the bread with some grappa, which made her sputter, but not enough to shut her up. "How about the ravioli? Did you see those? Carolina said she was going to make them with boar sauce! I was curious to try that."

"The ravioli are there, all right. I put the pot on to boil, and the sauce is warming up," Allegra said, back to her usual servile self. "Who wants wine? I found a bottle of Barbera d'Asti. I liked the label, with this pretty tree on it."

"Show me," Inge ordered, and Allegra obeyed. "Ah, Gelsomora. It's from the same makers of the wine we had last night at dinner. I guess I could switch from grappa to that. Go ahead and open it."

Allegra uncorked the wine and poured, and the three women fell silent, sipping and eating, Josephine devouring her food, Inge chewing hers deliberately, Allegra picking at the few things on her plate, until Josephine leaned back in her chair and cried out, "This is torture! I can't take it anymore!"

"What's wrong, Josephine?" Allegra asked, rushing over to her. "Is it your ankle? What?"

"Well, that too!" Josephine groaned, hugging her abdomen. "But mostly it's these stupid *jeans*! I can't eat another bite in them! They're too *tight*! And so *soggy*! I can't stand them another minute!"

"I *told* you to take them off!" Inge said.

"I'm not taking them off until I have something else to put on! Something besides a *tablecloth*!"

"There's nothing in the kitchen," Allegra said, glancing nervously out at the raining and rumbling storm, for the moment without lightning. "But I suppose I could sneak upstairs to see what I can find," she added, taking a candle with her as she limped away again.

Despite her moaning and groaning, Josephine continued tearing off bits of bread, which quickly amounted to a whole slice. It was excellent bread though, Inge had to admit, and a lifeline for her stomach, which was drowning in alcohol. It also had the added advantage of keeping one's mouth occupied, thereby avoiding conversation. Inge glanced at her watch, possibly only to make sure something was still working the way it was meant to. She didn't know what time Rino was due back, but he was certainly late.

"I had to rummage through Giac's closet," Allegra said, returning with some clothes over her arm. "Here, put these on," she said to Josephine, handing her a pair of roomy sweatpants. "I brought some sweaters, too." After offering a man's V-neck pullover to Josephine, Allegra zipped herself into a knit jacket, certainly Carolina's, then approached Inge with a cozy cardigan, guiding her good arm into a sleeve then gently arranging the rest over her shoulders. Inge was thinking of possibly thanking her when Josephine cried out again.

"*Ugh!*" she grunted, trying to wriggle out of her jeans, shooting dagger eyes at Inge when she caught her looking. "No peeking!" But the scene was too comical to ignore. The jeans were stuck down by Josephine's knees, but because of her pudgy midsection, she wasn't able to bend forward enough to pull them off. After some more huffing and puffing, she cried, "Someone *help* me, for God's sake!"

"Do you care about those jeans?" Allegra asked.

"*No!*" Josephine cried, her face flushed as she wriggled and writhed. "I *hate* them! Get them *off* me!"

Wielding the serrated bread knife, Allegra carefully sawed through enough of the left pant leg to avoid further traumatizing Josephine's swollen ankle, then grabbed the pants by the waistband and pulled them off as fast as you'd tear a band-aid off a hairy man's chest.

"*Ayyy!*" Josephine wailed. Inge roared with laughter. Allegra, who'd been tugging so hard she fell over backward, began giggling too. Josephine, freed from the trousers of torture, howled with relief.

CHAPTER FORTY-THREE
Carolina

"Calling Giac! Do you read me Giac? Do you read me?" Carolina shouted, breathless from running and slipping and sliding through the woods under the pouring rain (not to mention freaking out with worry!). But she'd made it back to the beginning of the trailhead in record time, and now that the lodge was in view, she needed to know what to expect, what to say, and what to do when she got there. Her thumb on the push-to-talk button, her mouth so close to the receiver that she sprayed it with spit, she was trying desperately to raise her husband. When would he learn that cheap equipment was worthless? What the hell good was a walkie-talkie if it didn't let you walk and talk?

Suddenly, the crappy handset crackled with static. "I hear you! I hear you!" Giac's voice was muffled, but at least it was a voice. "You don't need to scream!"

"Are you guys back?" she cried. "Over."

"No, we're not back. Not even close to back!"

"Why not? Over."

"Quit saying '*over*,' would you?" Giac yelled.

Carolina rolled her eyes. The man had no respect for procedure. He'd see what "over" *really* meant, one of these days. "What's taking you so long?"

"You know that giant dead oak? It got hit by lightning, split in half, and crashed onto the access road. Took down the power and phone lines too. And now we're stuck on the wrong side of it."

"That same oak I've been telling you to cut down for what? *Three years*?" Carolina couldn't stop her tongue from lashing out. She didn't wait for Giac to say that that wasn't the point, that this wasn't the time. With him, it was never the point, or the time. "Can't you ram it out of the way with that macho truck of yours?"

"It's a goddam massive *tree*, Carolina. And besides, it's lying on *top* of that macho truck of mine. Slammed right onto the hood. Lucky thing we were all sitting in Rino's car. Ada made me get in to show me something."

"Can't you make those wusses walk up?" She didn't care if they all heard her. But no one said anything. "Giac? Do you read me?"

"I'm here, I'm here. I stepped out of the car to talk. Listen, Ada told me that when Rino blew out his tire he had a shit fit, and then he overexerted trying to repair it."

"Tell me something I don't know."

"He got really bad chest pains. He thought he was having a heart attack."

"A *heart attack*?" Oh God, could this day get any worse? Could it?

"Ada thinks maybe it was indigestion. They stopped at a bar and people kept bringing them stuff to eat. He says Rino must have devoured an entire foot-long salami."

"He stuffed his face with *salami*? While I was *killing* myself to prepare an exquisite meal?"

"Whatever. The fact is, I'm not gonna make the man walk if he maybe might have been having a heart attack. He doesn't want Inge to know, so don't go telling her."

"OK, I won't. Roger."

"You did find Inge, didn't you?"

"What?"

"Inge! You found her, right? And the other women?"

"What's that? You're not coming through!"

"Listen up! Send Allegra down in Ada's SUV like he told you to! I don't want to leave the guys here alone and it's raining too hard to walk anyway."

Carolina pushed the talk button, contracted her glottis, and said, "*ghoochaagh*." Pocketing the device, she said, "Over. And out."

These people were going to give *her* a heart attack! She needed a plan before everything blew up in her face. She always had a plan, she was the *master* of plans! Was it *her* fault if shit kept going wrong? Was *she* to blame if the shitheads kept screwing up? Panting and panicking, she made a run for the lodge, desperately trying to figure out what she'd do about finding the women once she got there.

CHAPTER FORTY-FOUR
Josephine

No one heard the latch click, but the door must have opened because someone stood in the shadows of the flickering candlelight, and that someone let out a shriek that froze the laughter on the lips of the giggling women. All three swiveled their heads around to see what the source of the scary sound was, Allegra still gripping the knife she'd used to slice through Josephine's jeans.

"What the *hell* is going on here?" the hooded person screamed, charging into the dining room. Allegra was the first to find her voice.

"*Carolina?* Is that *you?* Where have you *been?*"

"Where have *I* been? Where have *you* all been? Do you realize what kind of *hell* you put me through? *Do you?*" Carolina shouted. "I thought you were *dead!*"

"We would be if wasn't for Allegra!" Josephine cried. "We fell into this awful pit, but she saved us!"

"Compliments on doing such a superb job of booby-trapping those trails!" Inge said. "You belong in jail!"

"It's all *your* fault! You people can't just take off like that!" Carolina cried, pushing back her hood to reveal dark eyes glinting with anger. "*I'm* the one in charge here, and I specifically instructed you to check with me before going into the woods! I had maps to give you, and advice! But no, you all just ran off on your own, totally unprepared, with a storm on the way!"

"I can assure you that I, at least, am an *expert* mountaineer!" Inge retorted. "And I was perfectly equipped for a walk in the woods. You people are criminals for allowing access to that death trap! At least post some warnings, for God's sake!"

"For your information, *Frau Doktor* Expert Mountaineer, rocks roll! Land slides! That's why you have to stick to the marked trails like good girl scouts! What was I supposed to think when I found this?" Digging into her backpack, she pulled out one of Allegra's flip-flops, held it up high for all to see, then threw it to the floor with a grimace. "And this? And this? And this?" In quick succession, Allegra's second sandal was displayed and dropped, then her shawl, then Josephine's sweatshirt, all landing in a pile on the floor.

"Oh! Can I have that?" Josephine cried, her hand outstretched. She wanted to nuzzle her nose in her beloved blue sweatshirt and hug it to her chest; she wanted to check if by some miracle Nonna's rosary was still in its pocket; she wanted to feel the familiarity of Buffalo, with its detested climate and adored football team that had made it to four Super Bowls but couldn't field the trophy, and its greasy, spicy specialty of chicken wings with blue cheese dip and celery sticks on the side. But Carolina just stared at her. And what a stare! Evil as the devil himself.

"You can have it when *I* say you can have it!" Carolina yelled, the veins in her neck bulging as she jabbed her finger in Josephine's face. Josephine was so shocked that she couldn't even react. No one had treated her like that since she was a kid.

"Okay, *okay!*" Allegra said, raising her hands. "That's *enough!*"

"I risked my *life* for you!" Carolina said, jabbing fingers left and right. "And all the while you were holed up here having a *party!* You could have at least *called* to let me know you were *alive!*"

"*Called?* Who? How?" Inge said. "The reception up here is *appalling!*"

"Besides, none of us had phones, Carolina," Allegra said, with remarkable calm, smoothing the skirt of her tablecloth toga. "I wanted to call you on the landline but your office was locked."

"Damn right it was locked! Just like the kitchen should have been locked! Who told you you could go in there, huh?" Carolina was pacing back and forth, back and forth, then around in circles like a caged animal. She still hadn't taken off her slicker and was leaving little pools of water wherever she stopped. "Who told you you could help yourselves to *my* food after not having the decency to turn up for the meal I prepared? Don't you have any *respect?*"

"We were *starving!*" Josephine said.

"I'm the one who took the food," Allegra said.

"And who told you you could go into our *private* quarters and help yourselves to our clothes? *Who?*" Carolina grabbed a fistful of Allegra's knit jacket, unzipped it, and pulled it halfway off.

"We were cold and wet!" Josephine cried.

"I'm the one who went upstairs," Allegra said, calmly pushing away Carolina's hand.

"And that's *my* personalized chef's apron you're wearing under *my* sweater! See those initials? CC? Those are *mine,* not yours! And what the hell are you doing playing dress-up with my good Irish linen?" she yelled, tugging at the tablecloth. "*What?*"

"Leave her *alone!*" Josephine cried, throwing a fistful of gnawed olive pits at the back of Carolina's head.

Carolina spun around. Glaring at Josephine, she took a step toward her, then gave a sadistic kick to the chair that her injured foot rested on. Josephine saw stars, but bit her lip and stared back. Just play it cool, she told herself, while sweating up a storm in Giac's pullover. But as quickly as Carolina had attacked her, she backed off, shuffling away in that oddly lopsided way of hers. She stopped by the dismantled tables, her shoulders slumped, her head drooping. "Everything was so *perfect*! I waited for you for *hours*!"

Josephine suddenly regretted throwing the pits at her. Now she felt sorry for her, picturing her in the empty dining room, waiting to serve the delicious food she'd spent all morning preparing. Food that no one showed up to eat.

"And my *dishes*! Who broke my dishes?" Carolina moaned, kicking aside bits of pottery that skidded across the tiles. "*Who?*"

"*I* did!" Allegra said. "Just blame me for *everything*, okay? I'll pay for all of it. But calm down. *Please*!"

"*Enough*!" Inge shouted. "More serious things have been broken than your precious dishes! Things like *bones*! I need medical attention! We all do! So snap out of it, would you? Call Rino, call an ambulance, call the EMTs! But get help up here! *Stat*!"

Instead of replying, Carolina began pacing in circles again, her eyes cast downward as she finally took off her dripping jacket and slung it over a chair. "Look at my *floor*! I keep it so clean you could eat off it! And now there's mud and blood and who knows what else smeared everywhere! It's *disgusting*!"

"Forget the damn floor!" Inge snapped. "Call Rino and tell him to get his ass back here!"

"*Nein.* Not possible."

"What's that supposed to mean?"

"It means what it means." Carolina's voice was calmer as she stood in front of Inge, her hands on her bony hips, but her chest was still rapidly rising and falling. "It. Is. Not. Possible. We have no phone service and no power. The lines were knocked down by a tree that got struck by lightning."

"Oh no!" Allegra cried, her hand flying to her chest.

"How do you know that?" Inge asked.

"Giac told me."

"And where *is* the resident cowboy, if I may ask?"

"He went to pick up Rino and Ada."

"Oh, really? He gets around, doesn't he?" Inge said.

"What's that supposed to mean?" Carolina asked.

"It means what it means," Inge grinned. "But getting back to Rino and Ada, where are they?"

"The boys got a flat. You really should teach your husband how to drive. Among other things."

"What's that supposed to mean?"

"It means what it means," Carolina said, smirking.

"Enough of your games! Where are they? And why aren't they back yet?"

"You know that tree I mentioned? They're stuck on the other side of it. The road is closed. *Chiuso. Geschlossen.*"

"And they're just sitting there? Why don't they walk?"

"Seems as though they don't want to get wet."

"Well, go *get* them!" Inge ordered.

Josephine stared at Inge, feeling a surge of admiration, or at the very least gratitude, that she had both the energy and the attitude to conduct this conversation.

"*Not* a good idea," Carolina said, shaking her head vigorously.

"I'll go," Allegra said. "I'll take Adalberto's SUV."

"*No!*" Carolina screamed. Her black eyes darted from face to face until she slapped her palms over them, as if she couldn't bear the sight of the other women for one more second. When she finally opened her eyes again, her voice sounded eerily flat, as if someone had flipped a switch, from Crazy Carolina to Calm Carolina. "The men made me promise that we'd all stay put, right here, together. The road is dangerous, and more trees could fall. Besides, Ada said he has the keys to his car in his pocket. So everybody just sit tight. You're safe here with me."

Josephine really wished she could get her hands on that rosary. Or at least on the bottle of grappa.

CHAPTER FORTY-FIVE
Allegra

Except for the occasional joint she was coaxed into smoking with her parents, Allegra had never messed with drugs. Her head was all over the place as it was, always buzzing back and forth between fuzzy borders, never knowing for sure what was real and what was imaginary. Sometimes, when she had a problem that seemed unsolvable, she managed to meditate it away. So did that mean that the problem had existed only in her head? Other times, meditation opened her eyes to things she'd never seen. So did that mean it was her head that made them real? Right now that head was so confused that she couldn't even tell what she should be doing anymore. What she *wanted* to do, was sit in a dark corner and think about how to act around Adalberto when she saw him, which would be soon. But right now her priority was to keep caring for the injured companions she'd worked so hard to bring back to safety, and to prevent Carolina from spinning totally out of control.

"Carolina?" Allegra said, trying to strike a tone of voice that would placate her instead of setting her off again.

"What can I do for you?"

"I looked for the first aid kit in your kitchen, but that little white cabinet with the red cross on it was empty."

"You can thank Giac for that! He's always stealing my stuff and not replacing it!"

"Well, could we at least get some disinfectant for our cuts? I didn't want to go rummaging around in your bathroom."

Carolina glared at her but said nothing.

"And don't you guys have a generator up here?"

"Yes, we have a generator up here," she mimicked in a child's voice. "What do you *think*?"

"Oh, good! Do you think maybe you could start it up?"

"How am I supposed to start it up if there's no gas to run it? Huh? Giac keeps forgetting to fill the tanks and I'm *not* going to fall into the trap of doing all his work for him!"

"Oh. Well. How about an emergency lamp? You have to have one of those, right? By law?"

"Oh, so now you're going to turn me in, or what? The emergency lamps

I keep here – one in the kitchen and one in the dining room as per regulations – somehow always end up in the barn!"

Mention of the barn reminded Allegra of the chicken coop, which reminded her of the wolves, which gave her goosebumps. This probably wasn't a great time to tell Carolina about the horrific hen massacre. "I see. Well, candles are nice. You probably have plenty of those."

"I sure hope so!" Josephine said. "And could you at least contact the guys to let them know that Allegra and Inge are safe?" she asked. "They must be out of their minds with worry."

"And how do you suggest I do that? My cell phone isn't working, the landline isn't working, the internet isn't working and Giac's walkie-talkie isn't working," Carolina said hurriedly, tallying the casualties on her fingers. "Is that *clear*?"

"Well, maybe whoever sent that drone saw the landslide," Josephine suggested. "Maybe they'll send help."

"You *saw* the drone?" Carolina perked up.

"We did indeed," Inge said. "*Someone* actually thought it was a helicopter!"

"Ha! I *love* that! But I can tell you for sure that it was a drone, because it was mine!" Carolina said, grinning proudly.

"*You* have a drone?" Allegra said.

"Yes, I have a drone! No one was coming back, no one was answering their phones, and I was getting alarmed. Of course, Giac wasn't around to help, so I took matters into my own hands and sent the drone to recon the area, hoping to locate you."

"Well, aren't you the clever one?" Inge said. "You were on the right track. Too bad you chickened out so soon."

"The weather forced me to abort!"

"You must have been awfully worried about us!" Josephine said.

"Of course I was!" Carolina said, wringing her hands. "You are my responsibility, and I would never forgive you, I mean *myself*, if anything happened to you!"

"Well, you'd better brush off your hairshirt, then. As you can clearly see, something *did* happen to us!" Inge said.

"Oh come on, no one's in danger of *dying* here, are they, *Doktor* Egger?

"You shouldn't underestimate the risks of delayed treatment," Inge replied. "There's not only my leg and shoulder to be concerned about, but Josephine's ankle. And Allegra did get bit by a snake.

"Oh, don't worry about me," Allegra said, wanting to downplay the drama before Carolina got too worked up again. "But maybe you could find that disinfectant I asked you about? So we can at least clean our cuts?"

"Disinfectant isn't going to fix our broken bones!" Inge said. "We need to get to a hospital!"

"Broken bones aren't life-threatening though, are they?" Carolina asked.

"I'd say you'd be running a bigger risk being evacuated by chopper. With the road blocked, that's the only way out!"

"You wouldn't get me to leave a safe place with plenty of food to eat and wine to drink, to go up in any helicopter!" Josephine said, draining her wine glass of its last sip.

"Even if there were a pilot with enough balls to fly here in this weather, which I doubt, I wouldn't go either," Inge said.

"Very well then," Carolina said. "So now that we can put the idea of any men rushing to rescue you, let's take advantage of this time to focus on how, with my help, you can rescue yourselves. You came here for a transformative experience. Make no mistake, I will see to it that you get it."

Allegra had gone through so many transformations since yesterday that she could hardly remember how she'd felt driving up in the car with Adalberto, what they'd talked about, or what expectations she'd had for the weekend. It seemed like such a long time ago.

"I just might be all experienced out," Josephine sighed.

"I just want to get the hell out of here," Inge said.

"Not quite yet, my dear *Doktor*, not quite yet!" Carolina said. "But where are my manners? I do believe the refreshments need replenishing!" She disappeared into the kitchen, leaving the women in stupefied silence.

"Do you think she's going to bring the ravioli?" Josephine finally whispered.

But Carolina was back already, bearing a tray with another bottle of wine, a carafe of water, and a loaf of bread. "The perfect inspiration for transformation," she said, uncorking the wine, pouring it into fresh glasses, and passing them around.

"To us!" she said, standing in front of the three seated women, her eyes bright, too bright, maybe borderline feverish, if Allegra were to describe them. "To women who are strong enough to survive transformation, and thrive!"

Allegra, Josephine, and Inge stole glances at one another without diverting their attention from Carolina, who kept flicking her bangs out of her eyes as she stood there, glass in the air, staring at them expectantly. "Well?"

"To us!" they mumbled, afraid to find out what exactly they were celebrating.

CHAPTER FORTY-SIX
Inge

After a moment of uneasy silence, Carolina slipped away to her office, taking a candle with her. The sounds of keys jangling, a lock turning, and paper shuffling made the women glance at one another, in wordless recognition that whatever situation they were in, they were still in it together.

"I used up all my cartridges to do it, but I knew I wouldn't regret printing this out," Carolina said, returning to the group. Sitting down in a chair, she set a stack of papers on the table, lining up their edges so that they were perfectly even. Picking up the top page, she stared at it for a moment and smiled. "He's a very striking young man!" she said.

It wasn't clear who she was talking to, or about, or whether she expected a response. No one offered one.

"The resemblance is remarkable, too." Carolina tilted her head, making a show of studying whatever she was looking at from different angles, now and then casting a sidelong glance at Inge. "Rather uncanny, in fact." Finally flipping the sheet over, she held it up for Inge to see, then showed it to the others.

"But that's Carl!" Inge cried. "Where did you get that?"

"Where do you think? On the internet. This is his Facebook profile photo, but there are many others, and even more on Instagram and probably a whole bunch on some of those other platforms the young people use today to publicly make fools of themselves. I'm not into all those, but I did google him."

"Why would you google my son?" Inge asked, wincing as she pulled herself up in her chair.

"To help. Why do you think?"

"Help *who*? Help *how*?"

Carolina shook her head slowly, indulgently. "As I was saying, the resemblance is undeniable."

"Well, yes, lots of people say he looks like me. And he takes after me, too. He's big on science. I think he's set on becoming a doctor. I hope it doesn't break his father's heart," Inge said, but why? She was confused, caught off guard, and certainly a little tipsy. She clamped her tongue between her front teeth before she could tell this woman anything else.

"Au contraire!" Carolina said. "I daresay his father will be tickled." Setting the paper on the table, she picked up two new ones from the pile.

"That resemblance I mentioned, I don't really see it here, do you?" she said, holding out another sheet for Inge and the others to see. It was an image of Carl and Rino on a sailboat, both with wind-tousled hair and tanned skin and smiles as radiant as the summer sun, Rino proudly posing at the helm and Carl holding up a trophy. It was taken after they'd won a father-son regatta on Lake Como, Inge remembered the day well, despite not being able to attend. Though it seemed like yesterday, it must have been a few years back. Carl was still a lanky, smooth-faced adolescent, but already an excellent sailor.

"What a beautiful son, Inge!" Josephine exclaimed. "He and his father look so happy here!"

Inge glared at Josephine. "If I wanted to share family photos, I would have brought an album."

"Happy, maybe," Carolina said, ignoring Inge's comment. "But not alike, right? Personally, I think he looks more like *this* father than *that* father." After a pregnant pause, Carolina held up the second sheet, stared at it, smiled, then waved it in front of Inge's face.

"What do you mean by this?" Inge demanded.

"C'mon, Inge. It's just us girls here. You can tell us. Right, girls?" Carolina looked at Josephine and Allegra, who remained silent. "He's a handsome rascal, isn't he?" she asked, reaching out to show them the printed image from up close.

"Oh yes, he's a *very* handsome man," Josephine agreed. "He's a doctor, too, I take it from the white jacket and stethoscope?"

"Yes, I downloaded this one from LinkedIn. He's not into Facebook."

"What does it matter what that man looks like or what he does?" Inge snapped." It's none of anyone's business."

"Call me a fool," Carolina said, "but it looks like it might be Carl's business. And Rino's." Setting down the photo of Rino and Carl together in the boat, she then picked up the previous photo of Carl alone and held it next to the doctor's photo for Inge, then the others, to examine, as if she were introducing exhibits at a jury trial.

"You know, you're *right*, Carolina! If anyone were to ask *me*, I'd have to say these two guys really *do* look alike!" Josephine exclaimed.

"No one is asking you anything, Josephine! That's *enough!*" Inge cried. She knew that Carl looked more like him with each passing year, but she tried not to dwell on it. And she certainly never looked at their pictures side by side. Now that Carl was approaching manhood, anyone who saw them together would have no doubt they were related. But no one would *ever* see them together, not if she had anything to say about it.

"I don't know what you're insinuating, Carolina," Allegra said, "but Inge's family is none of our business."

"I'm not insinuating anything. I'm *exposing* it. I happen to know this man. He's originally from Imperia, down on the coast. He moved away as a medical student and never returned, though he made some very fond memories here. He was one of our first guests back when we opened, and came up whenever he could grab a few free days. Then at one point, he disappeared. I never heard from him again until last week when he called to request that I kindly take special care of a colleague to whom he'd recommended us as the perfect spot for some soul searching."

"And based on a friendly recommendation you took it upon yourself to dig up pictures of my family?" Until recently, Inge had rarely had any contact with Fabio Fustello. There was no point; that was their pact, and both knew it was better that way.

"Oh, his call had very little to do with it," Carolina said, with a wave of her hand. "It was all very coincidental, you see. When I was checking you in, I looked up Rino, a standard procedure of mine that enables me to get a better feel of who my guests are and what sort of personalized treatment I can offer them, especially if they're new and only plan to stay a day or two. Honestly, how can you get to know a person in such a short space of time? I figure why not take advantage of all the information people so generously put out there for our free and easy consumption? Anyway, as I was saying, when I looked up Rino and saw the picture of the boy, I looked up the boy. Honestly, if Dr. Fustello hadn't phoned me, I might have thought your son looked vaguely familiar, but I *never* would have made the connection. But then when your doctor friend called a second time, I looked him up, the way I do when someone from the past resurfaces and I want to get caught up without asking them a million questions, which some might mistakenly consider nosy. I have to say, I was *flabbergasted* when I saw that photo!" Carolina threw up her hands and shrugged her shoulders. "It was *fate*, I guess."

"*What* fate? *Whose* fate? What the *hell* are you talking about?" Inge cried. Her eyes darted from crazy Carolina to wide-eyed Josephine and flush-faced Allegra.

"Yes, my dear Inge. You poor, poor woman. You've been walking around with this tremendous secret all these years. What a weight to carry on your sorely overburdened shoulders! Admit it! Doesn't it feel better to have it all out in the open?"

"Have *what* out in the open? You have no idea what you're talking about!"

"Did you always know it was his and not Rino's?"

"What I know is I'm switching back to grappa! *Now!* Hand me the bottle, Allegra."

"Of course," Allegra said, looking lost.

Grabbing the bottle from her, Inge poured a generous shot of grappa into her wineglass and took a swig. Eyes closed, she tilted her head back and let the liquid slide over her tongue and down her throat, burning everything in its path.

Josephine cleared her throat. "It may not be my place to speak out here, but I feel a calling to tell you not to fear the truth, Inge," she began. "As Allegra said earlier, everything happens for a reason. This day has presented us with many unexpected challenges, though right now we might be asking ourselves, why *us*, why *here*, why *now*? If you feel troubled and need to clear your conscience, then I can't help thinking that maybe we've been brought together to help get you through it." Upon concluding her little speech, Josephine glanced at the others, looking both grateful and astonished that no one had interrupted her. "Now I think I'll have some more of that grappa too, please."

Allegra retrieved the bottle from Inge and was about to pour some into Josephine's wine glass when Carolina jumped to her feet. "For heaven's sake, if you're going to drink that rotgut, at least use the right glasses!" She stomped over to the credenza, brought back three cordial glasses, and handed one to each of them. Allegra poured two fingers of grappa for Josephine, but none for herself.

"Dammit all!" Inge muttered, taking another swallow of liquor. The rational part of her had always known that her secret would have to come out eventually, but she wasn't about to share it now! Not in this godforsaken place, under these ridiculous circumstances, with these pathetic people! Yet at the same time, she began to feel something inside her subtly and unexpectedly give way. That hard, cold blockage in the center of her chest that sometimes made it hard for her to swallow, or talk, or even breathe, seemed to be cracking with each sip of grappa, as if she were drizzling scalding water onto a slab of ice. "It's not like you think," she said, cringing at how lame it sounded.

"It never is, is it?" Carolina said, her dark eyes peering at her from beneath her lopsided bangs, as she tucked her hair behind her ears and smiled. Inge wanted to smack the woman across her grinning face and tell her to mind her own damn business, then go get herself some therapy. She didn't give a shit what Carolina thought of her, but for some reason it disturbed her that Allegra and Josephine might picture her engaged in some sordid affair, imagining some frenzied half-naked sex in the hospital supply closet. As if she didn't have control over her own body, even if she did have extramarital sex! As if having a baby wasn't a choice! Her choice!

"You don't have to say anything, Inge," Allegra said, "You have a right to your privacy, and no one can take that away from you."

"Someone already has," Inge sighed. But even as she spoke, she felt that ice in her chest creaking and cracking, melting and trickling, like springtime in the mountains. "But it is what it is, right? Isn't that what they say these days?"

"Shall I continue, or shall you?" Carolina asked.

"I told you, you are *way* off base," Inge said, downing her drink. "When you go poking around in other people's lives you should at least get the facts straight before you harm the innocent. So listen up. Rino was bent on fathering the heir his previous wife didn't provide him with. As for me, I was almost forty when we got married, and having a baby was nowhere near the top of my to-do list. I didn't see how any of that maternity business could fit into my busy schedule, but Rino was a decent man, and I'd promised him we could try. I see couples of all ages who can't conceive, but the older you get, the harder it gets, and the riskier it gets."

"It would take a *miracle*, for me," Josephine blurted, her arms crossed over her chest. Her unexpected comment caused everyone to glance at her as she brushed a tear from the corner of her eye.

"You're not missing much, believe me," Carolina said in a flat voice.

Allegra looked like she was on the verge of tears, too, as she reached over and took Josephine's hand.

"Could I please just get my part over with?" Inge asked. "Can we save the group therapy for another day?" Once she regained everyone's attention, she continued. "To make a long and complicated story short and simple, once I decided it was now or never, I couldn't get pregnant. We gave it our best shot, many best shots, but nothing happened. Rino, being a staunch Catholic at the time – he even went to the trouble of obtaining an annulment after his wife left him – didn't want to investigate why. We shouldn't question God's plan, he said, He would give us a child when the time was right. As for me, if I was going to do this, I needed to do it right away." Grabbing the bottle she was now cradling in her lap, Inge paused to pour some more grappa into her wineglass, ignoring the dinky little cordial glass. Whether or not it was because of the liquor, the ice block in her chest kept melting, and her tongue was nice and loose too, and it seemed like the more she talked, the easier the words flowed and the lighter she felt. "Naturally, being who I am and doing what I do, I was determined to resolve our problem. I captured a sample of Rino's sperm and ran some tests without telling him. Turns out, there was no way he could get me pregnant, no matter how much he enjoyed trying. Me, I didn't care much for the sex. I just wanted to get the job done."

"So you decided to have an affair? Just like that? In cold blood?" Carolina asked. "Or were you already in love with our Dr. Fustello?"

"No, I wasn't already in love with your Dr. Fustello. I was *never* in love with him. And no again: I did *not* have an affair with that man."

"And?"

"Well, as I said, Rino was against interfering with God's plan, especially since he was one hundred percent convinced that it corresponded to his own plan. I didn't have the heart to tell him he was infertile. Men often take that kind of news poorly, and he really wanted this child. Of course, we perform standard artificial insemination at my clinic in addition to IVF and all the more complicated treatments, but I knew Rino wouldn't go for that – he never even wanted to hear about what my job entailed – and I was certainly not interested in being impregnated by some donor. I wanted to give Rino the baby he wanted, but I also wanted him to, you know, stop *poking* me."

"Inge!" Josephine exclaimed.

"So what did you do?" Allegra asked.

"Well, around that time, Fabio – Dr. Fustello, that is – accepted a position in Turin, and I was promoted to take his place. During the transition, we spent many long hours together and he told me that when my name came up as his replacement there was a conversation about how it might be 'safe' for them to promote me now that my age made it unlikely that I would have a child. Apparently, I had been overlooked when a previous opportunity presented itself years earlier because they considered me 'at risk.' Needless to say, I was *furious*! And so was Fabio. Imagine a fertility clinic discriminating against women doctors! And against pregnancy in the workplace!"

"That's *appalling*!" Allegra said.

"*Shame* on them!" Josephine said.

"What *bastards*!" Carolina said.

"*Exactly*!" Inge said. "Anyway, we took that conversation to a nearby restaurant, and over dinner I told him about my predicament with Rino. He'd met Rino once at a reception and thought he was a nice guy. I remembered them talking about boats and cars, the usual small talk. He told me he felt sorry for Rino, that he would have made a good, old-style dad, the kind he'd always wished for but never had. I don't know who thought of it first, but at one point our eyes locked and we hatched a plan. Here I was, sitting with an exceptionally bright man, a gifted and compassionate physician, who happened to be an extremely attractive specimen. He was also gay, and although he had a partner, a rather well-known architect, they were both very passionate about their work and didn't feel the need to complicate their lives with the presence of a child and its demands, let alone tackle the bureaucratic hurdles the Italian government imposes on same-sex couples. I hinted that it would be a pity for his incredibly desirable genes to go to waste, which may have sparked some male vanity, I don't know, but by dessert we were shaking hands. In short, he offered me a donation, a direct deposit, if I may, no strings attached. The extra bonus of getting back at our directors for their discrimination made the idea irresistible."

"Wow!" Josephine said. "But isn't that unethical?"

"It was a friendly, consensual transaction between adult colleagues, no money or emotions involved," Inge said. "I insisted on paying for dinner, though."

"He's *gay*? How did I miss that?" Carolina asked, rubbing her chin.

"How did you pull that off?" Allegra asked. "I mean, in a practical sense."

"Well, because of my age and urgency, I put myself on a cycle of hormone therapy, to stimulate ovulation. A couple of months later I was settled into my new job, the board was extremely satisfied with my performance, and I was ovulating up a storm. I made an appointment with Fabio, he delivered the goods, and put them where they needed to be, via IUI."

"IUI?" Josephine asked.

"Intrauterine insemination. It's quite simple, the most basic form of assistance you can get. You can even perform it at home. They sometimes call it the turkey baster method."

"Turkey baster? Why is that?" Josephine still looked confused.

"Use your imagination, for God's sake! However, you don't really use a turkey baster. They sell kits with all you need for insemination without sex – except for the sperm, of course." For some reason – maybe it was the tension, or the grappa, or the image of Josephine trying to impregnate herself with a turkey baster – Inge found herself smiling.

"And it *worked?*" Josephine leaned forward, all ears.

"I had Carl, didn't I?" Inge said.

"Wow! That really *is* a miracle!" Josephine said, shaking her head slowly.

"Well, Josephine, not quite as impressive as the Virgin Mary's, but it was good enough for me."

"Clever, yet simple. Well done!" Carolina said, nodding at Inge with a combination of disappointment and admiration. After chewing her lip for a moment, she perked up, as if someone had whispered a suggestion in her ear. "But the problem remains."

"What problem?" Inge asked.

"How do we break the news to Rino? And to Carl?"

"*We* don't break *anything* to them!" Inge shouted. "*I* will break any news I want to break, *if* and *when* I decide to break it! *IS THAT CLEAR?*"

Inge glared at Carolina, holding her gaze for several seconds, until Carolina eventually dropped her eyes to the stack of papers in front of her. Inge then cast her menacing glance on Josephine, then Allegra, before taking another swig of grappa, feeling the warmth spread in her chest, relishing the rush of the thaw, hoping it wouldn't cause a flood.

CHAPTER FORTY-SEVEN
Carolina

Well, that had gone even better than expected! Especially considering she had no solid proof that Dr. Fabio Fustello (FF! another double!) was Carl's biological father, or that this juicy fact was still unknown to the cuckolded Rino the Rhino. How could she? Once again, Carolina's sixth sense had not betrayed her, and even if she was initially disappointed about not uncovering an affair, those stories were always squalid and usually about as mind-blowing as minced meat. The truth about Carl's unorthodox conception, on the other hand, was quite a tasty tidbit to chew on. A real first for her! She shook out her hands then tugged on her fingers, one by one, until the knuckles cracked, to get rid of that tingling sensation she got when she was onto something big.

Yes, if she must say so herself, she'd totally aced that! Her technique and timing had been infallible, and she'd instinctively known just how far to push Inge the Hun to make her spill the beans. She was so damn good at it, it was a pity she hadn't gone into law enforcement, which she'd briefly considered as a second career choice. It wouldn't have been as thrilling as flying a helicopter, but according to her pig-headed parents, it was almost as dangerous. Just as well. Even if they'd let her apply to the Polizia or, better yet, the Carabinieri, it wouldn't really have been her bag. She hated guns almost as much as she hated having men order her around (they were always the ones in command). Besides, she played by her own book of rules and wasn't interested in enforcing anyone else's laws. The only reason she'd gotten into all this investigating was to help her guests get their lives back on track, not to judge them or punish them (only someone as dense as Giac would accuse her of that!), and certainly not to send them to jail. In other words, she did what she did for the good of others. Take Inge. You could tell by looking at her that she was already feeling better after confessing. Sure, she still had some mega issues to resolve, and sure, she was pissed at Carolina right now, but she was an intelligent woman and knew she'd have to come clean sooner or later. Better sooner, better voluntarily. She'd be grateful to her in the long run. Though Carolina never expected gratitude, of course, even when it was well deserved. Call her an altruist if you must, but in the end, she was simply doing her part to make some individual worlds (hence the whole world) a better place. And maybe make a few new friends in the process.

Carolina knew that timing was crucial, so she waited for the ashes of Inge's blow-up to settle over her dumbfounded guests, meanwhile pretending to study the pile of documents stacked in front of her to add a touch of suspense. Eliminating the entire Inge section (there were pages and pages of printouts she hadn't even needed to use), she set them aside, squaring off the remaining papers separated by color-coded tabs, quickly calculating her next move. This was no time to rest on her laurels, not when she had back-to-back cases to handle.

Who to tackle next? She'd already treated Absent Allegra to an antipasto from the smorgasbord of Adalberto's lies, but the girl looked a little too out of it to respond with any spunk right now. Carolina wanted to see her reactive and combative, not resigned and accepting, so she'd follow that famous instinct of hers and let Allegra sit and wallow for now. That left Plain Jane Josephine. She was such an easy target that Carolina was a tad reluctant to start in on her, but it was also true that she had so little to go on that she'd be stabbing in the dark (or candlelight, in this case) for clues as she went along. That would even out the playing field a little.

"*Carissima* Josephine Fortunata," she began. Josephine stopped gnawing on a crusty heel (how much bread could that woman pack away?) and fixed her clear blue gaze on Carolina. She had that unassuming way of looking at you which made you wonder what she was thinking, that same kind of sidelong glance Lady Diana shot at people without turning her head. "Do you still feel *fortunata* after today's misfortunes?"

Josephine resumed chewing at a quicker pace so as not to answer with her mouth full, sputtering as she swallowed because there was nothing left in her glass to wash the bread down with. Normally, Carolina would have rushed over to remedy that, but between the wine and the grappa, the woman already had enough alcohol in her to loosen her tongue up nicely. And at this delicate stage of the interrogation, withholding comfort was always a good tactic.

"Well, um, *ahem!*" Josephine cleared her throat, her eyes tearing as she faltered a few times before finding her voice. "To tell the truth, I'm really more suited to city life. Always have been. But all's well that ends well!"

"I hope you're not suffering too much on account of your ankle."

"Not too much if I sit still," Josephine croaked. "It's been a scary day, and I'm just grateful to be back here."

"That's the spirit! I commend you on being such a good sport. I know you came here for some quiet time. When he made your reservation, Mr. Tomas mentioned his concern for you, and your need for tranquility. He said you are a very special person."

"Really? He said that?"

"Yes, he did. I wrote back asking if there were any particular needs I should be aware of. It helps to have a little background about a person's situation, like whether they prefer to be left alone or need extra attention, the same way I should know if someone is vegan, or vegetarian, or allergic to nuts. Neglecting details can prove fatal. Take anaphylactic shock, for example."

"Yes, um, you certainly do a very thorough job," Josephine coughed.

While warming Josephine up with small talk, Carolina sneaked a peek at the others. The posture-perfect Inge was slumped in her chair, looking dazed, while a bleary-eyed Allegra tried to stay focused on Josephine. They were beyond exhausted, full of food, and feeling the booze. The day had been no picnic for Carolina, either, and this session was extremely difficult for a perfectionist like herself who relied on a tried and tested technique for easing her guests into intimate tête-à-têtes after prepping them with adequate pampering. How was she supposed to handle three women at once, when there was so much work to do, and so little time?

"Thomas came across as a good man," she began, craning her neck in an exaggerated way to stare at the gold band on Josephine's right hand.

"Oh, he is. *Very* good," Josephine replied, following Carolina's gaze, as intended.

"And he's good to you?"

"Definitely."

"So why …?" Carolina let her words hang in the air a moment while she phrased her question, knowing the pause would make Josephine wonder what she was going to ask. "Never mind," she added, with a shake of her head and a wave of her hand.

"Why what?" Josephine asked. Good. She was a nibbler. No real surprise.

"It's just, well, maybe I'm out of line here, but I only speak up because I care. Why the separation?"

"What do you know about a separation? What did Thomas tell you?"

"Nothing, it's just that he wrote to me from America and you came from Rome. It would appear that you're not living together. Why is that?"

"We haven't lived together in years. We're both committed to our work, and we each go where it takes us. That's not so unusual these days, is it?"

"But why the wedding band on your right hand? You couldn't bring yourself to take it off yet?"

"No, I've always worn it there."

"Why should you care, Carolina?" Inge let out a tipsy titter. "Ha! Caring Carolina! That's a laugh!"

"But you don't even go by the same name," Carolina continued, undeterred. "I saw your passport, Josephine. Or should I say, *Marisa*? Marisa Tomas is your real name, isn't it? Why the double identity?"

"Many women in my line of work use another name. Mine's important to me, so I went the extra step."

"Oh, are you a performer, perhaps?" Carolina chuckled. A little teasing could go a long way with a sensitive person. It made them jump to their own defense by spitting out the truth. "One with a social media presence below *zero*? I checked out both names. Nothing. Zilch. Nada. It's as if you don't exist."

"Do I honestly look like a *performer*? I write and teach under the name Josephine Fortunata. You won't see my byline on any of the articles I publish, though. A man takes credit for those."

"Why Josephine? Why Fortunata?"

"Yeah, why?" Inge said, relaxing now that it was someone else's turn to answer the questions. "I'm curious, too."

"What does it matter to you? Or to any of us?" Allegra said, stirring from her semi-stupor. "Just leave her alone!"

"It's all right, Allegra," Josephine said, clearing her throat again. "Could I please have some water?"

"Oh, for God's sake!" Carolina said, filling her glass from the carafe. "Here you go."

"Thank you," Josephine said.

"Anyone else?"

Allegra nodded, holding out her glass. "Thanks."

"I'll stick to this," Inge said, holding the grappa bottle in front of a candle to check that there was still some left.

"We were talking about your name," Carolina said, scooting her chair closer to Josephine, abandoning her notes on the table. They were all based on speculation anyway. "Your *alias*."

"I have nothing to hide, okay? I just wanted to come here and be *myself*, no name needed."

"And that's *precisely* what I urge my guests to do. All I want to know is which self that is, so that I can help you. Who is this alter ego, Josephine Fortunata?"

"It's complicated."

"Complicated is fine. As long as it's quick."

"Okay, you asked for it. So, Josephine was a Sudanese girl whose life started out comfortable enough, thanks to her family's tribal standing. Everything changed when she was kidnapped by some Turks and sold as a slave."

"Wait – a *slave*?" Allegra said.

"Child trafficking is a thriving business in certain parts of the world," Inge said, tripping over the word "thriving."

"You two!" Carolina barked. "Quit interrupting and let her tell her story! Which better have a *point*!"

"I'm sorry, it's just that she feels so alive to me that I left out the part about it being the 1800s," Josephine said. "That poor girl was bought and sold so many times she didn't know who she was anymore. She *literally* did not remember her own *name*. Now we know her as Josephine, but her captors called her Bakhita. Sometimes she was treated decently, but more often she was beaten and tortured. It breaks my heart to think about it!"

"Let's stay focused and stick to the story, shall we?" Carolina said, on seeing Josephine's eyes fill with tears. While giving her a quick second to recover, she began tapping her foot on the floor but suddenly stopped. "Hold on! I know who you're talking about!" she cried, snapping her fingers. "That African girl was the only thing that came up when I googled Josephine Fortunata. I didn't read the whole story, but something caught my eye. You know the part about that mistress ordering her to be scarred by cutting? And then sitting there and watching while she made someone rub salt into the wounds? Talk about *sick*! But what does any of that have to do with you?"

Josephine shook her head sadly, then gulped some water, paused to clear her throat, then sipped some more, as if she had all the time in the world. "I'll get to it if you give me a minute."

Carolina tried not to groan. Maybe she'd adopted the wrong approach with this woman. She was hijacking the conversation, and frankly, how important was the origin of a stupid name that wasn't even hers? She'd give her exactly one minute before working a new angle.

"Anyway, the story goes that after changing hands a dozen or so times, she finally ended up in the possession of a Vice Consul, an Italian who was kind enough *not* to beat her. The good man actually *saved* many slaves. So when it came time for him to return to Italy, she begged him to take her with him. They embarked on a very long and dangerous journey, and when they finally arrived in Italy, the man gave her away. The family she ended up with put her to work as a nanny."

"That was a step up, anyway," Inge said. "Without pay, I assume?"

"What do you expect? Paid holidays and sick leave? A full benefits package?" Carolina snapped, resuming her foot tapping. "Please get on with it."

"Well, wouldn't you know, that family had to go to Sudan on some kind of business!"

"They didn't drag her back down there, did they?" Allegra said.

"No," Josephine said. "They left her with the nuns, in Venice. But then that family came back and *reclaimed* her! At that point, she didn't want to go home with them. She'd been learning about God from the nuns, and wanted to keep studying with them."

"Did the nuns let her stay, or were they forced to give her back?" Allegra asked.

What was *with* her, suddenly all alert and asking questions, when Carolina should be doing that? The problem was, this subject wasn't inspiring her *at all*. If she wanted a history lesson, she'd read a book. "Cut to the chase, please!" she ordered.

"Let her *talk*!" Inge said. "You started it, and now I wanna hear the rest of the story."

"And you will," Josephine said. "Anyway, there was a big fuss over the case, and all kinds of authorities became involved. In the end, she was saved by a loophole. As it turned out, slavery had already been outlawed in Sudan before Bakhita was even born, which meant the original sale was invalid. Plus, slavery was a no-no in Italy!"

"So she was finally a free woman!" Allegra cried.

"How was an ex-slave supposed to fend for herself in nineteenth-century Venice? Prostitution?" Inge asked. "Did she think that was better than being a nanny?"

"She didn't turn to prostitution, Inge! Why would you think such an awful thing? She stayed at the convent with the nuns. She was finally free to choose the life she wanted to lead, and that was her choice."

"Sounds like a waste of freedom to me," Inge said.

"Summing it up," Carolina began, "after all that, now we know where your fake name Josephine came from, for whatever convoluted reason."

"Wait! I still have to explain the Fortunata part."

"Oh, for God's *sake*!" What torture this monologue was! And the slower Josephine spoke, the faster Carolina's heart raced. But the women were all chummy and relaxed now, and if she started yelling at them they could turn hostile and clam up. The foot tapping was not doing the trick anymore, though; unable to take another word, she jumped to her feet and started pacing. She tried to listen to what Josephine was saying, but all she could hear was a droning, buzzing sound in her ears and she needed it to s*top Stop STOP*!

"The Arabic name Bakhita translates to Fortunata in Latin. So that's the name she was given when she was baptized Josephine Margaret Fortunata. And guess when that happened?"

Finally, a moment of silence.

"On January ninth! And January ninth happens to be my birthday! Anyway, Josephine eventually took her vows and remained with those nuns for the rest of her life."

"And that's the happy ending?" Inge said.

"At least it's an *ending*," Carolina said, rubbing her hands together. Her palms were itchy, her breath erratic. These women were going to push her over the edge.

"It's a sad story, Josephine. But inspiring." Allegra said. "I feel like I missed something though. Apart from the date, what's your connection with Josephine?"

Josephine looked down at the hands folded in her lap, sighing heavily. When she looked up again, her eyes glistened, and her chin quivered. She took a deep breath.

"My connection stems from the fact that I identify with what Josephine went through. I was abused as a child, too," she said, her voice surprisingly steady.

Carolina had to hand it to her for not going all blubbery and wasting more time sobbing. In fact, it sounded like she'd repeated those words many times in the past. Probably in therapy, she speculated, or worse yet, a support group. You couldn't pay Carolina enough to go to one of those. As if it wasn't bad enough to have a shitty childhood, a failed marriage, a toxic dependency, a chronic illness, or whatever; for some reason, people had to hash their problems over and over with other people suffering from the same problems. How could you ever forget and move on if you kept wallowing in the very shit you were trying to escape?

"Oh, *Josephine!*" Allegra cried, reaching over to hold her hand.

Sympathy was all fine and well, and of course Carolina felt sorry for the woman too, she wasn't heartless, far from it, but now her priority was to figure out how this bit of news could help her get to the bottom of Josephine's current crisis. Everyone knew that victims of abuse in childhood struggled with relationships as adults. Maybe that was at the root of her marital problems with Thomas. Like most men, he was probably so self-centered and emotionally tuned out that he didn't get where she was coming from.

"Does Thomas realize how that abuse must still affect you, even now?" she asked. "Does he even *try* to understand?"

The women looked at her as if she'd asked if they preferred pasta or risotto as their first course.

"Who cares about *Thomas?*" Inge said. "Let's hear the rest of Josephine's story."

"Thanks," Josephine said. "I don't usually talk about this to strangers. But after all we've been through together, you women seem like sisters."

Not just friends, but *sisters!* Of all the things for Josephine to say! Now Carolina was the one who risked getting all sloppy and sentimental if she didn't keep her wits about her. She'd always wanted a sister more than anything in the world. She still dreamed of having one, a ready-made friend to confide in, to support, and who would always support her. That desire for sisterhood was at the very root of her commitment to helping other women. But straightening out a sister could be tricky business.

"You asked about Thomas, Carolina," Josephine volunteered. "The answer is yes, he does know what I went through. He went through something similar."

"You were *both* abused as children?" Carolina asked. "So did you meet at some support group?"

Josephine tilted her head. "Support group? Why, no. I've known him since he was born. Thomas is my brother."

"Thomas is your *brother?*" Carolina repeated.

"Yes. My little brother. Why are you so surprised?"

"Nothing! Never mind!" Carolina managed to say. Now she was the one with the shaky voice. Dammit! She should have held off on Josephine, with so little information to go on. Damn this whole emergency, and the storm, and the landslide, and the injured women, and the stranded men! It was one big conspiracy to throw off her timing, to force her to act too fast or fail in her mission. How was she supposed to stay *calm* in these circumstances?

"I'm so sorry you both suffered like that," Allegra said.

"Me too. But I'm sorrier for him, you know? I'm fortunate enough to remember more than he does."

"Why would you want to remember *more*?" Inge asked.

"Sorry, I'm not going in order. I remember my parents better, because I was six when they died, and Thomas was only three. The bad part came later."

"You lost *both* your parents? You poor sweethearts!" Allegra said. "How did they die?"

"In a helicopter crash."

"*No!* My poor Hans died in a helicopter accident, too!" Inge cried, cupping a hand over her mouth.

"How tragic!" Allegra exclaimed.

"Were they *pilots*?" Carolina asked. Before this weekend, she'd never met anyone who knew anyone who died in a helicopter accident, and now she knew two! Maybe her parents were right about piloting not being a suitable job for a woman who intended to raise a family. Or for any woman who wanted to stay alive.

"My Hans was hanging from the helicopter, on a rescue mission!" Inge said. "He was slammed against the mountain!"

"And my parents were reporters," Josephine said. "It's not like they were covering a war or anything. My father was shooting footage for a documentary my mother was directing. They never flew together, but at the last minute he convinced her to go along."

"She probably hated being left behind," Carolina said, imagining the scene. "Who wouldn't choose a helicopter ride over being stuck home with two little brats?"

"*Carolina!*" Allegra cried.

"They didn't have any close relatives," Josephine continued, ignoring the comment. "And at their age, who ever thought of appointing a guardian? So the court did. We were bumped around, living in a series of foster homes, some good, some bad. Some kept us together, some split us up. One in particular was awful enough to make me relate to Josephine's story the minute I heard it."

"But what caused the crash?" Carolina asked. "Mechanical failure? Human error? Bad weather?"

"Who cares about *that*?" Inge snapped. "All the investigations ever focus on is who was to *blame*! When my Hans was killed, no one filed a report on how his death would ruin *my* life!"

"Just because it's not important for you to know, doesn't mean it's not important for the rest of us to know!" Carolina said. "If one of your couples lost a baby you helped them to conceive, you'd be way more interested in knowing why, rather than in what happened to the poor couple afterward!"

"We're talking about two *orphans* here!" Inge said. "Two defenseless children whose lives were *ruined*!"

"I don't want to get into what happened to me over the years. Let's just say it put me off men," Josephine continued, her calm voice defusing some of the tension. "Things improved when the Tomases adopted us, but by then the damage was done. They were a nice Catholic couple and I took to Catholic school like a duck to water. To start with, mine was an all-girls' school. And we wore uniforms, which helped me blend in and feel like I belonged. The nuns taught us right from wrong, and those clear-cut lines told me where to stand if I wanted to stay on the safe side. I was fascinated by the prayers, the rosary, the masses. By the candles and incense. By the seasonal rituals of Advent and Lent, leading up to my favorite holidays. And by the nuns who were my teachers, especially Sister Josephine, who took me under her wing. She was the one who told me about Josephine Fortunata."

What the heck was Carolina supposed to say to that? This story was taking her way off track. She'd been expecting to hear about a philandering husband, a stale marriage, a midlife crisis. All she had now was a boring brother and a bunch of nuns!

"It's a miracle you didn't become a nun yourself!" she muttered.

"Yeah." Josephine smiled. "Maybe not a nun. But a sister. I'm Sister Josephine Fortunata."

"You're a *nun*?" Inge said. "Holy *shit*, I'm sorry, I mean –"

"Hello, *Sister* Josephine!" Allegra said, squeezing the hand she'd never let go of. "I'm very happy to meet you."

"I wish your brother Thomas had had the *decency* to share such an important detail with me!" Carolina spat, her face flushed. "You don't withhold that kind of information from your host. It's not *fair*."

"As I said, I wanted to come here as a regular woman struggling with a serious relationship problem. I needed to get away from it all to try and work out some important conflicts going on in my conscience, and in my heart."

Now something clicked! All was not lost! "I should have *known*!" Carolina cried, snapping her fingers again. "You're having an *affair*! With a *priest*!"

"No, I'm not having an affair with a priest," Josephine sighed. "The relationship I'm referring to is with the Church."

Josephine's soft, round shoulders slumped after pronouncing the words. Her chest rose as she drew in a fresh breath, a breath that caught her voice on the way out. "I'm struggling with my calling. I'm thinking of leaving the sisterhood."

CHAPTER FORTY-EIGHT
Josephine

"What's everybody staring at?" Josephine asked, looking from one pair of probing eyes to another. She'd been gawked at her entire life: for being the pitiful orphan, the homeless ward of the court, the nervous new kid in countless new schools, the awkward adoptee, the naive novitiate, the white-skinned inner-city sister-teacher, the outsider, the foreigner. Well, maybe it was time to start staring back.

"You can't just leave the convent!" Carolina said.

"Why is that?" Josephine said.

"You took vows, didn't you?"

"Yes, I took vows. But that doesn't mean I'm locked up for life." If there was one thing that destabilized Josephine more than the *feeling* of not having a say in her life, it was being *perceived* as a woman who had no say in her life. Maybe it was time to change that, too. "I *can* actually leave." There. She'd said it. It was a real thing. A possibility.

"Oh. I always thought – well, never mind. So if you want to go, and you're free to go, just go!" Carolina said. "What's the problem?"

"You've been asking lots of questions, Carolina," Josephine said. "Can I ask you one?"

Now everyone stared at Carolina. She was perched at the edge of her chair, her eyes darting around the candlelit room, as if checking for an escape route. "Shoot."

"Do you love your husband?"

"Giac? Of course I do."

"Do you ever think of leaving him?"

"*Hee-hee!*" Carolina giggled, in a high-pitched twitter. "At least once a day."

"So why don't you?"

"I was *joking*. We're together because we're meant to be together. We fell in love and got married in under six months! And I've put an *enormous* amount of energy into our marriage every single day since. We built all of this together. We raised two children together. Who we *are* is tied up in what we *do* together. We're *inseparable*, and he'd be *lost* without me."

"Well, why would you think I could devote decades of my life to a commitment every bit as serious as marriage and simply walk away, just because I'm not locked up in a solitary cell? Well, guess what? Neither are you."

"Exactly! This is what I go *crazy* trying to make women see! As long as we're alive we have choices!" Carolina jumped to her feet, speaking excitedly in a high-pitched voice. "There comes a time when you have to take a good, hard look at yourself from all angles and maybe see what you don't want to see. Love makes people blind, especially women."

"But not you?" Inge chuckled.

"What do you mean by that?" Carolina asked. Inge shrugged. Carolina turned her attention back to Josephine.

"Did you even know what you were signing up for?" she asked her.

"Probably more than you did, when you married a man you hardly knew and said yes to a whole list of vows until death do you part. It took me a good seven years to work my way up to my vows. First, there's the postulancy, then the novitiate, then the temporary vows, and, finally, the permanent vows. By the time I made it that far, my eyes were wide open to what I was getting into. What am I supposed to say now, that it was all a big misunderstanding?"

"People change."

"Do we really? Or does what we see change?"

"What are you seeing now that you didn't see before, Josephine?" Allegra asked.

"A lot of things. Like how I could be expected to not only teach but basically run a parish in a rough neighborhood with virtually no resources – not even our own priest, because they're in short supply, but they still won't let women in. I didn't mind the extra duties, but what I did mind, more and more, was the discrimination. Sure, I could distribute the host, but only after it was consecrated by the priest, that magical man with the God-given powers! Says *who*? Other *men*, of course. I'm sorry, but I don't think God would agree. And I know I don't. Not anymore."

"Please! Don't get me started on the subject of equality," Inge said, shaking her head. "Switzerland's glass ceiling is so low it's more like a glass floor. Who would think that such a wealthy country would still have one of the highest gender pay gaps in the Western world? Why, women didn't even have the right to vote there until fifty years ago! And in the canton of Appenzell Innerrhoden, women weren't granted full voting rights until 1990!"

"You get what I mean then," Josephine said. "The resentment started eating away at me, but the more I prayed over it, the angrier I got. I simply could not hear God's voice telling me to accept the limitations of my role. Thomas saw how it was affecting me and convinced me to take a break from Buffalo. That was when I applied for a temporary transfer to our Rome community, where they needed an English teacher. Here, I actually get to teach instead of breaking up fights all day. And I also get to do some writing, too."

"What do you write about?" Allegra asked.

"Who cares?" Carolina said, standing up, pacing in a circle around her chair, then sitting down again. "This is not what we're supposed to be talking about here!"

"I came up with an idea for a column in our newsletter," Josephine said to Allegra. "It's about the mystics. I started with my favorite, Julian of Norwich. She was an anchorite, who wrote the first book by a woman ever to be published in the English language. I also wrote about Catherine of Siena, then Joan of Arc, and Clare of Assisi. But I've recently been given orders to focus on the mainstream male mystics."

"Who would want to read about that stuff anyway?" Carolina asked.

"As it turns out, lots of people. So that makes it even more rewarding. Especially for the priest who signs his name to the articles, now that they've been picked up by a nationwide Catholic publication." Josephine sighed, looking down at her empty glass.

"So some high-handed priest takes the credit for his sister's work?" Inge said. "Unbe*liev*able."

"Believe me, it happens all the time," Josephine said, shaking her head, then turning to Carolina. "Boy, I could sure use a drink now, but that grappa is vile. Do you have any more wine?"

"Haven't you had enough, *Sister* Josephine?" Carolina said.

"Are you worried about leading me astray?" Josephine asked.

"Well, it's weird for me, all right? I went to a Catholic school and had nuns for teachers. But I don't go to church anymore."

"I grew up Protestant. Swiss Reformed Church," Inge said. "At least they ordain women. I don't go to church anymore either."

"I grew up confused," Allegra said. "And stayed that way."

"Sadly, the universal message of love has been hijacked," Josephine said, watching Carolina open the bottle with her usual flair, sniff the cork, and pour, as if they were normal clients sitting down for a normal evening, instead of a bunch of wrecks. Allegra skipped this round; Inge stuck to the grappa.

"Why is it that men are so afraid of relinquishing even a *little* bit of their power?" Josephine asked, swirling the wine in her glass as if searching in the ruby-red liquid for a revelation God had withheld in prayer. "I don't want to *steal* anything from anyone, I just want there to be *balance*. And *justice*. And *love*. Power interferes with love. It's the *enemy* of love!" Taking a sip of the wine, she tasted its fruity tartness on her tongue, let it slide slowly down her throat. "Jesus preached love. And they killed him for it."

"Love needs to be governed," Inge said. "Relationships would fall apart if we let love take over. And so would society. We'd be too vulnerable."

"I *always* feel vulnerable," Allegra mumbled.

"I know what that's like," Josephine said. "But if you're lucky, someone comes into your life and sees you for the human mess that you are, with all your qualities and faults, and they accept the whole package and love you anyway.

"That sounds ideal," Allegra said. "But does love like that exist in real life?"

"Yes, it does," Josephine said. "And I've found it in Rome, with an Italian sister."

"Ah *ha*! You're in love with another *nun*!" Carolina cried. "Of course! I always knew kinky things went on behind convent doors!"

"*Basta*, Carolina!" Allegra groaned.

"It's not how you think," Josephine said, shaking her head. "Love and sex are two different things. You can have one and not the other. But even leaving that part aside, our relationship is still a problem for us. We're not supposed to form special attachments, and when the Mother Superior confronted me about spending too much time with Lucia, I denied I had feelings for her out of fear I'd be sent back to Buffalo." Josephine's eyes glistened as she looked around at the others. "Can you *imagine* that? I denied loving another person to stay out of trouble! As if love could ever be *wrong*! I don't want to live in an environment that makes me do that. I can't blame the environment for the words I did or didn't speak, though. I can only blame my own lack of courage. The thought of being separated from Lucia made me realize how much I love her, and denying that felt like a profound betrayal. Is it so wrong for me to desire the love of a flesh-and-blood person? Is it so selfish of me to want to finally rest in someone's arms at this stage of my life?"

"I suggest you find out if she snores before making any rash decisions," Carolina muttered. "I haven't had a good night's sleep in over twenty years!"

"You *deserve* that love, Josephine," Allegra said.

"What about this Sister Lucia? Is she supposed to break her vows, too? Just like that?" Carolina asked. "If she ends up regretting it, you know who she'll blame!"

"She tells me not to be so American, that everyone in Italy has clandestine relationships, so why can't we? But to me, that's tantamount to disobeying, and I've always been a rule follower. Even when I don't like the rules."

"That's why I'm a boss," Inge said, taking a swig from her bottle. "I get to make the rules."

"I don't want to hide my feelings anymore. I either have to obey or leave," Josephine added, then paused to drain her glass. "Thinking about this, day after day, has been torture, but talking to you women on the outside makes me feel more normal."

"Wait a minute! Not so fast! We need to find out more about this Lucia," Carolina said, already on her feet again, picking up her notebook and pen.

"Give me her name and I'll look her up as soon as I can get online. And I want her *real* name, not her *nun* name! We know she's Italian, right? How old is she? Younger than you? Is she beautiful? Because, let's face it, temptation is out there! And once you fall, it's easier to slip up the second time around."

"Thanks but no thanks," Josephine said.

"You have to be careful what you give up in the name of love!" Carolina said, sitting down, then standing up again. "All my life I've had to give up what I wanted to do, and how and when I wanted to do it. First on account of my parents, then Giac, then my kids! Well, the giving up stops right here! Right *now!*"

"Calm down, Carolina," Allegra said. "This isn't about you."

"It's *never* about me, is it? All I do is worry about other people, every *friend*, every *sister*, who comes here! I open women's eyes, help them see what they need to see to move on! Like I'm doing with you!"

"Oh, come on! All you're interested in is snooping around in other people's lives!" Inge said.

"I only do that so I can see the things you women don't want to see, and help you open your eyes! The people closest to you never have the courage to do what I do!"

"What if I have the courage to open *your* eyes to something *you* don't want to see?"

"If you have something to say, come out and say it!"

"As you know, I'm an expert hiker," Inge continued. "I don't just trip and tumble down hills and slide into pits and break my bones for no reason!"

"Don't you go trying to blame *me* again! You should have stayed on the trails!"

"The reason I fell was that I was being *chased!*"

"What do you mean, chased?" Carolina said. "By boars?"

"*I* was being chased by boars!" Josephine interjected.

"And *I* was being chased by a dog! And a man!"

"What dog? What man?" Carolina asked.

"A howling hunting dog!" Inge said. "And a man with a shotgun!"

"You saw a hunter? Hunting is prohibited up here! I'll have to call in the Guardia Forestale! Can you tell me exactly where he was?"

"Of course."

"Hold on a sec, I want to get all the details right." Carolina picked up her pen and paper again, then sat down, poised to take notes.

"Let's see now ..." Inge said, taking her time. "There was a little stone hut."

"Right. It must have been one of those crumbling old shepherds' huts. Was the hunter hiding out there?"

"This particular hut was patched up pretty nicely," Inge squinted her eyes, as if to take a better look at her memory. "There were even some flowers on the window sill. The mule kept trying to eat them."

"Wait – a *mule*?" Carolina stopped scribbling and looked up.

"The mule was with the man. A good-looking specimen he was, too. The man, not the mule. And so was the girl. A pretty young thing with a hot little bod."

"*What* girl?" Carolina cried, slamming her pen down on the table.

"How should *I* know?" Inge said. "But she did have a foreign accent."

"Was she *Albanian*?" Carolina asked, jumping to her feet so abruptly she knocked the table over.

"I was hiding in the trees, Carolina, not checking passports!"

Carolina began pacing. "So what were the two of them doing while you stood there spying? I want *details*!"

"I wasn't *spying*. I was just so surprised to see anyone up there that I froze in place. When the girl started taking her shirt off and ran inside I knew it was time to get moving."

"She took her *shirt* off?" Carolina bent so close to Inge's face that their noses practically touched. "What about that *pig* who was with her?"

"He was already shirtless," Inge said, pulling her head back.

"*What*?"

"Oh yes. And he was already following the girl inside when my phone rang."

"That was *me*, you idiot! Why didn't you *answer*?"

"Watch who you call an idiot! That phone call made the guy come after me with a shotgun! He must have been pretty darn worried about being seen! And he would be, if *you* opened *your* eyes!"

"My eyes are *wide* open, don't worry! I know perfectly well you're talking about that rat Giac! And now I know why he's always checking on those stinky goats! And why he was so pissed about me flying my drone! He's scared of being caught sneaking around with that tramp Jada!"

"And Jada is …?" Inge asked.

"A girl I hired to work here! I gave her and her husband a chance to earn a decent wage when no one would, and after he left for another job, she thanked me by slinking around behind my back, always turning up wherever Giac was! I finally had to kick her tight young ass out of here! I should have gotten rid of her for *good*! And I *will*!"

"Wait, what do you mean by that?" Josephine asked, sincerely worried. Carolina looked crazed enough to kill Giac, or Jada, or both of them. Or maybe she'd take her anger out on her prisoners instead?

"I should have reported her! She wasn't supposed to be working here, but I wasn't supposed to hire her, and she knew that! So I just told her to get out and never come back. I assumed she went back to her husband, down in Ventimiglia.

"It hurts to have your eyes opened, doesn't it?" Allegra asked, speaking up for the first time in several minutes.

"Don't you dare try to compare my situation with yours!" Carolina cried. "I'm in *control* of my life and my man! You'll never be able to keep an eye on yours, because you can't even keep an eye on yourself! Take a look in the mirror, would you? You look like a half-starved hag, traipsing around braless and barefoot, with that witchy mop of hair! Is that supposed to make you feel like a free spirit or something?"

Allegra just sat there, her cheeks burning, her chin trembling.

"See? You're so passive you can't even defend yourself! You have nothing to say! *Nothing!*" Carolina shouted.

Josephine reached over to take Allegra's hand in hers. "Leave her alone, Carolina."

"You're a *fake*, and you're a *failure*! Men don't need a woman like you! Your father abandoned you, and so will Ada! What ever made you think that a man like him could be happy with a nobody like you?"

Allegra bowed her head, covering her ears with her hands.

"That's *enough*, Carolina!" Inge said.

"I know when it's enough! It's enough when she opens those dewy eyes and takes a good, hard look at reality! Men don't learn unless you *punish* them, Allegra! Passivity and acceptance will get you killed! I'll make Giac pay for his behavior, and you'll do the same with Ada. But first, you have to expose the truth! And since *you* won't do it, *I'll* do it for you!"

CHAPTER FORTY-NINE
Allegra

Allegra did not want to take a good, hard look at anything, especially not at Carolina's pacing and ranting and finger-pointing. This time she couldn't run away, this time she was too weak to move, too afraid to go back out into the storm. Her only escape was to close her eyes and silently chant her mantra, hoping it would tune out her attacker's voice.

"Are you with me or aren't you, Allegra?" Carolina shook her by the shoulder until she opened her eyes. "I can't do this without your participation."

"What do you *want* from me?" Allegra asked in a tired voice.

"For now, just sit back and listen while I give the ladies here a little background. They don't know you as well as I do," she said, picking up a sheaf of papers and clearing her throat. "Introducing Allegra Verseau, the little orphan Annie who was brought into the world by a French mother and an Italian father. At least that's what she says."

"I never said I was an orphan!" Allegra said. If Carolina was already starting in with the lies, she'd better stay alert.

"I wasn't being *literal*, Allegra. I was *joking*."

"You shouldn't joke about orphaned children!" Josephine said.

"And you should be listening, not talking," Carolina snapped, pausing to glare at Josephine before continuing. "Anyway, we'll skip your pathetic childhood, we've all had one of those. Let's talk a little about your mother, instead. Any regrets there, Allegra?"

Allegra sighed. "What does my mother have to do with anything?"

"Mothers always have everything to do with anything. Yours didn't live long after you left her, right?"

Allegra had been over this so many times in her head it made her ill. She considered remaining silent, but Carolina was a bulldozer when it came to digging, and wouldn't relent until she got the dirt she wanted. It would be over with faster if she humored her, and at least she wasn't screaming anymore. For now, anyway.

"No," she answered. She should have left it at that, a simple yes or no was all that was required, but it was more complicated than that. "I didn't know she had *cancer* when I left, and neither did she. My parents weren't exactly the types who went for annual check-ups. By the time she had symptoms, it was too late to do anything. She died the way she wanted to, at home."

"Home? What do you mean by home?"

"*Home*. Where she lived. With my father."

"Was that in Provence? Or Brittany? Or perhaps Normandy? It's hard to keep track."

"It was wherever they decided to stop."

"So while you were off gallivanting with that herbalist from Grasse, your mother was wasting away in an old hippy van, like some homeless bum?"

"I was *apprenticing*, not gallivanting. And my mother was *not* a bum. She actually owned her own house, up near Dijon. It was left to her by her parents, but she didn't want a piece of property tying her down. She sold it so she and my father could keep traveling around. It was her choice."

As a child, she'd heard her father talk about that "embarrassingly bourgeois home and its frilly furnishings" as if it were a source of shame, but that hadn't stopped little Allegra from fantasizing about it. At night, she'd often imagined sleeping in a real bed and waking to the smell of breakfast wafting up to her room from the cozy kitchen. She'd dreamed of sitting at a giant table surrounded by all the relatives she'd never met, on all the holidays she'd never celebrated. Sometimes when people asked where she was from, she still replied "Dijon," which was at least partly true. A few years back, she'd even driven up there to look for the old *maison* Verseau, but with so little information to go on, she'd ended up cruising the streets in a state of confusion, feeling as lost as the fat, hot tears rolling down her cheeks in search of something specific to grieve for.

"*Her* choice, you say? Are you sure? I mean, how many women really *choose* their lives?" Carolina aske. "I'll bet it was your father's idea to sell the house and live off her money. Your grandparents would have certainly wanted the house to go to *you* someday."

"I wouldn't know. I never met them. Whenever I asked about grandparents or aunts and uncles my parents told me I didn't have any. The only exception was *Oncle* Léon from Lyon, who was already dead, on account of being struck by lightning."

"You must have *hated* them for depriving you of a family!"

"Do we have to talk about this now? Can't you just say what you have to say and leave me alone?"

"First answer my question! It's for your own good!"

"I didn't always agree with them, but I didn't *hate* them," she replied, honestly. Then she went a step further, for some reason wanting to explain who they were before Carolina could paint a picture even worse than reality. "They did what they thought was right for me. They believed that families were toxic. It was a general attitude they had toward all institutions, like marriage and religion and school and government. They said they were all inventions created to limit personal freedom."

"How very *evolved* of them!" Carolina smiled indulgently. "So, no strings attached, right? You were free to abandon your dying mother, without giving it a second thought."

"That's *not* how it went! My parents refused to own a phone, so I couldn't call them, and they never tried to get in touch with me, even though they had my number. You have to understand who we're talking about here," Allegra said, turning from Carolina to look at Josephine and Inge. She didn't want them to think she was an awful person. "I was born because my parents loved *each other*, not because they wanted *me*. They didn't *need* a child to be happy, and they didn't *need* me hanging around. They wanted me to be free and independent, even as a child!"

"Still, you must have felt so shocked and guilty when you found out your mother was dead!" Carolina persisted.

Allegra tried to sip some water, but her throat was so constricted that she couldn't swallow. What was she supposed to say? That she would feel shocked and guilty every single day of her life until she died too?

"That's *enough*, Carolina!" Josephine said. "Have your fun with me, if you want!"

"Fun? You call this *fun*? I'm doing this for her own good! Now stop interrupting me, or we'll never finish!" Carolina grabbed a couple more sheets from the pile on the table and waved them in front of Allegra's face. "We'll let your poor mother rest in peace now, and take a look at your father. Why don't you tell me how his Indian adventure came about?"

"He was fixated on India," she mumbled. "He always talked about taking my mother to live in this community he knew of down there, but she didn't want to go with a child. Basically, they were waiting for me to get out of the way."

"Maybe your mother wasn't so keen on that idea, anyway. Maybe she preferred to *die* rather than go along. Which she conveniently did." Carolina paused to scour her documents by candlelight, letting her cruel comment sink in.

"I don't want to talk about that," Allegra mumbled, rubbing her arms.

"Very well," Carolina said, looking up. "Now then, you go by the name Allegra Verseau."

"That's my name. Of course I go by it."

"Yes, unlike some of our other guests, you use your *legal* name," Carolina's eyes shifted toward Josephine and back again. "Let's hear the story of how you got that name."

"You've already heard it because I've already told you. But if it will speed things up, I'll tell you again. My parents both swore I laughed instead of crying when I was born, so they decided to call me Allegra and leave it at that.

"Yes, I remember, that's very cute, but what about your surname? Verseau came from your mother, not your father, correct?"

"They wanted me to just be Allegra, but by law, they were forced to register my birth with a surname, too. Of course, they weren't married, and back then you couldn't choose which parent's name you wanted to use. So my father stepped aside, in protest against our patriarchal society. He said that since I was blood of my mother's blood, and since I'd been carried and birthed by her body and would be nourished by her milk, I should bear *her* name."

"Bravo!" Inge said, attempting to clap despite her sling.

"The point here is," Carolina said, flashing her dark eyes at Inge, "that Allegra's father didn't assert his paternity. Don't any of you find that *strange*? I mean, we're talking about an Italian male of Calabrese provenance! Unless of course his free-thinking was an alibi and what he was really against was taking responsibility for his child. Not even your own *father* wanted you, Allegra!"

"That's not *true*!" Allegra cried, though she'd been telling herself exactly the same thing for as long as she could remember.

"If you say so," Carolina said, finally dismissing the topic with a wave of her hand. After a quick glance at her papers, she smiled, but the corners of her mouth twitched with trouble. "I had to go back a few years to find this next tidbit. But, as I always say, perseverance pays off! It takes some expertise to navigate foreign bureaucracy, but if you know the ropes as well as I do, you can access all kinds of information. Such as the criminal record of one Diego Scalzo, who confessed to helping one Josephine Verseau kill herself! The man was imprisoned in the French penitentiary of Les Baumettes, in Marseilles, for mandatory psychiatric care."

Allegra's cheeks burned with a sharp, sudden sting, as if Carolina had smacked her face with a good, hard slap. "What he did was put an end to my mother's suffering!" she cried.

"So you think that what he did was *normal*?"

"Everyone has a different normal."

"Let me get this straight. You believe that your father *killing* your mother was *normal*?"

"He didn't *kill* her. She was *dying*, and he made it easier for her to leave her diseased body. He only got all that attention because he went on a hunger strike after his arrest, and a pro-euthanasia movement picked up the story and fed it to the press."

"This is where I admit to feeling a little lost, Allegra. Where does daddy's India escapade fit in? Was that before or after prison?"

Allegra sighed, cradling her burning cheeks in her icy hands. "It was *instead* of prison. My father is convinced he's in India. It's a coping mechanism."

"Ah, I see. And what's your excuse for lying about it to everyone?"

"It helps *me* cope, too. India was our code name for Les Baumettes. I couldn't stand the thought of him being locked up with psychopaths and criminals! Even after they shut down that nightmare of a place and transferred him to another facility, he still wouldn't let me visit. If I went there, we wouldn't be able to pretend anymore."

"So you lie?"

"I don't *lie*, I just avoid talking about him."

"What does Ada think about all this?"

"I don't know. Nothing."

"You hid it from him, too, didn't you?"

"We never talk about my family. He knows my mother's gone and there's no one else. So what if he thinks my father's in India?"

"Relationships must be built on solid ground, Allegra! Not on the slippery slope of lies! You have to tell him the *truth*! And *he* has to tell *you* the truth, too! Or I will!"

"Just spit it out, would you? What *truth* does Adalberto have to tell me?" Allegra cried.

"It can be summed up in two words. Gisella Giostra."

Allegra regretted telling her anything at all about that woman, and she regretted allowing Carolina to shame her into running away. And now she was going to embarrass her in front of the others.

"Wait, now you're losing me," Inge said.

"I know *giostra* is Italian for merry-go-round," Josephine said. "But I've never heard of a *gisella giostra*."

"Gisella is a person, Josephine, and Giostra is her last name," Carolina said.

"She's just a friend of Adalberto's," Allegra hurried to add before Carolina could elaborate.

"Oh," Josephine said, looking confused, or apologetic, it was hard to tell, with that way she knitted her brows together and nibbled on her lower lip as if it were a favorite cookie she wanted to make last as long as possible.

"Right. A *friend*. How many of you people feel close enough to another person who is just a *friend*, to suddenly go out and get twin tattoos on your necks? Can I see a show of hands?" Carolina asked, scanning the room as if she were addressing a crowd of delegates in a convention hall.

"On the neck? Ouch!" Josephine said. "You'd have to be very close to that friend, I think. Or *drunk*. I have to confess – and I haven't told anyone this in years – I did get a tiny tattoo at the base of my spine before I joined the sisterhood."

"You have a *tattoo*?" Allegra asked.

"Just a little cross. No one can see it. Even I can't see it unless I look in the mirror, but I avoid those things as much as possible."

"A cross on your butt? Does your Lucia find that a turn-on?" Inge winked.

"That's *not* funny," Josephine said.

"Some of my patients disgust me with their dirty tattoos," Inge said. "Believe me, no part of the body is sacred these days. And I mean *no* part!"

"*Ladies!* You're getting way off track again! Take a look and tell me, would *friends* really do something like this?" At that Carolina produced the evidence she'd teased Allegra with earlier: images of Adalberto and Gisella from behind, flaunting identical tattoos, identically placed at the napes of their necks.

Josephine leaned in closer to look. "When you're young and pretty you can get away with anything, I suppose," she said.

"Oh, she gets away with quite a bit, believe me!" Carolina said.

"Cut the theatrics, would you?" Allegra said to Carolina, then turned to face Josephine and Inge. "That guy is Adalberto and that girl is Gisella. Carolina is dying to tell you some stupid story behind the tattoos, but I'll save her the trouble. Adalberto wasn't just her friend. They had an affair."

"Some friend *you* are!" Carolina cried. "You could have admitted that this morning, instead of running away! We could have talked it over then, just the two of us, like old times!"

"Oh, *Allegra!*" Josephine said, with a sad shake of her head. "He seemed like such a nice man!"

"Guess what? The world is full of nice men who turn into cheaters at the first opportunity!" Inge said. "Take *Giac*, for example."

"You leave Giac out of it!" Carolina said. "I know how to take care of myself, and I will! We're talking about Allegra now! She doesn't seem to get how important it is to keep an eye on her man!"

Listening to the women kick around her relationship like an old tin can while she just sat there hanging her head, Allegra could only imagine how pathetic she must look. It saddened her, but mostly it angered her.

"I'm not as oblivious to what goes on around me as some people think!" she blurted. "I knew about their friendship, and I knew about the affair! The important thing is that it's already over, and I'm already over it."

"How did you find out about this illicit little lark in the first place?" Inge asked. "These stories always fascinate me, because men can be so utterly stupid. They deserve to get caught!"

Allegra had absolutely no desire to recall the brutal lucidity of that horrendous moment when she put all the pieces together and simply *knew*, or to relive the unspeakable terror that she was about to lose the only man she'd ever really loved, and who claimed to love her, too. But she needed to prove that she wasn't a passive pushover who would swallow any story, that she'd had the strength to confront Adalberto and handle the matter with honesty and strength.

"As Carolina knows, I met the woman whose name I won't mention at an online seminar and discovered that she and Adalberto were friends. But my intuition told me that something was up. After that, his phone helped," she said.

"So you *did* snoop through his phone!" Carolina said, her eyes lighting up. "Good girl!"

"No, I certainly did *not*! It was a combination of little things, like when he started taking out the garbage two or three times a day and never left his phone behind. And sometimes when he received a message, his face took on these unnatural expressions, kind of like when someone who never smiles tries to look kind, or someone who always smiles tries to look mean. I'm a sensitive person. I pick up on things."

"Too sensitive for your own good," Josephine said.

"What does that even *mean*?" Carolina groaned.

"Thinking about it and doing nothing was making me sick. My suspicions were like toxins building up in my body. I got to the point where I couldn't stomach them anymore."

"So you finally came out and asked him?" Inge asked.

"No. I told him that I *knew*."

"And he admitted it?"

"Yes. He started by repeating his story that Gisella really was just a friend, who was going through a tough time and needed his advice. *Lots* of advice, apparently. He did also admit that something physical had happened between them, but not to worry, because that part was pretty much over before it started. Then he went on to say that I should be glad he could still be friends with her, that it shows he's a person who cares about women's feelings, instead of being an insensitive pig like so many men." Allegra realized that the last part didn't sound so noble, but those were his words, not hers.

"And you *believed* him?" Inge asked.

"Well, yes. It was hard to take, but he was completely *open* about it."

"Ha! It's easy to be open *after* you get caught!" Carolina said.

"How long did the affair last?" Josephine asked.

"He said it was so short that it didn't even qualify as an affair."

"An affair is an affair no matter what you call it!" Carolina cried.

"I don't want to hear any more about it, Carolina! It's between me and Adalberto, and it's a thing of the past! If he says they're just friends, they're just friends!"

"My dear Allegra, those two have been screwing around behind your back for at least three years! And it's *not* over! If you used social media like every intelligent woman out there, all you'd have to do is cross-reference their posts and track down when they were both in the same place at the same time to figure it out! It's child's play, especially when people are stupid enough to post where their pictures were taken!"

"Three *years*?" Josephine clucked her tongue. "Gosh, some *marriages* don't even last that long."

"If Adalberto told me it's over, it's *over*. I *believe* him. And there's no way it could have been going on for three years!" She crammed as much conviction as she could into her cracking voice, but she already knew it would come down to Carolina's accusations versus Adalberto's assurances, and the stack of papers at Carolina's fingertips suggested that her claims, unlike his, were well documented. And that was without considering all those texts she herself had seen his phone bombarded with that very morning! Allegra rubbed her sweaty palms on her tablecloth toga, hoping she wouldn't need to use it to catch her vomit.

"Did you *hear* me, Allegra? While you've been chanting, he's been cheating! For three whole *years*!" Carolina repeated, waving the photos in front of her face. "How is that even *possible*?"

Allegra stared at her, not knowing what to say, except to repeat that she trusted Adalberto. It would sound pitifully passive, she knew that, even though deciding to trust him again was one of the least passive things she'd ever done in her entire life. It had taken a superhuman effort, a monumental force of will, every single day they were apart, to not obsess about where he was and with whom, to not barrage him with questions or torture herself with suspicions.

"What have you been *doing* all this time?"

"I've been living my life!"

"On your own, or with Adalberto?"

"Both! He came and went, nothing strange about that! He does have an important job, you know, and a child in Turin!" Why was she still defending him now, when she herself wondered why, in addition to Turin, he needed to go off to his country house so often, always without her, to work on all those pressing projects he talked about? And why she couldn't sometimes go with him, especially if he had little Marcello with him? It would have given her such joy to help make the house cozier for them, cook meals for them, bake cakes for them, all those silly wifely things her parents would have scoffed at. But insisting would have made her feel pushy, and complaining would have made her feel whiny. And now she just felt like a fool.

"He came and went, all right!" Carolina said. "Here's a picture he took one of the times he went. And you know where he went? To a cocktail bar in Turin, overlooking the Po River, where he enjoyed this pretty orange spritz. And here's Lady GG drinking a spritz of her own, on that *same* day, three years ago, at that *same* bar!" Carolina waved the images in front of her face before Allegra could look away. "Coincidence? I think not!"

"That doesn't prove anything! Only that they've known each other for a while, and Adalberto already told me that. They met through the magazine! For an article he was writing!" Even as she spoke, she could already feel the trust she'd worked so hard to rebuild crumble as easily as those potato chips in the bowl between the spritzes.

"Funny, isn't that the same way *you* met him? He's got a good gig going, I'd say. *Anyway*, again courtesy of Ada's profile, here's some fresh powder on the snowy slopes of Sestrière, the week before Christmas a couple of winters ago, and here's a cute selfie of GG waving from a chair lift, on that *same* day, on those *same* slopes!"

"Friends sometimes ski together," she said, hating the fear creeping into her voice.

"Why weren't you invited, I wonder?"

Allegra was wondering precisely the same thing as she tried to choke back the sour reflux of all those gut-corroding doubts she'd hoped were flushed from her system for good. To think she'd been naive enough to suggest that Adalberto introduce them, if they were just friends! I don't ski," she managed to mumble.

"Well if you don't like the mountains, how about some summer fun in Savona? That's where GG lives, is it not?"

"*Savona?* I was just there yesterday!" Josephine said, leaning in to look at the image of a sandy beach with striped blue recliners and matching umbrellas. "I guess I was in the wrong part of town, though."

"*Really*, Josephine?" Carolina said. "Do you honestly think Allegra *cares?* What she cares about is that couple in the picture who can't hide behind their sunglasses, because we *know* who they are!"

"Look, can't you just leave the past alone? *Please?*"

"Very well, but if any of you other ladies want to browse through the rest of the pictures I'd be much obliged. I wouldn't want our Allegra to think I 'm fabricating things. Remember, Allegra, I'm here to *help* you, not *hurt* you. You're my *friend!*"

"Do you want me to *thank* you?"

"You will, sooner or later. Now, as your friend, I have to say it gives me no pleasure whatsoever to show you this photo that only dates back to last month. No squirming or averting your eyes this time, either!"

"Just get this *over* with!" Allegra cried, seeing Carolina's deadly combination of a grave expression and twinkling eyes.

When Carolina exhibited her next piece of evidence, it took Allegra a minute to realize what she was looking at. Then she read the caption scrawled at the bottom of the printout: Monforte d 'Alba. That was where Adalberto 's old farmhouse in Piedmont was located!

"Isn't that Ada's place?" Carolina asked.

"I guess so. Maybe. It looks different."

"Different from what? When was the last time you were there?"

"Well, what I meant was, different from other pictures I've seen."

"So when was the last time you were there?"

"Well ... never."

"You've *never* been to the country home of your boyfriend of, what is it now, *seven years?*"

"Yes. I mean no." Allegra was sick of justifying Adalberto's repeated retreats to her friends, to herself, to anyone who thought they had the right to ask and were blunt enough to share their theories with her. "I mean, that's where he goes when he has his son. But mostly he goes there to be alone. And if I went, he wouldn't be alone, would he?"

"Hmmm. Interesting. Considering I found that photo on GG's profile, not his."

"You must be confused."

"Me, confused? I think not. She posted these, too," Carolina said, calmly displaying a series of generic landscapes shot among some rolling green hills, all labeled "Monforte d'Alba," leading up to some picturesque vineyards, then a dimly lit wine cellar with neat rows of giant oak casks, ending with the romantic image of a wine bottle and a pair of goblets on the floor by a fireplace. Then Carolina paused, tilting her head to make Allegra look her in the eye. "Don't worry, there's only one more. But this one, well, it's a beauty!"

Carolina's final blow was like a perfectly placed punch to the gut that turned Allegra into a shivering, quivering, breathless blob of a non-person as she eyed the image of Gisella and a boy doubled over with laughter, splashing each other with paint. That woman was at the farmhouse Adalberto wouldn't allow Allegra to visit because it was in such ramshackle shape and had such bad karma that he blamed it for ruining his relationship with every woman he brought there! That woman was playing with the child Allegra wasn't allowed to spend time with because of his ex-wife's pathological jealousy and constant threats of custodial revenge! Allegra was too stunned to cry, too shocked to scream; her insides were too gnarled to bring up the bile that shot into her belly like venom. Her face grew hotter and hotter until her whole head was a ball of fire that blazed through her mind's attic full of musty dreams and crumbling compromises and overused excuses. Someone was talking but she couldn't hear whose voice it was or what they were saying over the roar of the flames that engulfed the beams and stuck their tongues out the dormers, lapping her face while she just sat there, paralyzed, watching it all burn until the timbers crashed and the roof collapsed and everything went black.

CHAPTER FIFTY
Inge

"Now look what you did, Carolin-*ayayay!*" Josephine jumped to her feet, only to topple over and land next to Allegra, who'd slid to the floor, senseless. "*Ayayay!*" she wailed, clutching her ankle.

"All I did was tell her the truth!" Carolina said, walking circles around the two fallen females as if they were calculated casualties she could do nothing about. "It was the *truth* that did that, not me! The *truth!*

"Stop your damn pacing and give me a hand!" Inge ordered her. Carolina snapped out of her funk enough to help Inge up onto her good leg, then down to the floor, where she began checking Allegra's vital signs. "Now go get her a blanket. A *real* one, not a tablecloth!"

"What's *wrong* with her?" Josephine asked, scooting in closer. "Will she be all right?"

"Don't crowd her like that! She needs space," Inge said, rearranging Allegra's limp limbs and tucking them under the blanket which Carolina unceremoniously tossed to the floor. "She's feverish."

"It's no wonder, after the awful shock Carolina gave her!"

"Words can't give you a fever!" Carolina snapped. "But traipsing through the woods half-naked and barefoot in the rain can!"

"Oh! What about the snake bite? What if it was poisonous after all?" Josephine cried.

"It wasn't. But any bite that breaks the skin can still be nasty. I'd like to start her on antibiotics as a precaution. Do you have any on hand, Carolina?"

"Nope. Not after that time Giac got us in trouble by giving amoxicillin to a woman who was allergic. The best I can do is ibuprofen."

"Fine. Bring what you have." Inge 's leg was throbbing, and so was her shoulder, and thanks to the grappa so was her head. If she'd been thinking like a doctor instead of a woman with a closetful of secrets, she'd have asked for the medicine earlier.

"Yes, *ma'am*," Carolina muttered, but obeyed, immediately disappearing through the kitchen door, her feet pounding up the stairs and back down in under a minute. She tossed a box to Inge, who caught it with her good arm. She wasn't about to become a fumbler.

"Here, Josephine," she said, popping some pills from the blister. "Two for you, two for me, and two for Allegra. Water, Carolina. And no throwing this time." After Josephine and Inge washed down their pills, Inge began giving Allegra little slaps on the cheek. "Allegra! Allegra!"

"God bless you, Inge! What would we do without you?" Josephine spoke in a reverential whisper. "But I can do something that might help, too." Clasping Allegra's hand, she closed her eyes and bowed her head. "Oh, Saint Joseph, you whose power extends over all our needs, who knows how to make possible –"

"Enough of that mumbo jumbo!" Carolina said, hovering over the trio.

"I'm *praying*! Saint Joseph will listen to a Josephine." Tightening her grip on Allegra's hand, she continued, "Where was I? Oh, yeah … who knows how to make possible for us the most impossible of things –"

« *Je me recommande … à votre … à votre … solicitude … paternelle*," Allegra mumbled, her eyes fluttering open.

"Allegra!" Josephine cried. "She woke up praying! In French! It's a *miracle*!"

"You!" Inge pointed at Carolina. "Go behind her and prop her up!"

Carolina grumbled something but knelt down behind Allegra and helped her to sit, as Inge held out the pills. "Here, swallow these."

"*Quoi?* What?" Allegra said, blinking. "Oh, I don't take pills."

"Today you do," Inge said, forcing the pills past Allegra's lips and onto her tongue, then clamping her jaw shut. "And you make sure she swallows!" she said passing her off to Josephine.

"How do you know the prayer to St. Joseph?" Josephine smiled, tenderly tilting the tumbler of water to her lips. "It's not exactly a yoga thing."

Allegra blinked a few times. "Mantras, prayers, what's the difference?" Then she swallowed another sip of water, staring off into space. "I have to tell you something strange! When I cleaned out my parents' van, I found a holy card hidden inside one of my mother's books. It was dedicated to her by my grandmother on the day she was baptized, and the *prière à Saint Joseph* was on the back. I've never heard anyone recite it before."

"Another sign that the two of us were meant to meet!" Josephine said.

"Why? So you could end up back down on your asses together?" Inge said.

"All *three* of us are back down on our asses," Allegra said, smiling weakly at Inge.

"Make that *four* of us," Carolina said, from behind Allegra's head.

"Oh, Carolina. I didn't see you there," Allegra said, without turning to look at her. "I can sit up on my own now."

"That's okay," Carolina said. "I've got you."

"Yeah, right where you want me. At your mercy."

"You act like I'm your enemy, but I'm on *your* side! Can't you see that you were brought here to me for a *purpose*?" Carolina cried, leaning over her shoulder.

"You *invited* me!"

"And you came! With Ada! And *that's* where I want you!"

"Everybody quiet, please!" Josephine said. "I think I'm having a revelation!"

"First, it's a prayer meeting, now it's a revelation?" Carolina sighed.

"I'm starting to see something I couldn't see before. The same thing happens to me when I fast, or try to anyway, then I eat something I really love, like *cannoli siciliani*, or *pastiera napoletana*, or practically any dessert made with ricotta."

"And that's your divine revelation?" Carolina said. "Ricotta?"

"Never mind, I didn't expect you to understand. It's about heightened awareness. About not really tasting, then tasting fully. About not really seeing, then seeing clearly. What I'm seeing now is that it wasn't just Allegra and I who were meant to meet here this weekend. I'm seeing that we were *all* meant to meet."

"Could you ask the mighty wizard or whoever is revealing all this to you why we couldn't just have a chat over coffee?" Inge said. "Why we needed to fall off a cliff and break our bones in order to connect?"

"Maybe that was *exactly* what we needed! Something to really shake us up! To make us take stock of where we are, how we got here, and where we want to go from here!" Josephine stretched her injured leg out in front of her, mirroring Inge's position on the other side of Allegra.

"*Finally!*" Carolina chimed in. "Someone who *gets* what I've been trying to tell you all!"

"Oh, and while you're at it, Josephine, ask the wizard how long we're going to be held hostage by the world's craziest host!" Inge said, jerking her thumb at Carolina.

"Watch who you call crazy, you cuckoo quack!" Carolina said. "Crazy is what you did behind your husband's back! Don't you ever feel guilty when you look him in the eye? *Huh?*"

Inge massaged her pounding temples, hoping the ibuprofen would kick in soon. Of course she felt guilty, she'd already admitted that, but worse than the guilt was the fact that deceiving a respectable man like Rino made her feel morally inferior. And feeling any kind of inferior was something that Inge did not like one bit.

"I've received some more insight!" Josephine said excitedly. "Now Inge, I know this may sound strange coming from a sister, but the more I think about it, the less serious your offense seems to me. You put yourself through an awful lot, out of love for your husband. You wanted to make him happy, and you found a way! I actually think he'd understand, and even be grateful. I mean, it's not like you had *sex* with that other man."

Inge heaved a long, heavy sigh, staring at the floor in the center of their circle.

"Inge?" Josephine said.

"Oh. My. *God!*" Carolina said. "You did! You *did* have sex with Fabio!"

"Just once," Inge mumbled, her eyes still downcast.

"So you made up the whole story about the turkey baster?" Josephine asked. "Why?"

"Because she's a pathological *liar*, that's why!" Carolina said.

"Why, why, *why*? If you shut up for a minute I'll *tell* you why! Because when I met Fabio for dinner a second time and told him that I wasn't pregnant, he ordered champagne anyway. And honestly? Because he was really *hot* – imagine, I don't know, the *opposite* of Rino – and because I was all jacked up on hormones, and because one thing led to another and we figured we'd give the plan another shot, while giving ourselves the gift of *enjoying* it."

"Didn't you say he was *gay?*" Josephine asked.

"Yes, he was. And still is," Inge said. "But he liked me. I was tall and strong and athletic, just like him. Our bodies clicked in an amazing way and we both got the baby-making bug out of our systems. Think of it as a workout if you will, only more fun. *Way* more fun. And we made Carl in the process."

"Oh, *man!*" Josephine said. "That changes *everything!*"

"Not really. He wasn't my *lover*, he was still just my *donor*." Inge paused, allowing herself the forbidden luxury of thinking back on that encounter, which she would have been more than happy to repeat. No sense telling these people that, though.

"Yes, you made Carl, who happens to be the spitting image of the handsome Dr. Fabio Fustello!" said Carolina, who had abandoned her post behind Allegra and weaseled her way to a place in the circle, where she sat at Allegra's feet, wedged between Inge and Josephine.

"Forget you *ever* heard *any* of this, Carolina!" Inge glared menacingly at her. "And don't you *dare* mention that name to my husband!"

"Then you'd better do it yourself!" Carolina yelled. "If you can't own up to what you did, you deserve to live a tormented life!" After clearing her throat, she sat up straight, looked Inge in the eye, and continued in a creepily calm, almost robotic voice. "But that's not what I want for you. None of us can change the past, but we can decide how to face the future. My mission is to provide women with the information and support they need to take control of their lives and reach their fullest potential. It's called empowerment. What you do with it is up to you."

"Your *mission?*" Allegra said, tenting the blanket over her head and crossing her legs in the lotus position.

"*Empowerment?*" Josephine blinked.

"Bullshit," Inge said.

"I'll pretend I didn't hear that, dear *Doktor,*" Carolina said. "Now do you want help figuring out your future, or not?"

Whether it was the fumes of grappa fogging her ability to think clearly, or her prolonged, profound befuddlement over what to do while time relentlessly ran out, Inge realized that she desperately needed something she wasn't used to asking for: advice. "The donor contacted me recently!" she blurted.

"Is that bastard trying to blackmail you?" Carolina asked. "If so, just say the word, and I'll put him in his place. We go back a long way, and I happen to know a few things about him, too! One also wonders what his architect partner would think about all of this!"

"No, it's nothing like that. It's about our agreement."

"What agreement?" Josephine asked.

"Well, when we tried the first time, we signed a pact stating that if I got pregnant he'd renounce his paternity, but that if he so desired, he could reveal his role to the child once he or she turned eighteen."

"Why in the *world* would you sign anything like that?" Carolina asked.

"Because in Switzerland, artificial insemination using donor sperm is only accessible to married couples, and by law, any offspring have the right to know who their biological father is once they reach the age of eighteen. So even though we didn't go through official channels, following that guideline made it seem more legit. And even though it wasn't the AI that impregnated me, the method of conception wasn't specified in our agreement."

"How old is Carl now?" Allegra asked.

"I can figure that out in a second," Carolina began. "If he was born in –"

"Thank you, Carolina," Inge said, glaring at her. "But I'm quite capable of keeping track of my son's age. He'll turn eighteen in November."

"At least that gives you a couple of months to decide how to handle it," Allegra said.

"Not exactly. As I was saying, the donor contacted me recently. Now he doesn't want to wait until November."

"Don't you just love the way men think they can change the rules whenever they want?" Carolina cried. "You had a signed agreement!"

"I bet you wish you had a copy of that to wave in Rino's face, don't you, Carolina?" Inge cried, then fell silent for a moment before continuing. "He's always kept his end of the deal, hardly ever calling me after I had the baby, once he knew we were both fine. The reason he's suddenly in such a hurry to meet Carl is that he's dying. When we made our pact, back at that first dinner, we joked about whether we'd even be around in eighteen years, you know, the way young people do. 'I may already be dead by then!' I remember him saying before draining the bottle of pricy Bordeaux I'd splurged on. But it's not a joke anymore; now it's a very real possibility. You see, he's been diagnosed with a glioblastoma, an aggressive type of brain tumor."

"Wow!" Carolina said, shaking her head. "Now *that*, I didn't know!"

"God help him!" Josephine said.

"Poor man!" Allegra said.

"What about poor *me*?" Inge said. "Now he's pushing me, and I can't stall forever!"

"You can't stall at all!" Carolina said. "This is about facing the *truth*, not getting away with a *lie*!"

"It could have worked in my favor, if he'd just gone ahead and died without telling me," Inge muttered. It was true that she'd fantasized about such a clean and simple solution more than once, but saying it out loud made her sound like some kind of a monster. "I don't wish him dead, of course," she hastened to add. "But let's face it, if the secret went to the grave with him, we'd all be safe."

"But *would* you?" Allegra said. "Now that you know he's dying, could you live with yourself if you denied him the desire to meet his only son? And deprived Carl of his last chance to meet his biological father?"

"No, I couldn't," Inge said, shaking her head. "That's just some selfish voice talking in my head."

"Maybe now you can finally see that's why you need *me*," Carolina said. "I'm the other voice. The voice of *conscience* you so rudely keep telling to shut up."

"The thing is, I had everything figured out. Rino got his heir without going through procedures he didn't feel comfortable with. And I resolved the matter quickly without jeopardizing my career."

"Swiss logic saves all!" Carolina said.

"The thing about conscience is that it adapts to the company it keeps," Inge continued.

"Absolutely! Holy people feel holier when they're surrounded by holy people," Josephine said. "Even though Jesus preferred the company of sinners."

"Cheaters feel less like cheaters when they hang out with other cheaters," Carolina said. "Giac and Ada are probably sitting in the car bragging to each other even as we speak."

"What I mean is, we each have our own reality and our conscience adapts to that reality," Inge said. "My daily reality is played out at a fertility clinic where thousands of inseminations are performed every year. None of my colleagues would think me a monster the way a layperson might. But I could still lose Rino and Carl. What if they don't understand? What if they don't *forgive* me? Those two mean the world to me."

"Sometimes we don't appreciate the people we love until we risk losing them," Josephine said.

"Then maybe we realize we don't need them anymore," Carolina said.

"Or how much we expected them to be who we wanted them to be, instead of who they really were," Allegra said.

"For the first time, I feel a sense of, I don't know, *shame*," Inge said.

"You did what you felt you needed to do at the time, Inge," Josephine said. "It's too easy to judge yesterday's version of ourselves based on today's knowledge. The only way to move forward is to clear your path of the past, or you'll keep stumbling over it. Confessing what you did can be a turning point for you."

"I wish I could turn back time and start over."

"You can't. No one can," Josephine said. "But all will be well because your actions were prompted by love. "I'm sure Rino couldn't imagine a world without Carl."

"Absolutely not. But could he imagine a world without *me*? Can't any of you help me find a way out of this mess without ruining my life in the process?"

"I'm pretty sure I can dig something up on Rino," Carolina said.

"*Carolina!*" Josephine said, glaring at her. "You can't right a wrong with another wrong! You have to promise to let Inge handle this in her own way, in her own time. And Inge, you may be in for a surprise when you talk to Rino. Asking for forgiveness will free you."

"Asking for forgiveness will make me vulnerable."

"It takes a strong person to be vulnerable, Inge. You can do it."

"Hey, did you hear that?" Allegra said, sliding the blanket off her head.

"I don't hear anything," Josephine said.

"Me neither," Carolina said.

"That's what I mean," Allegra said. "No thunder. No rain. The storm's over!"

CHAPTER FIFTY-ONE
Josephine

Silence was exactly what Josephine needed after all that tumultuous talk about lovers and traitors and turkey basters. As a woman used to living with other women trained to hush their voices, swallow their feelings, and suppress their sexuality, it made her wonder what kind of world was out there, and whether she really wanted to be part of it. Her head was reeling after sharing her own confidences while doing her best to prevent the whole free-for-all from degenerating. Okay, so maybe the wine had something to do with her wooziness. And the grappa. And her general state of exhaustion. On the upside, Carolina finally seemed to have run out of ammunition, at least temporarily, leaving the women dazed and pensive as they sat silently in their little circle contemplating the candles, some still burning brightly, others flickering, others sputtering in the final throes of wick and wax.

Just as the meditative mood was settling over them, it was shattered by the banging of a door and the appearance of a man bursting into the dim dining room. Blinded by the beam of a flashlight, the women gasped and squealed and squeaked in surprise. Carolina alone was alert enough and fit enough to make a move. "Giac!" she cried, jumping to her feet. "You're back!"

"No thanks to you!" he bellowed, stomping over on filthy work boots. Looking up from her spot on the floor, Josephine thought he looked like an ogre, towering over his wife like that. It made her wonder whether he ever mistreated her in other ways, besides cheating on her with that girl.

"Allegra Amore? Are you here?" That had to be Aldalberto's voice, gushing with concern. The guy rushed past Giac, panning the scene with the light of his phone.

Wheezing and panting, the last person to enter could only be Rino, who shuffled cautiously across the tiles in a pair of mud-caked moccasins.

"What took you so long?" Carolina was asking Giac.

"We were waiting for a ride, remember?"

"My assistance was needed more here! As you can see, we have casualties!"

"Yeah, well you should see my truck!"

"Oh, gee, your poor truckie-poo has a boo-boo! I'm so sorry. But these three women need urgent medical attention!" Carolina said.

"Urgent or not, no vehicles are getting through until I can clear the road, which isn't going to happen until tomorrow. *If* I can fix my chainsaw."

"You *still* haven't fixed that thing? Were you *waiting* for disaster to strike?"

Josephine shifted her attention from the bickering couple to her friend on the floor, who was joined by Adalberto, already kneeling by her side. Rino rushed over to Inge as fast as his legs would allow, then collapsed into a chair. All around her voices were babbling with worry about cuts and breaks and bruises, with questions about where and how and when, with remonstrations, with indignation, with irritation. No man hurried over to Josephine, but that was okay with her, after all she'd learned today about life in a steady relationship, and knowing what she knew now made it fascinating to watch how the couples interacted. She alone was unaffected by the arrival of a partner, so she alone was lucid enough to take control before things could get even more out of hand.

"How about getting that flashlight out of our faces?" she said to Giac in her tough teacher voice. Though she was uncomfortable around that sort of man, she wasn't intimidated by him. After standing up to her share of Buffalo bullies, she'd learned that macho males were just weaklings with attitude. And now *her* attitude was getting the attention she needed. "If you'll all listen up for a minute, I'll bring you guys up to speed. The landslide knocked out a giant chunk of hillside and opened up a treacherous pit in the middle of the woods. I won't get into how or why we ended up in that pit, but Inge fell in first, then I fell in trying to help Inge, but since we both had leg injuries and couldn't walk, we were trapped down there. Talk about easy prey for the boars and wolves! Luckily, Allegra came to the rescue and dragged us back here, as you can see. Alive, but not so well."

"*What* landslide?" Giac asked Carolina.

"The one I was *trying* to survey with my drone, you idiot!" she retorted.

Ignoring their quibbling, Josephine turned to Rino and said, "Your wife is a courageous woman and an exceptional doctor. You should be proud of her." Although he was already affectionately patting her arm and rubbing her back, it seemed like a good idea to give Inge's reputation a little boost, considering the beating it was bound to take.

"Allegra was phenomenal, too, Adalberto," she continued. "A real miracle worker! Inge and I wouldn't be here if it wasn't for her. Anyone else would have left us behind, but not Allegra! Instead, at great cost to herself, she hauled us back here, encouraging us every step of the way. The scary storm didn't stop her, and neither did that awful snake bite!"

"What snake bite?" Adalberto cried. "Let me see!"

"I'm fine," Allegra said, tucking the blanket tightly around her crossed legs.

"But you're burning up!" Adalberto said, his hand on her forehead. "You have a fever!"

"Other things besides snake bites cause fevers. Like lies, for example," Carolina said, glibly reversing her previous position on the power of words.

"Enough of your crap!" Inge said to Carolina, then turned to address the others. "Yes, we're injured and yes, we're in pain, but we're strong women and we're handling it. What you men need to do is to calm down, make us comfortable, and do everything in your power to get us out of here as soon as possible. Oh, and by the way, what Josephine said is true. Allegra's determination to drag the two of us back here in our condition was nothing short of heroic."

"I'm totally aware of what an exceptional woman Allegra is," Adalberto said, clasping her hand.

"Oh yes, a real *gem*!" Carolina said. "And you don't deserve her!"

"Easy, Carol!" Giac said from the table, where he'd gone to sit alone. "Lay off the guy!"

"You stay out of things you know nothing about!" she cried. "And don't call me Carol!"

Josephine didn't want to hear those two squabble. What she wanted to hear was Adalberto praise Allegra to her face. "You were saying, Adalberto? About Allegra?"

"Yeah, well, like I was telling Rino and Giac down in the car –" he continued.

"Ha!" Carolina cackled. "It doesn't take much of an imagination to figure out what you guys would talk –"

"*Carolina!*"

"Thanks." Adalberto flashed his dazzling smile at Josephine. It didn't do much for her, but she could see how a woman could fall for him. Even more than one. Allegra may have been thinking the same thing, because Josephine saw her brush a tear from her cheek as she looked away, as if she couldn't stand the sight of that smile. Who could blame her? "As I was saying," Adalberto continued, "I didn't plan on talking about it with these guys first, but being stuck down in the car, I just *had* to tell someone. And now I'm just so *freaked* out that Allegra was in danger, and just *seeing* how wiped out she looks, and how *defenseless*, I just really can't hold in what I want to say a *minute* longer!" Placing a finger under Allegra's chin, he tilted her head toward him. "I'm already down on my knees and I'm just gonna go for it here. Allegra Amore, will you marry me?"

"Ha! That's a good one!" Carolina said. "You know she's on to you, so you're trying to placate her! Well, you don't get off that easy, no *signore*!"

"Carolina! *Basta*!" Josephine snapped. "Stay. Out. Of. It."

"What's going on here?" Adalberto asked, looking from Carolina to Josephine to Allegra. She hadn't said a word, but the tears rolling down her face didn't look much like tears of joy. "Allegra, say something! Please! Isn't this what you wanted?"

"What's going on is that no woman in her right mind would want to marry a man who's already having an affair with another woman!" Carolina said, happy to fill in the blanks.

Josephine groaned. If that woman wasn't going to back off, she'd have to be quicker than her and get this over with in the most humane way possible. As the Italians said, "*via il dente, via il dolore.*" Out with the tooth, away with the pain.

"What Carolina is trying to say, even if it's absolutely *none* of her business," she began, "is that she came across some information that she shared with Allegra in the presence of us all, which has left her convinced that you are carrying on a relationship with a certain Gisella, um ... what was it? Something about a roller coaster, no wait, a merry-go-round ... yes, that's it, the *giostra*, Gisella Giostra."

"Gisella's a friend of mine," Adalberto said. "Allegra knows all about her."

"Not *all* about her! Just what you *want* me to know!" Allegra cried. "Turns out there's another side to your tattoo story!"

"What?"

"She has a tattoo just like yours!" Allegra blurted. "And now every time I look at your neck it'll remind me of her! Of the two of you together!"

"All right, I guess maybe I didn't think it through enough, but there is no 'two of us together'! I was researching tattoos for my column, like I told you. And I just got really inspired by that butterfly, for my own private reasons, if that's okay with everyone here!"

"Excuse me!" Carolina said, raising an index finger. "Would your own private reasons have anything to do with the fact that your initials, AA, and Gisella's initials, GG, are tattooed inside both of your dirty little butterflies? I saw the photo! We all did!"

"Oh, for God's sake!" Adalberto said, turning to Allegra, who averted her eyes. "I can explain. That butterfly has a special meaning for me. And for Gisella, too. But it's not what you think! I'll get mine removed if it bothers you that much. Gisella is specialized in laser removals."

"Stop sullying my home with that name!" Carolina spat. "Allegra has put up with tattoos her whole life, so I'm pretty sure she can put up with yours! What she won't put up with is a *cheat*! Do you want to tell her about who you've been inviting to your hideaway in Monforte, or shall *she* tell *you*?"

"Butt out, Carolina!" Giac yelled. "A man has a right to his privacy!"

"Oh, does he now? Well, hold your horses, cowboy! We'll get to you, too!"

"I saw pictures of Gisella at your house! With Marcello!" Allegra cried, her lower lip quivering like a little girl's. "You never take me to your house, and you never bring Marcello to mine, and now I have these images in my head, of you and your boy, there, with *her*! No matter what you tell me, I won't be able to un-see what I saw!"

"Where the heck did you ever see any such pictures?"

"On the internet! Carolina found them on that woman's Instagram site!"

"On her *profile*, you mean?"

"I don't *care* what you *call* it! They were there for the whole world to see! Carolina showed them to me!"

"Gisella had no business taking any pictures there, or posting them, and Carolina had no business digging them up or showing them to you!"

"And you had no business being there with her!"

"That's where you're wrong! It was precisely because of business that I was there. As know-it-all Carolina must have discovered and you are already aware, Gisella is a dermatologist. She was kind enough to come to the house and take a look at Marcello's fungal infection while I met with her husband, Gilberto."

"What?" Allegra caught her breath on a half-formed sob. "She has a husband? Why didn't you tell me that?"

"Because she didn't have one when we first discussed her existence, but she has one now. What was I supposed to do, forget about Gisella and never mention her again, or give you daily status updates about her life?"

Allegra sniffed, glaring at Carolina. "And how about *you*? Why didn't you tell me she had a husband?"

"I didn't see anything about a husband!" Carolina said. Even in the penumbra, Josephine could see the flush in her face, almost feel its heat. "I needed more *time*!"

Adalberto glared at Carolina. "God only knows what you told her about the *baby*!"

"*What* baby?" Allegra gasped, clutching her stomach. Even Josephine felt like vomiting.

"*Whose* baby?" Carolina cried.

"Everybody please be quiet and listen up for a minute!" Adalberto said. "Gisella has a husband. Gisella is going to have a baby. Gisella's husband is the father of that baby. Gisella's husband is also an architect, who happens to be from Alba. He's a bit of an expert on *feng shui*, so I hired him to manage the renovation project for the house in Monforte. *Our* house, Allegra. I always knew the flow and energy were all wrong, but the work took longer than I expected and I took longer than expected to take this step. You can't rush real transformations. They take time. But the house is ready for you now. And so am I."

"So that's what the butterfly stands for!" Josephine cried. "*Metamorphosis*!"

"Yes! You got it, Josephine!" Adalberto said, reaching over to high-five her, but Josephine wasn't *that* easy.

"But why does Gisella have one just like it?" she asked.

"Because we went through our transformations together. We met a few times while I was looking into tattoo reversals, as relating to the concept of permanence. You see, people today are still attracted to the *idea* of permanence, but only if they know there's a way out. One day in the middle of a discussion Gisella burst into tears and opened up to me, the way women tend to, for whatever reason." Here he inserted a well-timed pause, complete with a smile and a shrug of the shoulders. "The poor girl was depressed and confused, and we ended up confiding in each other about our respective relationships, in particular our doubts about making a lifelong commitment. Seeing as that's not exactly something your *partner* wants to hear you talk about, we used each other as sounding boards."

"So while I was home all by myself, struggling to respect your need to be alone, you were off skiing and swimming and having cocktails with *that* crock of crap as an excuse?"

"We did the things friends do, in the light of day."

"*Really?* You must have made some beautiful memories together! Especially going to your house together, and feeling its *energy* and who knows what *else* together?" Allegra cried.

"Listen, I admit that over time we developed a special bond, but we realized that it was a mistake to let it go beyond that. The thought of ruining what we had with our partners and losing the one person we truly loved terrified us both. That's when we made the butterfly pact and sealed it with a tattoo."

"The butterfly pact?" Carolina said. "Did you hear that Inge, you're not the only one with a secret pact!"

"Shut *up*, Carolina!" Josephine ordered, catching the panic in Inge's eyes as she glanced at Rino, who was polishing the lenses of his glasses, looking only vaguely confused.

"The butterfly was to remind us that we had two choices. We could either keep living like worms and wriggling out of our commitments, or we could break out of our emotionally comfortable cocoons and finally learn to fly." Looking immensely pleased with himself, Adalberto began stroking Allegra's tangled mass of curls as if she were his faithful pet spaniel, but she brushed his hand away.

"Yeah, right, but what about the initials?" Carolina asked.

"You can believe what you want to believe, but they could just as easily stand for Allegra and Adalberto, and Gisella and Gilberto."

"Ha! They *could*, but *do* they?" Carolina said. "And how the hell was I supposed to know there was a Gilberto in the picture?"

Instead of wasting his breath on an answer, Adalberto tried to turn Allegra's chin toward him again, but she pulled back. "I didn't mean to harm you in any way, Allegra Amore, believe me," he said. "But now you know everything there is to know. Can't we move on? Please?"

Watching the two of them grapple with deception and the hurt it inevitably caused, Josephine wished life were simpler, and people more straightforward, and that everyone could have their happy ending. The thought that maybe even she had a shot at one must have made her tear up, because her vision was blurred as she tried to discern the expression in Allegra's downcast eyes. She couldn't see much, but she heard some sniffling, and a whimpering sound, the kind a puppy makes when left home alone. It took her a moment to realize that the sound wasn't coming from Allegra at all, but from Inge.

CHAPTER FIFTY-TWO
Carolina

Great, now all she needed was for everyone to start bawling! If there was one thing that messed up interventions it was tears. The people who cried them were illogical and incapable of stringing two coherent thoughts together, while the people being cried at or cried over were thrown off balance, made uncomfortable, and would say anything to make the wailers stop. She hadn't pegged Inge the Hun as a woman who would play the sniffly female card.

"I didn't mean any harm either, Rino!" she sobbed. Her voice and her face were sobbing, anyway; the tears had yet to appear.

"What are you talking about?" Rino asked. "Did you have a hand in this story?"

"No, but –"

"But what?"

"I had a hand in something *worse*!" Inge cried. "Only it was more than a hand! It was a whole *body*! A whole *life*!"

"I'm not following you, Cara," Rino said, looking puzzled. "Have you received bad news from a patient? Did you lose a baby?"

It was driving Carolina crazy to stand there and listen to this drivel, but she had a well-established technique to respect and she must give Inge the opportunity to right her wrong. Besides, this was an extremely unusual case and she was very curious to see how it would play out. As long as it didn't take forever. She began pacing in circles, first in a clockwise direction, then counterclockwise, around the three women and Ada, still camped on the floor, and Rino, who hadn't budged from his chair near Inge.

"No, it's not that," Inge said. "It's not about a baby I *lost*, but about one I *found*!"

God, these people were a disaster at handling these conversations on their own! Instead of putting everything out there, and maybe making things sound even worse than they were so they could dial it down a bit after, they had to beat around every damn bush in sight!

"You *found* a baby? Where? When?" Rino asked, seated at the edge of his chair, his elbows on his knees as he leaned in closer toward Inge, who stared up at him with a tortured expression on her face, making another pathetic whining sound. Rino looked around at the others. "Can anyone tell me what on earth she's talking about?"

"I can!" Carolina said.

"Don't you *dare!*" Inge hissed.

"Hey, Carolina? Why don't you, I don't know, go make tea or something, and give these two a little *privacy?*" Josephine suggested. "I'm sure the men could use a hot drink after their ordeal. I'd go make it myself if I could walk."

"Tea would be simply *delightful*," Giac smirked. "Seeing as someone drank all my grappa." Holding up the empty bottle, he tilted it over his open mouth, pinky extended, catching the last few drops on that lying tongue of his.

"You have to *understand*, I had my reasons!" Inge cried.

"Hey, take it easy there, Inge! No big deal!" Giac said. "It was half-empty anyway. Lucky thing I have another bottle. Which I'll go get right now."

"She wasn't apologizing for drinking your damn booze!" Carolina called after him as he disappeared into the kitchen.

"Or, we could have French champagne!" Adalberto said, squeezing Allegra's shoulder. "I came prepared to pop the question! But not to wait so long for a yes. Come *on*, Allegra Amore!"

"Give the girl some space!" Josephine said. "Allegra will let you know if and when she wants to pop any corks!"

"You down there! Quiet!" Carolina ordered, then walked over to Inge, staring down at her. "Now's your chance. You know what you have to do. So *do* it!"

"Stop bullying her!" Josephine said.

"Could everyone please be quiet and let me speak with my wife?" Rino said. "Now tell me what you're talking about, Inge. What baby did you find?"

"*Our* baby! I finally found myself pregnant with a baby and I didn't tell you how it happened!"

Finally! Carolina stood still, staring at Rino, exquisitely aware that the future course of at least three lives was hanging in the balance, depending on his reaction to the next part of the story.

"Cara, I may not be a gynecologist, but I do know how that kind of thing happens," Rino chuckled nervously, clearly uncomfortable with the intimate nature of the discussion.

"But there's something you *don't* know! Something I wanted to tell you so many times, but you were so happy and I was so afraid you would hate me! What's worse, I was terrified that you'd reject innocent little Carl!"

"I don't know what you wanted to tell me, but I could *never* reject our Carletto, *or* hate you!"

"Ha! Wait till you hear the rest!" Carolina said.

"*Carolina!*" Josephine and Allegra cried together.

"Nothing my wife tells me will change the way I feel," Rino said. "In fact, don't tell me anything, Inge. I beg you."

"I *have* to!" Inge cried. "But I *can't*!"

"Yes, you *can*," Josephine said, patting her on the shoulder.

"And if *you* don't, *I* will!" Carolina said.

"*NO!*" Rino shouted, standing up at the same time Giac burst through the swinging doors, holding a bottle by its neck like a strangled chicken. "No one needs to tell me anything because I already *know!*"

"What … what do you mean?" Inge asked, the color drained from her face. "What exactly do you know?"

"First of all, I know that Carl is my son, and nothing you or anyone else can say will ever change that. Second, I know that I was not present at his conception. I do *not* require or desire further details."

"You *know?*" Carolina said, the first spectator to recover her voice and the only one who didn't feel awkward using it.

"You *knew* that all along and you never *said* anything?" Inge asked, her tone of voice subtly but surely shifting from apologetic to accusatorial. Boy, was she good at turning the tables! "All these years, I've been carrying around this burden! If you'd spoken up sooner we both could have been so much happier!"

"I didn't speak up because I was afraid that if everything were out in the open, you'd leave me. Hans was the one true love of your life, and I could never take his place, no matter how long he's been dead. I've tried to be a good husband, but I know I'm not an exciting man, and on top of that I couldn't even father a child. You acted strange during the whole pregnancy, as if it had nothing to do with me. Then, watching our Carletto turn into a young man who was neither a male version of you nor anything like me, was evidence enough. The accident was a godsend. A blessing in disguise."

"Wait – do you honestly think a woman in my profession would let an 'accident' like that happen? I *wanted* to get pregnant! I did it on *purpose!*"

Rino squeezed his eyes shut, wincing as the words sank in. He took a deep breath before opening them again. "You're gone so much of the time, I always assumed there was someone else. And now I have to ask. Is the affair still going on? Do you still love him?"

"*No!* I don't love him, and I never did! He was just a *donor*, a doctor I used to work with. There was no affair."

"Except for –" Carolina started.

"*CAROLINA!*" the female chorus cried.

Rino sat down again, heaving a heavy sigh. Leaning back in his chair, he tugged on the collar of his polo shirt repeatedly, fanning his chest. Beads of sweat dampened his forehead.

"Holy crap! Are you having another heart attack?" Carolina asked.

"What do you mean *another* heart attack?" Inge cried. "He's never had one before!"

"Giac told me he almost keeled over trying to change the tire!"

"And no one thought to tell *me* that?" Inge cried, grimacing with pain as she pulled herself to her knees, preparing to assist her husband.

"It was indigestion!" Adalberto said. "From all the salami!"

"How do you feel now, Rino?" Inge said. "Did you take your pills today?"

"I'm fine, I'm fine. It's just a lot to digest, in addition to the salami," Rino said, his nostrils flaring with each intake of breath. After a moment he looked Inge in the eye and said, "I want to meet him."

"What?"

"This man, this doctor-donor. I want to meet him. I want to thank him."

Inge inhaled slowly, deliberately, then exhaled with an audible sigh. "Um, sure, I suppose I could try to arrange it," she said. "If that's what you really want."

"This is *not* fair at all!" Carolina cried, clenching her fists and punching her thighs with them to stop herself from punching Inge. Things were working out well for that sly Swiss lady, a little *too* well. "I'm sorry, but your wife getting off *way* too easy!" she said to Rino. "The only reason she told you is that she was *forced* to!"

"We don't need anything more from you at the moment, Carolina!" Josephine said. "Now sit down and shut up!"

"Who died and left you Pope?" Carolina heard herself saying, cringing at how infantile it sounded. Fine, she'd shut up, if that's what everyone wanted, but she sure as hell wouldn't sit down. She resumed her pacing and punching, furiously, silently.

"Inge, you are truly blessed to have the love of a loyal man like Rino," Josephine said. "Isn't there anything else you want to tell him?"

"Nope," Inge said. "I'm good."

"Let me put it this way, then. Isn't there something you want to *ask* him? He's shown you forgiveness every day of your life for all these years, and that's a precious gift. Are you just going to keep on taking?"

Carolina looked on as Inge locked her icy blue eyes with Josephine's. It was the strangest thing, but she could swear she saw their color softening, then melting, finally filling that frigid gaze with tears. After nodding at Josephine, Inge turned to Rino, her chin trembling as she spoke. "I'm sorry, Rino. I'm sorry for hiding the truth for all these years. I'm sorry for every minute I've made you suffer. Please forgive me."

"Of course I forgive you, Cara!" Rino said in a broken voice, gently placing a hand on Inge's head. Clutching her husband's legs, Inge pulled herself closer, resting her head on his knees, and sobbed. This time with tears.

Carolina smiled smugly as she looked on, satisfied at the outcome, waiting for them to thank her. And thank her they would, sooner or later, one way or another, whether they liked it or not.

CHAPTER FIFTY-THREE
Allegra

Allegra wondered whether those pills Inge had forced down her throat were doing more harm than good, but at least she'd stopped shivering. Shrugging the blanket off her shoulders, she uncrossed her legs, gently rubbing her stiff knees. Wiggling her tongue around in her mouth, she rolled the tip up and back toward her throat, using its underside to massage the soft part of her palate. The practice of *khichari mudra* was said to offer protection from snake bites. Maybe it was effective against poisonous people, too. At any rate, it was preparing her tongue for the arduous task of releasing her repressed thoughts out into the world. With such a backlog of things to say, she didn't know where to start. Maybe she'd let her tongue take the lead.

"Remember when we first met, Adalberto?" she said.

"How could I forget, Allegra Amore! As soon as I saw you I knew –"

"Yeah, yeah. But we had dreams, you and I. Yours was to write that great novel, remember?"

"It seems like yesterday, doesn't it?"

"Yeah, but *seven years later* you still haven't written it! Or even started it! You spend all your time on the internet, and squander all your talent on that trashy column and ridiculous radio show! And then you mash everything up and recycle it in those stupid short stories and pathetic podcasts of yours!"

"*Wow!*" Adalberto said, struggling to keep his smile pinned in place. "And this is coming from where?"

"It should be coming from *you*! From taking stock of your life, deciding what's important, and going for it!"

"All those things I squander my talent on, as you say, are what pays the bills. And combined, they contribute to building up my online popularity. If people don't recognize my name as a *brand*, they won't buy what I *produce*."

"You're not *supposed* to be producing *gibberish*, you're *supposed* to be creating *literature!*" Allegra wanted to leave it at that, knowing that she bore some of the responsibility for always praising his work, thinking it would encourage him to push himself harder. "*That* was your dream!"

"But if no one knows who I am, no one will care about what I write! More followers equals more potential readers."

"Yeah, consumers of bite-size pieces of cheap entertainment! Not readers of great novels!"

"Before you say another word, listen to this," Adalberto said, his smile fully restored, a sign he was ready to move on. "I have some *amazing* news I was going to surprise you with, but I think you need to hear it now!"

"I've had enough surprises for one day, thanks."

"Oh, you'll *love* this one! So, I've been putting together an anthology of my short stories for a hardcover collectors' edition. It's slated for publication just before Christmas!"

"Gee, gosh, so now you're recycling short stories based on previously recycled content? What an energy-saving idea! Do they call that *green* fiction? *Eco* writing?"

"That's *not* how it is at all! If this book weren't something really special, I wouldn't be dedicating it to you, Allegra Amore!"

"Please don't," she said. "I hate short stories. Actually, I *despise* them. What I like are novels. Big, thick ones with complex characters. And depth. Layers and layers of depth. And a love story, with a capital L. Romantic Love, Sisterly Love, Brotherly Love, Fatherly Love, Motherly Love, Spiritual Love, *any* kind, *all* kinds, but there has to be *Love*."

Adalberto looked startled, as if he'd never heard her voice before.

"Great novels aren't the same thing as entertainment!" Allegra continued. "I love them because they stir up my *emotion*s! They challenge my *beliefs*! They make me *dream* and *laugh* and *cry*! They make me want to live inside them *forever*!"

"If I may?" Josephine raised a finger, clearing her throat. "I'm not familiar with Adalberto's work, so I won't venture an opinion about that. But it seems to me that what Allegra is trying to say is that she would like your *relationship* to be like a great novel."

Allegra gazed into the eyes of her new friend, wishing she'd met her sooner, feeling as though she'd known her forever. "That's *exactly* it, Josephine!" she said, straightening her spine. "But all I get is short stories! Adalberto comes and goes so often that I forget where we left things off, and by the time we get back into our story, *poof*! He's gone again!"

Adalberto stared at Allegra as she spoke, stroking his chin, then running a hand through his hair. "Why aren't you saying this to me instead of her?" Adalberto asked. "And why now?"

"I've brought it up before, but you never seem to grasp my meaning. Or even *try* to."

"You never put it that way before, though."

"I shouldn't need to explain certain things to you. You should *feel* them, the way I do. You should have a burning desire to create that great novel!"

"You inspire me, Allegra. I want to give you that great novel."

"Novels have thousands and thousands of words, you know. But the ones at the beginning have to be the *right* ones. Do you even know what they are?"

"I already asked you to marry me. What better beginning could you ask for?"

"A beginning that starts with words I've *never* heard you say. You found words to brush off the Gisella story when I first confronted you. No doubt you found words to justify being together when you were with her, and words to ease your guilt, provided you ever felt any, when you were alone. But you've never said the words that our big, fat, romantic novel of a lifetime needs to start with."

"I love you, Allegra! You *know* I do!"

"Not *those* words."

"What words, then?"

"The very same words Inge said to Rino."

"What? Come on, how many times do I have to tell you that I'm sorry?"

"Once would suffice!" Allegra sighed. "All I've ever heard you say was that you didn't mean to hurt me. As if you could ever *betray* me without *hurting* me, whether or not I found out! But you *never* said you were *sorry* for what you did."

"Okay then," Adalberto said. "I'm sorry. I'm such an ass."

"You're sorry that you're such an ass, or you're sorry for hurting me?"

"For hurting you. For all of it. I'm sorry. Can you forgive me?"

Allegra stared into his dark eyes, trying to fix in her mind this rare sighting of Adalberto Albertis, in vulnerable mode. Her impulse was to say that yes, of course she forgave him, then hug him and reassure him, as if he were the one reeling from the slap of betrayal. But now that her tongue was limber, she had a few more things to get off her mind.

"Your apology has been noted. Remember, though, forgiving you is one thing, and trusting you is another."

"What the hell do you women want from a guy, anyway?" Giac cried, taking a swig from the fresh bottle of grappa. "You break our balls morning, noon, and night! We do everything in our power to make you happy, and you do everything in your power to make us feel guilty!"

"Ha! As you *should*, but I'll take care of *you* later!" Carolina cackled, then switched back to a calm voice to address the others. "When do men ever feel guilty? Their guilt meter, if they even have one, is always set to zero. That's why if you forgive them once, they expect you to forgive them again and again! How many times can you do that? Once? Twice? Five times? Seven?"

"When Peter asked Jesus that question, He answered: Not seven but seventy times seven," Josephine said.

"Yeah, well look how that worked out for him!"

"Forgiveness is obviously not a concept you're familiar with, Carolina," Josephine said.

"Everybody! Please *stop*!" Adalberto cried, holding up his hands, waiting for silence before turning to Allegra. "Let me say this here and now, loud and clear, in front of everyone: I am sorry, *very* sorry, Allegra. It won't happen again, I *promise*."

"Promises are only as reliable as the people who make them," Carolina said.

"Promises give me hope," Allegra said.

"Hope is for the passive," Carolina said. "Action is what counts!"

"Spoken like a true commando," Josephine quipped, rolling her eyes.

"Marriage is a major promise," Adalberto said, taking Allegra's hands in his. "Will you make that promise with me?"

"I guess I could consider it," she said, allowing Adalberto to kiss the backs of her scratched hands, then turn them over to kiss the palms, before pulling them away. "And will you write that great novel for me?"

"I guess I could consider it."

"Another one bites the dust," Giac mumbled.

"Marriage is a holy haven for love, a marvelous institution, not a *prison*," Rino declared.

"Hold it right there, everybody!" Carolina cried, jumping to her feet.

"Repeat what you just said, Rino!"

"Me? Well, I said that marriage isn't a prison, that two people who promise –"

"That's enough. You had me at prison. I can't *believe* I almost let it slide! Isn't there something you should tell the man who wants to marry you, Allegra?"

"Oh, for God's sake, leave them alone, Carolina!" Josephine said.

"You see, Ada, Allegra has been hiding something from you, too!" Carolina said, cracking her knuckles as she walked back and forth.

"What's she talking about?" Adalberto asked.

Allegra couldn't believe that Carolina would put her through this now, on top of everything else! She'd already decided to tell Adalberto about her father, when the time was right. Then it hit her that she'd been doing that her whole life, always hiding things instead of talking about them out of fear she'd be a nuisance, be misunderstood, be rejected. It was time to stop. "She's right," she said, "But it's not what you think."

"How do you know what I think?" Adalberto asked.

"Because people always think that secrets are about love affairs."

"Well, what's it about then?"

"It's about my father. He's not in India."

"So? Where is he?"

"In Marseilles."

"Good! Now that he's back, I can finally meet him."

"That would be lovely!" Carolina chuckled. "You could have your wedding at Les Baumettes! With a fabulous open bar – oh wait, the bars there are all *closed*! As in floor to ceiling closed!"

"Must you really, Carolina?" Inge said, still clinging to Rino's legs.

"My father never went to India," Allegra said.

"Then why did you say he was in India?"

"Because it was simpler than saying he was in prison."

"In *prison*?" Unsurprisingly, Adalberto looked surprised. "*Why*? What did he do?"

"I'll explain it better later, but in short story format, my mother was dying and he helped ease her along. That's all. Except that it's illegal."

"Nice. Your father killed your mother. And *you* lied to me."

"Um, well, it was just the *passive* kind," Allegra began, wondering whether passive lies were even a thing. "You never came out and *asked* me if my father was in prison. I never would have *denied* that."

"When you asked me if I was having an affair, I didn't deny that, either. I told you the truth."

"I already had *proof* that something was going on. I even had a *name*. How could you deny it?" She was speaking the truth, but why did she sound so false?

"So what are we discussing here? Isn't a lie a lie, whether or not someone has proof?"

"Yes! I mean no!" Allegra took a minute to think. It was important for this to come out right. "What I mean is, that it's not the first thing you tell a man after you meet him, or after you fall in love with him, or after you find out his ex-wife hand-picks who their son can see when he's with him! Kids ask questions, and ex-wives milk their kids for information about new girlfriends. I was afraid that if it ever came out that my father was in prison, I'd *never* be allowed to see Marcello. It's hard enough as it is!"

"Of course my ex would gobble this up, but now you're justifying why you didn't tell me. You're not answering my question."

"I didn't *mean* to lie to you, Adalberto, I just told you the same story I was telling myself, and then I never found a way to tell you the truth. Oh, how I *hate* this! Why can't people – I, me, you, all of us – why can't we just be *open* and *honest* to begin with, instead of trying to *justify* ourselves when we get caught? What makes us *do* that?"

"Arrogance," Inge said.

"Insecurity," Rino said.

"Stupidity," Carolina said.

"Fear," Josephine said. "What have I been so afraid of, anyway? Leaving the order? Dying of cancer? Loving a wonderful woman who loves me?"

"What did I miss?" Rino asked.

"It's complicated," Inge said. "In a nutshell, she's a gay nun cancer survivor."

"Who is *done* being a coward!" Josephine cried.

"Wow!" Adalberto exclaimed, jumping to his feet. "Major plot twists all around! You know, I think I'm getting an idea for a great novel! And in my book, that's a good enough reason to pop a cork! I'll go grab that bottle I had Carolina put in the fridge yesterday! Hopefully, it stayed cold."

"You stay out of my kitchen!" Carolina said, trying to grab him by the elbow as he hurried past her, but catching only his sleeve.

"You know, I suddenly feel like celebrating, too!" Josephine said. Relief washed over her face, relaxing her features. "And I'm hungry, too! Imagine that! Any chance you have any ricotta cannoli in there, Carolina? They would taste *so* good with that champagne!"

Everyone was staring at Josephine, as if her craving for a dessert was the most shocking desire she'd expressed yet, when the lights flickered on. One by one, appliances whirred, devices beeped, LEDs blinked. Looking around at the little group, Allegra was struck by how haggard they all appeared in the harsh artificial light, so dirty and bedraggled, bent and broken, bloodied and bruised, huddled together in their candlelit circle, debating dreams and deceit, love and forgiveness. She opened her mouth to comment, but before the words could make it past her tongue, a wiry, rain-soaked man burst into the room, his shifty black eyes scouring the scene, his trembling hands gripping a gun.

CHAPTER FIFTY-FOUR
Inge

"No!" Carolina cried to the gunman. "Don't do it!"

"Here! Take my wallet!" Rino shouted, jumping to his feet. He raised his hands in the air, though no one had ordered him to, then twisted his torso to proffer his backside. "It's in my pocket! There's plenty of cash!"

"Sit *down*, Rino!" Inge said, tugging on his pant leg. All she needed was for him to get shot now.

"Whatever you're thinking of doing, *don't!*" Josephine cried.

Giac, who'd disappeared behind a partition to check the circuit breakers, came to see what all the commotion was about. "*Florian?* What the hell?" he shouted, his hands flexed in front of his face, as if they were endowed with a bullet-deflecting superpower, which would have been useless anyway, considering the gun was aimed at a much lower target, just below his belt.

"You messed with my wife!" the man called Florian cried, his pistol-toting hand shaking violently.

"Put that gun down!" Carolina ordered, as if the nut would obey her!

"You stay out of this!" the man shouted, waving the gun madly at her, then at the others, one by one, while never taking his eye off Giac. "And that goes for the rest of you, too!"

Every nerve in Inge's aching body buzzed with frustration. *She* was always the one to react in situations of peril, yet here she was being held hostage for the third time in one day! First by the pit, then by crazy Carolina, and now by an even crazier gunman! There was no way in hell she was going to let this *diem horribilis* end in a bloodbath, after all she'd been through! There was precious little she could do in her condition, but there was one person who could help. Keeping an eye on the kitchen door, she waited for Adalberto to appear. As soon as he cracked the door open to see what was going on, she shook her head as a signal for him to wait there. Luckily, he was smart enough – or cowardly enough – to stay put and keep quiet.

"You tricked me into sending Jada back here so you could have her all to yourself!" Florian screamed, the veins in his neck bulging.

"What the hell are you talking about?" Giac cried.

"As if you didn't know!"

"I *don't* know! All I know is that poor girl came back here after you abandoned her. She didn't have anywhere else to go!" Giac said.

"Why would she come to *you* for help, instead of *me*?" Carolina asked, glaring at Giac.

"Why would she come to *you*, when *you* were the one who kicked them both out in the first place? I felt bad for the way you treated them, so I gave the kid a place to stay in exchange for some work."

"She's not a *kid*, she's a *woman*! And I don't think '*work*' is the right word for the services she provides!" Carolina quipped fearlessly. Inge had to hand it to her, standing up to her husband *and* the gunman at the same time.

"You watch your mouth, or I'll blow it out!" Florian yelled, his falsetto betraying his inexperience. He shook the gun at her again, using his free hand to push away the shock of damp, dark hair that kept falling in front of his eyes. Unfortunately for those present, it was the amateurs who made the mistakes.

"If you care so much about your wife, why did you take off on her?" Giac yelled.

"I didn't take off! You don't know anything!" the man yelled back.

"Then why don't you calm down and tell me?"

"I got work down in Ventimiglia, but Jada hated it there. She likes animals! She likes nature!" Florian talked in a great rush, as if his trigger finger were connected to his words which were connected to a short fuse. "She told me that Carolina said she'd take her back till the end of the season, but that she had to come alone. Jada said if I tried to stop her, she'd go back to her mother in Albania."

"And you *believed* her?" Carolina said. "Why the hell would I want Jada back up here without you here to keep her in line?"

It struck Inge that maybe she should have kept what she'd seen up at the hut to herself, instead of letting Carolina anger her to the point of wanting to get revenge, thereby turning herself into a very inconvenient eyewitness!

"Oh, *now* I get it!" Josephine whispered to Allegra, as if they were safe and snug in a movie theater, trying to crack the plot of a mystery between mouthfuls of popcorn. "Jada must be the girl Inge saw at that hut!"

"And this guy's the *husband*!" Allegra said. "I've seen him here before."

"Shut your big mouths!" Inge hissed at them.

"What's going on?" Rino asked, bending close to Inge's ear.

"*Shhh!*" Inge whispered. "Stay out of it!"

"You women shut up down there!" Florian ordered, the rage glinting in his dark eyes. "This is between men! Between me and this ... this ... *bastard*!"

Inge recognized that kind of anger and knew it could go either way for Giac. Florian was shaking with passion and jealousy and possessiveness and rivalry, all rolled up into the corrosive kind of fury that rotted holes in a guy's gut, that stoked his brutal instincts to attack his enemy with savage punches and merciless kicks that would break his bones, disfigure his face, prolong his suffering, rather than end it with one quick shot, which would leave Giac dead, sure, but Florian still holding onto that red-hot ball of killer tension. She was observing how his fingers fidgeted, how his muscles flinched, how primed he was to lunge at Giac, when Adalberto crept out from the kitchen and snuck up behind him, brandishing the champagne bottle like a club. That was when Allegra gasped like a scared little girl, which tipped off Florian, who spun around to face him. While Ada swung the thick green bottle by its neck, an astonishingly agile Josephine made a side dive for Florian's ankles, knocking his feet out from under him. Panicking, he squeezed off a shot before falling face down on the floor, where Josephine straddled his hips to pin him down, as the wide-eyed Alberto slumped to the floor, landing on his stomach, across Florian's head and shoulders.

"Holy crap!" Giac shouted, while everyone stared, dazed and in shock, at Josephine twisting the man's arm behind his back and wresting the gun from his grip, then sending it sliding across the tiles with a swift kick. Time stood still in the deafening aftermath of the explosion. All were frozen in place, bracing for the blood, except for Florian, who flailed and fought furiously to free himself. "Oh *no*!" he screamed. "Ohnono*no*!"

"Well, Inge?" Josephine urged. "Aren't you going to do *anything*?"

Inge was so goddamn sick of emergencies! She was a pregnancy planner, for God's sake! One who also happened to be immobilized by her own injuries, in case anyone cared!

"Adalberto!" Allegra wailed, her bare feet slipping and sliding in the puddle forming around the pileup as she rushed toward him. Falling to the floor, she crawled to him on all fours. "Adalberto! Say something! *Please!*"

Adalberto glanced up without raising his head, looking stunned but very much alive. "His legs!" he moaned. "Get his legs!"

Allegra threw herself onto Florian's thrashing legs, positioning herself behind Josephine, who was positioned behind Adalberto, while tiny bubbles burst all around them.

"Stop!" Florian cried. "You're gonna *crush* me!"

"And don't *you* bother getting up!" Carolina screamed at Giac, who sat on the floor some distance from the action, while she tore a table lamp from its plug and hurried over to Florian, binding his hands behind his back with the electrical cord.

"I'm impressed, Sister Josephine!" Inge said, so distraught by the unfamiliar feeling of inadequacy that she needed to make light of something. "Did they teach you those moves at your convent?"

"I'm just an inner-city sister who teaches her girls self-defense!" Josephine said.

"Well done, people!" Rino sighed, mopping his forehead with a hanky. Realizing she'd been gripping onto his legs the whole time, Inge released her hold. "Though I might have grabbed a more effective weapon from the kitchen, with all those knives to choose from!"

"Knives are *not* my style!" Adalberto said. "As it was, I was afraid of cracking his head open with the bottle! I was swinging that thing so hard that I lost my balance when I went to hit him and he was gone!"

"So no one's hurt, right?" Carolina asked, her dark eyes darting around the room. The sight of her filthy, injured guests scattered around the floor of her trashed dining room in the company of a cheating husband and a homicidal intruder must have killed her. But damn if she would show it.

"I guess I'm good!" Adalberto grunted, sitting back on his heels. Allegra locked eyes with him, saying nothing, as she slid off of Florian's ankles.

"Great! Everything's fine then!" Carolina said, tucking her hair behind her ears repeatedly as she paced back and forth. "Everything's under control!"

"Hey, don't worry about me, it's just a graze!" Giac called out. He was pulling himself to his feet with the help of a chair, grimacing as he rose. There was a gash in his jeans and a dark red stain next to his right pocket.

"Oh, my God! You were *hit?*" Carolina cried, rushing to his side.

"Saved by my Leatherman!" Giac said, extracting a bulky multi-tool from his tattered pocket. "It deflected the bullet after it ricocheted off the ceiling."

"And you people don't believe in miracles!" Josephine cried.

"I gave you that knife our first Christmas here!" Carolina said.

"You're a very lucky man!" Inge said, more than a little relieved that she wouldn't be forced to treat a gunshot wound. "A bullet in the groin could have been extremely serious. It could have nicked your femoral artery, and externally, well, you know what's at risk there. Are you so sure you're okay?"

"It's nothing," Giac said, brushing aside his wife, who was trying to sneak a peek inside his pants.

"Maybe you should come over here and let me examine you," Inge felt obliged to insist.

"Take my word for it, everything's still hanging in the right place."

"Good," Inge said, before turning her attention to Rino, who was walking over to retrieve the gun Josephine had kicked out of reach. "And you watch out for that broken glass!" Bending over his bulging belly, he picked up the pistol with one of those little squares of felt he always carried around with him for good luck and returned to his seat.

"We're all very lucky that the only thing that got killed here was a bottle of champagne!" he said, staring down at the gun in his lap with a mixture of fascination and satisfaction, looking pleased to have done his small part to restore law and order.

"And I'm going to keep it that way. I'll take that off your hands now," Carolina said, snatching the firearm from Rino.

"No, *I'll* take it," Giac said, already behind her and grabbing the gun away.

"Actually, *I'll* take the gun until everyone here calms down," Josephine said, holding out her hand. "Thou shalt not kill. Or be tempted to kill."

Surprisingly, Giac complied.

"Are you gonna get off me now?" Florian groaned, still pinned in place by Josephine.

"Are you gonna cool off and talk about this like a reasonable adult now?" Josephine said, jerking his bound hands up and over his elbows.

"*Ayyy!* All right, all right!" Florian said. "But keep him away from me!"

"Listen up, Giac. You've had a shock and you are bleeding a little," Josephine said, sliding off of her charge. "So if you won't let Inge examine you, how about you go over and sit down in that chair, nice and quiet?"

"Yes, by all means, go sit still," Inge agreed. The guy could dress his own dirty balls, thank you very much.

"As for you, come with me!" Adalberto said, escorting the wiry young would-be assassin to a seat in the far corner of the room. Standing guard next to him, he rolled his muscular shoulders and tattooed neck, probably already imagining the reactions of his fans and followers when he described how he'd freed a group of hostages by downing the gunman with a bottle of champagne, omitting the detail that it was a nun named Josephine who got the guy to the floor.

CHAPTER FIFTY-FIVE
Carolina

No one was a quicker thinker than Carolina, but all this replanning of plots and rewriting of scenes and adjustments of tones and shifting of viewpoints was frazzling every synapse in her overworked brain! If people simply did what they were supposed to instead of following their most selfish, stupidest, basest instincts, this disaster of a day could have been totally different! Even the storm could have been fun! An adventure! An opportunity for people to get to know one another, dining by candlelight and chatting by the fireside while she pampered and protected them! But no, they were doing their best, every single one of them, to ruin everything!

"What do you have to say for yourself, young man?" Ada said, standing in front of Florian, his hands on his hips. Oh, so now he was Mr. Model Behavior?

"Ask *her*!" Florian said, pointing his finger at Carolina. "*She's* the one who told me to come!"

"I didn't tell you to come *now*! Or to come with a *gun*! I specifically said to wait until *after* the weekend, when everyone was gone and I had more *proof*!" Un-f'ing believable! Everyone was turning on her, even Florian, who was supposed to be her ally!

"What kind of man would sit home and wait, knowing his woman was with another man?" Florian cried.

"What kind of woman would sit home and wait, knowing her man was with another woman?" Allegra blurted, in that uncanny way she had of holding her tongue until the worst possible moment! "*This* kind! The *fool* kind!"

"That's totally different!" Ada retorted. "You were never threatened by her!"

"But *we* were! Your ego is so big you can't even see that! Well, guess what? You aren't the only person who gets to decide our future! So even if I didn't think you'd leave me for her, what I thought of you – what I think of you! – changed. For *good*!"

"So shoot me!"

"I don't want to shoot you! Josephine can shoot you! She's the one with the gun!"

"No one's getting shot on my watch!" Josephine said. "Everyone's safe, and we're going to stay that way!"

"Wait, wait, *wait*! Hold it right there, all of you!" Carolina shouted. She must resume control and get this unruly gang back on track, immediately. Florian had made a giant mistake by jumping the gun, but now that she stopped to think about it, everything could still work to her advantage. All of her hunches (even those about Giac!) had turned out to be right – or led to even more significant discoveries! Every single turn of events proved beyond doubt that she had a gift, a calling! *She* was the catalyst that sparked real change! *She* was the saving grace for people who were too weak or too blind or too stubborn or too lazy to save themselves!

Weeee-he-haw! Weeee-he-haw!

"Now what the hell is *that*?" Ada groaned, looking fed up with everything and everyone.

"A horse with a bellyache?" Josephine shrugged.

"Oh, crap!" Giac moaned, his head between his hands.

Carolina knew just as well as he did that the ear-splitting whinny belonged to Giac's stupid mule. Just like she knew by the flurry of commotion in the foyer that the beast hadn't come there on his own. She should have locked the damn door several visitors ago!

"Whoever has the gun, drop it right now!" Jada screamed, bursting onto the scene, armed with a shotgun.

"*You*! It's all *your* fault!" Florian said, springing up from his seat in the corner, but Ada grabbed him by the shoulders and pushed him back down.

"*Florian?*" Jada cried, swinging around to face him, her dark eyes clouded with confusion, her arms shaking as she tried to steady the barrel.

"What are you, crazy?" Florian cried.

"I heard a shot! Did you *shoot* someone?"

A sequence of images flashed through Carolina's mind faster than she could make sense of them: of Jada shooting Florian, of Josephine shooting Jada, of herself standing on the sidelines, waiting for events to unfold as they would.

"That's *enough!*" Josephine ordered, pointing the pistol at Jada. "You keep calm and drop that thing *right now!*"

"Why does that lady have a gun?" Jada cried, aiming her question at Florian, but shaking the shotgun at Josephine. "Did *she* shoot someone?"

"Don't worry about her, she's a nun!" Giac said, wresting the shotgun from Jada's hands. "And *this* is to ward off boars and wolves, *not* to shoot nuns!"

"A *nun* with a *gun?*" Jada asked.

"I'm a *sister*, not a nun!" Josephine said. "But make no mistake, I can shoot!" Without another word, she squinted an eye, straightened her arms out in front of her, drew in a breath, and took a shot at Giac's boar's head trophy hanging from the rafters. And just like that, she blew its snout off!

Weeee-he-haw! Weee-he-haw! Jack bellowed by the door that Jada had left wide open, as if she were still in the barn where she belonged! "*Ayy!*" "*Eek!*" "*What the hell!*" "*Holy shit!*" "*Are you crazy?*" people screamed out in shock, instinctively clapping their hands over their ears.

"You *lied* to me!" Florian shouted, unfazed by the defaced swine and the nun with the smoking gun that everyone else was staring at. "You said you were working for Carolina, but you were really sneaking around with her husband!"

"I didn't do nothing! I've been working!"

"My sister-in-law found you lots of work in Ventimiglia!"

"I'd rather clean stalls up here than other people's toilets in Ventimiglia! I'd rather shovel manure than wipe the butts of other people's parents! I'd rather mind the goats than babysit other people's brats!"

"And screw around with other people's husbands instead of your own!" Carolina cried.

"Giac only comes to bring me supplies and check on me!"

"Sure he does!" Carolina cried. "He comes to check how tight you can cram your ass into your jeans!"

"That's not true!"

"Let's ask *her!*" Carolina said, pointing at Inge with the cockiness of a prosecutor springing a surprise eyewitness on the court. Who cared if the witness herself had been caught in the lie of a lifetime? "This woman, a respectable Swiss doctor, saw you two up there! This very morning! So don't try to deny it!"

"And what exactly did you see, *Doktor?*" Giac said, coming to stand over Inge, tapping the toe of his cowboy boot as if it wouldn't cost him a thing to compound her fractures with a stomp or two. The sight of those mud-caked boots infuriated Carolina beyond belief, even if she did have bigger issues to deal with, even if everyone else had already trashed her floor! And the bastard knew it! And he did it on purpose! "You were spying on us, weren't you?" Giac continued. "Did Carolina send you? Because if she –"

"No one *sends* me anywhere! I go where I want to go! I was out on a hike, and I came across that mule out there. He was obviously with someone, because he was still bridled and wearing a saddle pad. A particularly colorful one, I couldn't help noticing."

"Hey Giac, was it the one made with Feltro Di Meglio felt?" Rino asked.

"Not *now*, Rino!" Inge scolded him.

"So what else did you see? Huh?" Giac asked.

"I saw a guy I didn't know was you, and this young lady I'd never seen before. I was already leaving when you came after me with a shotgun! It's your fault if I'm in this condition! In fact, you'll be hearing from my lawyer!"

"Objection! Irrelevant!" Carolina cried. All she needed now were cops and lawyers crawling all over the place! "Stick to the question, please!"

"Yeah, tell us exactly what were we doing that was so wrong," Giac said.

"I'm supposed to be asking the questions here, if you don't mind!" Carolina said.

"I do mind!" Giac snapped.

"At first, just talking," Inge said.

"Did you see us kissing? Or hugging?" Jada asked, in that tacky foreign accent some men probably found sexy, shifting her weight from one skintight boot to the other. Carolina should just kick them both out of her dining room, and out of her life, for good! They belonged with those stinky goats!

"I'll kill you both!" Florian said, squirming in his chair, his eyes darting at Josephine.

"Don't even *think* of getting up!" Josephine said, pointing the pistol at him.

"Well, I didn't actually witness any physical contact," Inge said. "Not of *that* sort, anyway."

"Of *what* sort, then?" Carolina maintained a steady voice, despite her urge to scream. She was not some jealous wife throwing a fit; she was the voice of conscience, the voice of truth, the voice of justice, and must pursue the values she represented, as she had done for the others, whatever the sacrifice to herself. "So tell us. When did they take their clothes off?"

"I never said they took their clothes off!"

"You said Giac was bare-chested!" Carolina had already seen how ably this Inge twisted the facts to suit her purposes! Well, her sly tactics might work with Rino, but they weren't going to work with her!

"He already had his shirt off. Remember how hot it was before the storm? It was so muggy you could hardly –"

"I didn't ask for a weather report!"

"I'm aware of that! But I pay attention to details, and so should you!" Inge huffed. "Giac was splashing himself to cool off, and then he splashed that girl and then they both started horsing around which was why they didn't notice me there."

"So it was during that so-called 'horsing around' that she took her shirt off, too?" Carolina said.

"I never *saw* her take her shirt *off*. I only saw her putting one *on* when she came running out of the hut behind Giac, who was running behind the dog, who was running after me, the innocent bystander, who was running like hell!"

"Why would a girl have to put a shirt on if she was already wearing one?"

"I didn't stop to ask about wardrobe changes! I just ran!"

"Since I'm the person who actually knows what I did, why don't I tell you?" Jada said. "I went in to put on a dry T-shirt because you could see right through the wet one."

"Oh, come on! Look how you dress! You were luring him! You've been hitting on him since day one!" Carolina said.

"I was dressed like this when you hired me! I've been dressing like this since the day I got here because this is how I always dress! Jeans and a T-shirt! This is me, it's who I am!"

"She looks too damn *sexy* for her own good!" Florian cried, his eyes blazing as he looked at Jada. "No matter what she wears! She drives me *crazy*!" He turned to Giac. "If you so much as touched her, I swear –"

"For the last time, there's nothing going on between us!" Giac cried. "If you people want a confession though, I'll give you one! I confess that I enjoy having a woman smile at me! And having a woman to laugh with! A woman who appreciates the simple things! A woman who doesn't criticize everything I do! One who isn't tormented by what someone else did, does, or will do, or what their motives are, or how she can change them! Jada has no security, but she's not insecure. She's been lied to and deceived – and don't you dare deny that, Florian, or you either, Carolina – but she's trusting! She's been treated like a slave, but has the dignity of a queen! She has nothing, but needs less."

"Meaning I'm not like that?" Carolina said. All that ringing in her ears made it hard to understand what exactly he was saying.

"No, you're not! Not anymore. Maybe you never were, and I was blind to it until we moved up here where I could see who you really were, with no filters, no distractions! And now the kids are hardly ever here, and it's just the two of us, stuck in our solitude. Just what we wanted, right? Idyllic, right? But there's no joy in it!"

"*Joy?* You expected joy from life? From work? From *marriage?*"

"Yes, I did! And I do! That's why I gave up my number-crunching job with a month's paid vacation and a Christmas bonus and an air-conditioned office to come here in the first place! I *love* what I do up here. I love spending the days outdoors, and I even love breaking my back when I can see the fruits of my labor. It gave me incredible joy to renovate this place, brick by brick, stone by stone, from a dream we had, a vision we shared! But now, the harder I work to build, the more determined you seem to tear everything down! Starting with *me!*"

"*I'm* the one breaking my back! The work *I* do is the money-making part of the business! I built that up with my hard work, good taste, and dedication to personalized attention! That's what our guests come here for!"

"But none of what you do would be possible, or make sense, without the rest! The lodge you take care of and the food you prepare, the animals I tend to and the land I look after – it's all part of an organic system! It's about the circle of life, the flow of energy! It's about harmony and balance! *That's* what makes people feel so good when they stay here! But your negativity is killing it all! And it's killing *me!* You are *poison!*"

"But you never say a word to me! You come home exhausted, you eat your dinner, you drink your grappa, and you go to sleep! And to make matters worse, you snore! And you stink like manure even after you shower! And you never listen to what I have to say, either!"

"You're right, I don't. It didn't use to be like that, but your constant criticism got so out of control that I had to tune you out if I wanted any peace at all. You talk, but I don't listen. I'm *done* listening."

"I talk because you *need* me to talk! You *need* to hear what I have to say! I'm your inner voice, your conscience, your guide! You'd be *lost* without me!"

"You know, Carolina, lost isn't always a bad place to be."

Giac donned his cowboy hat, tipped it to the group of bruised, betrayed, and bedraggled fellow humans, then turned to walk away, shotgun in hand. His uneven gait made Carolina wonder whether he was in pain from the bullet graze or if it was all just part of his performance.

"And this isn't a *barn*!" she cried, following him to the door. Damn if he'd get the last word! "So you better take those boots off before coming back in!" She stood there watching as Giac unhitched Jack in silence, then lead the mule off into the darkness. Then she slammed the door shut and leaned against it, grateful that no one could see her trembling. How *dare* he leave her like that, making her out to be some demanding, unreasonable tyrant, in front of everyone? Well, guess what? It was *life* that was a demanding, unreasonable tyrant, but she didn't run away from it like he did. That was the truth, and she had the courage to face it head-on. Just like she'd turn around and face the people in her dining room head-on, as soon as her mind cleared and her nerves calmed and her shaking stopped. She only needed a freaking *minute* for herself, was that too much to ask after all she'd given them today? Grabbing the broom she kept handy in a corner, she brushed some clods of mud into a pile, opened the door, and swept them out with one swift stroke, then shut the door again; firmly, but softly this time. She thought about locking it but didn't.

"You people must be *starving*!" she said, returning to the dining room. She smiled her most cheerful, gracious hostess smile at her guests: at Inge still leaning against Rino's legs; at Allegra, sitting cross-legged on the floor with her eyes closed; at Ada, moping like a lost dog with no one to guard, and even at the two uninvited outsiders, who were already sitting next to each other, holding hands. But she was stuck with them, and she'd be kind to them, showing everyone she was above their pettiness, impressing them all with her generosity of spirit and unwavering professionalism. All she had to do to pull it off was to get into her kitchen where no one could see her and start cooking.

"Well, you know me by now!" Plain Jane Josephine chuckled, breaking the ice. "Better than I expected you'd know me, but enough for you to know that I'm *always* starving!"

"Now that you mention it, it's been *hours* since I ate that salami! No wonder my stomach's growling!" Rino the Rhino said, patting his Buddha belly.

"Well then, let's see what I can whip up for you!" Carolina said with a clap of her hands. "Someone raided my kitchen earlier, so it may not be exactly what you ordered this morning at breakfast, but we'll make do!"

"Breakfast seems like a year ago," Adonis Ada said, looking glum. "A *lifetime* ago."

"I can help you," Jada said, perched on the edge of her chair, ready to rise.

"Thanks, but I've got this," Carolina said, brushing aside her bangs. She really had to cut them, before they drove her bonkers.

"Come on, we'll both help you," Absent Allegra said, groaning as she rose to her feet. How strange to see her looking stiff and sad instead of flexible and cheerful. It gave Carolina a twinge of satisfaction. Just a tiny one, though, and it didn't last long.

"And if you could please untie me, I'll seat the women and make them as comfortable as possible," Florian said as he walked over to Ada, his hands behind his back, dragging along the lamp still attached to the electrical cord, which made Jada giggle. "Back home I was an ambulance volunteer."

"Really? So was I, back in my college days!" Inge said.

"A volunteer with a gun?" Josephine said.

"A gun which I'll lock up in the safe right now," Carolina said, taking the revolver from a reluctant Josephine. "My house, my rules."

"Just so you know, the gun belongs to my brother," Florian said, rubbing his wrists and shaking out his hands. "He only let me borrow it because he knew I would never shoot anyone. I didn't mean to fire! Honest!"

"The only way you can be sure of not shooting anyone is to not carry a loaded gun! Especially in the state of mind you were in," Josephine said. "Sorry I had to sit on you. I must weigh twice as much."

"You did what you had to do," Florian said, walking over to her. Dropping to one knee, he wrapped his arms around her, and with a surprising show of strength and skill, raised her up onto her good foot, then eased her into a chair.

"That's the last I *ever* want to see of guns at my lodge!" Carolina said, calling the attention back to herself. Holding her back straight and her head high, she walked purposefully to her office, trying not to limp too noticeably, and closed the door behind her. Alone at last, she sank into her swivel chair, letting out a long, private sigh; she was surprised to hear how heavy it sounded, and how ragged. God, it was stifling in this damn cubbyhole! She looked up at the low ceiling, then at the four close walls, one with that tiny window she could crank open if she wanted some air, but she didn't, because she knew nothing would ease that feeling of suffocation. Nothing. Looking down at the gun, she realized she'd never spent any time alone with one, and it was strange, even a little scary, to feel its weight in her lap. Picking it up, she ran her fingers over its grip, toyed with its cylinder, caressed the cold metal of its barrel. She imagined kissing it, wrapping her lips around it, but the thought made her hands shake. She wondered how many bullets were left in the chamber, and whether Josephine had inserted the safety, and what would happen if she pulled the trigger. Even if she didn't aim it at herself (could she ever do that?), the bullet could ricochet off the wall and hit her, the way Giac had been hit. Maybe she'd be lucky, maybe she wouldn't. Maybe she didn't even know what lucky was. Because lucky was what other people were. People who had husbands who loved them and stood by them instead of demolishing them in front of their clients, and children who didn't desert them and force them to hire illegal help when the work was too much to handle all alone. Because *alone* was what she was, what she had always been and always would be. Because no one understood how freaking *hard* it was to listen to her head always *bossing* her around, telling her what to *say* and what *not* to say, what to *do* and what *not* to do, like how now it was telling her to maybe just try brushing her lips against the barrel of that gun to see how cold it was, but it was unexpectedly warm because she'd been stroking it with her hands, more like rubbing it really, once she got the feel for it, and then to lick the metal once or twice, just to see what it tasted like, then thinking the taste was familiar, like blood, and then to toy with the trigger and imagine what would happen if a shot accidentally (or not) went off, and how everyone would come running, and how Giac would regret it until his dying day if he really lost her, and –

"Carolina?" The voice sounded distorted, as if coming from someone talking underwater. There was a tap on the door, or maybe it was just the banging in her head. Either way, she didn't answer because she couldn't, because if someone was there, she wanted them to leave, but as usual what she wanted didn't matter because the person started banging on the door in short, sharp knocks, rapping harder and faster, insisting and insisting and *insisting!* "*Carolina!* Are you *okay?*" And then the door opened, and Allegra stuck her nosy head in, but Carolina was quick to swivel her chair around to face the opposite wall, the one with the safe.

"We wanted to get started in the kitchen, but we're waiting for you."

"I'm coming," she said, her voice thick, her breath short, her back squarely turned to the door until Allegra went away. In one quick gesture, she opened the safe, shoved the gun inside, and locked it up. Rubbing her sweaty palms on her thighs, she swiveled back around to face her desk. She stared at her idle computer, useless without an internet connection, then picked up the phone. The line was still dead. No surprise there, she was used to the things she relied upon most coming and going without any concern for her needs. By tomorrow everything would be back to normal, though, she'd see to that. Gripping the edge of her desk, she pulled herself to her feet and tucked her hair behind her ears a few times. Spotting a pair of scissors, she grabbed them, held her bangs between her index and middle fingers, and clipped off a good inch, letting the trimmings fall to the floor. Then she went back out into the dining room.

"The phone's still out and so is the internet," she announced to her guests, wringing her hands to hide their shaking. "You came here to disconnect anyway, right? But considering the special circumstances, I'll share a little secret with you. If you stand on a chair by that window over there, you may be able to pick up a signal. Unless of course the storm knocked out the antenna on the mountain, too. While I have your attention, may I also add that I regret any inconvenience caused to anyone and am happy to offer tonight's dinner and drinks on the house."

Eyes of all shapes and colors and expressions were focused on her, but she could ill afford any speculation about the thoughts behind their looks. She had guests to look after, a dinner to prepare, a lodge to run. She'd do her very best tonight, like she did every night. Yes, and tomorrow everything would be back to normal. Maybe even better than normal.

JOSEPHINE

Josephine was stretched out on her back, arms over her head, indulging in an unrestrained, multi-tonal, wide-mouthed yawn, a luxury reserved for those who sleep alone or have horrendous manners. Though it was very late by the time Florian helped her hobble to her room last night, the habits of the habit were not easily broken and she was still up with the hens, as they said here in Italy. Except that there were no more hens to be up with, poor things, one of the many distressing facts she'd blocked out of her mind until just this minute. She felt awful for what she was thinking now, but as a person who'd spent a hellish day fighting for her survival, better the hens than her, right? Oh yes, Josephine Fortunata was a survivor, she had the scars to show it, and now she also had a lame leg and a fresh battery of aches and pains to remind her of it.

If she had to suffer, she couldn't have found a more comfortable bed to do it in. Another thing she had to do as she lay there in the lap of luxury was laugh, because of the other thought that crossed her early morning mind, which was the priceless look on everyone's faces when she shot the snout right off that swine! What a thrill to finally show off her marksmanship to someone outside the firing range in Buffalo! If it hadn't been for her adrenalin high, she probably never would have pulled the trigger, but then again, maybe it wasn't only the adrenalin that made her do it. Maybe she wanted to prove to everyone, herself included, that there was more to this religiously confused, sexually challenged, frumpy schoolteacher than met the eye. But right afterward, it had seemed awfully disrespectful toward the already slain and stuffed boar, disturbing her to the point that she had to sit with her back to it during dinner for fear its face, mutilated by her gratuitous cruelty, would ruin her appetite. Speaking of appetites, she couldn't believe how much she'd had to eat and drink! The long day of physical exertion and emotional drama seemed to have made everyone else ravenous, too, except for Allegra, who just picked at some cheese, and Carolina, who looked a little zombie-like as she went about her hostess duties with that creepy smile plastered on her face. It wasn't that she did anything weird, which was already a big deal for Carolina, but she came across as a little too upbeat, a little too self-assured, after what must have been the worst day in the history of the Renovatus, if not of her entire life.

No one said another word about Florian and the whole surreal gun affair, but considering Carolina's undue instigation, the flight of the intended but essentially unharmed victim, Giac, and Florian's swift return to sanity and unexpected show of solidarity, the consensus seemed to be that no further action against him was required. At one point, Allegra and Jada were kicked out of the kitchen, and Carolina insisted that people sit down properly at their assigned tables, while she rushed back and forth to bring them bread and water and wine. Those who could walk showed no interest in making a trip to their bungalows before eating, maybe because it was pitch dark by now and the electricity kept coming and going, maybe because they didn't want to leave behind those who couldn't walk, maybe because they were afraid of missing something, maybe because they felt bound together by some weird force they feared they'd be excluded from if they stepped outside the circle.

After Florian seated her comfortably at her table, Josephine invited him and Jada to pull up chairs next to hers. Thanks again to Florian, Inge was settled in nicely at another table with Rino, who fussed over her incessantly. Adalberto was finally joined by Allegra at yet another table, though neither was very talkative. It wasn't just them, though, because as sometimes happens when there's too much to say, no one had anything to say, but then Josephine remarked how ridiculous it was, after everything they'd been through together, to sit there as if they hardly knew each other, and asked the men to rearrange the small square tables into one big rectangular table they could all sit around. Once Carolina had brought all the food out, they finally convinced her to stop bustling and sit down, and if she had any objection to Florian and Jada partaking of the supper with the rest of them, she kept it to herself.

Allegra had been smart enough, or possibly intimidated enough, to keep her hands off the ravioli and wild boar sauce during her earlier raid on the kitchen which had literally saved Josephine from starvation. Because of that, the food Carolina had begun preparing so many hours ago was finally enjoyed by everyone together, certainly not as she'd intended, but undoubtedly with even greater appreciation. They all agreed that the ravioli were exceptional, and the sauce was unlike anything Josephine had ever tasted, such a flavorful blend of tomatoes, herbs, and meat. It was undeniably a bit gamey, though, which prompted her to consider a future as a vegetarian, what with having encountered a real live boar in the woods, who had been kind enough not to eat her, and having treated what was left of the dead one on the wall with such irreverence. And to be honest, the same ravioli tossed with fresh sage, olive oil, pine nuts, and parmesan, had an even more refined flavor without overpowering the delicate herbal nuances of the stuffing. Praise for Carolina's culinary skills flowed sincerely and profusely from everyone, perhaps also out of compassion for her current predicament, God bless her tormented heart. Whatever the case, the barrage of compliments made her cheeks glow a rosy pink and her smile twitch with well-deserved pride.

Maybe it was just Josephine's impression, but breaking bread together at the end of such a traumatic day seemed to give each individual a sense of being accepted and of being open to acceptance, a sense of being forgiven and being able to forgive. At the same time, there was an almost palpable, lurking awareness that the hard part would come when the drama died down and they would all go their separate ways, return to their ordinary lives and singular struggles, perhaps still hurting but perhaps already healing, perhaps in some way enriched and wiser; perhaps humbler, perhaps kinder. At least that was what Josephine liked to think. She wondered whether Allegra would continue her relationship with Adalberto, and didn't quite know what to wish for her, only that she find the serenity she deserved, with or without him. She already knew she'd miss her new friend horribly, and she also knew they would vow to stay in touch. But would they? As for what would become of Carolina, that was harder to imagine. Josephine would remember to pray for her, though, and strange as it may seem now, she was pretty sure she'd even feel some gratitude toward her.

After supper, Florian and Adalberto had managed to pick up a phone signal in that special spot by the window, except that they were forced to climb on a stepladder instead of a chair, and even then had to use a selfie stick which a previous guest had left behind. Florian was nice enough to stand up there and make a call for Josephine and even gave her his ear pods so she could speak via Bluetooth using his phone while sitting down, since she was in no condition to be climbing on anything. She fully intended to call Thomas, until the instant she dictated the last digit of his number to Florian, when she asked him to start over and gave him Lucia's number instead, surprising him that a person, one he probably considered ancient, could store two phone numbers in her brain's memory, and surprising herself with a more urgent need to hear Lucia's voice than her brother's. Without telling Lucia the whole story, which would have taken all night and alarmed her needlessly, she said that she'd sprained her ankle on a hike and wouldn't be able to drive her rental car back to Genoa. Lucia immediately replied that she'd arrange to come and get her, she'd find a way to be there the very next day, come hell or high water, Josephine could count on that.

Josephine decided that instead of rising and reciting her usual prayers, silently citing her swollen ankle as an excuse to whoever may be listening, she'd lie right there in that divine bed and think for a spell. She felt a little less like a lost lamb than when she'd arrived, but maybe Giac was right. Maybe lost wasn't such a bad place to be. Especially if you believed you were in the hands of a good shepherd.

INGE

Saying that she'd spent a comfortable night would be an exaggeration, and Inge was not one to exaggerate. However, for someone who favored falling asleep in a prone position, it was a miracle – God, now she was sounding like Josephine! – that despite having to lie flat on her back with an immobilized arm and leg, next to an overly solicitous Rino who started every time she stirred, she'd actually managed to doze intermittently. She could thank Florian for that, really, because after supper he'd driven his jalopy down to Rino's stuck car to retrieve her medical bag, which enabled her to pass out antibiotics to those who needed them, and also to pop a painkiller in the early morning hours, once the effect of the alcohol wore off. After that, Florian had also assisted her in fashioning splints for her leg, impressing her with the skills he'd learned from his volunteer work and YouTube videos, and responding correctly to her quiz regarding the possible type of fracture and the bones involved, though only an X-ray could confirm the diagnosis.

During their conversation, Inge learned that Florian's ambition was to become a paramedic. It had been Jada to suggest they should come to Italy to work and save up for his training, and maybe even find an opportunity to become certified here. But now that he was making good money working with his brother building dry stone walls, Jada was afraid that he'd give up his dream and stick to the back-breaking work his father, and all his father's brothers, and all his father's brothers' sons back in Albania did, because there were hundreds of kilometers of crumbling stone walls in Liguria and very few Italians willing or able to fix them. After their last and most furious argument on the subject, Jada had headed for the hills, *not* to sneak around with Giac as accused, but hoping to drive her point home. At least according to her.

As she lay there in bed sipping the cappuccino Rino had brought her before going out, Inge began mulling over the possibility of helping Florian achieve his dream. Maybe she could finance his studies, set up some kind of Dr. Fabio Fustello scholarship fund in honor of the man who'd made a very important donation to her own very personal cause, allowing her and Rino to become parents to a precious little boy, while neither expecting nor gaining anything in return. Who could tell, Florian might even want to go on to become a doctor. Everything in due course.

While he was placing phone calls in that sweet spot by the window, Florian had also managed to contact his brother in Ventimiglia, who had a friend with a tow truck who'd agreed to come and get Rino's car in the morning, despite it being a Sunday, and drop it off at another friend's tire shop. Among his many current skills, Florian also knew how to repair Giac's chainsaw, and had already rounded up the guys to go down and free the road blocked by the fallen oak tree. Initially, Rino had been reluctant to leave Inge alone, but after seeing how his eyes lit up at the prospect, she'd insisted that he go along, knowing that each episode of this weekend's escapades would turn into a story he'd repeat to his buddies at the golf club, yacht club, and whatever other clubs he frequented.

Once Rino's precious car was finally towed back down to civilization, they'd still have to wait for those special-order high-performance replacement tires to be delivered, but surprisingly, neither one of them was worried about the delay or in any hurry to get home. Once the tree was out of the way, Florian himself would drive her and Rino to the hospital in San Remo for an X-ray of her leg and, to be on the safe side, of the dislocated shoulder Allegra had reduced for her. From there, she and Rino would check into the luxurious five-star hotel they'd stayed at on their way up, one with so many rooms and constantly changing staff members that no one would know or care about their identity, their past, or their personal lives. Rino might even have a go at the roulette table; he deserved a little relaxation after all he'd been through – after all she'd put him through. She'd even try to look interested, no, to *be* interested, in what he had to say if he couldn't avoid talking about felt, a subject which, now that she reflected on it, seemed to have a comforting and reassuring effect on him – and maybe on her, too – a bit like felt itself.

Savoring the final sip of cappuccino, Inge wasn't too concerned about the fracture in her leg; the pain would pass, and the bones would mend. She hoped the same could be said about her marriage, a chronic source of suffering whose misaligned structure had been left untreated for so long. On her part, she was determined to do everything in her power to make amends, to be kinder to Rino instead of transferring her guilt onto him and then resenting him for it. Above all else, she worried about the inevitable injury she would cause the other person directly involved, the most important person of all, their son Carl. She hoped that if they told him the truth in an honest, loving manner, he would take it well, possibly even understand. He was bright, and sensitive, and belonged to an open-minded generation. But he was still a soon-to-be eighteen-year-old male, about to have his carefree world turned upside down by the existence, for whatever brief time remained, of a previously unheard-of biological father. Instead of terrifying her, the thought of introducing Carl to Fabio now filled her with a bittersweet sense of pride for the exceptional young man their genes had produced, whom she and Rino – especially Rino, she must admit – had raised with such love and devotion.

Though she was grossly appalled by Carolina's methods and highly skeptical of her motives, she was immensely relieved that the story of Carl's paternity was out at last. Who could have known that the truth could be so liberating, that it would have the power to lift the tremendous weight that had been crushing her for so many years? Who could have known that Rino would accept that truth, that he had in fact understood it long ago, that he'd been suffering doubly because of his doubts about her loyalty? If only she'd known that his forgiveness had been waiting there for her all along, if only she'd been humble enough to ask for it.

Taking a deep breath, Inge felt a lightness in her chest, feeling it rise higher than it had been free to rise in years. She became aware of a tingling sensation, as if a peculiar type of energy were flowing into her, similar to the way she used to feel at the top of a snowy slope, the tips of her skis pointing expectantly downhill, anticipating that final nudge of the poles as she breathed in the icy mountain air, poised for a challenging run. She didn't know whether to call it optimism, or hope, or possibly even happiness, but it made her feel good, and a bit lightheaded, almost giddy. Looking longingly into her empty cup, she used her index finger to wipe up the foam clinging to its sides, then licked the foam off her finger with her tongue, like she used to do as a child when she was lucky enough to deserve a mug of hot cocoa and whipped cream on a cold and snowy Swiss winter's day.

ALLEGRA

Allegra awoke with a start, the left side of her face squashed against the pillow, a little patch of drool beside her open mouth. Blinking, she tried to bring into focus her surroundings and figure out how she fit in there. Even her body felt unfamiliar, so stiff and uncooperative when she tried rolling over onto her back. Everything ached, from head to toe, including every inch of her skin. Looking up at the ceiling, she automatically counted the rafters like she always did at home. Here there were thirteen, while in her bedroom there were ten, that much she remembered. Placing her stiff hands on her abdomen, she saw that they were horribly scratched, their nails jagged and dirty. Peeking under the covers, she was shocked to see how much of this strange person's body was covered with grazes and gashes, bruises and contusions. It was dirty, too, the same kind of filthy dirty she used to get when playing in the woods as a child, with gobs of mud and drops of blood caked onto her skin by the end of the day. It had been a very long time since she'd gone to bed in such a state, and she was still feeling confused about why she had now, when she remembered Adalberto struggling to undress her and saying something about a shower, but that she'd collapsed on the bed and refused to budge, fending him off with furious little kicks until he finally gave up and tucked her in.

"Adalberto?" she called out, in the silent room of the silent bungalow. "*Adalberto!*" she repeated after a few seconds. Still no answer. A jolt of panic made her sit up in bed, her heart racing. Had he given up on her completely? Gone away and left here there? Tossing aside the covers and swinging her legs around, she tried to get up, but her feet were too swollen and painful, and she was too lightheaded. After a few minutes of controlled breathing, she felt calmer and realized that she actually *wanted* to be alone, that it was a *relief* to not have Adalberto around right now. That was when she noticed the note on her bedside table. *Allegra Amore, I went with the guys to clear the road. Be back soon. Let's get the hell out of here. A.*

The note made the hand that held it tremble with anger. Was it the tone? The words? The assumptions? Exactly why it had that effect on her didn't really matter, she supposed, just that it did. Bits and pieces of the previous day's drama began bobbing to the surface of her memory like flotsam after a shipwreck, but before she could even *think* about thinking about any of that stuff, she needed to reconnect with her body. Limping stiffly into the bathroom, she reached into the oversized shower stall to turn on the tap and when the water was good and hot she stepped inside. She stood for several minutes under the rainfall spray, comforted and revived by the gentle jet of water cascading over her hair and body, and when the shampoo and soap and water had done all they could do, she turned the water off and stood there dripping in the fog-filled crystal cubicle for a few minutes. It was then that it hit her. Precisely what it was that hit her, she didn't know. All she knew was that one minute she was standing there, grateful to be clean again, and the next she was feeling too naked and wounded, too pink-skinned and vulnerable, too crippled by her cut and throbbing feet to venture outside the steamy stall. Tears welled in her eyes, but instead of fighting them, she welcomed them. She was sick of hiding her emotions behind the veil of detachment, exhausted from burying her needs under the pretense of acceptance. Standing there, nude and alone, an overwhelming sadness washed over her, stamping out the fire of her anger, racking her body with sobs, beating her down until she was doubled over, her arms clutching her stomach. It wasn't her stomach that hurt, though, the pain came from somewhere deep inside her, convulsing her whole body, making her collapse onto the wet stone tiles and curl up into a ball. She couldn't say how long she stayed that way, but when the sobbing finally subsided, she breathed in great gulps of the clammy air and tried pulling herself to her feet. The first time, she slipped and fell over, banging her hipbone, but she tried again, more slowly this time, and when her feet finally found enough strength to support her, she turned the water back on, as cold as she could make it for as long as she could take it. The icy jolt revived her, but she still felt incredibly weak, almost too weak to lift the giant bath towel she wrapped herself in as she stepped slowly out of the stall and shuffled to the sink. After wiping a circle of steam from the mirror with the heel of her hand, she was again shocked by what she saw. Who did those puffy red eyes belong to? And that scratched freckled face? Carolina was right, she did look like a witch. Reaching for her bottle of almond oil, she dribbled some into her cupped hand and dipped two fingers in, smoothing the liquid across her forehead, down the bridge of her nose, over her cheeks. Pouring out another generous dose, she rubbed her hands together, then ran them over her neck and shoulders, up and down her arms. Picking out one last stubborn twig still ensnarled in her dripping curls, she distributed some oil on her hair too, then turbaned it in a towel and made her way slowly back to the bedroom. Perching on the edge of the mattress, she drizzled oil over her aching legs, too, and then her poor feet, noticing that the site of the snake bite was still red and inflamed, but not any worse. The ritual of caring for herself soothed her, both physically and emotionally, and she decided that all things considered she was lucky. Her external injuries were minor and, for the most part, would resolve in a matter of days. Some deeper gashes had reopened and were oozing a bit after her shower; these would form scabs and take longer to heal, then the scabs would come off and new scabs would form, shrinking a bit each time, until finally a smooth patch of pink would appear in their place, becoming the scars that may or may not fade away completely. The important thing was to be patient, to let the healing take all the time it needed, to resist picking at the scabs before they were ready to be shed.

It was a bit more difficult to gauge when internal wounds were healed, and the main thought that emerged from the murky memory of yesterday's events was that she'd been overly optimistic about pronouncing herself cured of hers. Over the past several months she'd devoted chunks of her days to self-examination and meditation, until the bitter disappointment and humiliation of Adalberto's betrayal gradually dulled to a chronic ache. It had taken all that time to realize that her shortcomings were not to blame for his behavior, that although she couldn't change how he was or what he did, she could change how she reacted. Eventually, she'd learned to stop feeding on the pain and start letting it go, in however small bits she could manage, for as long as it would take.

Then along came Carolina, picking at the wound she'd nursed with daily devotion, and there it was, just below the surface, still raw and angry and not healed at all. But Carolina wasn't to blame for Adalberto's behavior, either. In her own cruel way, she'd done Allegra a favor. Only now she'd have to start the process all over again, this time faced with the reality that she'd been lied to on more occasions and over a longer period of time than she'd previously believed. She'd always known that loving Adalberto with all her heart and trusting him implicitly when everyone warned her against it would leave her more vulnerable to suffering, but she did not know how to be any different; she only knew how to be Allegra. Deep down in that childish, fragile, and scarred heart of hers, Allegra already knew that she'd forgive Adalberto for the pain he caused her, whether or not she still wanted him in her life. This time she'd put the pain to good use, though, not because she believed suffering would make her a better or more noble person, but because it would give her a much needed kick in her passive butt, and make her move on to another version of herself. One where she wouldn't expect Adalberto, or any man, or any person at all, to provide her with the roots her parents had denied her. Her root was within herself, at the very base of her person, her foundation, her core, her *Mūla*. That was something she was born with; no one could give it to her, and no one could take it away from her. She must hold on fast to it, nurture it, respect it.

That would be down the road, though. At the moment, her heart was too numb with disenchantment to know how it should feel, her mind too muddled to know what it should think. Carolina's cruel again-kind again behavior confused her, and the rustic luxury of this place confused her, and everyone's motives and lies and justifications confused her, and the mountains trapping her here in this place where she didn't belong confused her. While Allegra continued massaging her body with oil, deliberately but delicately passing from thigh to knee, from calf to foot and back up again, a plan took shape in her head. She needed to get this body back to the sea, back to the one place that always helped her put things into perspective, the place whose open horizons made her believe that anything was possible. Now it was *her* turn to take a break from Adalberto, *her* turn to deal with some renovations of her own. It was time to establish some order and honor in the House of Allegra.

As soon as Adalberto came back she'd tell him he was right about wanting to leave right away, and that he should definitely do so. He could take himself straight back to Piedmont, to recharge with all that *feng shui* energy she'd never experienced in the house she'd never seen, to focus unencumbered by her presence on all those things he always needed to do that he'd never involved her in. She, on the other hand, would drive Josephine's Panda down to meet Lucia, retrieve her own car, and arrange to drop off the rental in Savona instead of Genoa. Then she'd drive the three of them up to her little house in the hills of Dolceacqua, whose pure and natural energy suited her perfectly. There they could spend a few days or weeks or as long as they wanted, away from anything and anyone that tried to exert pressure on them. Caring for others would be a way of caring for herself, but she'd give the two women all the space and privacy they needed, and all the gentle yoga practice they wanted. Meanwhile, she'd harvest what was left of the vegetables in her kitchen garden, which she'd combine with products from the local farmer's market to prepare some delicious meals for them to share, together with that lovely Rossese she bought from a local winemaker by the demijohn and bottled herself. The zucchini season was drawing to an end, and the last tomatoes were shriveling on their vines, but mushrooms and fennel and chicory and chard and cauliflower and cabbage and squash and a host of other greens would be coming around to usher in the autumn. She wondered what she'd be doing in artichoke season this winter, and after that, in asparagus season, but all she was interested in now was the present. She had a garden to replant, and a father to reclaim.

There were so many things she wanted to ask Josephine about, spiritual matters she hesitated to discuss with her fellow yogis, who were sometimes so successful at emptying their minds from distractions, or at faking that dubious achievement, that she found them just that: empty. She imagined the three of them staying up until all hours, exchanging stimulating thoughts and inspiring ideas until their eyelids grew so heavy they couldn't keep them open. There would be no routines, no schedules, no rules to follow; they would each be free to do as they pleased while they gave Josephine's ankle time to heal and her heart time to find its direction. But Allegra had the feeling that each dawn would find the three of them meditating out in the open meadow, where there were no ceilings to prevent their intentions or prayers, pleas or thanks, hymns or mantras, cries or laughter, from reaching the compassionate ears of whatever Divinity was up there, or from keeping Love with a capital L from radiating down upon them with the first golden rays of the morning sun.

She couldn't wait to get dressed and go tell Josephine.

CAROLINA

The day couldn't have started in a worse way. For the first time in her life, Carolina had overslept, and it was easy enough to figure out who was to blame for that, namely, the guy who hadn't been next to her in bed, thrashing and snoring to make sure she stayed at the short end of the sleep spectrum. Yet even after waking at the scandalously late hour of six-thirty, she'd still felt so exhausted that it was all she could do to crawl out of bed and drag herself down to her kitchen. Those guests of hers could forget about her famously flaky croissants today, because she hadn't had the chance to prepare the dough yesterday (not her fault!), and there was no amount of rushing that could get the job done in time. She wasn't about to screw up this last breakfast though, and within forty-five minutes she'd downed four cups of coffee but had two dozen muffins cooling, an apple yogurt cake baking in the oven, soon to be joined by a ricotta and raisin cream pie which she'd invented on the spot, purposely to please Josephine.

She was loath to leave anything unattended in the oven, but calculating that there was just enough time, she'd decided to dash up to gather some freshly laid eggs and feed the hens, who also seemed to be oversleeping. On the way there she'd run into Jada, who, judging from the strands of straw sticking out of her hair, must have crashed in the barn, and insisted on helping her. Carolina wasn't one hundred percent sure the encounter had been coincidental, in fact, she'd bet her bottom dollar that Jada was lying in wait, hoping to catch the look on her face when they walked through the suspiciously open door to the coop and found there were no hens to feed, just a bloody, feathery, repulsive mess of what had been her beloved Leghorns! Had Carolina been a camel, that would have been the straw that broke her back. But a camel she was not. Nor did she have the luxury of mourning the loss of hens, with cakes in the oven and guests to feed. Leaving a tearful Jada alone to sweep up and hose down the site of the massacre had made her feel that a small dose of justice had been served – to Jada, if not to her sweet, generous hens.

After that, she'd been forced to swallow the lump in her throat and smile while serving breakfast to men so self-absorbed in plotting their escape with chainsaws and such that they couldn't even pause to appreciate the quality of the fresh baked goods they crammed into their mouths (just like her old customers at the bar!). They certainly didn't pay much attention to *her* as she waited on them, not even responding to her questions about how they'd slept and how they felt this morning, and definitely not asking a *damn* thing about how *she* was! Once the guys were out of the way, she'd made up trays for the women and delivered them to their rooms herself, and although she immediately informed each of them that she was too busy to stop and chat, she was pleased to note they were all very grateful for the unexpected luxury. Especially Josephine, whose big blue eyes lit up at the giant slice of ricotta pie she placed before her, together with the basket of bread with an assortment of honey and jams, the plate of cheese and prosciutto, and an entire carafe of steaming espresso with latte on the side.

The routine check-out procedure and settling of accounts had left her with a sour taste in her mouth, but what was she supposed to do, let these people off for free, after all the extra work they'd caused? Even Rino paid his bill in full, not saying another word about his stupid tires. As always, she saw all her guests off at departure time, but it took composure of granite to stand there and wave as trolleys crunched the gravel and people abandoned her without another thought. Seeing them leave and not knowing where they would go, what would happen to them, or whether she'd ever see them again had been about as uplifting as watching her own body being sealed in a casket and lowered into a hole in the ground. At least all the women had given her a little hug or squeeze, enough of a gesture to let her know, without wasting any words, that they understood how difficult it must be to be her (ha! they had *no* idea), and that they were parting as friends, which of course made her feel good, but also worse. Much worse. And empty. Very empty.

Adonis Ada had been the first to drive off in his Defender, spinning his wheels in a way that kicked up so much mud mixed with gravel that Absent Allegra, at the wheel of the Panda, had to wait until he was out of sight to leave. Next to her in the passenger seat sat Plain Jane Josephine, while the guitar Allegra never got to play lay silently behind them. Rino the Rhino, still proudly sporting particles of oak in his hair after his go at the chainsaw, was brimming with husbandly attention for Inge the Hun, who acted disconcertingly docile. It was hard to tell how much was just that, an act, because the doctor was a shrewd cookie and may be milking the fact that she was injured, just in case Rino revisited his stance on clemency. She'd certainly won the servitude of Florian, who spent the morning taxiing the couple around San Remo, while Jada was either hiding out in the barn or off kissing the goats. When Florian finally returned, she told him there was no need to rush off, that she'd pay them both cash up front if they'd hang around and help for at least a few days. It wasn't because she didn't want to be alone, not at all. It was because the lodge looked like a bomb had gone off in it, the cleaning lady was unreliable, and she could use some help getting things in order in time for the next round of visitors, who luckily weren't due until the following weekend. She'd have to talk over plans to hire more staff with Giac when he came back, because he would come back, she was sure of that. How far could he go on that ass Jack?

But by mid-afternoon, Jada and Florian were leaving, too, smiling falsely and mumbling promises about giving some thought to her offer. Florian was already pulling out behind the wheel of his brother's beat-up Fiat Uno, the sound of more crunching gravel like a kick to Carolina's gut, when he stopped the car and ran back up to her, which for a minute made her think he'd changed his mind. But he hadn't, what he wanted was his brother's gun, which she'd decided not to remind him about. It wasn't that she planned to keep it for any reason, of course, she just wanted to test him, to see whether he'd remember it on his own. After watching the pair drive off until they were out of sight, Carolina went back inside, where she took stock of her desolately empty dining room and stone-cold kitchen, with their floors waiting to be mopped, and dishes to be washed, and of course there were the linens to be laundered and the rooms to be cleaned, and next weekend's meals to be planned and provisioned for.

"No rest for the weary!" she said, trudging to the storage room where she kept her brooms and buckets. On opening the door and seeing her bright red drone there, all dry and shiny and fully recharged after yesterday's perilous flight, her heart swelled with tenderness, as if she were seeing a precious part of her that no one appreciated. Scooping the drone up in her arms, she took it out to the veranda which had so recently been populated by guests sipping wine and savoring food as they chatted, complimenting her on every dish she presented. How could they already be *gone*? But gone they were, every last one of them! Her hands were shaking a little when she powered up her aircraft and checked the connection with the transmitter, then throttled up enough to raise the drone to eye level and hold it at a hover in front of her. When she reached out to touch it, she quivered at the way it vibrated with energy, and was thrilled by the thought that she, and she alone, controlled that energy. Then she decided to practice some pitching and rolling and yawing to prove just how in control she was. She heard herself laughing a funny laugh, hoping Giac was someplace where he could see her show off her stuff!

"You just watch this, cowboy!" she cried. In a burst of daring, Carolina pitched the nose of her aircraft upward, then opened up the throttle and sent it out over the gorge. At one point she realized that she wasn't simply *controlling* that drone, she *was* that drone, flying out there free and high, thrilled by all that empty space above her, below her, and all around her. Ready to try her hand at a nosedive, she reversed the pitch, leaning her body one way then the other, according to the drone's movements, as it immediately and unquestioningly obeyed her commands. She let it almost get out of sight before she jerked its nose up again, making it circle three times overhead. She was so enthralled by her flight that she didn't notice her shortness of breath or sweating palms when she thrust the throttle forward again, sending the beautiful red creature soaring as high into the sky as it could go, watching mesmerized as it headed straight for the mountain. Walking over to the railing, she tossed the remote control into the gorge, then turned away and went inside to make herself some espresso in her three-cup Bialetti. When it gurgled to the top of the pot, she poured its entire steaming contents into her favorite mug and went into her cubbyhole office, closing the door behind her. A woman was entitled to a little privacy, wasn't she?

Grabbing the scissors, she snipped another little bit off her bangs, tucked her hair behind her ears, and began tapping on her computer keyboard, bringing up the website she checked daily for reviews. Noticing three new five-star ratings, she pulled herself up tall in her chair and took a gulp of coffee, unconcerned that it scalded her mouth and gullet. She read:

*****
"A weekend that defies description!"
*****
"A life-changing experience! I'll never be the same again!"
*****
"In a word: Unforgettable!"

Leaning back, Carolina slowly sipped the remainder of her coffee, swiveling from side to side in her chair. Then she rose to her feet, ready to attack the mess the others had left behind.

THE END

MORE BOOKS BY THIS AUTHOR

Gently, Jolene

Explore the Cinque Terre's cliffside vineyards, hike up and down its spectacular trails and swim in its crystalline waters with Jolene, as she adapts to life in the country she has dreamed of making her own but which catches her off guard with a series of disturbing challenges. *Gently, Jolene* is the inspiring story of every woman's need to hope, to learn to let go of the past, take a second chance, and find the courage to follow her heart's path.

"A warm and inviting story of hope and discovery."
"I have been to the Cinque Terre three times. Reading this book felt like the fourth time. The writing is so descriptive I felt like I was there...I highly recommend this book!"
"A lovely story about holding on and learning to let go. A story of being a stranger in your own life."

Iris & Lily

An engrossing and heartwarming, family saga, this bestselling three-volume novel series was co-authored by Angela Scipioni and her sister Julie.
A story of two sisters struggling to survive in a male-dominated word, it has been acclaimed as "a book every woman should read."

"Delightful, touching, deep and wise."
"Hard to put this book down!"
"I thoroughly enjoyed this gem!"
"I laughed, I cried, I empathized."
"My new all-time favorite!"

Learn more at www.angelascipioni.com